A.L.I.V.E.

R.D. BRADY

BOOKS

Vinci Books

vinci-books.com

Published by Vinci Books Ltd in 2025

1

A CIP catalogue record for this book is available from the British Library.

Paperback ISBN: 9781036700287

By R.D. Brady

The A.L.I.V.E. Series

"There are some hundred billion (10^{11}) galaxies, each with, on the average, a hundred billion stars. In all the galaxies, there are perhaps as many planets as stars, 10^{11} x 10^{11} = 10^{22}, ten billion trillion. In the face of such overpowering numbers, what is the likelihood that only one ordinary star, the Sun, is accompanied by an inhabited planet?"

- Carl Sagan, "The Shores of the Cosmic Ocean," *Cosmos*, 1980

"If aliens visit us, the outcome would be much as when Columbus landed in America, which didn't turn out well for the Native Americans."

- Stephen Hawking, *Into the Universe with Stephen Hawking*, 2010

Chapter One

Seven Months Ago

FOUR MEDICS RAN ALONG NEXT to the stretcher bearing Devon Shantz.

"Make it stop!" Devon screamed, his skin pale despite his tan. Sweat and blood soaked through the blue Oxford he wore. Blood pooled on the stretcher, dripping over the side, leaving a trail to follow to the infirmary in spite of the bandages being used to stem the ever increasing flow.

Martin Drummond followed the blood trail as he walked behind the moving medical emergency. A black suit with a white shirt and black tie covered his tall, gaunt frame. His dark hair was long and pulled back behind his ears. He knew that the nickname Angel of Death had been attached to him back at Langley, in part due to his appearance but also his skills. But today as he followed Devon, the name was not hyperbole.

His aide would not survive those wounds. He'd seen the man's intestines through the rips in his skin and he knew they had ruptured as well. If he didn't die of blood loss, sepsis would undeniably set in and kill him.

Ahead, the doors to the medical unit at Lowry Air Force Base stood open, waiting for its newest patient. The medics hustled the stretcher into the unit and right to the waiting doctors, already gowned.

"Get him on the table," the female doctor ordered.

Martin stepped into the unit. A flurry of medical individuals in blue scrubs blocked Martin's view as they worked frantically to save Devon's life. Martin pulled a pack of cigarettes from his coat pocket and lit one up as he leaned against a wall. An older woman in a nurse's uniform pursed her lips and started to walk over, but she was intercepted by another nurse who spoke urgently to her after a quick nervous glance back at Martin.

The first nurse glanced at him again, this time with traces of fear before she headed out the other door.

Martin took a long, satisfying drag, his feet crossed at the ankles, picturing the attack on Devon. It had happened so fast. The guards with them had been stunned. Martin had his weapon cleared of its holster before they'd even begun to react. But even then, he'd known it was too late for Devon.

Dr. Hasan Verma, the head of the medical unit, walked into the room. He glanced over at the flurry of activity around Devon before making his way to Martin. "Mr. Drummond, are you all right?"

Martin took a slow drag of his cigarette and blew the smoke out. Most of it hit the doctor in his face. Dr. Verma pulled his head back with a grimace but said nothing.

"I'm fine, but I cannot say the same for my aide."

"We have the best medical staff here. They will do everything in their power—"

"He won't make it. You know that as well as I do."

Dr. Verma nodded. "Most likely. But were you hurt in any way?"

Martin shook his head. "No."

Dr. Verma's gaze flicked to the bottom of Martin's shirt. Martin followed his gaze and noticed for the first time the dark blue spot that had spread there. Surprise flashed through him. *I didn't realize it had gotten so close.*

He met the doctor's gaze. "Obviously *that* blood is not mine."

"A med unit was dispatched for the creature as well."

Martin raised an eyebrow. "Why?"

The doctor frowned. "To—to see if it could be saved."

Martin dropped the cigarette and smashed it under his shoe. "Then tell them to stop and make sure the thing is dead."

"But, sir—"

"Dead, Dr. Verma, tell them to make sure it is dead." With one last look at Devon, he strode for the doors, pulling out his phone, careful to make sure that no one saw him smile.

Chapter Two

DAYTON, OHIO

Today

THE HORSE'S *hooves thundered across the field, her flank damp with sweat. Maeve Leander's fingers ached as she clutched the reins. Alejandra's dark mane flew behind her, as did Maeve's own hair. She'd pushed Alejandra hard and had nearly been thrown a few times. But she didn't dare slow down. Instead she silently begged*—please, my friend, go faster.

She'd heard about the raiders when she had been in town. She'd crossed through Copper Canyon to avoid the roads and cut her time in half. But now the road was her only option. Caution dictated she slow down but fear wouldn't let her. She knew she had already pushed the old girl too hard. But she still urged Alejandra to go just a little bit faster. And the horse responded as if she too understood what was at stake.

As soon as the horse gained traction on the dirt road, her pace picked up. But not before Maeve saw that which she was dreading— hoof prints. Lots of them.

No, no, no. *Terror slid over her. The reins became slick in her hands.*

A waft of gray smoke drifted over the hill in the distance. Disbelief and fear fought inside of Maeve, each trying to gain the upper hand.

She leaned forward, keeping her focus on the hilltop, not letting herself think what the smoke meant. It can't be. It cannot be, *she repeated to herself as Alejandra began the climb. She kept up the mantra as they ascended. Finally, she reached the peak, and her family's farm came into view.*

Maeve reined Alejandra in sharply. Her breath left her body in a gasp just as sharp, and the fear she'd been shoving away broke free, threatening to swallow her whole.

A pyre of flames burned brightly in front of the barn, gray smoke wafting up angrily from the blaze. Even from this distance, she could make out the red shawl being engulfed by the flames, the body it still clung to already burning. Tears streamed down her cheeks and a hole developed in her chest, threatening to split her in two. "Mama."

No one else was in sight. Just her family's home and the barn, watching in silent horror as her mother left this world in ashes. Maeve wanted nothing more than to turn Alejandra around and flee. But she knew she needed to check.

She needed to be sure her mother was the only one they had found.

MAEVE LEANDER'S eyes flew open. *Mama.* She reached up and felt the tears on her cheek. She stared at the ceiling, her reality coming into focus as the dream faded. But the feelings of grief remained, raw and deep. She swiped at the tears on her cheeks, but new ones replaced the old. And this time it was for her own mother, not the girl in the dreams.

Alice Leander had died over a year ago from breast cancer, but at moments like these her death seemed like it had occurred just yesterday.

A vision from the dream returned, the red shawl

covering the body as it burned in the pyre. Maeve shivered at the memory. Her dreams had been so vivid lately. And they all revolved around the same place—Mexico. She'd never been to Mexico in her life, and she couldn't understand the source of the dreams. Her subconscious was obviously trying to tell her something. But what?

The alarm clock on her side table blared to life. Sitting up, Maeve fumbled for the button to switch it off.

She sat with her head in her hands for moment, her dark wavy hair tumbling over her shoulders. With an impatient gesture she pushed it back.

She's gone, but she would want you to be happy. She would want you to keep going.

She knew her affirmation was right, and she wasn't one who gave up. But sometimes she just missed her so much. She sat for a moment staring around the Spartan one-bedroom apartment. A delivery person had arrived last week with the bed and asked if she'd just moved in. Maeve had told him yes, even though she'd been here for five years. But her life was not spent here. Here was where she slept, occasionally ate, and showered. Her real life occurred at Wright-Patterson Air Force Base.

A small face appeared in her mind, chasing away her feelings of grief. She wasn't alone. And there was still someone counting on her.

Pushing herself from the bed, she crossed the short distance to her windows and pulled back the room's darkening curtains. Bright sunlight streamed in and Maeve blinked hard, taking a step back. She glanced at the clock. 4:02 pm.

Time to go to work.

Chapter Three

MAEVE SAT near the front of the bus reading her book as she and twenty others who worked at Wright-Patterson Air Force Base were driven toward the base. Security on the base was incredibly strict, especially for the research divisions. As of three weeks ago, no personnel were allowed to drive in. They were bussed from a parking area set up outside the base perimeter. All bags were checked before entering the bus and before leaving the installation. And no unauthorized personnel were allowed within three miles of the base. They said it was for construction, but Maeve was pretty sure it was a new security measure.

From behind her, she felt a tap on her shoulder. She turned around.

Greg Schorn pushed the dark hair from his eyes, pushing his glasses up his nose. He nodded out the window. "What's that?"

Maeve looked up from her book with a frown. "What?"

Greg nudged his chin toward the front of the bus.

Maeve looked past the driver and saw the familiar fence of the base. But today there was something new—protestors.

"Never seen that before," Greg murmured. "I wonder how they managed it?"

Maeve was just as baffled.

Wooden sawhorses had been set up to keep the protestors from blocking the road. Military police lined up along the sawhorses as well.

"I don't get it. Why didn't security just run them off?" Greg asked.

Maeve read a few signs as they passed.

Stop Animal Abuse.

Animals Are Not Disposable.

The protestors ranged in age from college students to senior citizens and all raised their fists towards the bus. Some yelled, although the heavy glass windows made their words impossible to discern. *An animal rights demonstration?*

"I wonder which project they're protesting," Greg said.

She wanted to turn around and ask Greg if he knew anything about the protest but she didn't. One of the biggest rules of working at Wright-Patt's National Air and Space Intelligence Center (NASIC), formerly the Foreign Technology Division, was that you never asked questions about what was happening on base unless it was absolutely necessary. In fact, Maeve had ridden the bus with these same twenty people for the last three weeks but she had known their faces for much longer. But she didn't know what project a single one of them worked on—not even Greg, who she'd been friends with for years.

The departments were all completely separated. Maeve herself had top-secret clearance and she simply assumed no one else did. It was just easier that way. Who the others worked for and what their clearance was she didn't know and simply couldn't risk finding out. Anyone who spoke with someone outside their project parameters about their research would be immediately dismissed.

Maeve knew of three people that had been dismissed for violating that rule. And Maeve had way too much at stake to break it.

But despite that precaution, she and Greg maintained the friendship they'd developed in college. In fact, Maeve was the reason Greg applied for the position at Wright-Patt. And Maeve enjoyed having a friendly face around, even if neither of them ever mentioned their work.

The bus pulled up in front of Hangar One, and three people got off. Wright-Patterson Air Force Base had been established back in 1948 with the merging of Wright and Patterson fields. In fact, the base had its origins with the fathers of aviation: the Wright Brothers Huffman Prairie Flying Field. In 1917, it was established as a military installation. Since that time, the US military had used that same piece of land as a testing site for aviation. Now it had grown to cover almost twelve square miles and employed over twenty-seven thousand people, both military and civilian.

Greg leaned forward. "Hey, did you do anything good this weekend?"

Maeve shook her head. "I was here."

Greg shook his head. "You know, I'm dedicated to my research and all, but you take it to a whole new level."

You have no idea, Maeve thought but just smiled as the bus pulled up to her stop. "Lunch this week?"

"Yeah. Let me know what's good for you."

"Will do," Maeve said as she headed for the door.

With a nod of thanks to the driver, Sam, she stepped out into the cool night air. Building 23 stood fifty feet away. It was a square brick building only three stories high, one wall almost completely made of glass and dark metal framing. It looked completely unassuming and identical to another dozen buildings or so on the base.

Maeve moved quickly up the short path and placed her hand on the palm plate at the front door. The door popped open and she stepped into the vestibule. A guard sat at a desk at the back of the foyer with a thick wall behind him. A steel door stood to the guard's left, which led to the upper floors, and another one stood to the right, which housed another security detail. But even those guards weren't allowed into the building itself unless there was an emergency.

There were only two other doors in the entryway, one on either side of the hallway.

A quick nod at the guard and Maeve turned into the women's locker room on the right. Grabbing a pair of pale blue scrubs from the shelf on her right, she quickly stripped off her clothes. Donning the blue scrubs, she folded her clothes and put them in her locker, securing the lock.

She exited the locker room through the back. After sliding her ID through the scanner, the steel door by the guard slid open. Bypassing the elevator, she quickly made her way to the stairs. She jogged up the two flights to her lab, and at the landing of her floor, she waved her ID over another scanner. The door buzzed and she pushed through. Her floor had bright white walls with gray tile and was lined with eight doorways. To her left was a small lounge, the cafeteria, a med room, the security office, and two bathrooms. To her right was only one room: her lab.

She turned right. Another wave of her ID over yet another scanner and the light above her door bloomed green. She pushed through and pulled on a lab coat hanging by the door.

Her 'lab' actually consisted of five rooms with only one entrance. This part of the lab contained a large room with two large, long tables. Along the back wall was a couch and her desk. To the left was a large glass wall, beyond which was the control room, which housed a series of computers and monitors. Beyond that was another glass wall.

Maeve glanced over but the lights beyond the second glass wall were still dark. Inside that room were three doors leading to an additional three rooms—a medical suite, a physical therapy room, and a living space.

Maeve waved at Greta Schubert, who sat behind a console and a row of screens beyond the first glass wall. Greta had worked at the base for as long as Maeve could remember. Greta smiled, her brown hair, lined with only a few hints of gray, was pulled back in a bun. She wore a blue turtleneck that contrasted with her white lab coat and brought out the blue in her eyes. Greta gave her a quick wave before turning back to the console.

Maeve glanced at the clock and the still, dark room beyond Greta. *Good. I should have about an hour.*

She made her way to her desk, which was neat, just how she liked it. The only adornment was a picture of her with her mom and a small *E.T.* doll that Greta had picked up for her one birthday a few years back.

Maeve grabbed the reports that had been printed out by Greta during the day. She took a seat on the couch, flipping through them. EKG readings were normal, as were the sleep pattern readings. She frowned a little at the neuro-transmitter levels. They were a little low, especially the dopamine, serotonin, and norepinephrine. She'd have to check that.

She hopped on her computer and quickly wrote up her views on the lab reports. She was just replying to an email from the head of NASIC when Greta called her through the intercom.

"He's waking up."

Maeve smiled and pushed back from the desk. She pushed through the glass door into the control room. "Hey, Greta. How are you?"

Greta smiled. "I'm good. And he was quiet all day. Did you see the neurotransmitter levels?"

Maeve nodded with a frown. "Yeah. I'll re-run the test to make sure it's not just a blip. Did you see anything that indicates a problem?"

Greta shook her head. "No, but he tends to sleep when I'm around."

Maeve nodded and headed for the door on the opposite side of the room.

"You want me to put the lights on?" Greta asked.

"Yes, but only at ten percent."

The room that had been pitch black on the other side of the control room came into view with the dim light. Through the glass in the door, Maeve could see the bed, side table, small desk, and couch. Everything sized down for a child except for the table, which was regular sized. The color scheme was white with splashes of blue and red.

Maeve smiled at the old Raggedy Ann and Andy dolls sitting on a shelf next to a collection of matchbox cars. "Open one," Maeve said.

A buzz sounded at the door. She pushed through, making her way quietly to the bed. The figure beneath the blanket stirred. Maeve sat on the floor next to the bed and waited.

The figure turned toward her. Its small mouth opened and breathed out. The face that lay on the pillow was gray with a slight tinge of pink underneath. He had no nose, just two small holes. On either side of his head were two more small holes with the smallest of skin flaps for ears. A pinched mouth and large eyes that were currently closed completed the face. Slowly the eyes opened, revealing large black orbs without any white. The ends of the small mouth turned up when the being caught sight of Maeve.

Maeve smiled back. "Morning, Alvie."

Chapter Four

GREG WATCHED Maeve get off the bus and disappear into Building 23. He knew the history of the building. Back in the 1940s, it had been Hangar 23. Then the Roswell crash debris had been brought here in 1947 and the floor of the hangar had been removed. The ship had been placed inside and a new building had been constructed over it.

Greg turned his eyes back to the front. Of course, that's what the UFOlogists thought. But Maeve couldn't be involved in anything like that. She was too normal. He liked her—he had since they'd met in college. He'd tried to ask her out back then but she had shot him down, nicely, of course. But ever since that point, they'd been good friends.

It was tough not to talk about his research with her because she was bright, smarter than him, which took a lot for him to admit. The only problem with Maeve was that she worked so hard. He knew her mom's death had really hit her hard. He'd been worried about her, but Maeve just kept going. She didn't take any time off, which seemed weird.

"You getting off, Greg?" Sam called from the driver's seat.

"What?" Greg looked up and realized the bus had stopped. He grabbed his satchel and hustled down the aisle, nearly tripping over his own feet. "Sorry, sorry."

"Careful there," Sam said.

"I'm good." Greg felt his cheeks burn. When he'd been twelve his mom had assured him that he would grow out of his clumsy stage. Seventeen years later, he was beginning to think she'd lied. "Have a good one, Sam."

"You too, kid."

Greg stepped onto the sidewalk and his pulse picked up a tick. Leslie Cole, dressed in her crisp Air Force uniform, was waiting for him as always. Five foot eight with dark skin and light eyes and with a physique that kept Greg's imagination happy if unfulfilled, he viewed her presence as an absolute perk of the job. For the last two years, she had been assigned as his guard. Before that it had been Skeet Hamilton—an overgrown frat boy. Greg much preferred Leslie.

"Hey, Les."

She smiled. "Hey yourself. How was your weekend?"

"It was good," he said as he fell in step next to her.

"Red hot nights?" she teased.

He pictured the Dungeon and Dragons marathon he and his old college buddies had played online. "Um, yeah. Hot."

Leslie stepped in front of him to swipe her card at the reader, and Greg took the opportunity to stare at her perfectly shaped ass—not an ounce of fat, just like the rest of her. In fact, he was pretty sure even her boobs were muscular too.

And he had zero problems with that. Standing at five

foot nine and tipping the scales at one hundred twenty-five pounds, the idea of a dark-skinned Amazonian woman by his side gave him more than a little thrill. Of course, he doubted she got the same pleasure from the idea of a scrawny geek standing next to her. But, hey, his imagination was his to do with as he pleased.

"Greg?" Leslie looked back at him, the door held open.

He felt the blood rush to his cheeks as if she could read his thoughts, which he wouldn't put past her. "Right, sorry." He hustled through the door. Ten minutes later, they'd been through security and had switched into lab gear.

Two more guards stood outside his lab. They nodded at him as he approached. "Dr. Schorn, Lieutenant Cole," the one on the right said.

Smiling, Greg nodded back. "Hey guys." But they kept their serious expressions. Greg sighed. He loved his work, but these guys all needed to loosen up a little bit.

One of the guards keyed open the door and Greg stepped in. Leslie followed him in, taking up her position by the door. Greg went over to the computer and checked to see if there was anything that needed his immediate attention. A few of his results had come in during the day but, sadly, they were all negative. He looked over at the glass with a frown.

Making his way to the Keurig in the corner of his lab, he made himself a cup of coffee. "Les, you want one?"

"I'm good," she said.

Greg took a sip as he headed over to the glass.

Leslie left her position from the door and approached as well, her hand resting on her gun. Whenever he went near the enclosure, she was always near.

He stepped up to the glass and nodded to the being in the back. "Hi, Hank."

'Hank,' official designation Kecksburg-AG2, sat crouched on his perch at the back of the enclosure. His reptilian eyes narrowed, and he pulled back his lips, drool dripping onto the floor. Hank slithered from the corner, and the lights glinted off his dark green scaly skin.

Hank lowered himself from the perch using strong arms attached to a long torso. Thick legs with talons at the ends touched down on the floor, and at one point he stretched to his full six-foot height. Then he rushed the glass. The chains on his wrist yanked him back at the last second, keeping him a foot from the glass. A low growl sounded from his throat, his eyes staring into Greg's.

Greg took a sip of coffee, used to Hank's greeting. Hank was a second-generation creation of A.L.I.V.E. He had been created from remains found at a crash site somewhere in the US. It was beyond Greg's pay level to know which one, but he knew the original clone had had difficulties with the atmosphere especially sunlight.

The second generation's DNA had been merged with crocodile DNA to alleviate its skin's difficulty with the environment. Greg wasn't sure an aggressive animal like a crocodile was the best choice, but no one had consulted him. He had been brought in to observe and record. And that's what he did. Each day, he ran Hank through a myriad of tests to determine his abilities, intelligence, personality, and most importantly, his weaknesses.

And although Greg kept all his reports clinical in their detailed description, he knew that one term best described the creature in front of him: psychopath. Hank was a violent psychopath with no apparent empathy or interest in befriending any human.

And as for weaknesses, Greg hadn't found any besides the obvious: he needed oxygen, food, and water just like any living being. His skin was nearly impervious—a combination of the crocodile and the being's natural physicality. His bite radius was stronger than an earthen crocodile's. And he was fast and extremely strong.

Whatever race this thing had come from, the world had better pray it never showed up in force.

Greg watched Hank as he stepped back into his corner, his eyes scanning the enclosure. And that was the scariest part about Hank: his brain. Because he apparently had the same mission as Greg—to find whatever weaknesses he could.

Greg stepped back, thankful for the reinforced glass separating them. And Maeve once again floated into his mind. Yup, whatever Maeve did on the base couldn't possibly be as cool as this.

Chapter Five

LANGLEY, VIRGINIA

MARTIN DRUMMOND WALKED SLOWLY down the hall at CIA Headquarters. The last time he had been here, Devon had been with him. Devon hadn't been married, and his parents had been informed that he had died in a training accident. Just yesterday, his body had been cremated without allowing any viewings beforehand, even though his death had occurred over a month ago. Martin had ordered the body examined with a fine tooth comb before he'd released it for cremation.

It was a shame, though. Devon had been a good agent, if a little too docile. But his death would aid the cause, and that was all that mattered.

The aide to the CIA Director for Military Support caught sight of Martin and quickly moved to open the door to the office behind him. The man kept his gaze down as Martin passed, and just the slightest tremor was obvious in the man's body. Martin smiled. He liked that his reputation preceded him.

He stepped in the room and Robert Buckley looked up

from his desk. The years had been kind to Buckley. But then Martin had often thought that life in general had always been kind to Buckley. Robert came from a rich Southern family. His golden boy looks and family connections had opened many doors.

Martin, however, had been kicked in the teeth by life on the regular. A tall, skinny kid from the small town of Blackwater, Arizona, he'd never met his dad, and his mother had been a barely functioning alcoholic. Unlike Robert, Martin had earned, sometimes violently, every opportunity presented to him.

Yet the two shared a desire to protect the United States by any means necessary. Robert stood slowly, his expression somber, and held his hand out to Martin. "I'm sorry to hear about Devon. He was a good man."

Martin accepted the handshake, keeping his face equally somber. "Yes. His death was a true tragedy."

"Take a seat," Robert said, indicating the chair in front of his desk. "So, what can I do for you?"

Martin raised an eyebrow. Years ago, Robert wouldn't have had to ask. He would already know why Martin was here. "We have a situation."

Buckley's blue eyes scanned Martin, trying to read any and all tells in his body language. Martin gave him nothing to work with.

Buckley put down his pen. "What is it?"

"A sighting."

"Where?"

"Ellsworth."

Buckley raised an eyebrow. "Ellsworth? Weren't we doing some testing there today?"

Martin nodded. "Apparently someone decided to come see the show." He pulled his phone from his pocket and walked over to the TV in the corner of Buckley's room. He quickly linked up his phone. "This recording was taken from their control room."

"Who's out there?"

"Major Adam Juno."

"He's a good man."

Martin struggled not to roll his eyes. *A good man—what a useless phrase.*

The screen came to life, and the control room of the tower at Ellsworth Air Force Base came into view. Six people were on screen. One, a tall, slim man, faced four of the room's occupants. "You are all sworn to secrecy, understood?" Major Adam Juno asked.

"Yes, sir," the four individuals in front of him said before exiting the room. Juno turned to the one person left in the room—the radar operator.

"Who's she?" Buckley asked.

Martin paused the recording. "Nancy Stall, Airman First Class. Married, two kids, been with the Air Force for five years. Good at her job."

Robert nodded a smile on his face. "Good." And Martin had thought the same thing when he'd done the background check on her. She had people that were important to her, people that would keep her quiet. Martin hit play again.

"Report," Juno said.

Nancy Stall spoke clearly, without any emotion. "Taggert reported an unknown object at 1600 hours at his three o'clock."

"Heading?"

"South, away from him. He's been following it for the last few minutes."

"Has the object interacted with him?"

"No. Taggert describes it as a long cylindrical object."

A male voice cut in. "Sir, the object is stopping."

Juno hit a button on the console. "Is it landing?"

"No, sir. It's hovering."

Juno and Stall turned their attention to the radar screen. Sure enough, the object had stopped moving and remained in the same spot. Something no jet should be able to do.

"Sir? Orders?" Taggert asked.

"Keep it in sight."

"Holy crap. Did you guys see that?" Taggert said.

The light on the radar moved off screen.

"That thing had to be doing Mach 9 or 10, and from a standstill," Taggert said.

Juno hesitated for only a moment. "Taggert, return to base. A special unit is being sent to you for debrief. You speak with no one but them about this. Am I clear?"

"Yes, sir."

Martin turned off the recording. "That was two hours ago. They're getting bolder."

"Who knows?" Robert asked.

"Everyone in the room was sworn to secrecy. They'll be monitored to make sure no one talks. And the usual safe-guards are being put in place should one of them do so."

Martin had agents combing through each person's life, looking for any string to unravel in case they went public. Family members, vices, anything that could be used to discredit them.

Martin was sick of it. Not intimidating hardworking Americans—he considered that a perk of the job—he was sick of the lack of response to these invasions. They weren't joyriding—whoever was invading their air space was checking their defenses and forming a plan. Martin had no doubt about that.

22

And we need to be doing more.

Years ago, the US government had agreed to clone the alien bodies in their possession to learn their weaknesses. But it had taken years to fine-tune the cloning process for it to be fit for the alien DNA. And even then, they ran into more problems than answers. Most of the beings had been incompatible with the hosts they were bred within. A few clawed their way out only to die as soon as they escaped, their bodies too underdeveloped to do much else. Others lasted through birth only for their systems to fail once exposed to the Earth's atmosphere—gravity, oxygen levels, air quality, acid levels—the list of problems went on and on. It was one failure after another.

Yet after the first successful creation, he'd had such high hopes. And then Dr. Alice Leander and Senator Billingsley had managed to stop all their progress in its tracks. And Martin had been forced out. For years, he'd sat on the sidelines watching, letting others run the show. Letting others screw up the greatest chance the Earth had to protect itself. But not anymore.

Three years ago he'd finally tracked down all the files Senator Billingsley had held over him. And then Martin had held a crowbar over the senator. The official report said car accident. Martin had taken a great deal of pleasure in smashing both the senator and his prized Bentley.

But all that was in the past. "We need to increase the pace of the A.L.I.V.E. Project."

Robert raised an eyebrow. "Why? A.L.I.V.E. has been a success. And with the exception of Devon's death, it has been a safe process. The world does not know what is happening and we are learning more each day. Martin, nothing's going to happen."

Martin narrowed his eyes. He wasn't surprised by

Robert's response but he was disappointed—just as he had been for the last few years. Something had happened to Buckley. Maybe it was the grandkids he had been incessantly showing pictures of for the last few years, but he'd grown soft. He no longer viewed the alien threat as just that —a threat. He believed they could be simply observing.

Martin shook his head. The Robert Buckley who had brought him into the CIA would have laughed in the face of *this* Robert Buckley.

"Devon's death proved that is *not* the case. The threat is real. That creature broke out quickly, before anyone had a chance to realize security was down. That's smart—*that's* intelligence. With that one situation we learned a great deal about the creature and its capabilities."

Robert narrowed his eyes. "So what are you suggesting?"

"I suggest we allow to creatures to be who they are. We need to expand—"

"No."

Martin paused, waiting for Robert to continue, but apparently he was done. "No?"

"The project is moving forward at a pace we are all comfortable with. When and if we decide the project needs to increase its pace, we will make that decision, not you, Martin. Remember, you're not in charge."

Inwardly, Martin seethed, but outwardly he remained as unflappable as ever. He stood. "Of course, Robert. I just thought I should bring it to your attention."

"I'll take it under advisement. Now go out and get some fresh air. You're looking awfully pale."

"Will do." Martin turned and headed for the door.

"Oh, and Martin?"

Martin paused, his hand on the doorknob.

"Speak with Leonard on your way out about a new aide."

"Of course." Martin let himself out of the room. Leonard jumped to his feet, but Martin glared him back into his chair as he passed. Robert had lost his edge. There was a time when he was a man to be feared. But no longer. Now he was just a man in the way.

And Martin had always been very good at getting men out of his way.

Slipping his hand into his pocket, he wrapped his fingers around the small remote he'd used to release the creature at Lowry. Devon's sacrifice would make the world a better place. Martin's actions had actually been a gift to Devon and to the world. A picture of Buckley sitting at his desk filled his mind.

Perhaps Buckley needs a present as well.

Because apparently Martin was the only one who saw the true danger. And that meant he was the only one who could do something about it.

Chapter Six

One Month Later

THE PHYSICAL THERAPY room was silent. Alvie stood waiting at the starting line, his blue scrubs matching Maeve's. Standing at just under four feet, he looked top heavy, his head disproportionately large for his slim build. His arms were also disproportionately long for his torso by a few inches and were extremely slim. His torso was pear shaped, coming almost to a point at his thin neck.

Weighing in at thirty-eight pounds, Maeve knew his thinness wasn't the result of malnutrition, but design. His bones weighed a third of a human's but were extremely strong. Alvie's bones had fibers woven into them and the origin of the fibers was still unknown. In fact, his small build hid a reserve of strength and an agility that she still couldn't quite understand but could appreciate.

"Ready?" Maeve called.

Alvie held up a hand, his four fingers in the air.

Thumb poised above the button on the stopwatch, she grinned. "Go."

Alvie burst into motion. He sprinted toward the pommel horse and leapt over it with ease. As he ran for the cargo net, Maeve held her breath. The cargo net's movement sometimes gave him trouble.

Alvie grabbed onto the net.

Maeve forced herself to keep her face neutral, aware of the cameras in the room. *Come on, Alvie.*

After one fumble, he started to move up with ease. Maeve had to keep herself from cheering and covered a smile she couldn't contain behind a fake cough.

Alvie reached the end of the net twenty feet up and walked carefully along the beam at the top of the net, his balance perfect.

Reaching the end of the beam, Alvie knelt down and grabbed the rope. Lowering himself down, he ran over to the rings. He climbed the box in front and leapt up to grab hold of them. Then he swung with complete confidence across the series of rings, looking like a small Tarzan. Dropping to the ground, he ran to the track that surrounded the room and started on the last obstacle—two laps around the room measuring a half-mile.

Maeve moved next to the finish line. As soon as Alvie crossed, she clicked the button on the stopwatch and then grinned. "That was your best time yet."

Alvie smiled and headed for his water bottle.

Maeve recorded the time on her laptop and then turned off the camera. She walked over to Alvie and hugged him. "You did great. We need to sign you up for American Ninja Warrior."

He looked up expectantly, his small mouth turning up,

and Maeve cursed herself for getting his hopes up. Jokes were something he didn't always get, even with his high intellect. Maeve shook her head. "No, not seriously. But you would be great at it. Now, what do you want to do to reward yourself?"

He grinned and pointed at the computer. Maeve groaned good-naturedly. "Fine. As soon as we're finished, you can look at some puppy pictures. Let me—"

Alvie stepped away from her and let out a shriek, falling to the ground. Maeve dropped to her knees as Alvie shook, almost as if he was having a seizure. "Alvie!"

He stopped shaking but stared straight ahead, drool slipping from the corner of his mouth. She gathered him into her arms, wiping his mouth. She checked his pulse, which was racing, and she knew it wasn't from the obstacle course. His heart rate always returned to normal mere seconds after completing any physical task.

"Alvie, look at me. Look at me, Alvie."

He stared straight ahead.

She put her hand on his cheek. "Please, Alvie."

He didn't change his expression, but a single tear slipped from the corner of his eye. She wiped it away, keeping her hand on his cheek and turning his head gently so she could look into his eyes. "Alvie."

He blinked and his breath stuttered. He held his hand over hers and sadness washed over her. She pulled him into her chest and held him tight. "What's wrong, Alvie?"

Of course, he didn't respond. He had no vocal chords and couldn't speak. And later she'd try to get him to type out what had happened, but he never shared what caused these episodes. And they were happening more and more often, although never as extreme as this.

She glanced over to where the camera sat, the green light off, and thanked god she had turned it off. So far she had kept these incidents out of her reports. Until she knew why they were happening, she couldn't let anyone else know. But she was running out of time because they were happening with greater frequency. And soon someone was going to see.

And if she didn't have an answer, they would replace her with someone who did.

Chapter Seven

FIVE LEVELS UNDER EDWARDS AIR FORCE BASE, CALIFORNIA

MARTIN WALKED DOWN THE HALL, his footsteps echoing through the empty space. Ahead, a light glowed from underneath the one door in the hall. It was the meeting room for the Majestic 12. The Majestic 12 had been created by executive order by President Harry S. Truman after the Roswell crash and a rash of UFO sightings. The committee was composed of scientists, military and intelligence agents whose sole focus was preparing the United States to defend against the alien threat.

Technically, the committee had been decommissioned only a few years after its inception. But the real power in government, the one that didn't require election every few years and didn't need to answer to the public, decided the committee was too critical to disband and had moved it into the shadows.

Martin had been affiliated with the program for over thirty years. Robert had brought him in, setting Martin up to be his replacement on the committee back when Robert had a spine and some vision. Martin was supposed to replace him when he either retired or died. After their last conversation, Martin had decided that thirty years was long enough to wait for Robert to decide to take either option. So a week ago, he had helped him choose.

Martin opened the door and stepped in. It was in this very room that Martin had attended his first MJ-12 meeting. Martin didn't give in to nostalgia very often, but when he had decided to call this meeting, he thought it only fitting that he attend his first meeting as a full-fledged member in the same room he'd learned of the committee's existence.

Twenty-two sets of eyes followed Martin's progress to the other side of the room as he took the one remaining chair at the round table as the twelfth member of the committee. The other eleven members sat in a ring behind each of the members they would one day replace. Each member was a power broker within their own sphere: the NSA, FBI, Homeland Security, the State Department, each branch of the military, and scientists from the top programs and labs across the country. And Martin, of course, represented the CIA.

Barbara Freely of the NSA stood. "The committee recognizes Martin Drummond as a member, replacing Robert Buckley. We are sorry for your loss, Martin."

Martin nodded. "Thank you."

"Funny," Albert Brenner of the FBI said from the other side of the table, "I knew Robert Buckley for nearly forty years. Played golf with him once a month for the last twenty, and he never mentioned a word about having a heart condition."

Martin eyed him across the table. "Not all medical conditions are known, I suppose."

Albert narrowed his blue eyes. He was a redhead who still retained his football build from his college days and the freckles from his youth. "Is that so? It seems you also lost your aide not that long ago. Quite a bit of death seems to be following you around these days."

"It's a dangerous world." Martin held Albert's gaze for just a moment longer than necessary. "But the incident at Lowry only highlights what Robert and I have been discussing over the last few years—these experiments cannot continue to be performed the way they are. Too many people are placed at risk. They all need to be moved to a more secure location."

"They've never been located in one location," Michelle Danner of Homeland said.

"But that was never intentional, was it?" Martin asked. "At one point, almost everything was located in Nevada. Before those idiots irradiated the whole area."

"Is that true?" Brenner asked.

Martin looked at Dr. Harry Nagin. Of Japanese descent, Nagin's specialty was, among other things, the deleterious effect of the US's history of nuclear testing. Nagin nodded. "Yes. One of the tests over at the Nevada testing site was too strong and too close to 51. It irradiated the base, shuttering it for years."

While the world at large may have forgotten the testing that happened in Nevada, the Majestic 12 had not. From 1945 to 1992, over one thousand bombs had been detonated, a majority of them in the western part of the United States. Over two hundred of them had been exploded in the atmosphere, underwater, and in space.

There had even been a plan in 1958 to bomb the far side of the moon—Project A119. Ostensibly the detonation was justified by saying it would answer questions about planetary astronomy, but everyone in the know knew that the real impetus behind the detonation was to demonstrate

America's might to the world. Luckily that plan had been squashed.

Idiots, Martin growled as the history of America's stupidity rolled through his mind. *Why not just send out an invitation to the rest of the universe that didn't know we were here to come on by?*

Because the United States' unrestrained testing of nuclear weapons did not concern the Majestic 12 from a strictly environmental or even physical standpoint. One could say their greatest interest extended from a more galactic viewpoint. In the early 1950s, the committee had come to the conclusion that it was the setting off of the first atomic bomb that had increased alien interest in Earth, and the continued testing beyond that had kept their interest here.

After the first bomb was dropped, the number of sightings exploded. The MJ-12 believed it was the human race's violence or potential for violence that intrigued our interstellar neighbors. There had however been a number of valid sightings prior to the foo fighters. In 1897, an alien craft was rumored to have crashed in Aurora, Texas. The good people of Aurora found the alien pilot and gave him a Christian burial, albeit in an unmarked grave. One of the factors that lent the incident a high sheen of plausibility were the reports of something flying in the air over Aurora a year prior to the crash, which was also twenty years before the Wright brothers first took flight.

The violence of the second World War may have been the factor that first attracted galactic interest. Alien craft were first sighted in November 1944 in World War II Germany. They were called foo fighters by allied fighters. Fast maneuvers, glowing but also non-threatening, they appeared multiple times over the theatre of operations in

Europe, and documented sightings by military personnel went back to 1941. But those sighting were only the tip of the iceberg.

And with this increased activity, there inevitably were crashes. A few cases had been made public—Roswell, Kecksburg, Ontario. But the disinformation campaign had done an incredible job of throwing a blanket of doubt over any reports. The public remained largely unaware of the alien activity over their heads. And the alien subjects in the government's custody.

Everyone in the room was well aware of that history, so Martin knew there was no need to reiterate it. There was a need, however, to change how they presently conducted their research.

"Regardless, now the risk is too great," said Martin. "The subjects must be moved. The risk of human life is one factor, but exposure is another. All these bases are less secure than Area 51. There is simply no safer base in the United States."

Barbara shook her head. "Martin, you've shadowed this committee long enough to know that this proposal of yours is moving too fast. You just got here. We need to think through all the logistics. We act with cool logic, not rash impetuousness."

Martin scanned the room, meeting each of the members' gazes before speaking. "With all due respect, the world has changed radically since I first joined this group. Now everyone has a cellphone with a camera, from the highest level officer on a base down to every member of the janitorial staff. It is only a matter of time before someone takes a picture of something they shouldn't. And that is not the only security issue. *They* are stepping up their game. We need to as well."

"They have made no aggressive moves," Barbara said.

Martin's tone was incredulous. "No aggressive moves? What about Phobos 2?"

"That has never been definitively proven," Barbara countered.

Martin shook his head. And this right here was the problem. Unless proof came in the form of a written confession from an alien race, this body did not believe the evidence. Phobos 2 was about as cut and dry as it got.

In 1988, two Russian probes were sent to investigate the moon of Phobos as it revolved around Saturn. For years, there had been rumors that Phobos was an artificial moon created by an intelligent alien species. The Russians were the first to get close. Phobos 1 orbited the moon without an issue.

But Phobos 2 was not so lucky. It failed as soon as it came in line with the moon. Some say it was destroyed. But regardless, right before it went offline it sent back a photo of a large cylindrical object between the probe and the surface of Saturn before it went dark.

But even that wasn't enough proof for these people, Martin thought derisively. He turned to a small dark haired woman sitting to his left. "But we have more tangible proof of their intent. Isn't that right, Dr. Park?"

Each head turned to Dr. Amelia Park from Harvard. Dr. Park rarely spoke at meetings but when she did, it was always critical information. "It's not just one alien race that is abducting our people," she said.

"What do you mean?" Barbara asked.

Dr. Park looked coolly around the room, her dark eyes devoid of emotion, her voice full of confidence but not arrogance. "Genuine abductions fall into two categories—

those where an individual's body is taken to a ship and those where only their mind travels."

"Their mind? Are you kidding?" Albert said.

Dr. Park frowned. "Of course I'm not kidding."

"Ignore him, Amelia," Barbara said. "Continue."

"The contradictory categories suggest that at least one race is able to telepathically link with its victims and dole out the same treatment—medical experimentation, interaction, and so on, but the victims never physically leave the Earth."

"But isn't that just a hallucination? Or a dream?" Danner asked.

Dr. Park shook her head. "No. The victims demonstrate the same signs of post-traumatic stress and in some cases, even evidence of a medical procedure."

"I don't see how that's possible," Colonel Juarez of the Joint Chiefs said.

Park shook her head, her face troubled. "I don't either. All I know is that it is. Whoever is abducting them is much more advanced than we are. Much more."

Barbara squirmed uncomfortably. But they all knew it was true.

Albert shook his head. "That's not really germane to the discussion. The discussion is about the security of our bases. We have had security breaches in the past at bases. They have all been handled."

Martin shook his head. "But now those security breaches could be made public within seconds. If someone posts a photo, a video—it would expose everything. In the past we had the luxury of people having to search out a platform to make their revelations known. That gave us the time to intercept them. Now the platforms are numerous and there is no time delay."

He scanned the room, knowing each and every person here was well aware of the dangers of cell phones. They were the bane of every law and intelligence agency. "And then how will we explain this to the public? How will we keep the public calm? We all know how the public reacted to the War of the Worlds. And that was only a short fictitious broadcast. What happens when the public realizes we have live specimens in our custody?"

"But moving all of them to one location? That is a huge risk to the projects *and* the people at the base," Colonel Juarez said.

Martin shook his head. "No. It's not. As you well know, everyone at 51 is aware of the risks of their jobs. They have signed away their rights. They were all chosen precisely because they keep their mouths shut, and many have no family to speak of. If something were to go wrong, there will be no tear-soaked pleas for information on TV. No viral videos on YouTube. There will be no demands for accountability. There will be the quiet disappearance of a patriot."

"And you're comfortable with that?" Marine Colonel Julie Reardon asked.

Martin's response held no hesitation, no doubt. "I am. This is the duty we signed up for—to protect this country. And I will do whatever is necessary to accomplish that goal. You are each a member of this committee because you hold that same level of commitment to our goals. This is the next move that must be made. Because if the worst happens and our people are at risk, isn't it better that it occurs somewhere *away* from the public? Somewhere where we have the greatest chance of putting down that threat?"

Albert sneered across the table. "But you'll need to convince Heig to make the move. You don't have that power on your own."

Martin smiled. "Thank you so much for you concern, Albert. But I don't think that will be a problem." He looked around the table. "I call for a vote. All those is in favor of moving all subjects to Area 51, raise their hands."

Ten hands raised in the air. Albert sat defiantly, his arms across his chest. Barbara nodded. "The motion carries. Project Vault is a go."

Chapter Eight

MAEVE HEADED down the hall to the lab. She had set Alvie up with his puppy program—an unending video of puppies at play—so he was happy. She needed to think for a minute. Alvie's episode, whatever it was, had terrified her. In all her years with him, she'd never seen anything like that. It had been a full-blown seizure or had given the appearance of it.

But she'd run an EEG and it provided no indicators of a seizure. So what was it? As she looked back, she realized something had changed about two months ago. One day, Alvie had been staring into space. When she called him, he didn't respond. She touched his shoulder and he seemed to come back to himself. But he had been reserved that whole afternoon. There'd been a handful of other incidents like that since then.

Are they connected? Are they precursors to what I saw today? Usually Alvie would simply zone out, sometimes with a slight tremor. *But today… Good God, what was that?*

As she walked down the hall, she realized her arms were shaking. She shoved her hands into her pocket and ducked into the women's room. She leaned against the wall, taking deep breaths.

She always worried that one day someone would take Alvie away from her. That fear had pushed her to excel in school and even finish her doctorate two years ahead of schedule. She'd crossed every 'T' and dotted every 'I' to make sure there was never a reason for anyone to even consider removing her from Alvie.

But her work was always overseen. Someone was always looking over her shoulder. She knew her appointment had caused some concern. She was young at twenty-eight to be running a project. But her familiarity with Alvie and her rapport with him had helped seal the deal. She'd made a compelling case that introducing someone new could derail all the progress they had made over the years.

It had taken three weeks for them to agree to appoint her. It had been the most nerve-wracking weeks of her life. Not only was she faced with the prospect of losing Alvie, but she had just lost her mother. One soul-crushing loss was all she was capable of handling at a time, and it took all she had to keep it together.

But that's in the past. I've demonstrated to them I can do this. Whatever that episode was, I'll find the answer, because no one knows Alvie better than me. Taking a breath, she opened the door and resumed her trip to the lab.

She pulled the vials of Alvie's blood from her lab coat pocket. She'd taken some of Alvie's blood to check the neurotransmitter levels and to see if the episode had affected any of his other levels. She handed them to the tech with a request that they be rushed.

She frowned as she thought about the chart she'd made to document his sleep disruptions. They'd begun around the time of his first episode. He had started having what she thought were nightmares. He'd wake up from a deep sleep screaming. Occasionally during the day, he'd pull away and curl into the fetal position, unresponsive.

The incidents would only last a few minutes, but they terrified Maeve. She didn't know what to do to help him, and afterwards, he would be much quieter than normal. Which might sound weird to say about a being who didn't talk. But it was as if he moved less, as if he was too tired to do so. She thought it might be his way of coping with the loss of her mom, but she couldn't be sure. If she was being honest, she really had no idea why he was reacting the way he was.

"Someone looks like they need a break."

Maeve's head jolted up and she felt a blush spread across her face. "Hey, Chris."

Captain Chris Garrigan, United States Air Force, walked over with a smile that made Maeve's heart pound a little faster, despite all her concerns for Alvie. Six foot five, with broad shoulders and what Maeve had imagined were washboard abs, he tended to drift into her thoughts even when she needed to focus—which was exactly why she had kept him at arm's length since he had been put in charge of Alvie's security two years ago. Alvie and only Alive needed to be her focus right now.

"I hear you did Tough Mudder this past weekend," Chris said.

Maeve looked up at him in surprise. She had specifically not told him because she knew he'd offer to help her train. "How'd you hear that?"

Chris smiled, showing off a row of perfect teeth, his blue eyes staring down at her. "I have my ways. How was it?"

Maeve smiled, thinking about the ten-mile-long obstacle course. She had run the course with three college friends. "It was incredible."

"Did you take a swim in the mud?"

She shook her head. "Not me. Up and over all the obstacles without fail."

"That's my girl." He paused and nudged his chin down the hall toward the lab. "How's our friend doing tonight?"

Maeve hesitated. Chris had been on the Air Force base commander's staff before he'd been handpicked by Colonel John Forrester for the A.L.I.V.E. project. He had top secret clearance as well, but she always felt weird discussing Alvie with anyone. But Chris *was* one of the few people that Alvie interacted with.

"I don't know," she said. "He seems a little down, but I can't figure out why."

"Well, I have no doubt you will. No one knows him like you do."

Maeve smiled. She had needed to hear that.

"Have you two eaten?" Chris asked.

Maeve shook her head.

"How about I join you guys? I'll bring the food."

Maeve smiled. "That would be great. Thanks."

Chris turned toward the cafeteria. Disappointment flooded her. *He's not going to ask.*

He paused at the door and glanced back at Maeve. Maeve's toes curled in response.

Chris smiled. "So are we going out this weekend?"

Maeve smiled. "Nope."

"Next weekend?"

"Nope.

"Maeve, I've been asking you out for two months now. Should I stop asking?"

She smiled again. "Nope."

Chapter Nine

Two Months Later

MARTIN SAT at a conference table in the office of the Secretary of the Air Force, Wanda Heig.

Wanda flipped through the papers in front of her. Tall with dark hair and a milk chocolate complexion, she was smart, decisive, and formidable. And she was one of the few people in this business Martin actually respected. She was meticulous in her attention to detail, and her work in the intelligence sector made her a person who understood how the world worked—for good and for bad. A fact which the science folks often seemed clueless about.

Wanda continued her inspection of the papers, giving the appearance of making sure she had covered everything. But Martin knew an act when he saw one. She was taking Martin's measure, looking for any subtle queues that would suggest he was not the man for the position she was looking to fill.

Martin gave her nothing, and he knew the file didn't

either. It was a whitewashed version of his history, only hitting the easily palatable events relevant to this position.

Martin sat on the couch and studied her. Although not military, she had an impressive background in Homeland Security. She'd been one of the founders of Homeland after 9/11 and had quickly and deservedly risen through the ranks there. Her appointment to the Secretary position four years ago had been well received.

Wanda pushed the papers in front of her aside. "So tell me, without any political double speak, why you think you are best suited to run BOSAC."

BOSAC—the Bureau of Scientific Advancement and Cooperation—was tasked with overseeing the United States government's most secretive biological counterstrike advancement projects. Over the last seven months, Martin had helped create the agency behind the scenes. But being declared the director, that took a little more push than he could do alone. He had, however, pressured every single contact he had with clout to support his application. Now he just needed to pass this one final test.

"I believe the nature of these projects requires a more careful inspection. They should fall under one agency, not be part of a catalog of projects within another agency."

Wanda studied him, and Martin made sure to keep her gaze while sitting back, seeming unthreatening.

"And what do you believe is the most critical aspect of these projects?"

"Secrecy."

Wanda raised an eyebrow. "Secrecy?"

He nodded. "Yes. The American public is not ready to handle what is being created in our labs. And keeping them from knowing any of that is the most critical component in making sure our scientists have what they need to move forward."

"And how would *you* ensure this secrecy?"

He met her gaze. "My background has shown me that there are times when violence is necessary, as I'm sure you're thinking. But it's also shown me that oftentimes, it is overused."

"How so?"

"People can be led. Violence should be a last solution and only in dire situations. No, disinformation is the name of the game. Anyone who attempts to break the story of the United States involvement with UFOs should be and will be quickly dealt with through ridicule, through slight of hand, or in some cases with a more final method. But humans are generally sheep, willing to be led along by any ridiculous story." He smiled, a look he'd been practicing in the mirror. "And apparently they think the US launches a ton of weather balloons, with the amount that sorry excuse is used and believed."

He saw the acknowledgement in the Secretary's eyes, the small smile breaking across her lips. He had her.

Wanda nodded and stood, offering her hand. "Congratulations, Martin. You are now the official head of BOSAC."

Martin stood as well as he shook her hand. "Thank you, Madame Secretary. I appreciate your faith in me."

"It will take you a few weeks to get up to speed. After that, I look forward to seeing what you can do,"

Martin smiled. *Oh, and I can't wait to show you either.*

Chapter Ten

Three Months Later

THE SOUND of Alvie's laughter made Maeve smile. He was curled up on his couch, reading a Calvin and Hobbes comic. His eyes were bright, his mouth was turned up, and every once in a while he would let out a little squeal. It was one of the only sounds he was capable of making.

It was hard for Maeve to focus on her own work when he was in such a good mood. All she wanted to do was watch him. Alvie let out another laugh, and Maeve couldn't help but laugh herself. A laugh came from outside Alvie's room and she caught Chris's gaze as he stood outside Alvie's room. He grinned back at her, and then his grin faded.

Maeve's head whipped back to Alvie as he stared off into space, the book dropping from his hands. Alvie screamed, bringing his hands to the side of his head as he rocked from side to side.

Maeve shoved herself back from the desk and was at his side in a flash. The incident was over by the time she reached him. She made it in time to catch him as he slumped to the floor.

Chris keyed himself into Alvie's bedroom and kneeled down on Alvie's other side. "Alvie?"

Maeve gathered Alvie into her lap and rocked him from side to side. "Shh, it's okay. Shh, I've got you."

Chris crouched down next to her and she looked up into his concerned blue eyes. "What the hell was that?" he asked.

Maeve swallowed, not knowing what to say.

"Maeve, what's going on? What just happened?"

Maeve looked up into his eyes, feeling all the fear she had shouldered alone these last few months slip out for a moment. "I don't know."

Maeve had searched every relevant and irrelevant possibility she could think of, trying to find a cause for Alvie's episodes, but nothing fit. She was beginning to wonder if there was a genetic link, maybe some inherited trait similar to epilepsy or some other medical condition. The human genome had been completely mapped by 2003 and since that time, they had learned an incredible amount about the role of genes in an individual's behavior. It stood to reason that Alvie's genome could offer her just as much information.

The problem was, she was not allowed access to it. In fact, all of Alvie's early history was off-limits to her. And if she asked to do a genetic screening, she would have to justify it. And so far, she had been able to keep Alvie's incidents to herself. Until today.

But keeping it to herself meant she had no one to discuss the possibilities with. She wanted to speak with Greg about it. With his background in genetics, he'd be a great person to bounce possibilities off of. But that wasn't an option either. In fact, the only people she could speak to about it had no background in the sciences, and any mention would get written in a report and sent up the chain of command.

"Just help me put him in bed, okay?" Maeve asked quietly.

Chris nodded, carefully lifting Alvie and placing him gently in his bed, pulling the blankets over him. Shaken, Maeve followed them over and sat on the floor next to Alvie's bed, running her hand over Alvie's head and back.

"Maeve?"

Maeve read the question in his eyes. She shook her head. "I don't know, Chris. I don't know what's happening."

"This has happened before."

She nodded. "Yes."

"Why haven't you said anything?"

"Because you know what can happen. If I don't have answers—" Her voice broke off, and she just shook her head.

"You don't know that, Maeve. They could—"

She wiped a tear from the corner of her eye before it could fall. "The US government does not care about how much I care about Alvie and how much he cares about me. They care about results. And if there's a problem and I can't solve it, well, then I'm of no use to them."

Chris sat on the floor next to her, blowing out a breath. "What do you want me to do?"

"Just don't tell anybody, okay?"

"Maeve…"

"Please. I just need more time. I'll figure it out. No one knows him better than me. Please Chris."

Chris looked into her eyes for a long moment before he nodded. "Okay."

"Thank you." And suddenly she felt like crying. She took a shuddering breath.

Chris scooted closer, wrapping his arm around her. "You're not the only one who cares about him, you know."

She nodded, not trusting herself to speak, so she just laid her head on his shoulder.

"You're not alone, Maeve," he said quietly.

Maeve looked at Alvie, who rested quietly in front of her, knowing it was up to her to find out what was going on with him. She lay a hand on his back. *Because I'm all he has.*

Chapter Eleven

ALVIE SLEPT for an hour and then woke up. Chris had stepped out to do his rounds and Maeve was glad to see him go. She trusted Chris, but he was proving to be more and more of a distraction When he was around she wanted to lean on him and tell him all her worries. But right now, she couldn't afford that.

Alvie seemed to have recovered from his episode, but his movements were a little more sluggish. Even so, he did extraordinarily well on the remainder of the physical tests. Some were new, most he had seen before. For the older tests he showed improvement in each one, and Maeve knew that when she ran him through the newer tests next week, he would also improve. Alvie's intelligence included learning physical activities. It was almost as if he had some form of enhanced muscle memory.

Now, as requested—yet again—she'd set him up with a program of puppy pictures. Lately, he'd even begun to ask her when he could meet one. Maeve was still trying to figure out how to make that happen.

She glanced at the clock. Alvie had another ten minutes and then she was going to test his mental abilities. A colleague at Cal Tech had created math tests for him. The professor didn't know who the subject of the tests were and Alvie's skills had outperformed Maeve's years ago. So she arranged for him to receive certain textbooks followed by a test to see how he retained the knowledge. So far, he picked up math and science incredibly quickly.

Literature, he enjoyed, but she could tell he struggled with the human condition, and works that had too much emotion stressed him out. It had taken Maeve a little while to realize it was due to his empathy. It had only grown over time, and even reading about someone struggling caused him pain. So she tried to keep the books towards the funny side. Comics were among his favorites, particularly Calvin and Hobbes. He'd read and re-read those comics so much she'd had to replace the whole set twice.

Her phone rang, interrupting her thoughts, and she glanced at the screen before answering. "Hello?"

"Please hold for Colonel Forrester."

Surprise flashed through Maeve. A few seconds later, Colonel John Forrester's deep voice came through the line. "Hi, Maeve. Long time no chat."

With a smile, Maeve slid down onto Alvie's couch, curling her legs up underneath her. "Hi, Uncle John. I know, I'm sorry. It's been hectic."

'Uncle' John was the base commander, but he had been a friend of her mother's for as long as Maeve could remember. And he had been her father's best friend up until his death before Maeve was born. A confirmed bachelor, he seemed to like trying out family life with her and her mom, and even sometimes Alvie.

John sighed. "I know you're busy. But you should be making time to spend with other people. Are you dating?"

Maeve groaned. "Really? You're asking me about my love life?"

"I promised your mother I would make sure you didn't spend all your time in the lab. And I intend to honor that promise. Don't be an old workhorse like me."

The pang of grief travelled through Maeve's body. She knew John missed her mother as much as she did. They never said anything, but Maeve had known they had been more than friends. She'd been happy for them and never really understood why they didn't go public with their relationship. Maybe it was because he was the base commander and they worried about how that would look. But whatever the reason, Maeve thought they had both missed their shot.

Like mother like daughter, Maeve thought as an image of Chris passed through her mind.

"Well, I happen to think you've turned out just fine, even if you are an old workhorse," Maeve said.

"Thanks, kid." His tone turned serious. "But I'm not actually calling just to needle you about your social life."

Maeve tensed, but she tried to keep her voice unaffected. "Okay. What's up?"

"I'm going to need you to give a video conference on Alvie—his abilities, your findings. Basically, I need you to sum up everything you know about him in about fifteen minutes."

Maeve sputtered. "Fifteen minutes? You can't possibly be serious."

"I am, and the conference is scheduled for tomorrow at 3."

"3 a.m.?" Maeve asked hopefully.

John laughed. "I'm afraid not. 3 p.m."

Maeve groaned. Working with Alvie meant her days were completely reversed from most people's. She slept while they were enjoying their lives, and she was wide awake when they were sleeping. A 3 p.m. meeting was the middle of her night.

She sighed but didn't complain. It would get her nowhere. "Who is the presentation for? And what's the rush?"

"I'm afraid I can't answer either of those questions."

Maeve sighed, knowing that was all the information she was going to get. But it didn't make it easier to swallow. She'd grown up around the base and all of its rules. Her mother joked that 'need to know' was the first phrase Maeve had ever uttered. Once Maeve had received her top secret clearance, though, she thought that meant she would have the answers to some of her questions. But she'd soon realized it only meant she'd have more to wonder about.

She glanced over to where Alvie had switched from the puppy to a computer coding program she'd introduced him to last week. Like everything else, he'd picked it up quickly, the logic clear to him. She frowned. Why would someone be asking about Alvie now? She had read people into Alvie's program every once in a while, but usually she knew who she was presenting to. Not knowing was a first. Did it have anything to do with the increased security at the base over the last few months?

"Maeve?" John asked.

Maeve pulled herself back to the conversation. "Right, just trying to re-work my schedule in my head."

She could hear the smile in John's voice. "Oh, come on, you could rattle off about Alvie all day long without any prep. You'll do fine."

"True, but confining that rattling off to only fifteen minutes is going to be the tough part."

John chuckled. "I'm sure you'll figure it out. So tell me what's been happening in your life."

Maeve chatted with John for the next few minutes about her weekend and his. But the presentation and what she needed to pull together was a specter looming in the back of her mind.

After they had said their good-byes and she had disconnected the call, Alvie walked over and sat next to her, looking up at her with his big eyes. She took his hand. "So apparently someone wants to know all about you."

Alvie tilted his head.

"It's okay. I have eight hours to pull together all the research that's been conducted on you over the last twenty-five years and synthesize it into a coherent presentation. Then power nap, and get back here. Completely doable."

Alvie looked at her, and even without sclera, she could read the concern in his eyes.

She forced a smile to her face. "It's okay, really. How about we go do a puzzle?"

Alvie nodded before hopping off the couch and heading for the shelves with the puzzles. Even before he reached it, she knew which one he would pick out—the thousand-piece puzzle filled with puppies. He always picked the same one.

I really need to figure out how to get him a puppy. Maybe I can call it an inter-species communication project.

But that would have to wait, because someone new wanted to know about Alvie. It always made her nervous when someone else expressed an interest. Alvie was not human. And she knew someone could view him as a threat if they didn't understand who he was.

Alvie's existence was a closely kept secret. As far as

Maeve knew, no more than two dozen people knew he even existed. And now someone new was being read in. At the exact same time that Alvie was showing signs of unpredictability for the first time in his life.

Maeve swallowed as she walked toward him.

Please let this be nothing.

Chapter Twelve

MAEVE FLIPPED THROUGH HER NOTES, keeping one eye on Alvie, who was playing a computer game. The computer was not attached to the internet, by the base's command. He looked content. Maeve glanced back at the results from the blood test this morning. All his neurotransmitter levels were still low, just as they had been for months.

Yet another thing to be worried about. Alvie was allowed certain privileges because his behavior was so predictable. Unpredictability tended to make the higher ups nervous.

Alvie stopped the computer game and turned away. The screen showed the game wasn't done.

"Alvie? Everything okay?"

He just looked at her without moving.

"Alvie?"

The number 872-AR flashed through her mind. Maeve jolted back.

What the hell was that?

She stared at Alvie, her heart beginning to pound. "Did you do that?"

Alvie just looked at her. Maeve had theorized that Alvie could communicate telepathically even though it had never happened before. She'd never even hinted at the possibility. He had no voice box, so vocal communication wasn't possible, but his race had to communicate somehow. She'd ruled out pheromones because he didn't have them, which left touch or some kind of telepathic ability. He was able to communicate his emotions that way but this was the first time he'd ever shared specific information.

872-AR

Maeve's heart pounded harder. "Alvie, was that you?"

He nodded his head, and she felt her legs grow weak. "What are you trying to tell me?"

The door outside the lab opened and Chris walked in carrying three lunch trays. Alvie turned away from Maeve and hopped off his chair. He hustled over to the table and quickly started scooping the puzzle back into the box. But Maeve didn't move. She just sat where she was, her heart still pounding. What had that been?

The only time she had seen that kind of notation was in reference to a building. Room 872 in the archives building. Why would Alvie's first communication involve that place? And besides, how would he even know about that building? It's not like he'd been given a tour of the base at any point.

"Hey, want to get the door?" Chris asked from the other side of the glass wall.

"Uh, yeah, sorry." Maeve got awkwardly to her feet, pushing aside her reports, and walked over to the control pad. With a whoosh of air, it slid open.

Chris walked in with a grin. "Lunch is served."

He placed the trays on the table where Alvie was finishing up putting the puzzle away.

"Let me help you, bud." Chris slid a long line of pieces into the box, then held the box for Alvie to do the same.

Even though Maeve was still trying to figure out what had just happened with the numbers, she couldn't help but marvel at Alvie's interactions with Chris. There'd been other individuals who had interacted with Alvie in the past but none of them had the rapport with Alvie that Chris had. To Maeve it was almost like a big brother little brother relationship.

Chris walked the puzzle over to the shelves as Alvie climbed into his chair. Chris slid a tray in front of him, taking off the lid. "Bon appétit, my friend."

He glanced over at Maeve. "You joining us, Doc?"

"Um, yeah. Sorry. A little lost there."

"You're going to do great with the presentation. Just show them that big brain of yours."

Maeve forced herself to focus on the food in front of her. "I'm sure you're right. The presentation's just distracting me."

"Well, if you need to work, Alvie and I can hang out. We're only halfway through Season 3 of *Chuck*. Right, buddy?"

Alvie nodded his head with a smile, and Maeve's heart melted a little. She forced a smile to her face. "Great. Thanks." She watched Alvie, but he simply dug into his lunch as if nothing had happened. But Maeve couldn't help but wonder and worry.

872-AR. Why did you show me that? And how did you do it?

Chapter Thirteen

MAEVE SPENT the rest of the night working on the presentation and on trying to keep her fears from Alvie. He was incredibly sensitive to other people's moods. In fact, his ability to read people's emotional states had increased dramatically in the last year. Maeve wondered if he wasn't actually developing into an empath—an individual with the ability to feel and even influence others' emotions. She hadn't mentioned anything about her suspicions in her notes because she knew any indication that Alvie could influence others was going to scare the hell out of people.

Just like it scared her—although not for the same reasons. Maeve trusted Alvie. There was no unkindness in him. But if he developed telepathic abilities, even empathetic abilities, and the military found out, she knew their first question would be about how to weaponize it.

But it was hours now since 872-AR had flashed through her mind, and she was beginning to wonder if she had just made it up. Alvie was his normal self, curled up next to Chris, watching TV.

Maybe I'm the one losing it.

Maeve blew out a breath, staring at her computer screen. She had finally determined the organization of her presentation and filled in the critical information she thought would be best. But now, she'd had enough. Closing her laptop, she pushed it off her lap. "Okay, that's it. I need a break."

Chris looked up from where he and Alvie sat on the couch. "About damn time. We've been waiting for you. I'll go let them know." He disappeared out of the room.

Maeve turned to Alvie. "Sorry—big presentation tomorrow. But I didn't forget. I never would." She held out her hand to him. "Come on. Let's get some air."

Alvie scrambled off the couch and ran over to her, a smile on his face as he took her hand.

They stepped out into the control room. Chris gave her a nod. "We're ready."

He opened the door to the hallway and Maeve stepped out. She could feel Alvie's excitement.

The hall was empty, but Maeve knew it wasn't just the hall—it was the entire floor. Ahead, the elevator stood open, waiting for them.

They stepped in and Chris hit the button for the roof. The elevator rose quickly and stopped softly at the roof.

Chris stepped out first and nodded at the guard there. He looked back at Maeve and Alvie with a smile. "All clear."

Maeve stepped out and Alvie pulled away, staring up at the sky. Maeve watched him for a moment before settling back against the wall, crossing her feet at her ankles. She knew from experience she'd be here a while.

Her mom had managed to get permission years ago to bring Alvie out here. Maeve tried to bring him up here once a month, but not any more than that. She didn't want to push it. After all, it took a lot of coordination and resources to make this happen. Each time they came out here security went on high alert to the extent that even F-14s were placed on standby. At the slightest hint of a problem, she and Alvie would be whisked back inside and these outings would be finished.

But so far, there'd never been any issues.

Maeve smiled, remembering celebrating her mom's last birthday up here with Alvie. There'd been balloons and cake. Chris had been here as well as Greta and John. Her mom had looked so happy, despite her gaunt frame. It had been one of her last good days. She'd passed away only three weeks later. Maeve swallowed down the moment of melancholy, not wanting Alvie to sense it and have it dampen his outing.

"Has he ever been out in the daylight?" Chris asked.

Maeve shook her head. "No."

"Security concerns?"

"Yes, but also eyes."

Chris frowned. "What do you mean?"

"He can't handle the sunlight as well."

"Couldn't you get him some sunglasses?"

Maeve laughed, imagining Alvie in some Ray-Bans. "We could. But it seemed wiser to just let him go out at night when he's more comfortable and when there's less chance of him being seen."

Alvie wandered along the rail of the building and then took a seat at one of the chairs in the corner. He sat silently, staring up at the sky.

Chris leaned against the wall next to her, his gaze also on Alvie. "What do you think he's thinking when he looks up there?"

"I don't know. He never shares his thoughts when he's up here."

"Do you think he knows he's from up there?" Chris asked.

"I don't think so."

Surprise flashed across Chris's face. "Why not?"

"We've never been allowed to tell him."

"What?"

"One of the cardinal rules of the A.L.I.V.E. Project—the subject is not allowed to know anything about how they came to be. So, no, he doesn't know." She swallowed down the familiar guilt and shame that accompanied her words. She didn't agree with the rule, but she wasn't in a position to go against it, not if she wanted to stay with Alvie.

"So where does he think he comes from?"

Maeve sighed. "I don't know. He's asked."

"What have you told him?"

"That I don't know. Because that's the truth."

"You don't know?"

Maeve nodded. "My mom knew, but she wasn't allowed to tell me. And I don't have access to those early records."

"Haven't *you* asked?"

Maeve nodded. "But I was told in no uncertain terms that it was beyond the scope of the project."

"Are you sure he doesn't know? I mean, I thought he was telepathic."

Maeve's head whipped toward Chris, her heart pounding. "Telepathic? What makes you say that?"

"He can't talk, which from what I gather is biological. His people must be able to communicate in some way."

Maeve just stared at him.

"What? I went to college."

Maeve gave a small laugh. "Sorry, I'm just surprised. No

one else has ever mentioned that before. And I'm not sure if he's telepathic. He can communicate his emotions and he can feel others' emotions. Sometimes he's been able to receive an idea from my mind, but I have to really focus to make that happen. And honestly, we know each other so well, he may just know what I want. I've tried it with Greta and he doesn't seem to understand what she's trying to communicate."

"So he doesn't know what he is?"

Maeve shrugged, feeling the sadness she always did at the idea of Alvie being the only one of his kind on a planet of over seven billion humans. "I don't think so."

"That's really sad—being the only one of his kind."

"Well, at least on this planet," she said.

Chris raised an eyebrow. "Any ideas which one he's from?"

Maeve shook her head. "We used to think our solar system was the only part of the big universe. Then in 1995, 51 Pegasi B was found—the first planet orbiting a sun outside our solar system. Soon we realized Pegasi was just the beginning. There were more planets out there—a lot more. To date, they've discovered over three thousand exoplanets. And even that number is a gross underestimate."

"An underestimate? Why?"

"Planets are found by the Kepler space telescope through the subtle dimming of a star's light from a planet's crossing in front of it. Larger planets will therefore be more likely to be noticed. Smaller planets may be too small for Kepler to detect. Even so, dozens of the planets we *do* know about exist in the Goldilocks Zone."

"The Goldilocks Zone?"

"An area of space just the right distance from a sun,

making the planet not too hot and not too cold. Just the right temperature to support life. They've found other Earth-like planets, some of which are huge. In the Milky Way alone, approximately 160 billion planets are estimated to exist. Of course, much like our solar system, most are believed to be without life. But what are the chances all are?"

She took a breath. "And thanks to Kepler, there are close to a hundred planets that we believe may be suitable for life. But even then, no one knows what type of life. It could be microbial—which is not exactly what people are thinking about when they mention E.T.s."

Chris was quiet for a moment. "How many types do you think are out there?"

"I don't know. I think Alvie's type exists. I'm guessing he's one of the grays you hear about in alien abduction stories. But even then, there seem to be variations in those descriptions, meaning there could be different types of gray aliens."

"So do you think it's just gray aliens?"

"No. But they could be as rudimentary in their technology as we are. There could be millions of types but without the technology to either go there or have them come here, we'll never know." She smiled. "Or there could just be two."

Chris grinned. "So where do you think Alvie's from?"

Her dreams popped back into her mind, but Maeve shoved them away, not sure why she'd be thinking about that right now. "I don't know. Sometimes, he seems so human, you know?"

"Yeah."

"But then when you watch him on the obstacle course

or play on the computer you realize exactly how different he is."

Chris looked around, making sure the other guard wasn't close enough to hear. "Have you figured out anything about his episodes? Do you think it's related to how down he's been lately?"

Maeve focused on keeping her breathing even and her face neutral. She was surprised Chris had noticed, but she shouldn't be. Chris was extremely perceptive. And empathetic. He and Alvie are a lot alike. "No, but he has his ups and downs like anyone else."

Chris studied her face for a moment. "You're sure?"

Maeve looked up into his eyes and saw the concern there. And she wanted more than anything to tell him her fears about Alvie. But she turned away. "Yup. You haven't told anyone about the episode, have you?"

"I told you I wouldn't. But if he's having them regularly, you know it's only matter of time before somebody realizes what's happening, right?"

Maeve looked away from him and watched Alvie sitting along the rooftop, his face blissful as he looked up at the night sky.

She wasn't nearly as blissful. Because she knew Chris was right. It was only a matter of time. And she was no closer to finding the answers for his episodes now than she had been when they first began.

Chapter Fourteen

TUGGING on the collar of her suit, Maeve stared at her reflection in the locker room's mirror. She'd never made it home last night, or more accurately, this morning. She had slept in the lab, figuring it would give her a little extra time to get the presentation together. Greta had swung by her apartment before coming to the base and grabbed Maeve's presentation suit.

And no doubt stocked Maeve's refrigerator with groceries while she was at it. Maeve smiled. Her mom had gotten Greta to promise to look after her as well. After Maeve's grandmother had passed away, they'd had no other family—it had only been the two of them. So her mom had created an extended family that they could call on, and more important for her mother, that would look after Maeve when she was gone.

No. No more thinking about Mom. You need to focus, she warned herself.

Forcing her thoughts to the presentation, she turned to inspect her suit in the mirror. She rarely wore it. She wore scrubs all the time at the base or her regular clothes when off base. Suits were only necessary for the rare meeting. And seeing as she couldn't publish any of her findings, having a professional wardrobe wasn't really that necessary.

She smoothed the black jacket down over the matching skirt. A red blouse underneath and black heels finished the outfit. It was simple and sophisticated, or at least that's what the sales woman had said when Maeve had bought it.

Maeve pulled her hair back into a chignon and turned around to glance over her shoulder. *Well, I guess this is as good as it gets.* She'd put on a little extra make-up today to hopefully hide the dark circles under her eyes and to make her look a little older. Compared to other scientists running projects, she knew she was on the young side.

Grabbing her notes, she stepped out of the locker room and headed for the elevator.

A low whistle stopped her.

Chris grinned. "You sure do clean up nice, Doc."

Maeve felt the heat rush into her cheeks. "Thanks."

"So now's the big presentation, huh?"

Maeve nodded, stepping into the elevator as the door opened. "Yup."

"Nervous?" Chris asked as he stepped in next to her. "Yup."

He hit the button for the third floor. "You'll do great. Just show them what the rest of us see every day and you'll have them eating out of the palm of your hand."

Maeve glanced over to check if he was joking, but he didn't look like he was.

He looked down at her, his blue eyes serious. "It's going to be fine. No one knows him better than you, and no one is better suited for this project than you."

Somehow Chris always seemed to know exactly what to say. "Thanks, Chris."

The doors opened and they headed down the hall. Maeve paused outside the door to the conference room.

Chris stopped with her and leaned down. "You've got this."

Maeve nodded, swallowing her fear and squaring her shoulders. *Right. I've got this.*

Chapter Fifteen

MAEVE STEPPED into the conference room, surprised when there was only a technician inside. He stood up by the large screen, fiddling with some wires and glancing at his computer.

"Um, hey, Gabe, am I in the wrong place?" Maeve asked.

Gabe looked up, and his glasses slid from the top of his head onto his face. He pushed them back up. "Hey, Maeve. No. It's just you today. The rest will be linked in."

"Okay. Where are they being linked from?"

"Sorry, can't tell you that. In fact, you won't even be able to see them." He rushed on. "But you will be able to hear them."

Well, gee, that's great. Maeve's butterflies increased. "Oh, okay."

While she didn't like giving lectures, she liked the idea of giving a lecture in an empty room to faceless individuals even less.

"But they'll be able to see me, right?" Maeve asked.

"Yup."

"Well, that's ... fun."

Gabe gave a small laugh as he fiddled with the screen and a Department of Defense emblem flashed on. Maeve frowned. *The DOD?*

"Okay," Gabe said as he turned. "We're good to go. Someone will notify you when you can start. Should only be another minute or two."

"Where should I stand?"

Gabe nudged his chin toward the front of the room where a podium had been placed at the end of the table. "Right there. Camera's trained on it. Good luck."

"Thanks," Maeve said as Gabe headed for the door. As the door closed behind him, she turned and studied the room. She had pictured a few people in here.

Okay, no biggie. She headed for the podium. She pulled her papers from her pocket. She wouldn't need the notes, but she liked the security of having them. She unfolded them, straightening them out on the podium.

"Dr. Leander."

Maeve's head jolted up and she looked at the screen. It still had the DOD emblem. "Um, yes?"

"We're ready to go when you are."

"Yes, of course." Maeve took a breath, gathering her thoughts for a second before speaking. "My name is Dr. Maeve Leander. I have been the lead scientist for subject #1 of the A.L.I.V.E. Project for three years now, though my knowledge of the subject actually spans over two decades."

"How is that possible?" a female cut in.

Maeve paused, not sure what to say. She had thought everyone would have been briefed on her history with Alvie. She quickly ran through it. She paused but no one said anything.

"Okay, well, Alvie is approximately twenty-seven years old. He stands at three and a half feet tall and weighs in at thirty-eight pounds. He has no nasal cavity, a larger cranium than a human of a comparable height. In fact, his brain is a third larger than a human's."

"Is he more intelligent?" a male voice cut in. There was a nasal quality to it, and Maeve pictured the speaker as a modern-day Ichabod Crane: tall, dour, pale.

"That's difficult to say. He picks up on things quickly. Just yesterday he did a thousand-piece puzzle in under two hours. I helped a little." She smiled, but she had no way of knowing if anyone smiled back.

She cleared her throat. "Right, well, due to his physiology, vocal communication is not possible. He has no voice box."

"So he can't communicate?" the woman asked.

"No, he can't *vocally* communicate. He provides nonverbal physical indicators of his wants and needs, and his face is actually very expressive."

"What about telepathy? Have you considered that possibility?" Ichabod asked.

Maeve forced herself to keep her tone normal as the number 872-AR flashed through her mind again. But she wasn't ready to mention that. "No, no indications as of yet. His emotions come across clearly but as for his actual thoughts, that has not been confirmed. But he does mature at a slower rate than humans so it's possible in time he will in fact develop the ability at some point in the future. Even though biologically he is twenty-seven, in terms of maturity he's closer to thirteen or fourteen."

"What about his physical capabilities?" The female asked.

Maeve smiled. "Despite his shape, he is surprisingly agile. I've run him through obstacle courses to check his reflexes and his physical capabilities and I am always amazed at how fast he is and how well he can maneuver around obstacles. He looks like a child doing parkour really, really well."

"His strength?" Ichabod asked.

"He's strong but not exceptionally so. But definitely more than one would expect from his physique. His arms are very small, thin, although longer than a human's proportionally. He also has four fingers rather than five, which means he cannot write well."

"But he does write?" The man asked.

Maeve nodded. "Yes. He understands English and can write at a college level, maybe even grad school."

Silence greeted her response and it was impossible to determine if they were shocked by her words or simply waiting for her to continue.

"He can write at a college level?" the man asked.

Shock it is, Maeve thought. "Yes. Like I said earlier, he is smart."

"And is he a danger?" the man asked.

Surprise flashed through her. Had these people not read any of the notes on Alvie? She frowned. "No. He's never demonstrated any aggression towards anyone. In fact, he's only demonstrated the opposite—empathetic compassion. He is in a word, sweet."

"And what about his sleep disturbances?" the female asked.

Maeve had known they were going to ask about them. Greta had been on duty during most of those incidents. She struggled to keep her tone neutral. "I believe they are nothing more than nightmares. When he's awoken, while he *is* scared, he's not aggressive. In fact, he's looking for comfort, assurance."

"And what about his neurotransmitter levels? How do you account for that?" Ichabod asked.

"I—I'm not sure yet. It's possible he's experiencing some mild depression. But even that would be natural."

"Natural?" the man asked, and even without the face, she could hear the disbelief in his voice.

"He's been relatively isolated his entire life. As he matures, he may want to experience more than he currently has been able to. Think of it like a teenager wanting more independence or an inmate serving a life sentence. He needs something to help him adjust as he matures in his environment."

"And *how* are you planning on doing that?" the man asked.

"I intend to try to increase his experiences—in a controlled setting, of course," Maeve said.

"Are you talking about taking him out?" the woman asked.

"No, of course not. I was actually thinking about beginning an inter-species interaction analysis. The idea would be to begin with pictures of other animals and record his responses. And then, possibly bring in live animals that he would see first through glass and perhaps eventually actually allow him to touch."

"And what would the goal of this be?" the woman asked.

"Alvie is an incredibly empathetic individual. I've been wondering if that empathy extends beyond humans. This project would allow us to determine that."

And maybe get Alvie a puppy.

"I see. And what happens if the subject demonstrates aggression towards the other species?" Ichabod asked.

Doubt it. "Well, that will tell us something too."

No one spoke for a long minute, and then the voice that she had heard at the beginning came back on. "Thank you, Dr. Leander. That will be all."

"You're welcome." Maeve waited until the DOD emblem disappeared. Then she stepped away from the podium with a frown. They seemed awfully concerned about Alvie's potential aggression. But Alvie had never demonstrated any. Generally when she did these presentations her audience was fascinated by the subject. And while they asked about aggression, they didn't dwell on it. After all, Alvie was guarded round the clock. He had been his entire life. If he was aggressive and placed anyone at risk, it would be handled immediately. But there had never been a moment of concern.

She hadn't been able to recognize the man's voice, but the female voice had been undeniable—Secretary of the Air Force, Wanda Heig. Maeve had presented to her before. *But why all the secrecy now?*

Maeve gathered her notes, the butterflies still flying around in her stomach. She'd thought that after the presentation she'd feel a sense of relief. But that's not what she felt at all. It felt like something was about to happen. And whatever it was, she didn't think it was going to be in Alvie's best interest.

Chapter Sixteen

WASHINGTON D.C.

THE SCREEN WENT dark and Martin sat quietly in the guest chair in front of Wanda Heig's desk, mulling over Dr. Leander's response. There had been something there. Something she was trying to hide.

Wanda turned off the screen before returning to her seat behind her desk. She nodded to Martin. "What do you think?"

Martin took a moment to compose himself before answering. This was the last telecommunication conference they needed to have. So far, they had spoken with every single scientist working for the United States government who was running an A.L.I.V.E. project. But this one was the project that elicited the most emotion from Martin—and that emotion was hate. The former Dr. Leander had been the reason he'd been forced to the sidelines for years.

He shoved that old anger and resentment aside. In a few days, it wouldn't matter. Everything would be in place and neither Leander would be worthy of his thoughts.

As far as he knew, Wanda knew nothing of that particular history, but until he had everything in place, he needed to make sure she didn't.

He put his hand to his chin, pretending to mull over her question. "I think the project is interesting, but too many chances are being taken with these subjects. Wright-Patt is only eighty miles northeast of Dayton. Dayton has a hundred and fifty thousand people. If one of those things were to get out, it would be a bloodbath."

"You mean Alvie?" Wanda asked. "What Dr. Leander said about his history is true: he's never demonstrated any aggression."

"But that's not the case for all of them housed at Wright, is it? The Kecksburg-AG2, the one they call Hank, imagine all the damage it could do in a short time."

"True," Wanda conceded. "But Wright-Patt has a long history of keeping things wrapped up, in fact, they have since the very beginning. Blue Book was housed there. The Foreign Technology Division. All of it has remained secret."

"You mean while it was going on. But there *have* been leaks. The eye of the world has turned toward Wright-Patt. UFO buffs all know about the wreckage from Roswell arriving there, and they even suspect the wreckage from other crashes have been stored there. And some of the Wright-Patt people have talked."

Of course, that was at the end of their lives, or they had something released after they died—much to Martin's annoyance. After all, it was pretty hard to threaten a dead man. But the damage had been done. The worst case was former Wright-Patt secretary, June Crain. In 1997, Crain claimed to have seen not only alien spacecraft but also alien bodies at Wright-Patt back in 1942 and 1953. And due to her job as a stenographer who understood science, she actually had top-secret clearance while on the base, lending her quite a bit of credibility.

The most infamous individual to make claims, though, had to be former senator for Arizona, Barry Goldwater, who during his political career was the chairman of the U.S. Government's Senate Intelligence Committee, and the Republican Party's nominee for President in 1964. From 1974 on, Goldwater spoke about his attempts ten years earlier to access the Blue Room at Wright-Patt and Hanger 18 to see what he believed to be evidence of alien crashes. He was denied, but publicly spoke about his attempts and his strongly held beliefs that there was something at Wright-Patterson Air Force Base.

Damned senators, always getting in the way, Martin thought. But when he spoke, his voice gave no inkling of the storm of information swirling through his mind. "The base has done well, but that was before everyone had a camera on their phones. That was before everyone knew about what's *hidden* at Wright-Patt. And even though they've managed to keep things contained, some things have slipped out. And it's only a matter of time before the public no longer wonders, but instead demands transparency. And if the files on the A.L.I.V.E. Project or any of its precursors ever get opened, all the dirty little secrets at Wright-Patt will be spilled. Even school children know about Hangar 18."

Although the number repeated in the public sphere was wrong, everything else about the infamous hangar that had made it into the public eye was correct. The wreckage from Roswell had been shipped to Wright-Patterson AFB shortly after it was collected. Five of the bodies had been moved to the base. And the bodies had been extensively studied.

Martin couldn't blame the public entirely. After all, the military had stated that the Foreign Technology Division's directive was to gather and analyze specialized global intelligence on current threats from the air and space realms. As a result, it didn't take a lot of imagination to figure if there was alien aircraft, the FTD and later the NASIC was where it would be taken.

Wanda nodded. "Making these changes is going to be dramatic, though. I mean, the movement of the staff alone is going to be a logistics nightmare, especially all at once. So I am asking you, do you really think Project Vault is the right call? That could be equally as dangerous."

"It could be, but at least if there is a problem, we have more of a cushion to respond. Even today, there were reports of intruders on the base. The site is no longer secure."

Three animal rights demonstrators had made it through the fence at Wright-Patt. They'd been stopped, but not before they had spray-painted a few choice slogans across two buildings in the research area. Martin had had to dip into his black budget to make that little bit of security failure happen.

"And after Lowry, I'm not willing to take any chances. Allowing these projects to be spread all over the map—" He shook his head. "We've been lucky so far, but we can't count on that being the case forever. And 51 is more heavily guarded than any other base in the United States."

"But Project Vault is a little extreme," Wanda said.

"So is the subject." Martin interwove his fingers, creating a teepee on his chest. "And you know there is an even greater danger than just a few human lives on the line should these activities come to light."

Wanda met his gaze with a nod. The public at large had never been read into the alien situation. It had been decided that the release of that information would result in widespread panic. The radio broadcast of War of the Worlds aptly demonstrated that point.

On October 30th, 1938, Orson Welles led a broadcast of a fictionalized attack by aliens. They made a disclaimer at the beginning of the recording, but most people did not tune in until after the disclaimer, when the broadcast was well under way. An announcer broke into a song with news of explosions on Mars, then returned to the music. Another break-in occurred a few minutes later to announce a large meteor had landed in New Jersey. Soon the meteor was described as a metallic cylinder with aliens crawling out. The reporter stated that Martians had begun to attack humans with heat-ray weapons.

Radio listeners believed the story was true. Highways jammed as people attempted to flee. People called the police for help in defending themselves and to find out what was going on, overwhelming phone lines. Orson Welles cut in once they learned of the panic and reminded everyone it was not in fact true. But the damage had been done.

Granted that had been almost a hundred years ago, but Martin knew people hadn't changed. In fact, now, the range of a report would be much wider. Millions would panic. No, the general public could not know what the government knew. In fact, parts of the government couldn't even be trusted with what other parts of the government knew. But one thing all parts of the government agreed upon—the public could only learn a fraction of what the government was up to.

Wanda pursed her lips. "My one worry with you in this position was that you might miss the good these programs could do. The advancements they could provide us."

Martin nodded his head, conceding the point and

keeping the smile that tried to appear hidden. *Oh, but if you only knew exactly how much potential I do see.*

"Perhaps. But I think safety should trump any other concerns."

"And you're sure this is the safest alternative?"

"Safer than what we have in place now. Wright-Patt has all sorts of security issues. And it's not alone in their problems. Area 51 has had zero security issues and has complete control of the area surrounding it. It is far and away the most secure base in the United States' history."

"But all A.L.I.V.E. projects? Even cases like Alvie, which have never demonstrated any aggression, but in fact have demonstrated the opposite?"

"But we can't guarantee that pacificity will continue. For subject #1, the sleep disturbances are concerning, as are the neurotransmitter levels. And the doctor herself said he is still maturing. Who knows what changes that could bring?"

Wanda nodded but stayed silent. And Martin knew her well enough to know that she would not appreciate being pushed any further. So he simply sat and waited for her to come to the conclusion that he had led her to.

Finally, she sighed. "All right. Make it happen."

Chapter Seventeen

AFTER THE PRESENTATION, Maeve got changed quickly and headed into her lab. She felt like she'd hit a wall. All her worry about Alvie, the complete lack of sleep within the last thirty-six hours, it all seemed to catch up with her. She was done.

When she stepped into the lab, Greta had taken one look at her and shook her head. "Oh no. You need some sleep. Go crash on the couch for a little bit. When Alvie wakes up, I'll take care of him."

"Are you sure?" Maeve asked, even though the mere suggestion of sleeping made her want to weep with joy.

"I'm sure. How'd it go, by the way?"

Maeve smiled, even as her stomach clenched. "Good. No problems."

Greta studied her for a moment. "It will be okay. Don't borrow trouble." She waved her hands toward the couch. "Now scoot. Get some sleep."

"Yes, ma'am." Maeve initiated a sloppy salute that made Greta laugh before turning for the couch.

She lay down, her concerns about what the presentation meant rolling around in her mind. But soon exhaustion pulled her away into sleep.

MAEVE STRUGGLED *with Alvie in her arms up the canyon. They had barely escaped the raiders and they hadn't escaped unscathed. Alvie's blood coated her hands from the wound in his chest. His breaths came out in labored moans. She knew he was not going to last much longer.*

Her own breath caught at the thought. Tears stung her eyes. She looked down at him. "I'm so sorry, Alvie."

His eyelids flickered open, and for a moment all she felt was pure love. Then it vanished as his eyes closed. Maeve felt as if the sun had been chased behind the clouds. How could anyone think he was dangerous? How could anyone want to harm him?

She clutched him to her, ignoring the pain in her side and her own blood dripping down her leg. She knew she couldn't save him. She knew she would be unable to save herself as well. But she would place him somewhere he could at least rest in peace.

Maeve began to climb the side of the mesa. Loose gravel made it a tough climb. She hit an uneven spot and fell heavily to her knees, clutching Alvie to her chest, rock cutting into her skin at the knees. She gasped at the new pain and this time the tears did fall.

Alvie's little hand reached up to wipe them away.

She struggled to smile, pulling back her fear. "I'm okay. We're almost there."

Alvie nodded weakly, and Maeve knew he didn't have much longer.

Getting to her feet, she whispered in his ear. "Just a little farther."

Resolved, she made her way up the rest of the hill. She nearly cried with relief when she reached the small ledge outside the cave. Three tall boulders blocked the way, but she and Alvie could slip through with no difficulty. This had been their refuge from the world, their sanctuary since they were kids. They'd spent more afternoons here than she could count.

The boulders made it impossible to see from the ground. And they'd never run into another person any time they had come. And people had come to the canyon. She and Alvie had watched them, hidden safely away. Maeve would explain to Alvie what she knew of the world and what she hoped for her future and for his. It had been their classroom, their refuge, their church.

Maeve slipped through the boulders, pulling Alvie as close to her as she could. Once inside, she sank to the ground, leaning against the rock wall. "We're here, Alvie."

Alvie didn't respond. Maeve's gaze flew to his chest. It was still moving but agonizingly slow, and each breath seemed more labored than the next. Maeve let the tears fall. There was no need to be brave now.

She held on to his hand and began to sing the lullaby their mother had sung them each night when they were kids or even as they got older, when they were sick.

By the time she reached the end of the song, his chest was barely moving. Maeve sobbed, her tears mingling with his blood. She stayed like that as the sun dipped into the horizon. A wave of dizziness rolled over her and she knew she needed to finish the job. Gently she laid him down. Getting to her knees, she felt numb. The ground surrounding them was soaked in blood. Some Alvie's but most of it hers.

She pulled her knife from its sheath and stabbed it into the ground over and over again, breaking the soil. She tossed it to the side and used her hands to pull the dirt out. By the time she had a three-foot hole, she knew she couldn't dig anymore. Already she was having trouble seeing, and it was getting harder and harder to find her breath.

On her hands and knees, she crawled over to Alvie. She caught hold of his foot and dragged him toward her. She lay down, snuggling him close. She ran her hand over his head and then lay with him wrapped in her arms. "I love you, Alvie."

She felt his uneven breath, each second a struggle to stay alive. "It's okay to go, Alvie. I'll be right behind you."

She felt the barest of touches across her cheek and then nothing. His hand dropped and his chest went still. She tried to hold back the sobs because each shudder sent waves of pain through her. But it was too hard. She had lost too much. First her mother and now Alvie. And soon she too would be gone. She held him to her, cursing the men who did this to him and her family.

Exhaustion rolled over her in waves. Maeve started to close her eyes and then forced herself to keep them open. With great reluctance, she removed her arms from Alvie's waist. Sobs shaking her, she gently rolled him into the grave. With the last of her strength she pushed the upturned ground over him, each handful of dirt confirming that he was truly gone from her. She needed to hide him, even in death. She wouldn't let them take him.

Finished, she lay on top of the grave, her breaths labored, each more painful than the next. She didn't know how the raiders had learned of Alvie. They had always been so careful, keeping him away from people. But someone must have seen him and talked. And people destroyed what they didn't understand.

She looked down at the upturned ground. She had never been overly religious, but she always believed there was a life after this one. There had to be. This life was so hard at times, so cruel. It couldn't be all there was. There had to be a reason for all the suffering.

But now, as her life faded, she grew fearful. What if there was nothing to come? What if these were her last moments on Earth and she was alone? She reached through the soil and found Alvie's hand. And like he had done a million times during his life, he gave her comfort. The touch of him, even though he'd begun to grow cold, reminded her that life was not all cruelty. Not all hardship. There was beauty and kindness.

She closed her eyes, knowing her end was near. But now she didn't fear it. She looked forward to it. She clutched his hand.

I'll see you soon.

Chapter Eighteen

MAEVE WOKE UP, her heart pounding, tears streaming down her cheeks. Her hands reached for her side, surprised when they came back unbloodied. The dream had been so vivid, so real. Just like the others. Frustration rolled through her. *Why am I dreaming this?*

Her eyes strayed over to the glass. Greta was busy at the console and paid her no attention. Through the glass, Alvie sat on his bed watching Maeve, wanting something from her. She searched his face, trying to understand.

What are you trying to tell me? What can I do to help you? she asked silently, feeling helpless.

Those men had come for him, but it was just a dream, wasn't it? It wasn't real, was it? It couldn't be. She rubbed her eyes and stood. She made her way across the room and nodded at Greta. "Hey. I'm good. Thanks for staying."

"No problem. But I could stay longer if you want to sleep some more."

"Thanks, but no. Go get some sleep yourself."

Greta kissed her on the cheek. "Have a good night."

Maeve watched her disappear out the lab door before turning to Alvie's room. She let herself in, and Alvie sat waiting for her on the couch. She sank down next to him and pulled over her tablet.

"Did you dream?"

Alvie nodded.

"What was it about?"

Alvie took the tablet and typed. *I died. You did too.*

Maeve's breath hitched. "Did you share the dream with me?"

Alvie nodded.

"Why?"

Alvie took the tablet. *So it doesn't happen again.*

She looked at Alvie sharply. "Again? What do you—"

The door to the lab buzzed and Chris stepped in. Maeve quickly wiped the conversation from the tablet, standing up. "Hey."

Chris smiled from the other wide of the glass. "Sorry to interrupt, but the technicians said there was a problem with the blood sample. They need another one."

Maeve frowned. A problem? That had never happened before. "Uh, sure. I'll take care of it."

She looked down at Alvie, wondering what he had meant when he said he didn't want it to happen again. Nothing like that had ever happened to him. It was just a dream, maybe a shared dream. She must have misunderstood him.

But he gave no sign of being bothered by the previous conversation. He just sighed. She knew he hated getting his blood taken and she couldn't blame him.

"They need a salvia sample too."

Maeve frowned. "Why?"

Chris shrugged, putting up his hands. "Don't shoot the messenger."

Blood and saliva samples right after the presentation. Something was happening. She looked down at Alvie and he took her hand.

Maeve squeezed it. "It's okay." *I hope.* Maeve took the samples and handed them off to Chris for the lab. Dropping her gloves in the hazardous waste receptacle, she returned to Alvie, who had grown still.

"Alvie? Do you want to play Monopoly?" she asked. Alvie just stared at the wall. 872-AR flashed through her mind.

She went still, the hair on the back of her neck standing up. The same number as the other day. She had checked, and she was right, it was a room in the archives building. The room held all of the old files, maybe even Alvie's.

"You want me to go there, don't you?" she asked softly.

Alvie nodded at her.

"I can't, Alvie. I can't get there. I don't have clearance for it. If I get caught—" She sighed. He looked into her eyes, and for a moment she felt his pain and sucked in a breath. "Alvie, what's wrong? What's going on?"

He looked away and then curled up in his bed.

She sat next to the bed for twenty more minutes but couldn't get a response from him, except for the numbers in her mind. Finally, her cramping legs told her to take a break. She left the room, struggling to think of something she could do. She watched him through the window. He was so still. So sad.

All the terror of his episodes flew through her mind, along with the unusual presentation followed by the sample request. Something was happening. And she couldn't help but think she needed to learn the cause of Alvie's incidents to prepare for what was coming.

She stood there hearing the second hand of the clock tick down and she knew she needed to make a move. Finally, she reached over and grabbed the phone. She dialed the number quickly. "Hi. Could you ask Captain Garrigan to come down to the lab?"

A few minutes later, Chris strode in. "You rang?"

Maeve smiled. "Yes. Um, I need a favor."

"If I can do it, I will."

"I need to see Alvie's old files."

Chris went still. "What?"

"His old files."

"Why?"

"The other night you mentioned his sleep disturbances. Well, they're concerning me, and I thought if I could see his old files—"

"You don't have clearance for that."

"But you do, don't you?"

Chris shook his head. "Maeve, I can't do that. I can't just look at files without permission. I would lose my job. Hell, I would lose my freedom. You know that, right?"

"I know, but it's just—"

"No, Maeve. I'll mention it to John, but I can't go behind his back. And you can't ask me to do that."

"You're right. I'm sorry. Look, I'm just tired. If you could ask John, that would be great. It would save me from having to fill out the paperwork and wait for days for a response."

Chris looked relieved. "No problem. I'll make the request."

Maeve watched him leave, knowing John would say no

and hoping just asking to see them didn't send up any red
flags.

Chapter Nineteen

A FEW HOURS LATER, Maeve looked up, her eyebrows raising with concern as Colonel John Forrester strode into her lab. Presentation, tests she didn't order, Alvie's attempt to get her to look at old files, and now her Uncle John visiting her in the lab—no, things were definitely not okay. But she smiled as he opened up his arms. She walked over into them. "Hi, Uncle John."

John looked down at her, his blue-gray eyes twinkling in the corners. "My favorite scientist."

She laughed, because she knew it was true and because she was pretty sure very few other scientists or people on the base saw this side of him. "My favorite commander."

"So, I hear you've been asking about Alvie's background."

Maeve nodded. She studied John, trying to discern how he had taken the request. She did love him. He'd been a surrogate father to her, but he didn't get to be commander by being a nice guy. "Yes. Alvie's going through some developmental changes and I thought there might be something similar in his past."

"Why now?"

Maeve gestured to Alvie's room. "Something's going on with him and I'm trying to find an answer."

John frowned and walked over to the glass. "What is it?"

"I'm not sure. His neurotransmitter levels are low. I think he's depressed. And I was hoping there might be something in the old notes that would help with that."

"What specifically are you looking for?"

"That's just it. I don't know. I've been through all my notes and the history I can access. But I still haven't seen anything from that first year. I don't even know how Alvie was created. I'm hoping there's something in those early files that might address the serotonin levels."

John studied her for a moment before shaking his head. "There's nothing in those early files that could relate."

"But—"

"Dr. Leander, there's nothing in the files."

Maeve stepped back. *Dr. Leander?* "Okay."

"Listen, Maeve, things are changing, and it's best not to rock the boat right now."

"Changing? How?"

"Some projects from NASIC have been moved into a new department."

Maeve's mouth fell open. "What does that mean?"

"It could be nothing. But whatever is happening with Alvie, figure it out without going beyond your clearance." He hesitated. "What kind of incidents is he having?"

"Nothing too bad. Just staring off into space."

"You need to find an answer, because the guy heading the new division, he's not someone you want to look too closely at your relationship with Alvie."

"Then let me look at the old files."

"No," John barked, and then his voice softened. "Maeve, everyone's going to be under the microscope now, including me. I can't let you into those files. Don't ask again. Now I need to head to a meeting, but I was hoping we could get breakfast sometime soon."

Maeve shoved her hurt aside, trying to smile. "That would be great. Do you want to say hi?"

He shook his head. "No, I'm in a rush. But give him a hug for me, all right?"

"Sure." Maeve frowned. "What's going on? You're worried."

"What? No, honey. It's nothing. Just the usual stress."

"Are you sure?"

"Yes." He kissed her on the forehead. "I'm sure. Don't worry about me." He paused. "But I need you to keep your head down. Don't make any waves."

She raised an eyebrow. "Versus my usual attention-seeking ways?"

He gave a small laugh. "I know, I know. Just humor an old man."

"Now I know something's wrong if you're calling yourself old. Is it this new agency?"

He watched her for a moment. "Just be careful, okay?"

She leaned in and hugged him. "Always."

"All right, well, I need to get going. Miles to go and all that."

Maeve knew stopping in was not easy for him. His days were usually pretty packed. "Well, thanks, for stopping by. And you're sure you're all right?"

"Yes. Just look after yourself and Alvie."

"I will. I always have."

"Yes, you have," he said lightly. "All right, I'm already late. And don't forget, breakfast next week."

She hugged him again. "It's a date."

He hugged her back, resting his head on hers for a moment. And then the moment went on too long. She frowned and opened her mouth to ask him again if everything was all right but he headed for the door and stepped out.

Maeve waited for a few moments, watching the door. Something was going on. Something had him worried. But she couldn't concern herself with that right now.

She pulled the security card she had pinched from his pocket. "I just hope you won't be too mad."

Chapter Twenty

MAEVE SAT at a booth in the back of Wings Lounge. She had headed straight there after Greta arrived, telling herself she was hungry and not that she was staying on base to sneak into the archives building. Now her eggs sat in front of her, slowly cooling to room temperature. Her hand slipped into the pocket of her coat, fingering the card she had taken from John.

I can't believe I did that, she thought for the millionth time. But now that she had, she wasn't sure what she planned. True, John's card would get her into different parts of the base, but they all had cameras and human security. Someone would notice she wasn't the commander. Besides, what was the likelihood they kept paper records on Alvie? The archive had to be digitized by now, which meant she needed a password.

She had nabbed the card and now she had nowhere to use it. And if she used it, she would end her career. Meaning Alvie would be on his own. But if she didn't try, Alvie would continue to suffer without any way for her to help him. And with this new agency in charge, who knew what they would think about his incidents? Because she knew it was only a matter of time before someone uncovered them. It was pure dumb luck that no one had so far.

She'd never officially asked where Alvie had come from. It might seem crazy to some that she hadn't questioned his origins. But the fact was, Maeve had grown up in a military installation. She knew questions were not taken lightly and were often seen as dissent. So any questions she raised had to directly pertain to her interactions with Alvie. And how he came to be did not fit within that area.

So even asking John for the records had gone against everything that had been ingrained into her since she was a child. She could still picture the look of fear on her mother's face, the harshness in her tone when she warned Maeve to never ask about Alvie's history. Her mother had warned her that they would lose him if she asked those types of questions. It had had such an impact on her that she had squashed down her curiosity and never breathed a word of it to anyone. But it didn't stop her from thinking.

Although her mother had never said it out loud, Maeve had gotten the impression that her mother had known him from birth. In Maeve's mind that left only two options: Alvie was found at a crash site right after he was born or Alvie's mother, assuming he had one, was caught just before he was born.

In the dark recesses of her mind, she wondered if he had somehow been created, but she couldn't imagine her mother being a part of something like that. And besides, Alvie was at least ten years older than the technology needed to create him in a lab. The first test tube baby was created in 1978, but that required having both a male and female subject, harvesting a viable egg, and fertilizing it outside the body before implanting it back in. Even with the improvements made in the past few decades, only 36% of IVF treatments result in a successful pregnancy. Thirty years ago, that percentage would have been much lower, and that was before taking into account the alien biology.

The most realistic option was that he was somehow stranded here as an infant. But there must be something in those early records that could give her a clue as to what he was going through now. A genetic profile must have been run on him at some point. And she knew in her heart that that profile and his early history could help her explain what was going on with Alvie.

Maeve gripped her coffee mug. *What the hell am I going to do?*

A shadow fell across her table and she looked up. Chris stood there, glaring down at her. "I need to speak with you."

"Okay. Take a seat."

"Not here." He threw a twenty down on the table and reached for her arm.

Maeve shrugged him off. "What are you doing?"

"What am I doing? What the *hell* are you doing, Maeve?" Chris hissed and then took a deep breath. "Let's go, because I don't think you want to have this conversation here." Chris headed for the back door without a word.

Maeve frowned but followed him. *He can't know. There's no way he can know.*

Chris held the door open for her, which led to a small alley behind the restaurant. As soon as she slipped through, he closed the door behind her. Arms crossed, he glared down at her. "Where is it?"

"Where's what?" she asked, forcing herself to not reach into her pocket.

"The commander's office called to say his ID had gone missing. He last used it at your lab."

"I don't know."

Chris ran a hand through his hair, looking like he wanted to yank it out. "Maeve, I cannot help you if you don't tell me the truth. If you get caught with it, you will lose your position. You will lose Alvie. Let me help you."

"I asked you for help." She spit out, her anger rising. "You said no."

"Damn it, Maeve, this is the military. There are things I can't do. And there are things you can't do. That's just the way it is. You have to accept it."

"Accept it? I have been accepting it my whole life! My *whole* life. But now Alvie's in danger. Something is wrong. And no one will let me look at his records to see his history. Something in there could help."

"Apparently someone thinks those records won't help."

Maeve let out a bitter laugh. "And they know better? Because there is no one on this planet who knows Alvie better than me. And I can tell you without a single doubt in my mind, something is seriously wrong."

"Look, I get that you take your job seriously, but—"

Tears crested in Maeve's eyes and she willed them back. "No, you don't understand. Alvie's not a job. He's family."

Chris frowned. "Family?"

Maeve nodded. "Family," she said firmly. Pictures from her childhood swam through her mind.

"But you've only worked on the project for three years."

"No, I've known him much longer than that."

He frowned. "How long?"

"Twenty-three years."

Chapter Twenty-One

Twenty-Three Years Ago

FIVE-YEAR-OLD MAEVE CLASPED *her mom's hand as they stepped out of the elevator into the long white corridor. Doors lined it, though none opened or had any windows.*

Two soldiers with guns stood on either side of the elevator door. They nodded at her mother but they didn't smile. Maeve moved a little closer to her mom.

The air conditioning kicked on and Maeve jumped.

Her mom looked down and smiled, patting Maeve's hand. "It's all right—just the air conditioning. Do you remember what I told you?"

Maeve nodded. "That he looks different, but inside he's like me."

Alice nodded. "Yes." She stopped at the last door on the right. She paused and then knelt down so she could look Maeve in the eye. "I would never let anything hurt you, you know that, right?"

Maeve nodded.

"And there's nothing to be scared of. Do you believe that?"

Maeve looked at her mom. It had always been the two of them, plus her grandma, who made her breakfast while her mom was at work. Maeve had asked her mom why she worked nights instead of during the day. Alice had hugged her and said her job was different than most people's and she could only do it at night.

For a while, Maeve had thought her mom might be a superhero who flew around the world saving people under the cloak of darkness. She'd told her mom that once, but she'd only laughed. "No, I work for the government." Then she'd paused. "But I suppose I might be helping save the world one day."

Now Maeve was finally going to see where her mom worked. What kept her away and what had been upsetting her lately.

"I believe that." Maeve looked into her mom's blue eyes, the same color as her grandma's. "Do you?"

Her mom ran a hand through Maeve's hair. "You are such a smart girl. That is going to take you places someday." She stood up. "Okay, let's go." Her mother punched a series of numbers into the keypad to the right of the door. A buzzer sounded, and then the door popped open.

Following her mother in, Maeve clutched her Raggedy Ann and Andy dolls. There was a wall of computers straight ahead, and to her left was a long glass wall that ran the length of the room. And two people stood in front of the wall, one of whom she knew. She smiled and ran over to him, wrapping her arms around his legs. "Uncle John."

John reached down and pulled her up, tossing her a little bit in the air before hugging her. "Hey there, snug bug."

Maeve leaned back to look in his face. "How come you're here?"

"I told your mom I wanted to be here for this." He smiled, but Maeve knew it was his worried smile. She looked at her mother, who was avoiding her uncle's eyes.

A woman stood up from the computers. "So this must be Maeve."

John lowered Maeve to the ground as her mother spoke. "Maeve, this is Greta. We work together. Can you say hi?"

"Hi," Maeve said, clutching her dolls and taking a step behind her

uncle. She looked into the dark glass in front of her. What was in there? And why was it so dark?

Alice led Maeve to the wall. "Stay right here for a minute, okay?"

Her mom walked to the wall of computers and few seconds later a dim light appeared behind the glass. A small bed lay against the far wall and a figure moved underneath a blue blanket.

Maeve looked back at her uncle, who nodded at her encouragingly, but she also noticed the bulge on his waist. He had a gun. Why did Uncle John have a gun?

"How is he today?" her mom asked.

"Good. Quiet," Greta said.

Her mother let out a breath. "Okay. Let's see how this goes."

Her mom stepped to a door in the wall and nodded at Greta. The light above the door glowed green. Her mom smiled at Maeve before walking into the other room.

Maeve pressed her hands against the glass, trying to get a better look. Her mother reached down to the bed and picked up the person in it, wrapping them in a blanket. The person was small, not much bigger than a baby. But why would they put a baby in a bed?

Her mom walked toward her, the smile still on her face. She knelt down at the opposite side of the glass and turned the bundle in her arms for Maeve to see. The being had big eyes that were closed and was a pale gray. For a minute, Maeve thought it was a doll, but then the eyes opened.

"Maeve, this is Alvie," her mom said.

Maeve stared at Alvie, her heart pounding, but it wasn't out of fear. Alvie stared back at her. Then slowly, he reached a small four-fingered hand out from underneath the blanket and pressed it against the glass.

Maeve pressed her hand to his from the other side. "Hi, Alvie," she whispered softly.

Chapter Twenty-Two

CHRIS STARED AT MAEVE, unable to believe what she had just told him. At the same time, it explained a great deal about their relationship. "You really met him when you were a kid?"

Maeve nodded. "Yes, but it was more than that. I spent almost every day with him. For the first year, we played through the glass together. After that though, everyone knew we weren't a threat to each other. So we played together."

Chris was dumbfounded. How had the military allowed it? "How—I mean, if you had told someone—"

"I went to school on the base. I had a perpetual shadow. Any time it looked like I was going to spill the beans I would have been whisked away. But I was never tempted."

"How's that possible?"

"Because very early on, it was made clear to me that if I told anyone about Alvie, I would never see him again and neither would my mother. And even as a kid, I understood that. And I couldn't risk him being taken away from us."

"That was a lot of pressure to be on a little kid."

"I suppose it was. But I understood that I was Alvie's only chance at a normal life. Without me or my mom, he was on his own. We were his family, the only ones that truly cared about him."

Chris watched her for a moment. "Why would they take the risk?"

"You have to understand—my mom loved Alvie like he was hers. And he wasn't doing well. He'd become withdrawn. There was talk about terminating him. And she knew him better than anyone. She knew he was lonely. She knew there was no risk to me. My mom figured there was nothing to lose—if Alvie didn't get better, she'd lose him. She thought he might be lonely and need someone his age to play with. He was a child surrounded by adults. And to the military, she was the expert. They listened to *her*."

Chris couldn't miss the bitterness in her voice. "I guess it worked."

Maeve nodded, a smile playing across her face. "He became my brother, my best friend. I eventually made other friends, but Alvie was always the first. My schedule was even switched so I went to school at night."

"But didn't you resent that after a while?"

"When I was a teenager, I had a bit of a rebellious stage. But for the most part, I was okay with it. Me, Alvie, my mom—we became this family unit. Dinner together every day, holidays. I'd flop on his bed and tell him my plans for the future."

"Did he ever talk back?"

Maeve shook her head with a smile. "No. But you can always tell when he understands. And he always listened."

"But weren't you lonely?"

"I was okay for the most part. Mom made sure I did

normal kid things—soccer teams, art classes, swimming lessons—I had other friends. And for about five years there was one other kid in school with me. She was the daughter of one of the military officers. She had a skin condition, so she couldn't go out in the sunlight. We became good friends. She's over in California now, but we still talk."

"I can't believe they let you do that."

"I can't either. But Alvie's important to a lot of people in different ways than to me and my mom. But the goal of my mom's research and mine is to see what Alvie can do, how he reacts. Introducing me was a reasonable approach. And honestly? I wouldn't trade it for a normal childhood." She paused. "But that's why I know something is wrong. I know him better than anyone, scientist or not. Something is wrong with him. He's in trouble. And I can't help him. And I need to find a way to help him before—" She went quiet.

"Before they try to take him away from you."

Maeve looked away, nodding her head, and Chris saw the tremble in her chin.

Chris looked away too, tightening his fists. He wanted more than anything to help her. And to help Alvie. He'd seen him looking depressed over the last few months and he'd begun to worry about the little guy.

But what she was asking him to do …

He shook his head. "I'm sorry. I can't. But let me help you stay with him." He held out his hand. "Give me John's ID."

Maeve stared up at him, looking as if her heart was breaking. And it killed him to tell her no. But she needed to understand that this approach was only going to cause her problems.

Slowly, she pulled out the ID and placed it in his palm.

Chris curled his finger over her hand. "We'll figure out a way to help him."

Maeve just shook her head.

Chris opened his mouth to respond, but his cell phone beeped twice.

Annoyed, Chris pulled his phone off his waist. Code 542. He went still.

"Chris?" Maeve asked.

"We need to go." He grabbed her hand and started to run back to the lab.

Maeve matched his stride. "What's going on?"

"It's a Code 542."

"I've never heard of that before."

"That's because it's never happened to you before." He glanced at her out of the corner of his eyes, knowing his next words were going to terrify her. "They're moving Alvie."

Maeve stumbled. "What?" Chris reached out a hand to steady her. But she shook him off, increasing her pace. "Where are they moving him?"

"Somewhere off the base."

Chapter Twenty-Three

THEY'RE MOVING *Alvie off the base.* The words tumbled through Maeve's mind as she sprinted down the hall. Men and women in Air Force uniforms strode by, boxes in their arms, some pushing dollies. The sight of them terrified her. For years, it had only been a handful of people who had access to this part of the building. And none of them were these people. *Oh god, Alvie,* Maeve thought, her heart pounding.

Chris had left her at the front door to return John's ID, and Maeve had barely glanced at him, her first attempt at theft completely forgotten at the terror of Alvie being moved.

She tore around a corner and just missed plowing into a young officer. He glared at her, but Maeve didn't apologize. In front of her door, two armed guards stood. But instead of barring her way, they nodded at her as she approached. She yanked her lanyard off and swung it at the keypad as she reached the lab.

Greta whirled around from her position by Maeve's

console, her face pale, her hands clutched together. "Thank God."

Maeve strode across the room, glancing into Alvie's room. He sat on his bed, following her movements. She forced herself to focus on the problem at hand and provide a calm exterior. "What's going on?"

Greta shook her head. "I don't know. They said we need to get Alvie ready for transport."

Maeve felt lightheaded. Did they know about his episodes? Or about her taking John's ID? Had she somehow caused this? "Transport? What about us?"

"We're supposed to be getting ready for transport as well."

Oh, thank God. "Where?"

"They won't tell us."

"How the hell can they not tell us?" Maeve was worried about where they were going. But honestly, as long as she was going with him, she didn't care. She could not, she *would* not leave Alvie alone. "When will they be here?"

Greta looked more frazzled than Maeve had ever seen her. "I don't know—any minute. There only seem to be a few buildings that are being evacuated."

Maeve felt a stirring of hope take root. "Wait. We're not the only ones?"

Greta shook her head. "No."

Maeve let out a shaky breath, her mind churning. *Okay, we're not the only ones. It must be the new agency. There must be other projects that fall under its umbrella, which means I just need to act like everything's fine and make sure they realize I am the only one qualified to look after Alvie.*

Behind the glass, Alvie paced anxiously. She met his eyes and could feel his fear. She turned to Greta. "Get the sedative ready. I'll go talk to him."

Greta gave her a nod before disappearing out of the lab.

Taking a breath, Maeve pushed open the door. Alvie flew across the room. Maeve knelt down and wrapped her arms around him. "It's all right. It's okay." She ran her hand over his back in circles, feeling him calm. "You won't be alone. I'll be with you."

But even as she said it, she wasn't sure how long her words would hold true.

Chapter Twenty-Four

MAEVE MANAGED to get Alvie calmed down and administered the sedative. She sat by his bedside holding his hand as he drifted off. She checked his pulse and his oxygen output. He was good.

She adjusted the blanket over him. He tended to get cold easily. *Where are they taking you?*

"Maeve, I need you out here," Greta called over the speaker.

Maeve looked through the glass. Eight uniforms were now in the room, and with some relief she saw Chris was one of them. With one last look at Alvie, she opened the door and stepped out, letting it shut behind her. "He's out. Now where are we going?"

"That's classified." The name Rivera was typed across his black uniform and Maeve had never seen him before. Nor had she seen the uniform. Who the hell were these guys?

Maeve frowned, looking between Rivera and Chris. "But aren't I going with him?"

"That is still being determined," Rivera said.

"Still being determined? Alvie is my subject. I have been with him for years." She took a deep breath, reminding herself to calm down. "Who is making that determination?"

"Central Command. You will be reprocessed, and if you are cleared you will be allowed to accompany the subject."

Maeve had to practically bite her tongue off to keep from yelling at the cold man in front of her. They couldn't just send Alvie off to God knew where and inform her she *might* be allowed to accompany him. But a warning glance from Chris helped her swallow down her complaints. "Okay. Well, we'll get Alvie on a stretcher and—"

"We'll take care of his transport," Rivera said.

Only then did Maeve notice the box that resembled a coffin in the back of the room. They pushed the box forward. Inside was a smaller stretcher with chains attached to the sides.

Maeve shook her head. "Restraints aren't necessary. Alvie's—"

"Not human and not to be trusted," Rivera said. "He *will* be restrained. I will not have this evacuation compromised. Do *you* have a problem with that, doctor?"

Maeve's mouth fell open, but before she could respond Chris stepped forward. "Sir, I am familiar with the subject. I'll restrain him."

Rivera gave a nod. "Good. Doctors, you have fifteen minutes to grab what you need or we leave without you."

Chapter Twenty-Five

WRIGHT-PATT WHIRLED by Maeve as she sat in the back of an Air Force Jeep with Greta next to her.

"It will be all right," Greta said.

But Maeve wasn't sure about that. They hadn't let her accompany Alvie. And they had put him in box—*a box*. "What happens if he wakes up during transport? He'll be terrified."

Greta patted her hand, keeping her voice low and nudging her chin toward the driver, a reminder they weren't alone. "Don't focus on that. It's out of your hands, and if you complain too much, you could be removed too. Let's wait until we know what's going on and see what's really worth making a stink about."

Maeve knew Greta was right, but Alvie had looked so tiny in that box, and so still. And Maeve couldn't shake the thought that it looked an awful lot like a coffin. At least Chris had been the one to place the restraints on him. He had been extremely gentle. But he was another issue—

would he still be assigned to work with Alvie? She hadn't had a chance to ask him.

The Jeep pulled onto the runway rolling past a military transport plane. The plane's engines had already started. On the other runway, another military cargo jet stood, also idling. Coffins similar to Alvie's were being loaded on.

Her eyes grew large and her mouth dropped open. Who the hell was in those? Why are they doing all this out in the open? Secrecy had been drilled into them from day one. What the hell had happened?

Greta nudged her shoulder as they pulled to a stop at a hangar. They stepped out of the Jeep and a soldier gestured for them to head to the back of the hangar where a group of about a dozen people stood.

Maeve realized that she recognized almost all of them. A dark-haired man turned, surprise flashing across his face. "Maeve," Greg said.

"Hey," Maeve said, scanning the rest of the occupants. Some she'd seen on the bus. And she knew some were from other shifts.

Why are we all together?

A tall woman in her early thirties in the same black uniform Rivera had worn strode out from the office, twelve officers following in her wake and lining up next to her in front of the group.

"Attention. Your projects have just been re-classified. Your work on them is under review and your continuation on the project will need to be re-evaluated. If you are cleared for the project, you will be transported to your project's new location."

Maeve felt her disbelief growing, and her fear. What if she didn't pass?

"Where's that?" someone called out.

The woman glared. "You will be informed of the location *after* your clearance has been vetted."

A tall gray-haired man raised his hand. "I've already been vetted."

"New requirements have been put in place. You will need above top-secret clearance to work on these projects. You will need to meet these new requirements to be allowed to continue your work. Your clearance has already been in process for the last few months."

Maeve's mouth dropped open. *New* requirements? She knew security clearances took months to come through. But if these clearances had been already going on, they had been done without her knowledge. *Without any of our knowledge,* she thought as she saw the mixtures of anger and surprise flashing across everyone's face surrounding her. *What the hell?*

Greta took her hand and gave it a gentle squeeze. "It'll be all right."

Maeve nodded, feeling numb, her mind focused on what would happen if she somehow didn't pass. She'd had security clearance of one kind or another since she was a kid. She wouldn't have a problem, would she?

Maeve swallowed. *And what happens to Alvie if I do?*

Chapter Twenty-Six

MAEVE SPENT the next three hours being processed in the hangar. She tried to keep her impatience and worry buried, but apparently she wasn't doing a good job.

"Is something wrong, Dr. Leander?"

"Hm, what?" Maeve asked, turning her attention back to the unsmiling man in front of her. He hadn't introduced himself when he'd called her name, just indicated that she should follow him. She'd followed him to a card table with two folding chairs on opposite ends and a laptop on top. He'd gestured for her to take a seat and the questioning began in earnest.

"I said, is something wrong?"

Maeve shook her head. "No, just concerned about the condition of my research subject. Any kind of trip can be very taxing."

The plane they had seen when they first arrived at the hangar had taken off almost two hours ago, and Maeve's nails had now dug crescent-shaped moons into her palms.

Alvie had never been without her or her mom or even out of his building.

The man curled his lip. Throughout the process he had made no attempt to hide his dislike of her research. "I'm sure the subject's fine."

And that was the other problem. The guards that had come to take Alvie, this processing guy—that was nine people who now knew about Alvie. He'd been a well-kept secret for years. Why the hell were all these people now being allowed to know of his existence?

But Maeve said nothing about her concerns. Instead, she nodded, keeping her tone even. "Yes, I'm sure you're right. But I've put a lot of time into his care. It's difficult to entrust my work to someone else."

"Yes, well, we're almost done."

Maeve had decided as soon as she saw the people doing the processing that she needed to present an emotional distance from Alvie. She was pretty sure if she acted like she actually cared for him, it would mean that she was automatically declined clearance.

But despite her outward attempts at presenting a detached persona, inside she was shaking with fear. Alvie was a sensitive soul. He was used to kindness and he responded to it. None of the people she had seen so far indicated any sort of kindness.

The man in front of her hit a few more buttons on his keyboard. "Okay, Dr. Leander, you've been cleared. Now there is one final step." He handed her a document thick with pages. "You will need to sign these."

Maeve glanced at the first few pages and immediately knew what it was—a release. If she signed it, she was saying she would never speak about her work, would never sue the government if she was ever injured during the course of her work, and that should she in any way, shape, or form mention her work to anyone outside the accepted lines of secrecy, she would be incarcerated for twenty-five years to life without a trial.

Hand shaking, she signed. Part of her told her not to, that it was too big a risk without even knowing where they were sending her. But the other part knew that it didn't matter where they went; she needed to protect Alvie. And she knew signing away her constitutional rights was the only way she was going to be able to do that.

Maeve pushed the papers back across the table. The processor accepted them and handed Maeve a badge. "Keep this with you at all times."

Taking the badge as she stood, she was scanning the area. "Thank you."

"The plane will be leaving in a few minutes. Head out the back door of the hangar and wait with the rest of the group."

Nodding, Maeve tried to keep from sprinting to the door she'd seen a few other people disappear through. And she knew she was one of the lucky ones. Eight people had failed the new clearance requirements. Greta had been taken to a different area, so Maeve wasn't sure whether or not she had passed.

As Maeve slipped out the door the processor had indicated. She joined three people waiting, along with the four guards with them. Almost as soon as she joined them, the guard waved them toward the waiting plane. She climbed the tall metal staircase and ducked under the door and into the cabin.

Greg looked up from the second row. He indicated the seat next to him, but Maeve shook her head. If she sat next to him, the impulse to talk would be overwhelming. And she couldn't risk it. She couldn't chance anyone pulling her away from Alvie. "I'm going to sleep."

Greg stifled a yawn. "You and me both, sister."

Maeve gave him a smile, but it slipped from her face as soon as she passed him. She made her way to the back of the plane and took a seat in an empty row. She pulled her headphones out and quickly put them on, turning on some music. She stared out the windows. From her vantage point she could see they were loading another plane. More coffins were dropped and wheeled into the large cargo plane.

Her hands began to shake and she clasped them together. *Hold on, Alvie. I'm coming.*

Chapter Twenty-Seven

MAEVE FELT *the pressure in her chest first. It was dark, pitch black. She opened her eyes but she couldn't see. Terror tore through her.* I'm blind. *She tried to reach up for her eyes but she couldn't seem to make them move. Her heart was racing already so the realization didn't cause it to speed up. In fact, she didn't think it could speed up. It felt sluggish, like it was struggling for each breath.*

She squirmed. What is going on?

"Sh, sh, it's all right." A familiar voice whispered. Mom? *She thought as she felt a warm presence next to her. She was pulled in tight to something and then she began to rock. And despite her fear, she found comfort in the movements, the familiarity in the voice.*

"It's all right. It will be all right, Ben."

Maeve frowned. Ben? Who's Ben?

Maeve's eyes flew open and she jolted upright, her chest heaving at the unfamiliar surroundings. *I'm in a plane. Why am I—*

And then it all came back to her—the move, the new clearance and all her fear for Alvie. The lights came on in the cabin as she heard the wheels lower for landing.

She sat upright and wiped her eyes, lifting the window shade next to her. Bright sunlight glared in at her making her blink. A glance at her watch confirmed that they'd been travelling for five hours, which made it the middle of her night. But according to this sun, it was late morning for wherever she was.

Maeve did a quick calculation in her mind. Traveling at a normal air speed of five hundred miles per hour, that placed them about two thousand miles from Dayton. The plane touched down and outside, the ground was arid, with little covering.

She went still. *No freaking way.*

People began gathering their things as the plane came to a stop, and a short time later the cabin door opened. An officer, yet again all in black with no insignia indicating his branch of service, stepped on the plane. "Good morning. You will be exiting this plane and getting on a bus for a short ride to the next plane."

"Another plane?" someone called out.

The man gave them a brief smile. "Don't worry. It's just a short trip. But before that. please take out the bag that was placed in the seat pocket in front of you."

Maeve frowned as she pulled out the cloth bag.

"Please write your name on the front and place your cell phone inside."

"Our phones?" someone asked.

The man nodded. "Cell phones do not work at the base. And no one is allowed to carry one. They will be returned to you when you leave the base each day."

Grumbling filled the cabin, but Maeve just wrote her name and slipped her phone in. The soldier walked through and gathered them before returning to the front of the plane. "Thank you for your cooperation. Now follow me, please."

Maeve followed the crowd out of the plane and onto a waiting bus. It was only a short ride to the other side of the airport. When they disembarked from the bus, a white 737 with a red stripe across the side sat only a hundred yards away. Maeve stared at it for a moment.

I'm taking a Janet flight.

Greg hurried to catch up with her as she headed for the plane. "Well, that was fun."

Maeve smiled, trying to act at ease. But her concern for Alvie was making that difficult. One of the guards frowned at them. Greg waved back at the man. "Man, these guys are a little stiff, aren't they?"

"Well, considering where we're going, I'm not really surprised."

Greg smiled. "So you figured it out too."

Maeve nodded. "Yup."

The smile on Greg's face was huge. Maeve struggled to smile in return. But inside she was terrified. Because she knew exactly where they were heading, and now the release she had signed basically giving away her rights blanketed all other thoughts. She climbed the ladder to the plane and looked around the cabin.

A Janet flight—flights that were never officially confirmed by the US government because the base they led to was never officially confirmed until 1999.

Maeve swallowed as she took a seat, feeling numb.

They took Alvie to Area 51.

Chapter Twenty-Eight

AREA 51, NEVADA

OUTSIDE THE BUS WINDOW, hills rose on every side of the base. Chris knew that the base extended ten miles by six miles. And that the border was further enhanced by both the nuclear testing site that rested to the west and Nellis Air Force Range that bordered the base on its north, west, and south sides. The government controlled all of the land for over fifteen miles within this part of the country. And even without that, the nearest town of Rachel was dozens of miles away with a population of only 200 to 300.

Chris caught sight of the long runway that had been created by the salt plain known as Groom Lake. The base's location had been chosen because the salt bed provided a natural runway. Created by the CIA in 1955, that long runway was necessary for the U-2 spy plane they had in development. Over the years, as the planes became more advanced, the runway had been extended until it reached 12,400 feet, although about half of the runway was closed now.

Area 51 was the site where most of the United States

government's experimental planes were developed. The U-2 spy plane had first been tested, as had the stealth bomber. Both had been denied by the US government until their existence had become undeniable. And that was the key to the base—everything about it was denied. It had been that way since it had first been established.

With satellite imaging and the creation of planes like the U-2, it was possible for other governments to photograph US bases without their knowledge. In fact, the U-2's job was to do just that to Russia, all while the United States denied ever engaging in such activities. All those denials blew up in the United States' face however, when a U-2 plane was shot down on May 1, 1960 in Russia.

And yet, the US government had refused to acknowledge its existence, even going so far as to digitally remove it from satellite photos. The denials continued, in spite of the mounting evidence through the years, including Russian satellite photos which clearly demonstrated a base did in fact exist at Grid 51 of the land survey.

Originally, pilots, engineers, and agents lived in little more than tents. But over the years, more and more buildings had been added, including scoot and hides, which allowed aircraft to be quickly moved under cover when the wrong satellite came within range. Chris knew that part of Area 51 was built to stay permanently out of the satellites' range. Area 51 was also a DUMB base—deep underground military base.

Finally, in 1999, the United States government admitted that Area 51 existed. But that didn't mean the government was opening the area up to visitors. The security at the base was all-encompassing. The roads surrounding the base were all monitored, motion sensors were buried in the land surrounding the base, some even along public lands.

And then there were the camo guys who patrolled the hills. F15s or armed helicopters were regularly scrambled when a threat was detected—a threat as simple as a civilian with a camera or even without one. Reports of strong-arm tactics to remove anyone who came too close were rampant.

And that was just off the base. On the base, security was even stricter. No one was allowed to drive into Area 51. Most people were flown in from Vegas on unmarked planes known as Janet flights. No one was allowed on the base without an extreme background check. And often, the people working on projects lived on the base. There were thirty-three dorm buildings available to house the employees on the base.

Individuals were not allowed to know what anyone else was working on, and it was not unusual for people to be blindfolded when being taken to certain parts of the base. Occasionally, employees would be required to pull down the blinds to their windows and stay away from them for a certain period of time, or they'd be moved to a windowless room.

And yet, people continued to sign up to work at 51. Because in the world of aeronautical and extraterrestrial research, there was no one doing more cutting-edge research than the scientists here.

Chris stepped off the bus in front of a brick building. The building looked like it was one of the older buildings on the base. A sign indicated that it was the former base head-quarters, but thanks to the briefing on the plane ride over, Chris knew it had been refitted to accommodate the incoming projects. Chris glanced at the edges of the building, looking for any hint of the structures that were buried well below it, but it gave off no indication of the twelve sublevels of floors that would house some of the most critical projects in United States history.

To the north, he could just make out the large quick-kill radar array. It would be deployed to intercept any missiles that were aimed at the base. Behind it, built to a smaller scale, were the radar arrays and support buildings that monitored the skies. The entire base was a no-fly zone. In fact, the no-fly zone extended for 215 miles. Anyone who violated the no-fly zone would be swiftly and uncompromisingly dealt with.

Chris kept his face neutral, but as he looked around, he couldn't help but worry. He understood the need to keep Alvie a secret, to keep the government's work secret. But Alvie didn't deserve to spend his life here. He didn't think the people here were going to allow him to take any more rooftop breaks. He wasn't even sure they were going to let Maeve stay on the project, not once they learned about how close she was to Alvie.

He glanced to the west, where the nuclear tests had been conducted, and a chill ran through him.

It's not like the place has a history of putting human concerns above national security.

While Trinity, the first atomic bomb test in 1945, occurred in Alamogordo, New Mexico, many of the later tests occurred at the Nevada testing site that borders 51. As the testing continued, they moved the tests underground with Project Neva to address public concerns. But the coal tar epoxy seals were notorious for leaking.

And the people affected by the testing even had a name for themselves: Downwinders. Downwinders were the people living in the areas surrounding the Trinity testing site, ranging from Arizona, New Mexico, Utah, all the way up to Washington State and Idaho. And in many of those communities, the cancer rates were much higher than the rest of the country. The soldiers at the test sites had double the cancer rates compared to soldiers stationed elsewhere. And that's what they exposed their soldiers to. What would they expose an alien to?

"Man, they'll let anyone into this place."

Chris glanced over at the tall, muscular African American woman who had spoken. He grinned, extending his hand, feeling some relief at the familiar face. "Tell me about it."

Leslie gripped his hand and Chris struggled not to wince. "So, kind of crazy these last few hours, right?"

"That's an understatement."

At Wright-Patt, there'd been strict protocols in place to keep all lines of research, researchers, and even their security separated. Here, that was all blown to hell. Chris didn't like to think about what that meant for Alvie.

He lowered his voice. "Any idea why the big shakeup?"

Leslie glanced around, making sure no one was listening. "It's got to be the change at Command. The Foreign Material Division has been brought into the DOD under the Bureau of Science Advancement and Cooperation, BOSAC. I'm guessing it stems from that."

Chris frowned. "What the hell is BOSAC?"

"A new division, freshly minted."

"Oh, crap," Chris groaned. Any time a division, agency, or task force was developed, everything was in limbo. New heads always wanted to flex their muscles. Meaning no one seemed to know their ass from their elbow. It usually took months for all the kinks to be smoothed out.

A commotion by the doors drew their attention. The double doors were held open by two uniformed airmen. A woman in her late forties strode through, her dark hair pulled tightly back. She was followed by another officer. Chris squinted, trying to read their tags—Commander Regina West and Mitch Roberts—no title was on the man's chest. West stopped in front of the building.

Roberts stepped next to her. "Fall in," he barked.

All the soldiers immediately arranged themselves into three lines, ten people long.

West nodded. "At ease."

Along with the rest, Chris eased his posture but kept his attention on West. He'd heard about her. She was a force to be reckoned with. She was moving up the ranks quickly. She had an encyclopedic knowledge of military affairs, made quick but sound decisions, and was by the book. He was not surprised she had been tapped for this kind of duty.

West's voice carried across the space. "I realize this move was abrupt. I assure you, it was unavoidable. Having said that, you are each here because you carried out your duties faithfully at your last assignment. You are being offered the same opportunity here. I realize that for some of you with families and ties back in Ohio, this may not be convenient. For the rest of you, if you agree, your belongings will be packed up and shipped here. An apartment will be provided for you until you can find your own lodging. Unlike many assignments in the military, this one is purely voluntary. Think hard about your decision. But I will need it in fifteen minutes. Those who elect not to join us will be escorted back to Wright-Patt."

She turned and headed back out.

When she had disappeared, murmurs began to rumble through the room. "What do you think?" Leslie asked from next to him.

"I don't know. That was really—" he paused, "Unusual."

127

"Yeah. And the military tends not to do unusual."

Chris nodded. One thing he loved about the military was how consistent they were in their approach. "You know what that means."

Leslie nodded with a frown. "Yeah—the military's not calling the shots. Somebody else is."

Chapter Twenty-Nine

THE JANET FLIGHT had taken about an hour. Now Maeve sat next to Greg on the bus that had been waiting for them.

"Well, this is cozy," he muttered.

"Not exactly going out of their way to make us feel welcome, are they?" Maeve said.

The plane they had flown in had the shades pulled down for the entire trip. It had none of the usual signs indicating which airline it belonged to. There had been no flight attendants, just some rather severe-looking guards wearing the same unadorned black uniforms as the men who'd shown up to take Alvie. As soon as the door to the plane had closed, they had each been given a manual to read—the rules and regulations of Area 51. The manual was three hundred pages long. And it included lots of information about what would happen to someone who broke the rules—physical injury and incarceration were mentioned often. Needless to say, Maeve had not been reassured.

But what really hit home was that all correspondence would be monitored and all calls from the base had to be approved. Before the door was opened after landing, the manuals had been collected with the explanation that a manual had been placed in each of their offices. No manuals were allowed to leave the base.

When they'd disembarked, Maeve had only had a brief glimpse of the surrounding area. They were in a valley and the runway was extremely long. High hills surrounded them with very little vegetation. In the distance, she could see dozens of buildings. So many that it looked like a small town. But a few factors ruined the illusion—the giant radar dish was one, and the dozens of hangars and Quonset huts was the other.

Once they landed, they'd been hustled onto a waiting bus. The bus they were riding on had blacked-out windows with chain link across them. More chain link divided the riders of the bus from the driver and two guards who sat up front.

"Did you hear what happened to Rob Kinney?" Greg asked.

Rob had been a classmate of theirs in school. Maeve shook her head, wondering why on earth Greg would bring him up now. "No. What?"

"You know how he started up that lab?"

"Yeah, he was looking into how to replace damaged cells with healthy ones, right?"

Greg nodded. "Yup. And he apparently figured it out. He just sold the lab for a cool billion. Then he bought a yacht and now he's sailing the world."

"Wow. That's awesome." Maeve glanced at him and raised an eyebrow. "Any particular reason you bring that up now?"

"Just comparing the differing paths our lives took." Greg fingered the chain link on the window. "Think they got this from a prison? Maybe at a going-out-of-business sale?"

Maeve smiled in spite of her fears, although she'd made the prison comparison herself. "I'm pretty sure prisons don't have going-out-of-business sales."

Greg grinned at her. "It would be pretty cool if they did though, wouldn't it?"

Maeve shook her head but couldn't keep from smiling again. She was glad Greg was here. He was keeping her distracted, which she truly appreciated. But she couldn't help but wonder what project he was working on. He didn't seem even slightly worried about his work. Could there be another Alvie somewhere on the base? She'd never thought about it before. Her mother had assured her that Alvie was the only subject of his kind.

But recalling those coffin-like boxes, she wondered if her mother told her the truth or if she even knew it. The bus pulled to a stop and Maeve looked up. One of the guards unlocked the gate and gestured for everyone to move forward. Maeve grabbed her bag and followed Greg off the bus.

A tall, muscular female soldier walked up to Greg almost immediately. "Hey, Greg. You're with me."

Greg smiled, and Maeve couldn't help but notice how much. *Apparently Greg's got a little crush.*

"Leslie," Greg said. "I was worried we were going to be separated. I know how difficult that would be for you."

Leslie rolled her eyes. "Yes, my life would lose all meaning."

Greg turned to Maeve. "Maeve, this is First Lieutenant Leslie Cole, my perpetual protector."

"Protector?" Maeve asked.

Leslie narrowed her eyes at Greg before turning to

Maeve. "It's a pleasure to meet you, Dr. Leander. I've heard good things."

"You have?" Maeve asked.

Leslie smiled. "I have."

Chris walked up. "Yup, I've been singing your virtues to all who will listen."

Maeve felt the blush spread across her cheeks and relief flood her system at the sight of him. "Um, thanks?"

Chris nodded to Greg. "Dr. Schorn."

Greg shook his head. "How come you all know who we are?"

Neither Leslie nor Chris answered him. Chris took Maeve's arm. "You're with me."

"With you? What does that mean?" Maeve asked.

"All scientists have been assigned a personal guard," Leslie replied.

"Why?" Maeve asked.

"Uh, because that's how it's always been done?" Greg asked.

Chris tugged her forward. "Come on, Doc, your project is all set up."

Maeve's gaze flew to Chris's face but he shook his head, warning her not to ask. The four of them started toward the large building in front of them. At the elevator bank, Chris stepped to the right and Leslie to the left, each inserting their security cards to call up the elevator. Maeve noticed they were both heading down.

"Can't we just share an elevator?" Greg asked.

Leslie shook her head. "No. We're going to different floors."

"And they want to make sure I don't learn all about your evil project." Greg cackled, rubbing his hands together.

Leslie frowned. "You really need to stop talking that way. Here, it could really get you in trouble."

The smile dropped from Greg's face. "I'm just joking."

Leslie's face softened. "I know that. But not everyone appreciates your unique sense of humor."

Greg placed a hand on his chin as if mulling over her words. "It's true—I *am* an acquired taste."

The elevator door slid open and Leslie none too gently shoved Greg in. "Oh, enough."

Maeve laughed as Greg waved at her. "See you later."

"Later," Maeve said as their doors slid shut and the other car's doors slid open. Maeve stepped into the car next to Chris and as soon as the doors closed, turned to him. "Have you seen him?"

"No. But there's a lot going on right now."

"When did he get here?"

"I don't know. I wasn't part of his transfer. The planes with the research subjects were pulled into hangars and unloaded inside. Then they were transferred through underground tunnels to this building and one other building."

Underground tunnels? Maeve felt a chill crawl over her skin. And for the first time, she realized they were heading down and not up. What had she and Alvie gotten into?

"What were in those other crates, Chris?"

"I don't know." His eyes were troubled. "You need to be prepared for some changes."

"Changes? Like what?" She glanced at the keypad again. "Where are they keeping him?"

"Five floors down."

A few seconds later, Maeve stepped off the elevator behind Chris. The hallway was a gray-blue color with bright lights, but there was an antiseptic smell to the place.

133

Don't prejudge. It could be—she looked around the dark hallway —*fine*.

They passed two doors on the way down the hall. One read 'STOCKROOM' and the other read 'LOUNGE'. From down the hall, Maeve heard a wail, and her heart plunged.

Alvie.

She ran to the last door on the right, Chris right behind her. He flashed his badge at the door. It stayed red.

Maeve clenched her fists. "Come *on*," she said as Alvie wailed from inside.

Chris flashed his card over the screen again. The light above the door bloomed green with a buzz. Chris pushed the door open.

Maeve hurried in and then went still, her hand to her mouth.

No.

Chapter Thirty

THE ROOM WAS DIM, with a jail cell to the left with glass walls and air holes taking up half the space. Alvie's container had been placed inside the cell, and no one had bothered to let him out. Alvie's cries could be heard through the covering. Maeve sprinted across the room. The door was locked. She flashed her badge and the door sprung open.

She ran to the container with Chris right behind her.

"We're here, Alvie. We're here," she said, struggling with the locks. Tears sprang to her eyes as she met Alvie's gaze through the window in the coffin. He looked terrified.

"That's the last one," Chris said, pulling open the lid.

Maeve reached in and stroked Alvie's head. She wiped away one of his tears and then leaned her forehead to his. "I'm sorry, Alvie. I'm so sorry."

She unwrapped one of his wrists while Chris undid the restraints from his legs. Maeve removed the last restraint and Alvie leapt from the coffin and into Maeve's arms. Maeve let out a breath, struggling to keep her tears back as Alvie trembled.

She snuggled him to her as she leaned back against the glass wall. Sliding down, she sat on the ground, her head resting on Alvie's. She rubbed his back in a circle. "It's okay, it's okay. I'm here. Everything's okay."

But Alvie continued to shake. And Maeve didn't know how to comfort him. Because she had a feeling that she was lying and nothing was going to be okay again.

Chapter Thirty-One

MAEVE WASN'T sure how long she stayed on the cold floor with Alvie wrapped in her arms. Her butt had grown numb and her arms had grown tired, but she couldn't let him go. She and Alvie might have been born within year of each other, but he'd matured much slower. Her mother believed that meant his lifespan would be extremely long. It also meant that right now, he was a terrified child.

She leaned her head down so it rested on top of Alvie's. "It's all right, Alvie. It will be all right." She'd been repeating the same phrase over and over, hoping that at least one of them would believe it.

The door beeped and with a rush of air, Chris walked in. He'd been on the other side of the glass the whole time, giving the two of them some privacy. Now, he knelt down next to her. "How is he?"

Maeve didn't miss the concern on his face. "He's a little better. How could they do this to him?"

Chris shook his head, gently rubbing the back of Alvie's

head. "They don't know him like you do, like I do. They only see an alien."

Maeve knew he was right. But how could you spend that much money on watching Alvie and not read any of the reports? Watch any of the tapes? He obviously wasn't a threat.

"Listen, there's a new chain of command. Each building has a commander."

"Okay."

"This building's commander is Regina West. She is career military—mom, dad, brothers, grandfathers. All were in the military. She will not understand about Alvie. And if you want to keep working with him—"

Maeve eyes flew to Chris's face. "*If?*"

Chris nodded. "Yes. She makes the final decision. You have to be clinical, no emotion."

Maeve closed her eyes, holding Alvie close. An image of his old room wafted through her brain. She hugged him tight. "I know. I miss it too," she said softly.

"Maeve?" Chris asked.

She looked up at him and nodded. "Yeah, yeah. Professional, detached, unemotional. I've got it."

But that could wait. Today, she'd make sure Alvie was okay, and tomorrow she'd worry about being a scientific automaton without feelings.

Chris touched her shoulder. "Good, because she's coming. She'll be here in five minutes."

Chapter Thirty-Two

REGINA WEST STRODE down the hall wanting a shower. The last alien species she'd seen could actually change from solid to liquid at will. *Why the hell are we keeping these things alive?* The whole project made her skin crawl. So far, she'd seen aliens that made the Hollywood version look like fluffy bunnies.

Each new species she observed reinforced the importance of her job. They needed to know these creatures' weaknesses. They needed to know what they were capable of.

And most importantly, as far as she was concerned, was she needed to know how to control them or kill them.

She paused at the end of Hallway 5C. She held out her hand. "Tell me."

Her lieutenant, Mitch Roberts, handed her a tablet. "This one is the first of the experiments. He was created twenty-seven years ago."

Regina raised her eyebrows. "And he's still alive?"

Mitch nodded. "He's unlike the others. There have been

no signs of aggression from him at all. In fact, the researchers interact with him without guards or any form of restraints."

Regina quickly scanned the file. In grade school, she'd learned how to speed-read. She'd honed that skill over the course of her life and it gave her an edge over her colleagues. But halfway through the second page she stopped reading, her eyes growing wide. "She brought her *child* in to play with the thing?"

Mitch nodded. "Yes, the previous Dr. Leander was worried about the being's mental state. It was deteriorating at a rapid rate. She was worried they would lose him. She thought perhaps the being was lonely."

"Lonely? Are you kidding?"

"No, ma'am. While it was an unorthodox approach, the introduction of her daughter did work. The being began to thrive. In fact, it opened a whole new avenue of further research. It demonstrated the being's emotional capacity as well as its communication skills."

"It communicates?"

"Yes. It can't speak, but it can read and write. And it also uses some form of emotional telepathy."

Interesting and terrifying. None of the other subjects had demonstrated any sort of communication abilities— although she had to admit a few of them seemed to be able to communicate hate pretty well.

West finished reading the rest of the file. The second Dr. Leander was impressive. She finished college in only three years and completed her doctorate four years later. Then she'd begun work with the subject and taken over when her mother had become ill; her status became official after her mother's death. Which meant the doctor had a long-term relationship with the subject, which could be problematic. If

Dr. Leander had grown attached to the being, well, that just wasn't going to work.

But this one subject seemed to provide a wealth of information compared to the others.

I suppose that's why it was chosen for Project Progeny.

"All right, let's get this over with." She gestured ahead and Mitch hustled down the hall to key in his security code at Leander's lab. He held open the door.

West strode through. In a glance, she took in the room. Captain Garrigan stood at attention over by the glass wall. She'd read up on him as well. He had an impressive record. Personally she thought he was overqualified for his current position, but that was not her call.

Garrigan initiated a crisp salute. She saluted in turn before turning her attention to the small woman next to him. From the file, Regina had expected the doctor to be some geeky little lab scientist, like the rest of them, but she wasn't. She had a healthy glow to her skin and muscle underneath the baggy lab coat. And she looked even younger than her file suggested.

West's gaze drifted past the doctor and her guard to the subject behind the glass. She stiffened when she saw it. She knew it would be small. But it looked back at her with big, dark eyes, giving it a childlike appearance even though she knew it was close to thirty years old. She shook her head, knowing its innocent appearance had undeniably fooled more than one person. But she would not be so easily fooled.

"Why is the subject unrestrained?" she asked.

Maeve opened her mouth, but Garrigan cut her off. "Ma'am, Subject 1 has never needed to be restrained. He is cooperative."

"Captain Garrigan, Subject 1 is not human. You cannot predict what he will or will not do. He is an unknown—"

Dr. Leander cut her off. "With all due respect, Commander, he is not an unknown. I have worked in close contact with the subject for over two decades. He has never made any aggressive moves towards anyone. Even if he did, he does not have the musculature to do damage."

West eyed her. *A little gumption in this one.* That could either be a very good thing or a very bad one. "And if he ever does?"

"That's why I'm here, Commander," Chris said.

Regina watched the two of them. They were close. It could be just from working together or it could be more.

She glanced back at the being. It sat quietly on the cot. She read no menace off the thing, but she did get a sense of sadness. She shook off the idea. These things did not have the same emotions as humans.

But it was true there had been no reports of physical violence from the being in its entire time in captivity. But she wasn't about to be the one who allowed the first to occur. "It will be restrained. There will be no exceptions."

"There's no call for that," the doctor said. "You'll push back all the progress we've made."

"Doctor, I have no interest in hindering your research, but I will not allow one of these things to gain the upper hand and harm one of my people. And like it or not, you are now one of mine as well. If you wish to continue on this project, you will follow the rules outlined regarding it. If not, you will not remain on this project."

The doctor held her lips firmly together and gave a brief nod.

"Good," Regina said. "Now, I see in his file he is nocturnal."

The doctor nodded.

"Is there anything else about him that is not in the file?"

"No. My work speaks for itself."

"Very well. You have each received a packet including the rules for this facility. Any breach of those rules will result in immediate termination. Ignorance is not an acceptable excuse."

"Yes, ma'am," Chris said.

The doctor said nothing.

Well, she doesn't like me.

But the thought didn't bother Regina. You didn't get to her position without developing a thick outer shell. "Very well. I'll leave you to your work. Dr. Leander, I look forward to your first report."

Chapter Thirty-Three

MAEVE WATCHED the commander leave flanked by her lieutenant, her distaste growing. As soon as the door closed she turned to Chris. "Thanks for the backup."

Chris sighed. "Maeve, how can you not understand how the military works after all the time you've spent on bases? You know if I said anything, all I would accomplish would be getting re-assigned or worse."

Maeve looked away, trying to rein in her temper, knowing he was right.

Chris's voice softened. "Look, we follow the rules, we show them who Alvie really is, and then we can work on getting the rules loosened."

Maeve nodded. She knew it was the right call. But it was hard to agree that Alvie should be restrained like some kind of animal.

She turned to the glass wall. Alvie had curled up on the cot and was staring at the wall. She rested her head on the glass, watching him, her heart breaking. He'd never asked for any of this. He had no choice in any of it. Yet he had never done anything but show them compassion and trust. And as a reward, he was treated as a criminal.

The sob caught her by surprise. A tear rolled down her cheek. "I'm so sorry, Alvie."

Chapter Thirty-Four

GREG STEPPED off the elevator on the eighth floor next to Leslie, practically bouncing. He was working in Area 51. He couldn't say it was a childhood dream because he'd never imagined it happening, but he could barely contain his excitement just imagining what research might be happening in this building.

He glanced over at Leslie, who was not looking as excited as he was. She was always more serious. He smiled. "So did you watch the latest episode of *Dragon Quest*? I saw it on the plane. It was insane."

Leslie rolled her eyes. "How many times do I have to tell you I don't watch that stuff?"

"Oh, come on. I can totally see you clad in armor facing down a beast."

Leslie stopped and turned, narrowing her eyes. "You better not be picturing me wearing anything like that."

"Well, if you'd prefer to do it naked, I can—"

"You are so lucky I am not allowed to hurt you."

Greg grinned. "Hey, when you're a beautiful woman,

you have to put up with the fantasies of us poor schlubs who are so far below your league that we're playing a different game altogether."

Across the room, the sound of a throat clearing could be heard. Both Greg and Leslie looked over at the middle-aged man who watched them with disapproval stamped across his face. The soldier standing next to him looked more amused.

Greg felt like he'd been caught flirting with a girl by his dad. "Oh, hey, didn't see you there. I'm Greg."

The middle-aged man inclined his head. "*Dr.* Schorn, I'm Dr. Sheridan. I have overseen the transfer of data files and arranged to have the subject moved into the cell." He nodded toward the glassed-in room to his right.

Greg walked over to the glass and peered in. The silver container lay still. "Hank still out?"

Sheridan narrowed his eyes. "Yes—*Kecksburg*-AG2 is still out. The sedative should last for at least another three hours. It had to be re-administered in flight."

"Okay, well, let's get our boy out of there and locked up before he wakes up, shall we?" Greg stepped toward the door.

"I believe that falls under your purview. Now if you'll excuse me, I need to check on a few more labs." Without another glance, the doctor brushed past Greg and exited the room.

His guard trailed after him. "And the fun continues," he muttered as he passed Greg.

Greg smiled. "Poor guy. See how lucky you are to get assigned to me? And I more than lucked out getting you."

"Oh, enough," Leslie snapped. "I get it—you think I'm hot. Can we stop with all the comments now?"

Greg felt like he'd been slapped. "Uh, sorry. I'm just joking. I didn't think they really bothered you."

"Greg—"

"No, hey, old sourpuss was right about one thing—I should get to work."

Greg walked over to the computer and pulled up the latest diagnostics on Hank. All readings indicated Hank was still under the influence. The cell was equipped with a crane that would allow Greg to remove Hank from his coffin without any help. He just needed to attach the crane.

Greg pulled on his gloves and keyed himself into the cell. He was working on automatic pilot, but inside he was a ten-year-old kid who'd just been laughed at by the pretty girl in class. *Stupid, so stupid. I should just keep my mouth shut.*

He unsnapped the locks on the one side of the coffin. He grabbed the handle and started to lift.

"No!" Leslie yelled. She sprinted into the cell and slammed her hands on the lid, holding it down.

"What are you—"

"He's awake!"

Greg whipped his head to the side. His eyes met the stare of Hank, who glared at him from the circular window in the lid. Two of Hank's fingers were curled around the side of the lid, trying to shove it open. It bounced.

"Do something!" Leslie yelled.

Greg scrambled around to the other side of the containment unit and slipped on the floor, banging into the edge of the unit. His elbow went numb. "Damn it."

The lid started to rise. Leslie jumped on top of it. Hank let out a screech as its fingers were crushed under the lid, but he didn't let go.

Greg punched at the computer console, his heart racing. "Hold your breath!"

He punched the execute button. White smoke drifted across the inside of the box. Hank locked eyes with Greg and curled his lip. Greg held his breath, but then the lid stopped shaking. Hank's eyes closed. Greg slumped onto the top of the coffin. "He's out."

"What happened?" Leslie asked as she slowly climbed down, keeping an eye on Hank's still form through the window.

Greg felt shaky. "I don't know. He should have been out for at least another hour, maybe more. I mean, I checked the readings—he was out, completely out. He's never just come to like that."

"Well, let's get him locked up before he awakens."

Greg shook his head as he walked toward Leslie. "No, I'll do it."

"Um, the chivalry is nice and all, but—"

Greg gave her a shaky smile. "Well, I'm glad you think I'm chivalrous. But it's not that. You need to contact the other labs and let them know their subjects may not be quite as out as they appear."

"What other subjects?"

Greg sighed. "Les, we all saw the other containment units. There're dozens of the things. Make the call."

She stepped back. "Fine, but I'll make it from in here. Just in case."

"Okay." And Greg didn't tell her how much better that made him feel. Instead, he stared at Hank through the glass before carefully lifting the lid. Hank's scaly skin glinted in the light. His chest moved up and down.

Greg's gaze traveled down the well-muscled arms and the incredibly strong, long fingers. Leslie had put all her body weight on top of the lid and yet Hank's fingers hadn't been crushed. They weren't even nicked.

The power of Hank was unbelievable. Greg had seen him crush a metal table leg with one squeeze. He didn't want to imagine what those fingers could do to a human neck.

After quickly fastening additional restraints around Hank's arms, Greg stepped back to activate the crane. As it lowered, he pictured Hank's face staring at him. He pushed stop on the crane mechanism and shut the containment unit again. He'd wait until Hank had a few more doses. He wanted to be sure there was no chance Hank would come to again.

As the crane raised back to the ceiling, he felt the tremors fall over him again. He imagined what Hank could have done if Leslie hadn't warned him. Leslie came and stood next to him.

"Everywhere else okay?" he asked.

She shrugged. "I don't know. But I warned them. I'm sure it will be okay."

Although he nodded, Greg wasn't so sure. Hank should not have been able to awaken that quickly. He'd had no inkling of that trait in him in the two years he had been working with him. So what else was Hank hiding?

Greg swallowed, his mouth suddenly dry as he pictured the other coffins he'd seen back at Wright-Patt.

And what the hell else is in this building?

Chapter Thirty-Five

CHRIS MADE his way to the dorms on the base that night. Although apartments were set up for them in Las Vegas, they were encouraged to stay on base the first few days as things got settled. It wasn't the military being nice. If there were problems, they wanted to be able to grab the bodies they needed to fix the problem.

When he'd left the lab, Maeve had still been there. Greta hadn't been able to leave Dayton immediately, which meant Maeve would either have to train someone new or take over the day shift as well. He had a sinking feeling he knew which she'd pick. As he was leaving, he had arranged for a cot to be brought in so she could be nearby if Alvie needed anything. Alvie's night guard had shown up ten minutes before Chris left. Chris didn't know his replacement, and he'd warned Maeve to keep her closeness to Alvie under wraps.

He hoped she could do it.

"Hey. You staying too?" a voice asked as Chris stepped into the front foyer of the dorm.

Chris looked up and caught sight of Leslie walking down the hall. He conjured up a smile. "Yeah. Things are kind of hectic. I wasn't really up for travelling again."

Leslie gave a giant yawn. "Me either. As soon as I hit my rack, I am going to conk out."

"Have a good night," Chris said as he headed up the stairs to the men's barracks. The dorm was only two floors. The women's rooms were on the first floor.

"Night," Leslie said as she headed down the hall.

As soon as Leslie was out of view, Maeve returned to the center of Chris's thoughts. He'd known her for two years. And he'd asked her out almost every week for the last few months. He'd started it as a joke, but soon it became more than that. He knew she felt something for him. At first, he'd wanted to get her to say yes for the challenge of it. But the more he watched her, the more he grew to admire her. She was brilliant, sexy, and tough in her own way. And brave. He'd watched her pick herself up after her mother's death and keep going. And with Alvie, he saw her heart.

But that big heart of hers was now part of the problem. Maeve was easily the smartest woman he'd ever met. He didn't even pretend he could match wits with her. He knew that. But she wore her heart on her sleeve and her love for Alvie was practically tangible.

If anyone finds out how much she cares about him …

He sighed. He just hoped it didn't get her booted from the project. Because he knew neither Alvie nor Maeve would survive that separation.

Chapter Thirty-Six

OH, *coffee, you are my best friend*, Maeve thought as she took a sip. It had not been a good night. Chris had had a cot moved in, which had been incredibly thoughtful, but he might as well have not bothered. She'd tried to sleep, but the new guard had put her on edge. She didn't like how he looked at Alvie or what he said about him.

Last night, before she'd attempted sleeping, she'd given Alvie a sedative. She knew he would need it after all the turmoil and that it would be safer if he didn't wake up while she was asleep.

When she'd stepped out of the room, the guard, Andy Henning, had shook his head. "I don't know how you can go near that thing. Gives me the creeps just looking at him."

Maeve had said nothing.

"They really should just put the thing out of its misery. An autopsy could tell you just as much, couldn't it?"

Maeve didn't even try to keep the revulsion out of her voice. "The subject is not to be harmed."

He narrowed his eyes at her. "You don't need to tell me my orders. I'm just making conversation."

"Well, I think I've had enough conversation."

He snorted. "Suit yourself."

Maeve had climbed onto the cot and pulled the blanket over herself a few minutes later, but she couldn't sleep. Every time Henning went near the glass wall she tensed. And she was pretty sure he knew.

Asshole, she thought, taking another sip.

"Morning, sunshine," he called from the other side of the room.

Maeve ignored him.

The door opened and Chris strode in. He took one look at Maeve's face and his jaw tightened. But unlike Maeve, he was more adept at hiding his emotions. An easy smile crossed his face as he nodded at Henning. "Morning."

"Hey, man."

"How was your night?"

"Uneventful."

"Well, I'll take over. See you in twelve."

"You got it." Henning left without a word to Maeve.

The tension in the room decreased as soon as the door shut close behind him. Maeve sank back onto the couch.

Chris walked over. "You okay?

She nodded. "Yeah, just didn't sleep much."

Chris glanced over at where Alvie still lay sleeping before turning back to Maeve. "Well, why don't you get some sleep? I'll wake you when Alvie's up."

"I'd love to. But there's a whole day full of testing planned."

Chris frowned. "You can't take a few minutes?"

Maeve shook her head. "No. There are some technicians coming to evaluate Alvie. I need to get him up and ready. And I need to go over all my test results from the last few weeks."

"Okay. Well, let me help. I'll get Alvie some breakfast and ready for the day and you can go through the paperwork."

Maeve smiled up at him, realizing they sounded like an old married couple splitting up the household duties. "Thanks."

Chris held his hands out to her. "Anytime. Now get to work, Doc."

"Yes, sir." Maeve placed her hands in his and he pulled her up. "I wanted to thank you," Maeve said.

"For what?"

"For being a good guy. Henning made me realize how we lucked out with you."

"I'm sure Henning isn't that bad a guy, once you get to know him."

Maeve shook her head, thinking about how Henning had watched her while she tried to sleep. A chill crawled over her. "No. He's a bad guy, Chris. Of that I'm sure."

Chapter Thirty-Seven

THE PLANE MOVED SMOOTHLY through the air after a bit of turbulence over the Midwest. Martin had the cabin to himself. In fact, he always had the cabin to himself. He'd written the purchase into one of his budgets years ago and no one had even blinked at the expense.

He took a sip of his kale juice as he watched the monitor in front of him. On screen, Martin watched the soldier throw herself on the transport while the scientist in glasses raced around the side, slipping in his haste. A few seconds later, Kecksburg-AG2 had been knocked out, but the two humans on screen looked terrified. Martin made a note on his file.

He hummed as he flipped through some of the other screens. The move had gone smoothly. But already, some of the creatures had shown some unexpected behaviors.

And that is exactly why Vault is called for. Finally, we're learning something about them.

His phone rang, and he reached inside his jacket pocket for it before he realized it wasn't that phone. He pulled the other phone from his briefcase. He quickly placed the signal scrambler on and the program that would disguise his voice. "Yes?"

"Mr. Smith? It's Andy Henning from 51."

Martin sighed. "Code names."

"Oh, right, sorry. Um, this is Eagle at Canyon."

"Yes, Eagle? You have a report?"

"Yes. I just left Leander's lab. And you're right—she cares about the thing. Although I can't see how."

Martin had had Henning assigned to Leander. He wanted someone to keep an eye on the good doctor to make sure she didn't cause any problems. Not that he expected her to. But he also hadn't expected the mother to be a problem, and that moment of underestimation had cost Martin dearly. "What about her day security?"

"Garrigan? He's a good guy. A straight arrow."

Another good guy. How nice. He was really beginning to hate that stupid phrase. "Keep an eye on her."

"If you need me to do anything more than watch her, I have no problem with that."

"I am well aware of that." He'd chosen Henning because he had a very pragmatic approach to violence. "Not yet. As of right now, she's not to be harmed."

Henning hesitated. "But that might change in the future, right?"

Martin smiled. "Oh, I can almost guarantee it."

Chapter Thirty-Eight

THE SMALL CONVERSATION Maeve had with Chris that morning had been the last moment of peace for hours. The powers that be wanted every test, physical and otherwise, run as soon as possible.

Alvie had even had to run another obstacle course. The technicians who were monitoring the course had at first been surprised at Alvie's agility and how calmly he'd allowed himself to be restrained and placed in and out of the containment unit for transport.

In fact, everyone that Alvie had been exposed to that day had been amazed at how cooperative Alvie was. While initially nervous around him, they soon grew more relaxed. But Maeve grew more nervous with each person he was exposed to. At Wright-Patt, she'd been in charge of all of Alvie's testing. Did the inclusion of so many others mean she would soon be pushed out?

Despite her concerns, in a lot of ways, the day had gone well. Alvie had settled down and seemed much calmer than when they arrived. Two other scientists had arrived to take blood samples. They had been very standoffish when they first stepped in the lab. The phlebotomists had been shocked when Alvie extended his arm to Maeve for the blood draw, and Alvie's cooperation once again won them over. It left Maeve thinking that maybe Chris was right—maybe they just had to show everyone what Alvie could do and then the restraints could be loosened up.

Alvie was sleeping now, and Maeve sat at the computer, making sure all the files from Wright-Patt had been transferred. She rubbed her eyes, feeling exhausted. She had gotten a note from Greta that she would join her in a few days when she packed up her world at home.

She had offered to pack up Maeve's place too. Maeve had been thankful for the offer, because to be honest, she hadn't even thought of her old apartment or any of the stuff in it. But if this *was* her new home, it would be nice to have some of her things around her.

Maeve had wanted to call John, just to hear a familiar voice, but she'd been informed that all calls on and off base were prohibited for the first week someone was on base. Internet usage was also restricted, and Maeve had the distinct feeling that it was not only Alvie who was currently locked up.

Another guard had replaced Chris, who was needed for some sort of debriefing, but he promised to be back before Henning arrived. The new guard studiously avoided looking at Alvie or talking to Maeve, and she had no problem with that.

Maeve rubbed her eyes, glancing over the icons on her desktop. All Alvie's medical files were here, his psychological reports, his dexterity and intelligence reports. Everything from his last three years.

Maeve frowned, noticing a folder she was unfamiliar

with. A thrill shot through her as she realized what it was—Alvie's early history. Everything she had been trying to find at Wright-Patt. With her higher security clearance, she was finally being given clearance to see them.

Well, at least one good thing's come from this move.

She clicked on the link and a data box with seventeen folders appeared. She settled back and clicked on the first file and started to read. An hour later, Maeve's exhaustion had all but disappeared. It was like travelling back in time, with her mother as a tour guide. She could read between her mother's scientific speak to see when she was scared for Alvie and when she was proud of him.

The subject has demonstrated the ability to read and comprehend the English language. His writing is almost illegible, I believe due to his lack of a thumb. However, his typing demonstrates his keen understanding. Although only eight years old, he easily demonstrates a grasp of subjects at a high-school level.

Her mother's pride came through loud and clear. And Maeve could remember when, as a child, she'd go see Alvie, a library book in hand, and Alvie would cuddle up next to her as she read to him. The books were probably too young for him, but he always wanted her to read to him, his head resting contentedly on her arm.

But I guess he didn't need me to read the books. Maeve smiled at the memory and then clicked on the last file. Unlike the others, it was only identified by a number and letter—G2.

Maeve frowned at the identification.

G2? What's that?

She scanned through the documents and shock took away all her thoughts. Her eyes couldn't seem to leave one sentence on the report: *The somatic cell was successfully transferred from Subject 1 to the emptied egg cell.*

Shaking, her eyes flew back to the beginning of the

report and the project title attached to it: B.E.G.I.N.—
Biological Experiment of Genetic Interaction Nexus.

Heart hammering, she re-read the report, trying to
reach some other conclusion. She started back at the beginning, reading the report through again and then again.

This can't be right. It's not possible.

Her horrified gaze flew back to where Alvie slept in the
enclosure. She had been wrong all these years. He wasn't an
alien who had been left behind or born to an alien mother
in captivity.

He was a clone.

Chapter Thirty-Nine

MAEVE STARED at the computer screen, seconds ticking away, her mind unable to comprehend what the file in front of her was telling her. A clone—he was not a unique individual. He was in essence a copy.

Maeve had never imagined it. And how could she? The first official clone wasn't created until 1996 by a group of scientists at the University of Edinburgh. Dolly the sheep had been hailed as the scientific breakthrough of the century.

And yet, Alvie had been created ten years earlier. Maeve knew the military had made incredible advances in multiple fields, but she'd never realized they had been this far ahead of the game—that *her mother* was that far ahead of the other scientists of her generation. But who had they created him from? Where had the original sample come from?

She stared at the date of his birth. Alvie was born almost a year after she was. The embryo was created from a stem cell three months after Maeve was born. Maeve's jaw dropped.

She couldn't. She didn't...

She scanned the file, looking for any indication that she was correct, but there was nothing to indicate where the stem cell had come from. But in her heart she knew the truth: her mother had taken one of Maeve's. In the late eighties, stem cells were not regularly collected. But she knew her mother had collected hers. And now she knew what had happened to at least some of them—her mother had used them to help create Alvie.

But who did they clone him from? She searched the files and finally found something: there was a notation about the original sample coming from a thousand-year-old skull found in Mexico.

Mexico. A chill covered Maeve as she remembered her dreams.

It's a coincidence. Maybe I heard Mom discussing the original sample or I saw a file.

But even as she thought about the possibilities, she knew they weren't true. She'd never thought Alvie was created—not like this.

So how come I dreamed about me and Alvie being in Mexico?

Maeve pushed back from the desk, taking a deep breath. What did that mean? What did that make her and Alvie? Siblings? Twins? Nothing?

She knew for cloning to work, the donor egg had to be emptied of all genetic material. So her cell would be only an empty vessel. But still, didn't that mean she and Alvie were linked somehow?

Is that why I'm having the dreams?

No. That was impossible.

Maeve felt overwhelmed by the revelations she was reading, but at the same time, she couldn't help but feel a flash of pride—her mother had been the one who had developed the process that allowed Alvie to come into being. She had been the first one in the world to figure out how to clone a living being.

Way to go, Mom.

Maeve returned back to the screen and she noticed a subfolder within the G2 folder. It was titled G1. A sense of foreboding fell over Maeve. She clicked on the folder and as she opened the first file and began to read, she couldn't help but gasp.

Oh, Mom.

The file detailed the birth and death of the first clone, Ben. He had died only a few weeks after birth. The team, which included her mother, realized that Ben aged quickly due to the maturity of the donor egg cell, which was the reason that they had used a stem cell for Alvie.

Maeve sat back when she was done, her hand to her mouth. *Oh my god—G2. Alvie was second generation.*

The first had died so quickly. Tears sprang to her eyes picturing how difficult that must have been for her mom. She stared over at Alvie. He had lived, in a way, at least twice before. The idea made her so sad. She knew he couldn't remember anything from those lives—cloning didn't work that way—but still, it was a heartbreaking thought.

And then she went still. She flipped through the file looking for her mother's notes on Ben's declining health. *There.* Heart failure, liver failure, and Maeve gasped. He was blind. Maeve's jaw dropped open as she remembered her dream from the plane. Her startled gaze flew to Alvie, who was sleeping comfortably. It wasn't possible. He couldn't remember his past lives, especially not as a baby. But where then had that dream come from?

I've never seen this file. There's no way I could have known.

And that left only one possibility—somehow he was linked to his past lives. The idea was too horrifying and heartbreaking to consider, and yet Maeve knew that somehow it was true.

She stared at the screen for what seemed like forever before she clicked back to the original folder, her heart taking about as much as she could manage. She clicked on each folder again to make sure she had read everything. She'd been so caught up in Alvie's history that she'd forgotten the reason she had wanted to read his history was to see if there was anything that would help her figure out why he'd been having his spells. But there was nothing there.

I guess Uncle John was right.

On the third to last file, she noticed a small file she hadn't checked that had been embedded in another file. She clicked on it, already knowing her brain was too full of new information. She needed to sit back and think for a while, synthesize everything she'd read before she added anything new to the pile of data.

But one look at the screen in front of her made any thoughts of ignoring the file disappear. It was a genetic profile. Her mother had ordered it run fifteen years ago. Maeve leaned forward, reading the findings with growing disbelief.

She knew what the findings meant even before she reached the conclusion of the report.

Subject 1 of the A.L.I.V.E. Project has genetic material derived from an unknown biological father, who does not match any of the profiles for any living being on Earth, and a human mother.

Maeve sat back, shock running through her as her hand

flew to her mouth. All these years she'd thought Alvie was an alien. But he wasn't.

He was a human-alien hybrid.

Chapter Forty

MAEVE SAT STARING off into space, trying to come to grips with everything she'd read. Alvie was part human, and he had been created from her stem cells. And her mother had been the one who had created him.

Oh my god.

Maeve didn't hear Chris return. Her first clue was when he tapped her shoulder. She jumped and looked up in shock. "Chris! When'd you get back?"

"A few minutes ago. You've been staring into space."

She looked up at him, barely registering his words. "Huh?"

"Okay. You're done," Chris said, steering her toward the cot.

"No. I just need to—"

He turned her so she was facing him. "Sleep. You need to sleep. Anything you write right now will not be worth much. So get some sleep."

The suggestion was enough to increase her drowsiness, even though her mind was spinning. "Okay, maybe for a few minutes." Relief flowed through her body as soon as she lay down, even while her mind churned. Alvie was part human. He hadn't been stranded here. The U.S. government had created him. But why?

Chris gently pulled the blanket over her. "Get some sleep, beautiful."

She smiled, already feeling sleep pull at her. *He called me beautiful*, she thought drowsily even as her mind struggled to stay awake and understand what Alvie's history meant for him today. And for her.

But her attempts were in vain. She'd slept very little in the last forty-eight hours. And her body was shutting down, with or without her cooperation. A picture of Henning popped into her mind, giving her a jolt. She wanted to make sure Henning left Alvie alone. She needed to stay awake to protect him, but the stress of the last few days and the lack of sleep outvoted her. As soon as her head hit the pillow and she closed her eyes, she was gone.

Chapter Forty-One

MARTIN TOOK a seat at the desk in his true office. He was in the building he'd created years ago in anticipation of Project Vault. It was an old warehouse sitting on the outskirts of the Vegas city limits. Most people wouldn't give it a second glance with its decrepit exterior of peeling paint and cracked windows. But that was subterfuge, carefully crafted to avoid interest. Inside, the warehouse was a state-of-the-art monitoring and security system. And all of it was unknown to anyone beyond a handful of trusted associates. And by trusted Martin meant people he had control over.

In front of him was the list of all the aliens currently in American custody. Some had been captured after a crash but most had been recreated after their bodies had been recovered. Even those that had been alive when caught had died shortly after. All had been carefully recreated through the A.L.I.V.E. Project.

And all were now housed in Area 51.

Martin smiled. He didn't doubt the importance of the project. Quite the contrary, from its beginning, he had seen the potential and the need for the program. In fact, he failed to understand how the other members of the government, and the MJ12 specifically, couldn't see the inherent danger that was creeping up on them. The increased sightings meant something was coming. And the human race was woefully unprepared. They needed to know what each species was capable of. The lab could only tell you so much.

Still, he had to admit they had learned a great deal.

But they needed more. The first generation had told them much of what they needed to know about the physicality of the creatures. But the second generation, those were the ones that Martin had taken the keenest interest in because those were the ones that offered him the first glimpse of how they could fight an alien presence.

Of course, for some of the creatures, that required some modification. One alien could only survive in a methane environment. They had been able to successfully create a hybrid with a gorilla that allowed it to breathe the Earth's atmosphere, and the results had been impressive. The Dulce-AG1, or Blue Boys as they were called, had incredible strength and the bite almost equal to that of an alligator. They were aggressive creatures. Martin smiled again.

And if that could be turned to our side, they'd be an incredible asset.

But even though everyone agreed with the purpose, the means to get there had been left to the scientists, and they were relying too much on the strength of the creatures. But Martin knew that the best soldier wasn't always the strongest. They needed to know how these guys interacted. How they fought. How they thought. Keeping them restrained 24/7 was not going to show you who they really were. You needed to put their backs to a wall and watch them react.

Or dangle a carrot in front of them and give them room to move.

But oversight always argued for safety. Martin knew one day they would understand how foolish their approach was, but by then it would be too late.

No, Martin knew what needed to be done—they needed to find the killers. They needed to see who they truly had to fear and how they fought.

He pictured the scientist who had created the first A.L.I.V.E. subject with distaste. Even all these years later, Alice Leander left a bad taste in his mouth. She was exactly what was wrong with the scientific approach. She had treated that thing like a child and apparently, her daughter was no better.

Martin knew that bending the aliens to their will was only a matter of time. But first they needed to know who to bend. And the modifications in this new generation were an area that still left questions. By necessity, the merged DNA was taken from Earthen animals, many of them domesticated—and that could be a problem. Domestication tended to dull the animal instincts.

But even the non-domesticated animals had been known to come to the aid of humans. There had even been a few cases where gorillas had come to a human's aid. In one case a toddler fell into the gorilla pen in an Illinois zoo. The three-year-old climbed over the barrier and fell twenty feet into the ape pit. Binti Jua, an eight-year-old female ape, picked up the boy, her own child on her back, and carried him to the zookeepers, keeping herself between the child and the other apes the whole time. Martin needed to know they didn't have any Binti Juas in his group of Blue Boys. He was not looking for kind-hearted gorillas in this particular group.

Although, if we could direct that to protecting the right humans, that could work. But that was a project for another day. They needed to stay on target and find the subjects that would be the best candidates for Project Proxy. They needed to know which breeds of the fifty-five aliens in their custody were killers—stone cold, without hesitation killers.

And Martin knew just how to pick them out of the bunch. He stepped up to his computer monitor and looked at the computer code his protégé had created for him. It had been carefully inserted into the security code controlling Area 51.

Martin didn't understand computer coding. It had never been his area, but he could appreciate the beauty in a new weapon. And this code was just that—a weapon, a truly beautiful weapon.

Martin scanned the list and his eyes drifted back to the map he kept on his office wall, all the military bases in the United States marked on it. His eyes drifted toward a base in the southwestern United States.

And now you're all in one spot. Just one more small thing to take care of and then I can focus on the bigger picture.

His desk phone beeped and Martin hit a button. "Yes?"

"Your transport is here, sir."

"I'll be right out."

Martin spent another moment in silence, letting himself appreciate the magnitude of this moment. Then he leaned down and hit enter.

He turned and strolled to the door, a genuine smile on his face.

Let it begin.

Chapter Forty-Two

CONSULTING HIS TABLET, Dr. Carlton Sheridan notched off another lab. Five more to go and he would have everyone squared away. Sheridan was a man of organization. Disorganization made him unhappy. Organization didn't make him happy, but at least he was content. The world was a better place when it was an ordered place.

He swiped to the next screen—Subject 198, code name Catalina-AG2. It required a self-contained burn unit along with the usual lab and medical requirements. The unusual request didn't cause Sheridan to bat an eye. He had no curiosity about any of the experiments being conducted on the base. His job was to make sure everything ran smoothly, and if anything fell out of that purview, well, it simply wasn't his concern.

He nodded at the guard, who keyed open the door. Sheridan stepped in. Two scientists were already inside along with their guards. He frowned. He liked to get in before anyone arrived but with so many arrivals in the last forty-eight hours, that just wasn't possible.

One of the scientists, a male in his early thirties, was in the glass enclosure next to the transport box. The second, a female in her late forties with strawberry-blonde hair, was crossing the room to the enclosure when she stopped to frown at Sheridan. "Can I help you?"

"I'm Dr. Sheridan."

"Oh, it's a pleasure. I'm Dr. Anna Gaddolyn." She extended her hand with a smile.

Sheridan looked at it with distaste. Why did people insist on a greeting whose only purpose was to spread germs? He grasped her fingers lightly. "Pleasure."

Dr. Gaddolyn frowned, looking down at her hand before putting it in her pocket. "Um, well, I think we have everything we need."

"I'll need to check the desktop and make sure that everything, including security protocols, were correctly installed."

Dr. Gaddolyn waved toward the desk area. "Of course. Dr. Aziz and I were just about to unbox the subject."

"Don't let me disturb you," Sheridan said as he strode past her.

He made his way to the desk, which was set up next to a large lab table and a console for controlling the environment in the room and in the glass enclosure. He quickly brought up the diagnostics, checking that each file was correctly installed before checking it off on his tablet.

A thunk followed by a curse pulled his attention. In the enclosure, Dr. Aziz was attempting to lower the crane, but it had only made it halfway down before stalling.

Sheridan frowned. That wasn't supposed to happen. The cranes had just been installed in almost all of the new labs, and he'd been assured by the crew that they all worked perfectly. He scowled. *This is why I check everything personally to make sure they're working properly—to avoid these issues. Rushing guarantees mistakes.*

He strode over to the glass enclosure and keyed his way in.

Dr. Gaddolyn whirled around. "Dr. Sheridan, you are not allowed to be in here."

"I am allowed to be anywhere there is a problem." He walked over to the control panel on the wall and quickly brought up the schematic for the crane. He glanced up at the ceiling, noting the small cable jutting out from the tile. "One of the power cables has been caught." He waved to his guard. "Bring the ladder in here."

The guard shook his head. "I'm not your lackey. I'm here for your protection only."

Sheridan glared at him. "Fine." He headed to the other side of the room. There should be a ladder in the closet. He opened it. *Yes. And this is why organization is critical.* As he pulled the ladder out, a scream pierced the lab.

Sheridan dropped the ladder and it fell back against the closet with a bang as he whirled around. A thick, dark gray tentacle was wrapped around the neck of Dr. Aziz. The doctor's eyes bulged, his face turning purple, and then with a snap, his neck was broken.

Dr. Gaddolyn stood frozen in place. "Get down," the guards yelled.

Gaddolyn dove for the floor, but not before a tentacle reared back and cut her along the chest with a long razor-like fin on the side of the tentacle. Blood poured onto the ground.

The guards opened fire. The creature leapt away at an incredible speed, wrapping itself around one of the guards and turning him so he faced the other two. The man's eyes grew large. One of the tentacles snapped out and caught one of the other guards at the neck. The man dropped his weapon and grabbed for his throat. Blood pooled through his fingers and drenched the front of his shirt.

Sheridan ran for the door.

"Do not open that door!" the remaining guard yelled.

Sheridan ignored him.

The guard backed out of the room, firing at the creature. He glanced over at Sheridan. "I said—"

And that small distraction was all it took. The creature whipped out its tentacle and wrapped it around the guard's leg. It yanked and he flew backwards, his head crashing into the hard tile floor. The creature pulled the guard forward, and Sheridan could only stare at the large blood trail that followed.

He fumbled for his keycard and slammed his hand on the alarm. Klaxons blared to life, though he knew they were contained to this floor. No other floor would know there was a problem.

He waved his card at the reader and it continued to glow red. He waved it again and again, but the telltale green of release never showed itself. He stared at his card in disbelief. They had assured him that it opened all doors, in an emergency state or not.

They lied to me.

A hiss sounded behind him. He turned. The creature was only four feet tall, but its six tentacles draped out another six feet. Its face looked like an octopus's with its round head and beak. But the beak was exceptionally sharp looking, and its skin was a blue green. It slid forward in an undulating fashion.

Sheridan backed up as far as he could, closing his eyes and turning his head. The being stopped only a few inches away and then leaned forward, smelling or inspecting him.

Sheridan wasn't sure which, and he didn't open his eyes to find out.

Yells sounded from down the hall and his eyes flew open. The creature was only two inches from him. Its eyes stared into him—all six of them. And Sheridan had the feeling that it wasn't just looking into his eyes but also his mind. The sense of violation was overwhelming, but Sheridan couldn't look away.

Then the creature turned, and faster than Sheridan thought possible, disappeared back into the glass room. It leapt onto the transport box and, using the half open crane, scurried up and into the ceiling.

Sheridan slunk down to the ground, his hands moving to his stomach. They came up wet. He glanced down in shock at the deep gash across his abdomen. He hadn't felt it. Still didn't.

It must have some sort of numbing agent in its tentacles, he thought, watching his blood flow out with an almost disinterest. *This room is going to keep housekeeping very busy.*

He heard shouts outside the door before it burst open. Soldiers poured into the room. One knelt down next to him. "Dr. Sheridan? Dr. Sheridan, what happened?"

Sheridan rolled his head toward him, the effort seeming inhumanly difficult. He almost giggled at the thought. *Inhuman.*

The soldier shook him. "Dr. Sheridan?"

Sheridan focused on the man with his serious gray eyes and serious weapon. He looked between the two. *But not serious enough.* Sheridan leaned into him. "It's out."

Chapter Forty-Three

MARTIN WALKED down the hallway to the bunker underneath Edwards Air Force Base, just a short helicopter ride from Vegas. He glanced at his phone as a text scrolled across it.

The doors are open.

He smiled, but imagining the group inside the conference room, his temper rose. They had forced him into this corner by dragging their feet. Enough was enough.

Taking a breath to tamp down his anger, he opened the door. Twenty-two sets of eyes turned to look at him. All members of the twelve were here along with their continuity of function members. Only Martin arrived without his because he had not chosen one, and he had no intention of doing so.

Martin walked in slowly, a smile on his face. "Ladies. Gentlemen. Thank you for meeting me again on such short notice."

Albert Brenner of the FBI sprang to his feet, his Irish complexion taking on a bright red hue with his anger.

"What the hell is going on? You can't just snap your fingers and expect us to come running."

Martin didn't bother sitting. He closed the door behind him and stood in front of it. "Apparently I can. The generation that sat at this table before you created the A.L.I.V.E. Project, they understood what was at risk. And it was run all over the country. I brought it under one roof. And just in time. Apparently one of the creatures has broken free of his containment. Deaths have been reported. If I hadn't moved the projects, what is playing out in Nevada would be playing out at military bases across the nation."

"It's just one incident," General Juarez, U.S. Army said. "And you ordered the removal of the subjects *to* Nevada. Without that move, that upset to protocols and routine, none of this would have happened. You have placed countless lives at risk," Juarez said.

Martin's words whipped out. "Countless lives have always been at risk and will be until we have a method to fight the aliens on their own terms. We can barely recreate their technology and we have no inkling of their physical capabilities. But now we are beginning to understand. And we need this information for when one of these species finally decides they are sick and tired of merely watching us and are ready to take us over."

Barbara Freely of the NSA shook her head. "The chances you have taken are too great. You have overstepped your place—gravely."

Michelle Danner from Homeland stood. "Which is why you have been officially reprimanded and will now be removed from the committee."

"Is that right?" Martin asked softly. "You eleven are a shadow of your predecessors. They knew what the risk was and they took whatever steps were necessary to secure our future. You are only concerned with covering your own asses. You have no courage, no conviction."

Albert snorted. "Say whatever you wish, Martin. But your time here is done. Your words are no more important than the buzzing of a pesky mosquito."

"That's where you're wrong, Albert. Because you see, in this scenario, I'm not the mosquito. You are." He nodded.

Each of the individuals standing behind the eleven members of the Majestic 12 stepped forward, pulling the garrote they'd been provided from their pockets and wrapping it around a member's neck. Albert's eyes bulged, as did everyone else's around the table.

Martin watched impassively as the members of the Majestic 12 flailed and struggled. But soon, none of the original eleven made a sound or a move. Martin nodded, meeting the eyes of the members of the new Majestic 12, one that Martin controlled. A move he'd known he had to make after the last meeting. He was done with oversight.

"Well done. Make sure the bodies are handled and the cover stories are in place. And no one contacts me. I will let you know when we will next meet."

He strode from the room, his footsteps echoing off the cement floor.

But don't hold your breath.

Chapter Forty-Four

CHRIS'S BEEPER WENT OFF. He reached over in the dark to grab it and nearly hit his head on the bunk above him. Other beepers sounded throughout the room. The sound of those other beepers in the dark, even though their sound was smaller and less obnoxious than his, brought him to full wakefulness.

Something's happened.

He rolled out of bed, pulling on his boots. He hustled for the door, followed by another half dozen soldiers. They thundered down the stairs to the first floor.

He could hear the other rooms in the barracks coming to life as well, and from a window in the stairwell he saw lights blare on in the dorm next door. As he reached the first floor, more soldiers emptied out of rooms. And while no one spoke, Chris had no doubt that everyone's thoughts were running along the same lines: what type of emergency could possibly require pulling in all the off-duty security?

A dark pit opened in the base of his stomach as he pictured all those crates that had been loaded into the plane at Wright-Patt. And he knew that Wright-Patt wasn't the only base they had gotten deliveries from. It was too much too quickly—ripe for a mistake. And as he glanced around at the men and women heading for the front of the barracks, he knew something had gone horribly wrong.

A vision of Maeve slipped into his mind and his gut clenched at the thought of her being hurt. But he shoved it aside. No use worrying before he had to. And the base was huge—it could be any of the projects or none of them that had initiated the alarm. It could even be a drill just to see how fast they responded.

Chris rounded the corner that led to the front foyer. A woman stood at attention, calmly waiting—Regina West. The commander in charge of the security for Building 34—the building Maeve was in.

Chris's heart began to pound as he came to a halt in front of the commander with a crisp salute. Another ten soldiers fell in behind him. Leslie was one of them, along with a few of the soldiers he knew from Wright-Patt

The commander looked over the group. "There's been a security breach in Building 34. You are going to back up alpha team. Gear up."

Next to the major stood a master sergeant with a rolling cart filled with high-caliber weapons. A breach. With this kind of weaponry that could only mean one thing—something dangerous had escaped or gotten in.

The master sergeant pointed toward the cart. "Grab what you need."

Chris grabbed, and then after a moment's hesitation grabbed a belt of grenades. West caught his eye and nodded.

Oh damn, this is bad.

"With me," the commander said as soon as the soldiers

were armed. She led them outside where they piled into a waiting van. The van took off the moment they were all in.

The commander turned from her seat in the front.

"We have a containment break. You have each been assigned to retrieve the—" the commander paused "—subject. This is a picture of our quarry." She handed back her cellphone.

Chris's eyes widened at the picture before passing it on.

"Are those tentacles?" a female soldier asked.

Commander West nodded, her face grim. "The tentacles have razors on them. Do not let them near you."

"Is this a capture or kill?" A male soldier asked.

"The higher-ups would prefer it was a capture. I prefer you all come home, so do what you need to do. The creature is currently contained in level nine."

"How did it escape?" Leslie asked.

"Through the ceiling."

Chris pictured Maeve, sleeping only a few levels away. "Are we sure it's contained to level nine?"

"To the best of our knowledge, yes. The building is in lockdown, no one in or out as a precaution."

"What does it want?" someone asked.

"We assume to get out." The commander's gaze did not waver. "You will *not* let that happen."

"Yes, sir," they responded in unison.

"Has anyone been hurt?" Chris asked.

The commander paused for only a second before nodding. "Five have been killed. One injured. Do *not* underestimate this thing."

The entrance to the building was a half mile away. Chris wished the driver would go faster, even though they were all being thrown about by his high rate of speed.

"Sir, how come we don't know if it's contained?" Leslie

asked. "This is the most secure base in the world. Don't they have cameras?"

"The cameras from level eight down have been deactivated."

"Did this thing do it?" someone asked.

"We don't know," West said.

"But it's intelligent, right? It might look like a weird octopus, but it is sentient, right?" Chris asked.

"That's affirmative."

No one said anything else. Questions swirled through Chris's mind. What if they were wrong, and it made it to another level? And what if they were wrong about what it wanted? What if it didn't want out? What if it wanted something else?

Chapter Forty-Five

THE ELEVATOR LOWERED the security group down to level eight. The alpha team was already on level nine doing a sweep, though there had been no sign of the creature. And they couldn't use thermal imagining because apparently the thing was cold blooded. In response, they'd ratcheted up the air conditioning to hopefully slow the thing down. But level nine was a labyrinth of labs and rooms. It covered over five thousand square feet. Searching the entire place for one dark, gelatinous creature was not going to be easy.

Chris glanced up as the elevator chimed. "Okay guys, here we go." The doors slid open.

Chris stepped out, his crew of five behind him, everyone's weapons tucked securely into their shoulders as they scanned the area.

No one was in the hallways, but they had expected that. In a lockdown everyone was required to stay in whatever room they were in or get into the nearest room and remain there. He nodded to three of his group. "You three, head right. We've got left. Stay in radio contact."

Hutch, who Chris knew from Wright-Patt, grinned. "No worries, Chris. All the good stuff is happening one floor away."

"Yeah, well, let's pretend it's happening here. Keep your eyes peeled."

"Yes, sir." Hutch grinned again.

Chris shook his head but turned his mind back to the task at hand. "Let's go."

Two of his soldiers, Franks and Schwartz, fell in line behind him. They moved forward. At the corner, he held up his hand. He didn't like this. It was too quiet. He peered around the corner. He could just make out a hand lying on the hallway floor.

Shit. Quietly he keyed his mic. "This is Bravo Unit One. We have a body in Hallway A of level eight. We're going to investigate."

The response came quickly over his earpiece. "Roger, Bravo. Use extreme caution."

Chris glanced back at his two comrades. He'd known them for only the two years he'd been at Wright-Patt. Franks was a gym rat from New Mexico who had an almost red cast to his bronze skin, a gift from his Native American relatives. Schwartz was almost the complete opposite—from New Hampshire, she was small framed, with glasses and a paleness to her skin that suggested the sun was not her friend. But regardless of how physically different they appeared, both were top-notch soldiers. He'd never gone into a firefight with them but from their files, he knew they could handle themselves. He nodded at them before turning the corner, his MP5 submachine gun tucked into his shoulder.

Chris nudged his chin to the door on the right. Franks tried it and shook his head. They moved forward. He nodded to the door on the left. Schwartz tried it and shook her head.

Together the three advanced on the body. It was a woman, lying on her stomach. She had a large circular red mark on the back of her neck. It almost looked like a large Lyme disease mark, except the red was raised much higher on the skin, looking swollen. Schwartz reached down and checked for a pulse. She looked up and shook her head.

Chris nudged the door open, stepping over the woman. The room was empty and undisturbed. It looked like the woman had been attacked leaving the office.

Why would you leave during a lockdown?

"What the hell made that?" Franks whispered.

"It looks almost like a sucker mark," replied Schwartz.

Chris nodded. He'd been thinking the same thing.

Franks frowned. "Did that thing have suckers? I don't remember that in the picture."

"I don't know. I didn't see any, but maybe they retract or something." Chris keyed his mic. "We have a body down with what appears to be a large sucker mark. Does the subject have suckers?"

"Hold on." The commander was back in just a few seconds. "That's a negative. There are no known suckers on the escapee. Keep your eyes peeled. Do you need medics?"

"No, sir. It's too late for that."

"Roger. Continue the search. We'll send someone for retrieval."

"Roger."

Chris moved past the woman, not letting himself think about who she was. Together, the three of them moved slowly, listening for sounds, trying doors as they passed. Ahead, a door was ajar.

Chris moved toward it, keeping an eye on the hallway ahead. Schwartz continually scanned behind them. Chris stopped just before the door, sniffing. What was that? It smelled like formaldehyde but different.

"Shit!" Franks yelled behind him.

Chris whirled. A pale yellow gelatinous glob five feet wide dropped from the ceiling, landing right behind Franks. It reached out for him, a large sucker on the end of its arm.

"What the hell is that?" Schwartz yelled as she yanked on the back of Frank's shirt, pulling him out of the creature's reach.

"Don't care," said Chris, opening fire. But his bullets passed right through the creature.

"Uh, I think we need another plan," Franks said, scrambling back, his bullets equally useless on the thing. The creature oozed toward them.

"This way," Chris yelled, leading them down the hall.

He scanned the signs. *Come on. Come on.* There had to be something.

"Yes," he said, pulling his card and swiping entrance to the third room. "Keep it busy," he yelled.

"Keep it busy? How the hell are we supposed to do that?" Franks yelled. Schwartz just followed Chris into the room and grabbed the first thing she could find to throw at it. It was a beaker. The glass shattered but some stuck in the thing. It paused.

"Okay," Franks said, grabbing a test tube and chucking it at the thing. It slid out of the way. "Oh, come *on*," he groaned.

"You need me to show you how to throw?" Schwartz asked.

"No. I got it," Franks grumbled, throwing a beaker, which landed and stuck. "Ha!"

Chris made his way to the back of the room, ignoring them. He grabbed the tank he'd been looking for. Liquid nitrogen. He wheeled it to the front, grabbing the hose and turning the nozzle. "Out of the way!"

A stream of liquid nitrogen flew toward the creature. It slid to the side, but Chris nabbed its tail end. It froze sold, and the creature let out a screech. Chris adjusted his aim. The frozen part was holding the thing back. He aimed for center mass. With a wailing cry, it shuddered and slowly hardened, all movement stopping.

Chris turned off the nitrogen.

Franks moved towards it. "Excellent—"

"Back away," Chris warned.

"What? It's frozen," Franks said.

"Yeah, but it's also not from around here. We don't know if frozen means dead. So let's contain it."

"Status, Bravo Team," came the call in Chris's ear.

Chris keyed his mic. "We have a subject immobilized. It is not, I repeat, *not* the subject that was released from level nine."

"Describe it."

Chris quickly rattled off a description. "Did you know this thing was out?"

"Negative."

Chris shook his head. How the hell was that possible? "Sir, we're going to need a containment unit to make sure it does not cause any more trouble."

"Roger, we'll send a team to you. Any idea where it escaped from?"

"No, sir. Not yet."

"Keep me informed."

"Will do."

"Um, Chris, I think we may have another issue," Schwartz said from behind him.

"Hold, Command." He glanced over at Schwartz. "What?"

She nudged her chin toward the large cylinders in the back of the room, her weapon at her shoulder. Chris had been so focused on the immediate danger he hadn't really taken time to consider what the cylinders meant. There were over a dozen of the things at the back of the room.

And they were all empty.

They stood five feet tall and had a pale yellow water in them. Electrodes floated in the liquid within them.

Chris scanned the ground and saw liquid spilled next to each canister. Then trails of liquid led to the air duct.

Oh shit.

Chris pulled his own weapon into his shoulder, scanning the room. "Control, this is Bravo. We have a new situation. Whatever was in the cryogenics lab is now out."

"Say again?"

"Whatever was in these giant test tubes has escaped. We think they're in the air ducts. Do we follow?"

There was a pause on the other end of the line.

"Negative, Bravo Team. Get out, get out now."

Chapter Forty-Six

MARTIN WALKED the catwalk that rimmed the entire ten-thousand-square-foot building. He didn't take pride in many things, but this building was his baby. He'd had the old warehouse converted two years ago when he'd first conceived of Project Vault. He had two dozen analysts with their monitors and computers at desks in the middle of the room, glass walls that could be darkened separating them. There were two offices made with drywall—his and a control room. Otherwise, Martin wanted to be able to see what every one of his people was up to with no exceptions.

He had dozens of analysts running security protocols on all government agencies as well as monitoring their chatter. He'd even managed to wrangle a SCIF room.

All on the dime of the American taxpayer and all without a single bit of government oversight. He smiled. *Thank you, black budgets.*

But Martin hadn't spent that money in vain. He'd known this day would come and he needed the right tools to be in place. Plus, he wanted to be close to the action.

His phone beeped as his assistant ran up the metal stairs

toward him. Hamish Rheinberg was sorely in need of both a diet and an exercise regime. But what he lacked in physical prowess he more than made up for in computer know-how. He'd first come to Martin's attention when he was twelve, when he'd hacked NASA looking for information on UFOs. Martin had been grooming him ever since.

"Sir," Hamish said, his breath coming out in pants, sweat stains underneath his armpits.

"What is it?" Martin asked.

Hamish smiled. "Director Fezza is on the video phone. There's a problem at the site."

About damn time. "Patch it through to my office."

"Yes, sir." Hamish held onto the rail as he hurried back down.

Martin took his time following him, even as his pulse jumped. He turned into his office, closing the door and making his way to his desk. He hit the button on his laptop that activated the video phone. "Director, what's going on?"

Obeid Fezza glared into the screen. "What's going on? All hell is breaking loose. Your projects have escaped. Some of my people have been killed."

Martin frowned. "Escaped? How?"

"We're looking into it, but it looks like the containment units failed. We've never had a break like this before."

"Which building? 34 or 39?"

"Both have reports of escapes."

Martin narrowed his eyes. "Both? How the hell is that possible? You assured me the projects would be safe at your facility. You are supposed to have a security system second to none."

"And we do," Obeid spit back. "I wanted to space out the projects arrivals. You wanted them immediately."

"And you agreed," Martin's voice was ice cold. "Whatever the security breakdown was, I expect you to find it and fix it."

"I will find out the cause of this failure."

"Has anyone been hurt?"

Obeid's voice was tight. "Yes. We have close to twelve dead."

"*Twelve?* Has the situation been contained?"

"No."

"Well, if people are still in danger, their safety needs to be our top priority."

Obeid nodded. "Agreed."

"Can the projects be rounded up?"

Obeid shook his head. "Initially we thought so. But we've had reports that the breakouts are growing. There are now multiple subjects out of containment. The situation is unmanageable." He paused. "We need to do a clean sweep."

Martin blew out a breath. Clean sweep—a destruction of all research projects. "That's an extreme response. Surely the projects still contained—"

"I do not believe you understand the gravity of the situation. The security protocols are breaking down throughout both buildings. We have reports that a minimum of thirty percent of the research subjects are loose. And we cannot guarantee that the subjects currently contained will remain contained. The safest approach is to remove that threat."

Martin sighed. "You're sure it's necessary?"

Obeid nodded. "The situation is unsalvageable. Unless we move quickly, the death toll will rise dramatically."

Martin nodded slowly. "I understand. Approval given for Clean Sweep. But when this is over, I want to know who is responsible for this. Someone must be held accountable.

We're talking years of research and billions of dollars that are going up in smoke."

Obeid's face was grave. "As soon as we have the situation under control I will initiate an investigation. I will find out who compromised my facility." Obeid disconnected the call.

Striding from his office, Martin headed toward the monitoring room. The creatures were out and people had been killed. Now the security force would move in and destroy any and all creatures.

Shifting from foot to foot, Hamish stood at the door waiting for him. "It's all queued up, sir."

"Thank you." Martin stepped in, closing the door behind him. Ahead of him were sixteen monitors showing feeds from Buildings 34 and 39.

As Martin pulled out a chair and took a seat, he grabbed the coffee that Hamish had left for him. Scenes of chaos were splashed across the screens. In the bottom right a group of white-coated humans sprinted up a stairwell. In the monitor above them, a creature with black stripes over white skin that looked like a very large dog chewed on something.

Zooming in quickly, the fingers at the end of the arm became clear. Each screen offered some display of terror or violence. On the ground level, soldiers were entering each building to secure the personnel and take out any creatures that crossed their paths.

Martin took a sip of his coffee with a contented sigh. *Perfect.*

Chapter Forty-Seven

ALVIE'S terrified screams yanked Maeve from her sleep. She shot straight up off the cot.

The lights blared on and she blinked hard.

"What the hell's wrong with him?" Henning yelled, his gun in his hand but still pointed at the ground.

"I don't know." Maeve ran for the glass enclosure, her gait unsteady. It was taking her a moment to come to. She had been in a deep sleep. Shaking her head, she reached the keypad by the door of the enclosure. Alvie stood on the ground, his head thrown back. The scream now turned to a wail. The last time he'd made that yell, her mother had died.

Tremors ran through Maeve. But Alvie wasn't close to anyone else besides her and—

Maeve's stomach dropped. *Chris.* Fumbling for her security card, she flashed it at the scanner before keying in her code. When the door buzzed, she pushed through. She reached for Alvie's restraints.

"Don't you dare remove those," Henning yelled from the doorway, his weapon now pointed at Alvie.

Maeve stepped in front of Alvie. "Put that down."

"No chance."

Alvie collapsed on the bed, small cries coming from his lips.

Maeve held her hands up. "I won't release him. But pointing your weapon at him will only make him more upset. The goal here is to calm him down, right?"

Henning glared at her before lowering his weapon. But he did not return it to his holster.

Maeve let out a breath. She stepped toward Alvie. "Alvie, what's wrong? What happened?"

A vision snapped into her brain. A soldier pulled out his weapon and shot. Maeve flinched and stumbled back with a gasp, as if it was aimed at her. What the hell was that?

"What is it?" Henning demanded.

"Nothing, nothing. Just a nightmare," she said trying to keep her tone even. Then she had a vision of a door plaque that read '11 AI1', followed by a sense of overwhelming sadness.

She moved back to the bed. "It's okay, Alvie. It's okay," she said even as she tried to make sense of what she'd seen. *Had* it been a nightmare? But what else could it be?

Behind her, she heard Henning's phone beep, but she ignored it, her focus on Alvie and trying to calm him down.

She knelt next to the bed and ran her hand over Alvie's back. "Alvie? Are you all right?"

The vision with the door plaque '11 AI1' reappeared in her mind. She looked down at him. "What are you trying to tell me? Is that a room?" she asked quietly.

"Doctor, step away from the bed," Henning ordered.

Maeve gritted her teeth, keeping her gaze on Alvie, whose breathing picked up a tick. "I told you, it's fine."

"Doctor, I'm ordering you away from the bed."

Maeve glanced over her shoulder. Henning had his weapon aimed at the bed. She jumped to her feet, planting herself in front of Alvie. "What are you doing?"

"Following orders. Now get out of the way."

Chapter Forty-Eight

CHRIS HELPED EVACUATE all personnel from floors seven down. He'd seen three more creatures in that effort. He'd taken out one and maybe wounded the second. The third had ghosted right in front of him—its body literally turning to gas as it escaped through a vent. And Chris still couldn't understand how things had gone to hell so quickly. It was a no man's land below seven. It seemed as if all the subjects had escaped at the same time. What the hell had happened?

Once he reached the surface, he reported to Commander West.

The commander nodded at him. "Good work, Captain. Now stand down until further orders."

"Sir, what about the rest of the building? Is it being evacuated?"

"Not at this time. Although I expect the call will come in to do just that."

"Does the rest of the building know what's happening?"

The commander's mouth tightened. "No."

"Sir—"

"I don't agree with it either, Captain. But that's the order." The commander turned away as another group exited the building.

And Chris turned and headed right back into it. Maeve was two floors away from some crazy outbreak, and the higher-ups were keeping that from them. And that was fine with him. But he was sure as hell going to make sure she was safe.

He stepped into the elevator as two soldiers escorted a man and a woman out. They both nodded at Chris. He nodded back, punching the fifth floor button as soon as the doors closed.

The image of a soldier taking aim at him filled his mind. And Chris recognized the soldier—it was Henning. Chris grabbed onto the bar on the wall. *What the hell was that?* A layer of sweat broke out across his forehead.

His pulse picked up, not sure what that had been but knowing in his gut it had something to do with Alvie. The elevator doors had just opened when the alarm on his phone buzzed. Chris yanked it from his waist as he headed down the hall. He stared at the message in disbelief.

Code 42—the destruction of research projects. It was the failsafe if an experiment was deemed too dangerous. This one was sent out base-wide. All experiments in Buildings 34 and 39 were to be destroyed.

Gunshots sounded from the other end of the hall. Chris's heart raced. He sprinted down the hall toward Maeve's lab. He knew he was expected to follow that order, which meant killing Alvie. But he also knew that with Maeve there, she would not step aside and let Alvie be killed. Henning would have to go through her first.

And Chris had no doubt he would do exactly that.

Chapter Forty-Nine

MAEVE STARED AT HENNING, not believing the soldier was actually aiming his weapon at her and Alvie. "What are you doing? Put down your weapon. He's not a threat. He's harmless."

"I have orders."

"Orders? What orders?"

Henning raised his weapon. "All research subjects are to be terminated. Now step out of the way."

Terminated? Maeve put up her hands, her mind racing. *Protect yourself*, she thought at Alvie, not sure if he could hear her. Sometimes it worked. Sometimes it didn't. She was hoping her terror would help the message get through. Although considering Alvie was still restrained, she wasn't sure what he could do.

Maeve walked slowly toward Henning, being sure to block his view of Alvie. "Okay. Just let me get out of here first."

Henning nodded. Maeve kept her hands in front of her.

Henning stepped back so she could step through, then he turned his back to her as he got back into position.

Maeve kicked at the back of his legs as Henning pulled the trigger. The shot went through the ceiling. He let out a yell as Maeve put both hands on his shoulders and yanked him back. He slammed onto his back, his head cracking onto the tile floor. He lay there dazed as Maeve kicked his weapon across the room and underneath the console. She ran for Alvie.

Henning latched onto her ankle as she passed. She crashed toward the ground, just managing to get her hands out in time to keep her face from slamming into the floor. But she still hit the ground harder than she would have liked, pain radiating up her arms.

She turned on her side and kicked Henning in the face with her free leg. His head jolted back. Inwardly, she cringed. Outwardly, she yanked her foot free and sprinted for Alvie.

Alvie sat on the bed, his eyes watching her closely, his little form shaking. She quickly undid the restraints around his wrists. "We have to go," she said, even knowing there was no chance they would escape alive. But she had to try. She couldn't just sit back and watch him die.

Alvie caught her wrist as she started to undo the restraints holding his legs. She looked up into eyes. He shook his head. And her heart broke.

"Alvie, they'll kill you."

The image of her as a five-year-old child holding her hand up to the glass flew through her mind as well as the joy that moment had brought to Alvie. Countless images of the two of them together over the years flew through her mind. Tears cascaded down her cheeks.

He held his hand to her cheek. Maeve placed her hand

over his. "I love you too, Alvie, but I can't do what you want, not this time." She shook his hands free and undid the last of the restraints.

She pulled Alvie into her arms and turned as Henning got to his feet. He stood in the doorway, blocking the exit, his eye already beginning to swell. He pulled his baton from his belt.

"You're going to pay for that."

Chapter Fifty

THE TAPPING WOKE HIM. Greg cracked open one eye, half his body already off the small couch that had been crammed into the corner of the lab.

Tap. Tap. Tap.

He frowned and sat up, looking for the source. "Where is that coming from?"

His guard on the other side of the room, Kinsey or Kenny or Smith for all he knew—Greg hadn't really been paying attention when the guy had introduced himself at the end of Leslie's shift—nodded toward the enclosure. "It's coming from in there."

Greg's heart began to race, remembering the close call earlier. Hank was still in his transport box. Greg was not interested in taking him out until he pumped enough drugs into him to knock out a dozen elephants. And he wasn't taking him out until Leslie was back. No offense to Kinsey/Kenny/Smith, but Greg didn't know him, but he knew Leslie and what she could do. So in the box Hank would stay.

Greg stood up, his back protesting his uncomfortable sleeping position. He'd been tempted to go to the dorms. But Leslie had been heading that way and he really hadn't wanted to walk with her. It was just plain awkward right now, and he'd rather face an uncomfortable couch than an uncomfortable walk across the secret base.

Greg stepped up to the computer monitor and looked at the record of Hank's vitals. All his levels were—

Tap. Tap. Tap.

The hair on the back of Greg's neck rose and he turned slowly to look at Hank's box. "He's awake."

Which should be completely impossible. Hank should be out for hours with the amount of drugs running through his system. What the hell was going on? Ever since they'd arrived here it was like everything he had learned about Hank had been turned on its head.

Greg turned on the video feed and he had a view of Hank inside his crate. Hank grimaced at the camera and Greg knew he sensed that it was on. Hank wasn't psychic, but he could detect electronic signals. Hank stared right into the camera and then raised his talon and tapped three times on the lid of the box.

Greg swallowed, clicking off the screen.

"You okay?" Kinsey/Kenny/Smith asked.

Greg wiped his eyes. "Yeah, just tired."

"Not sure how you managed to sleep at all with that thing in there."

"Well, safest base in the world, right? What's to worry about?"

Kinsey/Kenny/Smith smiled. "Damn straight."

Coffee. Coffee and the world will be brighter, Greg thought, making his way to the coffee machine. He held up the empty pot with a sigh. *The world hates me.*

Behind him, he heard Kinsey/Kenny/Smith's beeper sound. A sharp intake of breath caused him to turn. "What's going on?"

Kinsey/Kenny/Smith stared at the screen of his phone, his jaw tightening. He looked up. "All research projects have been ordered to be terminated."

Greg felt his jaw drop as shock flooded through him. "Terminated? You can't be serious."

Kinsey/Kenny/Smith put away his phone and pulled out his sidearm. "Afraid so, Doc. Please don't get in the way."

Greg reached the enclosure just ahead of Kinsey/Kenny/Smith and finally read the name on his uniform. *Windover—wow, I was really far off.* "What the hell happened?"

"I don't know. But whatever it was, it must have been pretty bad for them to order this."

Greg looked over his shoulder at Hank. A shiver ran through him. Did one of them hurt someone? "But we just got here. There has to be some kind of mistake. I mean, why would they make us come all the way out here just to terminate all the projects?"

"I don't know, Doc. But I'm going to need you to move out of the way."

"Just hold on a minute. Let me think."

"There's nothing to think about. Orders are orders."

Greg stared up at the soldier and knew the man would follow through with his orders. And Greg wasn't exactly unhappy with the decision, but what the hell was going on?

Windover looked down at him, raising an eyebrow. "You're protecting him?"

Greg put up his hands. "God no. But I am protecting

you. He's awake. Let me knock him out. And there's a kill switch in the program. We can do it from out here."

Greg made his way to the console, part of him wondering what the hell was going on and part of him relieved. This morning's display had terrified him. Greg had no problem with getting his future info from an autopsy. In fact, Hank's brain might tell him quite a lot right now.

Windover took up position next to him. Greg opened the camera feed in the bottom right of the monitor and then input a series of commands to activate the injection system in the box. Hank slammed his arms against the box and Greg jumped a good foot. Shaking, Greg punched enter. Hank flung himself against the hood of the box. Then it began to rock from side to side.

As he stared at the box, Windover's eyes widened. "Holy crap."

"Yeah, let's give the drugs a minute to work their magic. It seems the more humane approach."

Gradually the noises from the coffin slowed and then stopped altogether. Greg looked at the readings. Hank's heart rate was really low.

"He out?" Windover asked.

"He should be."

"Should be?"

"Well, earlier he came to really quick. But we just dosed him, so he should be out. You're sure this is the order?"

"Yeah, Doc."

"Okay." Greg input a series of codes. And then his hand hovered over the enter key. Guilt rolled through him.

Sorry about this, Hank.

He hit enter. A light smoke covered the inside of the coffin. Hank's body seized. Then seized again. Greg stared at the monitors, and with each second that passed, Hank's heart rate slowed until finally, none was discernible.

"It's done." Greg stepped back, his body shaking. He felt bad and he didn't know why. Hank had been a monster and yet Greg had killed him while he was captive. It didn't seem fair.

"You sure?" Windover asked.

Greg nodded. "Yeah. So now what?"

Windover shrugged. "I don't know—" Another beep from his phone cut him off. He glanced down. "Check that. Let's go."

"Go? Where?" Greg asked as the soldier grabbed his arm, pulling him toward the door.

"All levels from seven down are being evacuated. Let's move." Opening the door, Windover didn't wait. He hustled down the hallway, and Greg had no choice but to follow. They headed for the elevator at the end of the hall. They passed three labs and were passing the fourth when gunfire burst out from behind the door, followed by a scream. Windover shoved Greg behind him, pulling up his weapon.

Something heavy slammed against the door and Greg jumped. Behind them, the elevator opened. But so did the door. A man in a lab coat soaked in blood flew out of the room and into Windover. Greg slammed to the ground, Windover on top of him. All the air left his lungs and he gasped for breath, but nothing came. Windover fired and Greg turned his head, trying to see what he was aiming at.

It was a gray alien with a large head. But this was no tiny cute alien. This thing stood at least seven feet tall. The alien's body looked emaciated, his skin so dry it was flaking off. His eyes were black, but something seemed to roll through them as he looked at Windover. The soldier began to scream, grabbing his head.

And then the gray stumbled back as round after round slammed into him. The being crumpled to the ground, white liquid soaking the ground around him.

A hand grabbed Greg's arm, pushing Windover off him and yanking Greg up. "Greg, are you hurt? Greg?"

Greg gulped in air and yanked his gaze from the being. He stared into Leslie's deep brown eyes. "I love you."

Leslie rolled her eyes with a scoff. "Yup, you're fine." She pulled him down the hall as a loud thump sounded from the elevator shaft.

"Windover?" he asked.

Leslie shook her head. "He's gone." Greg turned to look, but Leslie stepped in his way, blocking his view.

"Les?"

"Time to go." She pulled him down the hall. "You got your ID?"

Running, Greg grabbed around his neck for the lanyard, but it was gone. He'd taken it off when he'd fallen asleep. "It's in the office."

"Shit. We're going to need it." Leslie stopped at the office door, swiping her card over the access panel.

"Why do we need it if you have yours?'"

"In case we get separated."

Greg stopped short. "What?"

"Go!" Leslie yelled, pushing him into the room.

Greg nearly tripped over his feet as he sprinted for the back wall. He grabbed the lanyard from where it lay on the ground next to the couch, slipping it over his head. He'd almost reached Leslie when he stopped dead, a cold sweat bursting out across his skin.

"Greg, what are you doing? We need to go."

But Greg ignored her, turning slowly toward the enclosure. The coffin was still in there, but it had crashed to the ground.

The door had been torn off. And he could see inside.

Fear poured through him as he turned back to Leslie. "It's Hank. He's gone."

Chapter Fifty-One

CHRIS'S HEART nearly jumped out of his chest when he heard the gunshot. There was only one lab in this section of the floor—Alvie's. He ran down the hall. He passed three people on his way—all of them were heading for the exit and none of them were Maeve.

As he reached the door, the emergency siren sounded. Chris paused. *Now what?*

He fumbled for his card and shoved open the door as soon as it buzzed. Maeve stood in the glass enclosure, Alvie behind her. Henning stalked toward her, his baton in his hand.

"Henning!" he yelled.

The soldier turned. Chris saw the beginning of what was going to be a nasty black eye. And the anger in his taut form was impossible to miss. Henning glared back at him.

Chris held his gaze, moving forward cautiously. He unstrapped his Taser, keeping his hand near it. "You all right, man?"

Pausing, Henning inclined his head toward Maeve. "This egghead thinks she can avoid orders."

"They never understand, do they?" Chris asked, trying not to look at Maeve's face as he forced a smile to his lips.

"Well, how about we show her?" Henning asked nodding toward Maeve.

Chris stepped into the enclosure. "You read my mind. Let me handle it, though. I've had to deal with her for months now."

Not answering, Henning gripped his baton harder, his knuckles white.

"Seriously, man, all hell's breaking loose. You should get moving."

Henning stared at Maeve, hate in his eyes. "Yeah, you're right. She's not worth it." He nodded at Chris. "I'll see you in a few."

"Yeah," Chris said as Henning headed to the door.

As the door closed behind him, Maeve closed her eyes, her shoulders dropping. "Thank you, Chris."

"You okay?"

"Yeah. What's going on?"

"They've ordered all projects terminated."

Maeve's mouth dropped open. "But that's got to be wrong. I mean, they can't be talking about Alvie."

"It includes him too," Chris said, his stomach rolling at the thought.

"Well, what are we going to do?"

Chris pulled his weapon from his holster. "I don't have a choice, Maeve. I'm a soldier and it's an order."

Chapter Fifty-Two

AS SHE STARED AT CHRIS, Maeve's mind could not truly accept what was happening. She kept thinking this can't be real. And all she wanted was to wake up. "Chris, they can't mean Alvie."

"It's base wide. That includes him."

Maeve noticed for the first time that Chris's sidearm was in his hand at his side. Her pulse rate spiked and she stared at him in disbelief. "What are you doing? You can't be serious."

"Maeve, I'm a soldier. I follow orders."

Keeping herself between Chris and Alvie, Maeve put her hands out. "What about moral objections? Aren't you allowed to object to an order you find morally wrong?"

Pain twisted Chris's face. "I'm sorry, Maeve. But if they want him dead, there's a reason for it."

"No, there's not. You said this is a base-wide order. They're not considering this on a case-by-case basis. They're throwing the baby out with the bathwater. Alvie's not dangerous. He's done nothing to anyone. He doesn't deserve to die."

Maeve made sure to keep herself in front of Alvie, not giving Chris a shot as she stepped toward him, realizing that she was stepping between Alvie and a gun yet again. "Please, Chris, you know him. You *know* him. And I know you. You can't do this. You won't be able to live with yourself after."

Chris stepped to the side, aiming his weapon at Alvie. "I'm sorry, Alvie."

"He's part human, Chris."

Tearing his gaze from Alvie, shock was splashed across Chris's face. "What?"

"Alvie. He's part human. He's not completely alien. His mother was human."

"Wait, but that—I don't understand."

"I was able to check his older files. There was a genetic profile in there. Alvie is a hybrid, part human, part alien. You cannot kill him. That's murder."

"Maeve, you can't just say things—"

"I'm not. It's in his file. He was created at Wright-Patt. But the genetic profile is clear: he has a human mother."

Chris's jaw hung open. Then it snapped shut and he shook his head. "Maeve, it's an order. I have to—" Chris's words cut off and he went still.

Heart pounding, Maeve moved toward him, but Chris's eyes were unfocused. "Chris?" She gently pushed the gun away from herself and Alvie, so it was aimed at the far wall.

Chris shook himself from his daze and stared at Alvie, then he lowered his weapon, his hand shaking.

"What happened?" Maeve asked.

"He—he showed me myself. And you."

The PA system blared to life. "Code 12. Repeat, Code 12."

Chris jolted.

"What's a Code 12?" Maeve asked.

"Base-wide evacuation."

Chapter Fifty-Three

GREG STOOD LOCKED IN PLACE, staring in horror at the tipped-over coffin. Had something broken in and stolen Hank? He stared up at the ceiling where part of it had been ripped away near the crane, looking for a clue.

But somewhere deep inside, Greg knew the truth: Hank had played possum again, and the drugs meant to kill him had just ticked him off.

"What do you mean Hank's gone?" Leslie demanded.

"We administered the death cocktail. He flat-lined. But his body's gone. He's gone."

The PA system blared to life. "Code 12. Repeat, Code 12."

"What's a Code 12?" Greg asked.

"Base-wide evacuation. So we'll deal with this later. We need to go." Leslie gripped his arm and yanked him out into the hall. At the end of it by the elevators, another one of the gray beings appeared. Leslie pulled Greg in the opposite direction and into the stairwell. As they entered it, her radio buzzed.

"You want to take that?" Greg asked as he started to run up the stairs next to her.

He'd reached the landing of the next floor when she put out an arm, clotheslining him in the chest. "Ow." He rubbed his chest, knowing that was going to leave one hell of a bruise.

"Listen," Leslie whispered.

He could hear some thumps from the stairs above and then a scream.

Leslie grabbed him, pushing open the nearest door, and shoved him in, quickly closing it behind her. She yanked her phone off her belt, reading the screen. "It's West. I'm supposed to meet my team out front."

A thump sounded on the landing just outside the door. This time, Greg grabbed Leslie's arm and pulled her down the hall at a run. "That sounds like a really good idea. They have lots of guns, right? Let's go find them."

Chapter Fifty-Four

CHRIS PACED MAEVE'S LAB, his gaze shifting between Alvie and the door. "We can't take him."

Maeve crossed her arms over her chest. "Well, maybe you can't. But I'm not leaving without him."

Chris honestly didn't know what to do. Destroying Alvie was an order. And never in his life had he disobeyed an order. But at the same time, he could not kill him. Even without Maeve intervening, he wouldn't have been able to do it. But now Maeve wanted to take him with them—to help him escape. The idea was ludicrous, even if the thought of leaving Alvie behind broke Chris's heart.

"Maeve, the hallways will be crawling with soldiers. Even if we somehow manage to get him out of the building, then what? Nothing's changed. He's an alien."

Maeve cut in. "He's only part alien."

"Yeah, but he looks *all* alien. We can't just run off with him."

"I know that. But they don't know him like we do. If

they did, they would never order this. We just need time to convince them. That's all I'm asking for—time."

Chris knew she would lay down her life for Alvie. Alvie himself stood holding onto Maeve's hand, his large eyes staring back at Chris. And Chris knew Alvie would do the same for her.

Maeve winced and rubbed her head.

"Maeve?"

"It's nothing. It's just a headache."

Looking between Maeve and Alvie, Chris had the distinct impression he was missing something. "Look, we can try, but you know this is probably not going to work, right?"

Maeve nodded, tightening her grasp on Alvie. "It will work."

But Chris knew that she was wrong. Getting Alvie out of the building was one thing, but convincing the powers that be that he should be allowed to live—that was an all-new type of miracle she was asking for.

The number eleven filtered through his mind, and Chris went still. "What the hell was that?"

Maeve bit her lip, glancing down at Alvie and then back at Chris. "He wants to go to level 11."

"No, absolutely not. That's where the breakout began."

Maeve's eyes grew large. "Breakout? Something got out?"

"A lot of somethings got out. Below level seven is complete chaos—violent chaos."

The number 11 slipped through his mind again. Chris shook his head. "Alvie, you don't understand. We need to get out of this building. You don't know what's roaming these halls. We need to go up, not down."

Then the number 11 began to waft through Chris's

mind on an unending loop. He stared at Alvie. "No, Alvie. No."

The number 11 practically shouted into his mind. Next to him, Maeve's hands flew to her head. "Ah."

Chris grabbed her. "What?"

"We need to go to level 11."

"We can't—"

"I don't know what's going on. But Alvie says we need to go there. And that means we're going."

Chris glared at her. "Maeve, you're not in charge, and he certainly isn't. Which means I am. And we are getting out, not going deeper into this building. Got it?"

Chapter Fifty-Five

JOHN HAD SPENT the morning running from meeting to meeting. BOSAC's move of all alien-related projects to 51 had really disrupted the base's routine. Not to mention irking more than one individual who had spent years working on a project only to be unceremoniously dumped from it when they failed to meet the new security clearance requirements. He was scrambling, trying to put out fires, calm people down, and all the while he cursed Martin Drummond.

It had been years since he'd thought of the man. And John was fine with it that way. The man had nearly killed Alice, Maeve, Alvie, even himself. Drummond had taken it upon himself to step beyond his bounds as a CIA agent. And without Senator Billingsley, John didn't know what would have happened.

But now Maeve was within Drummond's reach. And that made John awfully uneasy. His phone rang, and John looked up at the ceiling with a sigh.

Is five minutes of quiet too much to ask?

But he reached over and pushed the lit button. "What is it, Gavin?"

"Greta Schubert is on line one. She said it's important."

"All right, patch her through." John waited a second before the second light on his phone blinked and then picked up the call. "Greta, how are you? All packed?"

"No, and that's why I'm calling. I just received an email that my transfer has been cancelled."

John frowned. "Cancelled?"

"You didn't know?"

"No. You're one of about a dozen people who were supposed to head over next week. Was there a reason given?"

"Nothing. They just said the project was cancelled."

"The project?" John felt his chest tighten. If the project was cancelled, that could mean only one thing—Alvie was going to be destroyed. Maeve would be beyond devastated. Her mother's death had hit her hard. Alvie had been a huge part in her getting her through that.

He couldn't imagine what Alvie's death would do to her. But he knew it would probably hit her harder. Because in her mind, she'd view Alvie's death as a murder.

And John thought she was probably right on that count. "I'm going to look into it. I'll get back to you."

"Thank you, sir," Greta said before hanging up. John quickly dialed two of the other individuals who were supposed to be heading out to 51 as well. They both reported that they'd had their transfers cancelled. Which meant it wasn't just Alvie's project that had been cancelled. It had been all of them.

John called Maeve's cell, but his call was immediately directed to voicemail. He tried Chris's and received the same treatment. He wasn't overly surprised as he doubted their cell phones were even allowed on the base. He found the number for one of his contacts out at 51 and dialed. "Jim? John Forrester."

"John, how you doing?"

"Good, good. Listen, I've got some people that were supposed to be transferred out to 51. All their transfers have been cancelled. Do you know what's going on?"

"No, that just—You know what, let me call you back. I'll see what I can find out."

"Jim, Maeve's out there. I just want to make sure she's all right."

"I'll call you as soon as I know something."

"Okay." John hung up the phone, a fear taking hold of him and not letting go.

She's fine. Chris is with her. She's fine.

He had chosen Chris because he knew how capable he was. But he also knew he would be good for Maeve. Someone her age who would make her laugh, because Maeve's life was her work. And the fact that Chris was with her did offer him some comfort.

But he couldn't shake the feeling that something had happened. Something that was completely out of his control.

And that scared the hell out of him.

He might be the commander of Wright-Patt, but his control was not complete. There were some projects on his own base that even he was not privy to the details of. And Area 51 was the most secretive base in the world. As much as he wanted to believe Maeve would be fine, he knew that there was a dark side to America's military. He just prayed Maeve wasn't seeing that dark side up close and personal.

Chapter Fifty-Six

MAEVE, Chris, and Alvie paused in the stairwell outside of the door leading to level eleven. As Chris eased the door open, Maeve stood against the side of the wall with Alvie, the shotgun she'd taken from a downed security officer carefully tucked into her side while Chris scanned the hall. Flickering light illuminated the hallway.

"You know, when I said I was in charge I meant it. You two have no respect for authority," Chris grumbled.

"Well, we tried to follow you. But that didn't exactly work, did it?" Maeve asked.

She gave him a tight smile, feeling the fear holding her tight. She and Alvie *had* tried to follow Chris out of the building. But something had blocked their way when they left the hall. They'd escaped into the stairwell, only for something to block their way up. She hadn't gotten a good look at it, but the slither it made followed by a scream and then gunfire had Chris ordering them down the stairs as fast as they could manage.

Maeve had pointed out that since they were heading

down anyway, they might as well head to eleven. It's not like they could go up. Even so, it had been a nightmare-filled trip. She'd seen seven dead humans with different wounds—one was missing an arm, one had swollen up, looking as if they were going to burst, another had a huge gash in his chest.

Maeve didn't know what had caused those injuries, but she did know it wasn't just one alien. Which begged the question of exactly how many alien species did the United States have? And exactly how many were now free?

But even with the stairwell of nightmares, she wanted to head to eleven. She knew it wasn't the safest option. But Alvie was adamant about coming down here. She'd never seen him like this before. It wasn't just curiosity. He was worried about something down here. Chris had finally relented when he'd realized that Maeve was going to go with Alvie alone. And she would have, but she was very glad to have Chris along.

Chris looked back at them. "Okay. We're in and out. Got it?"

Maeve nodded.

"Alvie?" Chris asked.

He nodded as well.

Chris motioned them forward. The hallway expanded to the right and then left and turned another twenty feet down, leading to other hallways. The floor was a dark gray tile, as were the walls. And the entire floor was silent save for the sound of the air conditioning. The flickering lights did nothing to cheer the space up.

Chris turned right, but Alvie clutched his hand and motioned left. Chris sighed. "You're killing me, you know that, right?"

Alvie just looked up at him.

"Okay, buddy, you're in charge." Chris glanced at Maeve. "You're sure he's not leading us to some of his friends, right?"

"From how you've described them and what I've seen, I don't think they're his friends."

Alvie went still as they approached the corner and let out a gasp. Then he ran forward.

"Alvie!" Maeve reached for him, but he was gone.

Chris held her back. "Hold up."

He glanced around the corner before turning back to her. "Come on." He led her forward. Maeve itched to sprint forward and find Alvie, but the fear of what might grab her kept her tucked in behind Chris.

They reached the end of another hall, and Maeve's nerves were pulled so tight she knew they were going to snap at any moment. Behind them, she heard the door to the stairwell open. But it wasn't footfalls that sounded but a sliding sound.

She grabbed Chris's arm. "Chris."

"I hear it."

Ahead, she heard Alvie's wail.

"Damn it. Is he trying to get them to find us?" Chris muttered before turning the corner and hurrying down the hall. Alvie stood outside a door labeled 11 AI1.

"Alvie, we need to go," Chris whispered.

The number of the room flashed through her mind. "He wants to go in there."

Chris looked between the two of them. "You two know this place is crawling with aliens, right? No offense, Alvie."

Alvie just looked at him and the door. Chris winced. "Okay, not so loud."

Inside the room, something crashed. Alvie threw himself at the door.

Maeve reached out and pulled Alvie to her as Chris keyed open the door. "Okay. Okay."

As soon as it opened, Alvie flew in.

"No!" Maeve yelled.

"Shit," Chris said, pulling his weapon to his shoulder. Two animals were in the room. They were gorilla sized but they had no hair and were a pale blue. Their heads were round and bulbous, but when they turned they hissed. Maeve got an eyeful of sharp incisors.

Oh my god. Alvie sprinted past them for the glass enclosure at the back.

Maeve pulled her shotgun around and pulled the trigger. She caught one in the hand. Chris caught the other in the chest. It should have been a kill shot, if it had been a gorilla. Apparently the hearts of these things were located somewhere else.

Chris unloaded shot after shot, but Maeve's weapon stayed silent as she watched the being. There. Just above its waist on the right hand side she saw a pulse in the skin. She pulled the trigger and hit the exact spot. The being toppled over.

"At the waist on the right," she yelled.

Chris wasted no time following her instructions. The second creature fell.

Maeve's breaths came out in gasps and she felt lightheaded. She stared at the creature, both intrigued and terrified by their existence. They looked so much like gorillas. Had someone mixed DNA? She looked back at Alvie. Is that how he'd been created?

"How'd you know?" Chris asked.

She blinked, focusing back on Chris. "What?"

"The kill shot. How'd you know?"

"It's where Alvie's heart is."

At his name, she turned to where he was. His face and hands were pressed against the glass enclosure. Maeve moved to his side.

He looked up at her, tears running down his cheeks. Maeve gasped. "Alvie, what's wrong?" He looked back inside the cage.

Maeve did the same and went still, her world tilting out of orbit. Inside, three small beings only two feet tall were huddled in a corner.

And they all looked exactly like Alvie.

Chapter Fifty-Seven

WASHINGTON, D.C.

WANDA HEIG LISTENED as Mr. Lai, the Chinese delegate, explained his country's displeasure at the change in position of the Pacific fleet due to the landing of a military jet on China's man-made island, thousands of miles from China's borders, in the South China Sea. Most of the world viewed the island as China's attempt to extend its boundaries.

No one was more concerned about that expansion than the Philippines, as the area where the island was built was within an area that they claimed. But they weren't the only ones concerned. The sea lane where the island had been built was extremely busy with commerce, making the rest of the world take an interest as well.

Wanda rubbed the bridge of her nose as the translator from China explained that the Chinese government had no intention of using the island for military purposes.

"Mr. Lai, if that is true," Wanda said, "why was a military jet seen landing and departing from the island seven hours ago?"

Wanda waited while the question was translated, cursing China for pushing boundaries they didn't need to push.

"There was a humanitarian need for the jet to transport three ill workers from the island," the translator said.

"And it wasn't a test to see if the recently completed runway was long enough to accommodate longer military jets?" Wanda asked.

Ten seconds of silence followed while the translator spoke with Mr. Lai. "No, of course not, Madam Secretary. It was a purely humanitarian gesture."

Wanda watched Mr. Lai, but he simply looked back at her without blinking. "I see." She wrapped up the conversation within a few minutes. There was nothing more to be gained. And she had done what she had intended to—let the Chinese know that their actions were not going unnoticed, and therefore subtly issuing a threat with the movement of part of the Pacific fleet closer to the China mainland.

The Chinese had also gotten what they wanted—testing how well their actions were being monitored and determining the military possibilities regarding the island.

Back in her office, Wanda rifled through her papers on the island for a moment before she pushed back from her desk with a sigh.

Some days, it's just not worth it.

She walked over to her window and stared at the traffic below. When she'd been younger, this was not the direction she had expected her life to take.

But early on in her career at State, she'd learned she was good at two things—one, understanding what people were really trying to say despite their words, and two, getting whatever she needed to get done, done.

Both skills had served her well. And had landed her in this particular office.

But some days, she seriously considered dropping it all and opening up a nursery somewhere. Surrounding herself with flowers that had no ulterior motives sounded like heaven.

A knock at her door caused her to turn as her assistant poked his head in. "Madam Secretary? You received a call from Colonel John Forrester while you were meeting with the Chinese delegate. He said it was urgent."

John?

Surprise flashed through her. She hadn't spoken with John in two years. She had meant to call him when Alice died, but somehow never found the time. And then so much time passed, it felt awkward. "Did he say what it was about?"

"No, ma'am. But he sounded concerned."

Concerned? That was not John's usual state. He was unflappable. "Get him on the phone."

"Yes, ma'am."

The phone on her desk buzzed a moment later. "Colonel Forrester on line one, ma'am."

Wanda took her seat as she reached for the phone. "John. Good to hear from you."

"Wanda, good to hear your voice too. It's been too long."

"I was sorry to hear about Alice. I meant to reach out but—"

"It's all right. I don't deal too well with sympathy."

Wanda smiled, picturing John during their early years together at the Pentagon. "*That* I do remember. So how are you? Adam said there was some urgency."

The warmth left John's tone. "Yes. I have a dozen staff

members who have already been vetted for a spot out in Nevada. But they've been informed the positions have been cancelled. I haven't been able to learn anything about why."

Nevada—51. A chill stole over her. "Well, perhaps the projects have simply been cancelled."

"That's the thing, these projects have been going on for years. The people scheduled to head out there have been *working* on the projects for years. They'd never be able to get anyone up to speed in time. And I know that some of my people are working on the same projects out there already. They left a few days ago. But I can't seem to reach any of them."

Wanda didn't pause in her speech, but her mind raced. "There could be any sort of reasons for that. They could be trying out a new technology that blocks calls base wide. Honestly, out there anything is possible."

"Could you just check and make sure there's nothing else going on? It feels like something is up."

"I'll see what I can find out and get back to you."

"Thanks, Wanda. I'll be waiting for your call."

Wanda hung up the receiver. She punched the intercom. "Adam, get me Director Fezza immediately."

"Yes, ma'am."

She waited, drumming her hands on the desk. It was nothing. John was overreacting, although if she was being honest, she had never known him to do so.

Her intercom buzzed and she picked up the phone.

"Ma'am, I can't get through to Director Fezza's office. I tried some of the other offices and I was unable to reach them either. It seems like no calls are going through to the base."

Wanda hadn't been sure when she had nominated Martin for the BOSAC position that he was the right fit.

But agency heads across the spectrum had supported him—Buckley from the CIA, Freely at the NSA, Danner from State, even Brenner from the FBI, albeit grudgingly.

But she had seen glimpses of the man behind the mask, and those glimpses made her uneasy. And now after he'd moved some of the government's most secret projects, no calls were going through. Transfers had been cancelled. And if something had gone wrong, it wasn't Martin who should be blamed but Wanda. Her gut had told her something was off about the man, but she had let others sway her. *God damn it, Martin.*

"Find me Martin Drummond. *Immediately.*"

Chapter Fifty-Eight

GREG RACED up the stairs next to Leslie. "How did they all get out?"

"I don't know." Leslie put out a hand to stop him, putting a finger to her lips. They'd entered another stairwell and had made it only two floors. Above them, a sliding sound filtered down the stairs followed by a slurp. Whatever was coming toward them was not human.

Leslie grabbed the door handle and, pausing for a deep breath, wrenched it open, her gun pulled into her shoulder. Two bodies lay in the hallway. One was a soldier, one was a scientist, and neither was moving. Leslie reached down and checked the pulse of each of them.

She looked up at Greg and shook her head. Greg reached down and picked up the automatic weapon lying next to one of the soldiers.

"Uh, what are you doing?" Leslie asked.

Greg looked from the weapon to Leslie. "Preparing to defend us?"

"Have you ever *shot* a weapon before?"

"Hey, I've played Call of Duty and I'll have you know, I'm an incredible shot."

Leslie stared at him, her mouth hanging open before she shook her head. "We are so doomed."

"I got this, Leslie. Okay?"

She searched his eyes for something before she nodded. "Okay. So let's go."

Behind them, a thump sounded at the door. Greg's head whipped around, expecting one of the gray beings to show up. But the door didn't open. Instead, something pale pink and two feet wide slid underneath it. Leslie pulled Greg behind her, keeping her weapon trained on the thing. It looked like someone had started to melt a starfish and stopped halfway through the process.

It slid along the ground toward Greg and Leslie as they backed up. Greg grimaced as it crawled over one of the bodies, leaving a trail of wetness behind it. And then the body where the thing had touched it began to disintegrate.

"Acid. Its saliva is some type of acid," Greg whispered.

"Got that." Leslie opened fire. The starfish jumped back. One of Leslie's shots cut off one of its arms. But then the detached arm began to form another one of the melted starfish.

"Not working, Les. That's not working," Greg said, on the edge of panic. He looked at the thing, his mind scrambling to figure out a way to stop it. Bullets cut into it but it healed almost immediately and barely slowed down.

Leslie grabbed his arm. "Run."

Greg did, but his mind churned. There had to be something they could fight it with. Everything had a weakness. He glanced back. The starfish and its twin were gaining on them.

He looked around frantically but the hallway was empty

save for— *Yes!* He sprinted ahead, Leslie on his heels, and stopped at the fire extinguisher, yanking it from the wall. Pulling the pin, he aimed it at the first being. A yellow powder shot out from the extinguisher, coating the being. Its movements slowed and then stopped. Then it began to crystallize. Not waiting, he took aim at the second. It also crystallized.

"What the hell?" Leslie asked, her eyes large.

"It's a dry fire extinguisher. It coats something, preventing the oxygen from getting through. They basically just suffocated."

"Why the crystallization?"

"I don't know. It could be a defense mechanism or some sort of chemical reaction."

"Uh-huh." Leslie walked over and slammed the butt of her rifle into each one, smashing them into a thousand pieces.

Greg looked at her.

She shrugged. "Just making sure. Good job."

Greg blew on the end of the hose like gunslingers in old Westerns. "Wasn't nothing, ma'am."

Leslie smiled. "I don't know. I'd say it was something."

The door at the end of the hall rattled. The smiled dropped from Leslie's face. "Let's go. And bring the extinguisher."

Chapter Fifty-Nine

THE THREE LITTLE beings were crouched low in the back of the enclosure, huddled tightly together. Each of their heads was disproportionately large for their small bodies—their necks looked too thin to hold it up. But Maeve knew if they were like Alvie, their bones were strong and they were also light. Each of them had four fingers on each of their hands and their skin was a light gray color. They even wore the same blue scrubs that Alvie wore, albeit much smaller versions.

One peeked its head out, large black eyes staring at Maeve with fear, before ducking back down. The eyes dominated the face, proportionally larger than Alvie's, the same way all babies and young children developed. Scientists believed that large eye size was a means of upping the cute factor, making humans and other beings more responsive to babies.

"Oh my god. They're babies." Maeve moved toward the door. Chris intercepted her before she could try to open it.

She looked up at him. "What are you doing? We have to get them out of there."

"We don't even know what they are."

"They look just like him. They're the same as Alvie."

"That means nothing. This is a whole new world, Maeve. They're mixing everything down here. We need to know what they are made of *before* we open that door."

Maeve took a breath, realizing he was right. "Okay."

With one last look at the three little figures, she headed for the console, knowing that was where the answers would be. But her mind was whirling at the existence of more beings like Alvie. She stared at the console for a moment before shaking herself from her thoughts and clicking on the mouse. A prompt popped up, requesting she slide her ID card through the reader. She slid her ID through but she was denied access. The console was ID specific. She looked back at Chris. "It won't accept my ID."

Chris walked over to a body in the corner of the room. Maeve blanched. She hadn't even noticed it. Chris pulled the card away from the man's neck, wiping the blood on the card on the man's shirt. He walked over and handed it to her. "Here."

She bit her lip and took it gingerly before running it through the reader at the bottom of the screen. The card prompt disappeared, replaced by another box. "It needs a password."

"What was his name?"

"Um." She flipped the card over to read it. "Ignacio Alvarez."

"Try Alvarez11AI1."

Maeve typed it in. The password box disappeared and the desktop screen appeared.

Maeve looked at Chris in disbelief. "How'd you know that?"

"You were all assigned temporary passwords that combined the room and your name—which you were supposed to change. But most of you scientists are so scatterbrained, I figured you guys haven't changed them."

"That's a gross assumption."

"Have you changed yours?"

"Not the point." Maeve turned back to the computer and pulled up the file for the projects. She scanned the file names before zeroing in on one that looked hopeful— Project Progeny. She pulled it open.

"They were created a year and a half ago. But they were born seven months ago." With a jolt, she realized that was exactly when Alvie had started having his disturbances.

And when I started having the dreams.

She paused, her mind racing. Had Alvie somehow known they were born? Was their birth somehow connected to his episodes? Was it possible? If he'd known that, was he linked to them?

Is he linked to me through my stem cells?

She quickly checked the files to see if anything had been done to one of them the day of the obstacle course. There —shock therapy. Her jaw dropped open.

Oh my god. They're linked. Somehow Alvie knew what they were going through.

"Where'd they come from?" Chris asked.

"Uh…" Maeve pulled herself from her thoughts, scanning through the files. "They were created through something called Project Progeny. They had a cow as a host prior to birth."

"They're part *cow*?"

Maeve shook her head, a smile ghosting across her face.

"No. The cow—she was only the host. It doesn't say who or what they were created from. Hold on." She scanned to files again before her hand went still. Toward the bottom of the list was a file with her last name—the Leander Process. With a shaky hand she clicked on the icon. A PDF appeared. She read through it quickly, her disbelief growing.

"Oh my god."

"What?" Chris asked.

"My mom…" Maeve felt ill.

"Your mom what?"

"She created them."

Chapter Sixty

GREG AND LESLIE had ended up heading down four more flights instead of going up. Each avenue they'd attempted to escape had led to more unfriendlies.

And more bodies.

Greg had counted thirty humans down and at least twelve different species of aliens. It was like being trapped in a zoo where all the animals had been set free—all the really terrifying man-eating animals.

"You all right?" Leslie asked.

Greg looked over her. Her shirt was torn. She had a cut on her bicep and she had fought off at least five aliens. And yet she looked just as fierce and determined as the first day he'd met her.

He didn't know if she came back to get him because it was her duty or because she wanted to make sure he was all right, but he knew he would not be alive if it weren't for her. And right now, even with the massive crush he still had on her, which to be honest had only increased after watching her in battle, he felt more gratitude toward her than he could remember feeling for any human on the planet.

He nodded. "I'm good. Thanks to you."

"Just doing my job."

Somehow I doubt that's all it is. "Well, this poor schlub is more than grateful that you do your job so well."

"You're not, you know."

"Not what?"

"A poor schlub. You shouldn't run yourself down so much."

Greg's mouth dropped open and then he hastily shut it. "Uh, I don't mean anything by it. I just…" He shrugged. "I don't know."

"Well, you're a pretty good guy. And you've held up better than a lot of other people would under these circumstances. I've seen seasoned soldiers who haven't held up as well as you. You should give yourself some credit."

Greg put a hand to his chest. "You know, you're right. I'm awesome. The world rarely takes notice."

"And he's back," she muttered, but the grin tugging at the corner of her mouth took the sting out of her words. "So what do you think's going on with all these things? What do they want?"

Greg had been puzzling over the same issue. And he didn't like where his mind was heading. "I'm not sure. But some of these deaths—they look like overkill. And these things have been following us at times. They're not just going through the obstacles in their way."

Leslie stopped walking, turning to face Greg. "Wait, are you saying they're tracking us down?"

"I don't know. I mean, in our world, humans were thought to be the only animals that committed murder. But now we know that's not entirely true. Male lions will kill all the new male cubs in their pride. Ant colonies will go to war against one another. Even chimps have been known to kill."

"So are they just killing in self-defense or is there something more calculated at play?"

"It could be either. Until we can sit down and observe what's happening, we won't know. I mean, we don't even know if all these guys come from the same planet or if they're pure alien or some sort of hybrid."

"Hybrid? As in someone mixed alien DNA with something else? Why would someone do that?"

Greg looked at Leslie and realized she didn't know how Hank had been created. That he had been cooked up in a lab.

"I'm guessing the animal couldn't survive in Earth's atmosphere," he said. "Or there was some other weakness or even a missing patch of DNA. There're all sorts of reasons. But regardless, I think it would be wrong to underestimate them. They're not animals. I mean, Hank, as much as he looked like a walking crocodile, had some intelligence underneath there. And from what little I've seen of these others beings—which has been more than enough, by the way—there seems to be some intelligence at work. So I don't know if they're trying to kill us because we're a threat or because they really just want us dead. Maybe it's revenge for the way they've been treated."

He swallowed hard, remembering that Hank might be running around the building somewhere. And if they were motivated by revenge ...

"Well, that's comforting," Leslie muttered.

Greg shrugged. "Or maybe they're all looking for a way out and have a really lousy sense of direction. And we just happened to be in the way."

"Well, we haven't seen any for a while."

Greg nodded. "And I will be perfectly happy if I never see another one."

"I hate to break it to you, but I'm pretty sure we're going to see another one."

A picture of Hank staring at him through the window in the containment unit floated through his mind. Greg adjusted his grip on his weapon, his hands slick.

Please don't let them be motivated by revenge.

"Yeah, I know," he said.

Chapter Sixty-One

CHRIS SPOKE SLOWLY. "Maeve, that's not possible. You said they were created a year and a half ago. Your mom was in no shape to work on a project then. She couldn't have created them."

"I know, but she created the process." Maeve sat down in a chair, her eyes focused on the screen. The Leander Process—her mother's procedure for cloning a living being.

And for the first time, Maeve wondered who else had used her mother's process. Her mother had created Alvie. It was awe-inspiring and terrifying. Had her mother also created all these other beasts? Even if she hadn't been directly involved, her technique had made it possible. Maeve's gaze flew to Alvie. How could she do this? How could she play God?

"Is that even possible?" Chris asked.

"What?" Maeve asked, not sure what Chris was referring to.

"Your mom—is it even possible for her to have created them?"

Maeve nodded. "Indirectly." Her gaze strayed to the three little figures hunched over in terror. The figures that all looked just like Alvie. Shock tore through her.

Oh god, no.

She scanned the files, looking for the original donor, the DNA that had been used to create them. She found it and felt sick to her stomach.

"How could they?" she mumbled.

"How could they what?"

She slumped into a chair, staring at nothing. "They're Alvie."

Chris grabbed her shoulder. "Maeve? What do you mean they're Alvie?"

Her gaze flew to Chris's face. "The three little ones— they're not his kids or his cousins. They're him. They're clones too."

Chapter Sixty-Two

LAS VEGAS, NEVADA

MARTIN STARED at the screens that lined the wall in front of him with a smile on his face. He had learned so much in the short time he'd been watching the action at 51.

I should have done this years ago.

His phone beeped, interrupting his thoughts, and he frowned before answering it.

"Hamish, I'm in the middle—"

"Secretary Heig is two minutes out."

Martin sat up quickly, nearly knocking over his coffee. "What? She's here?"

"Yes, sir."

Shit. Martin stood up quickly, exiting the room and pocketing his phone. Hamish stood right outside the door. "How the hell did she find us?"

"I don't know, sir."

Martin growled. *God damn it, when I find out who leaked this place, I'm going to roast them on a spit.* "Send her to my office when she arrives."

"Yes, sir."

Martin walked into his office, taking a seat behind his desk. He pulled over a file and flipped it open, pretending to read while he seethed. He had better things to do with his time than play politician. This was why he should be given full autonomy. Oversight was simply an annoyance that got in the way of progress.

I guess I should have gotten rid of Wanda when I got rid of the other pests.

He looked up as Wanda stormed through his door. He stood up. "Madam Secretary, what a nice surprise."

"Cut the crap, Martin. What the hell is going on at 51?"

"What do you mean?"

She slammed her palms on the desk. "Don't give me that crap. You moved all the subjects to Area 51 and not twenty-four hours later, all hell breaks loose. How could there possibly have been a security breach this big?"

Martin shrugged. "It was some computer thing. But it's being handled."

"*Handled?* I'm getting reports of multiple deaths—both human and otherwise. Complete floors are overrun. They're evacuating the base. That does *not* sound like it is being handled."

"You've heard about that? *Who* exactly have you heard from?"

"It should have come from you, god damn it. In fact, why wasn't I informed about the breach?"

Martin shrugged. "Information is tightly controlled, you know that. There was no need to inform you."

"No need?" Wanda's voice was deceptively soft. "I am the Secretary of the Air Force. Everything that happens involving the Air Force is my concern."

"Bullshit. You know as well as I do that there are a myriad of projects spread across the branches of the military that the higher ups have no knowledge of. You are now a paper pusher. You are not part of the inner circle."

Wanda narrowed her eyes. "Funny you should mention inner circle. There have been rumors for years about a group operating outside the restraints of the government, controlling black projects related to alien interactions."

"So?"

"So some of the people who have been rumored to be part of this group seem to have disappeared. Two, in fact, are confirmed dead just today. That's quite a coincidence."

Seems I underestimated you as well, Madam Secretary.

He sat back, his hands teepeed in front of him. "Careful, Wanda. You are treading in waters that are way over your head, and there are sharks in these waters. Besides, it's not all bad."

"Not all bad? Are you insane? The inmates are not just running the asylum—they are destroying it. Our people have been killed. And if these things get out—"

Martin waved away her concerns. "They won't get out. There are safeguards in place to avoid that. And we shouldn't look at this like a problem but an opportunity. We can now see how these subjects react when not restrained. We can see how they do against our security operations."

A look of horror crossed Wanda's face. "You realize people are going to die."

Martin shrugged. "True, but the knowledge we gain will be invaluable. We'll learn how they attack, how they communicate, how they think and strategize. All things we can't learn with them locked up behind glass walls."

Wanda paused, her eyes narrowing. "It's quite a coincidence, a *second* coincidence, that the security system broke down just as all the subjects were getting settled in. Area 51 has never had a security breakdown like this before."

Martin smiled. "Yes, it *is* quite a coincidence, isn't it?"

Wanda paled. "Martin, how could you? All these people, they placed their trust in us. They signed on to—"

Martin's voice whipped out. "To do what is necessary to understand this threat. And that is exactly what they are doing. They agreed to the risk. They signed away their constitutional rights to work on this project and at that base."

"You've created a war game between humans and aliens."

Martin smiled. "With one big difference—we know exactly how this one is going to end."

Wanda's mouth fell open. "The Manhattan Protocol."

"Like I said - they won't get out. As soon as there is any chance of them escaping, the entire facility will be bombed. No one will escape. No one will talk. And most importantly, no one will know but us," Martin said, keeping his smile in place.

"Are you even trying to get the staff out?"

"The base has been evacuated of all non-security personnel outside of Buildings 34 and 39. And any personnel who make it to the surface from 34 and 39 will also be evacuated. I'm not a monster."

Wanda reared back and stared at Martin, her mouth hanging open for a second before she closed it. "How could you do this? It's beyond reckless. It's criminal."

Martin narrowed his eyes. In that moment, Wanda represented every paper pusher who stood in the way of real progress. They could be years ahead in research if the powers that be had some vision, had any idea of the stakes of their failure to act.

Just thinking of the years they had wasted made Martin's blood boil. His voice lashed out. "We've had these aliens in our custody for what? Ten years? Twenty? Thirty? And what do we know? Their resting heart rate. That they prefer the dark to the light or vice versa. This is not a *zoo*. We need to *know* the type of threat they possess. We need to *know* how they defend themselves and how they attack. And we can't learn that by taking their damn temperature."

"But you are putting human lives at risk!"

"They are already at risk! Humans are being grabbed every year and you damn well know it. Sightings indicate this threat is only growing bolder. There will be a point when the aliens stop watching and start interacting on a much larger level. So we can study how they fight now or when it's too late. And I'd rather do it now."

Standing at him, Wanda pursed her lips, her fists clenched. "This is murder."

"This is *science*. And our government has a long history of using its citizens to further the goals of science." Martin stared at Wanda, his contempt barely contained. "You appointed me to this position because you know I *could* and *would* make the tough decisions."

"I won't let you get away with this."

Martin laughed. "What are you going to do? The facility is under my control. No one can infiltrate it. By the time you cut through all the red tape and muster up some pitiful little security team, it'll be weeks from now. The experiment will already be concluded. And the site itself will no longer even exist. It will be an irradiated crater that will take years to clean up. This is done, Wanda. You can thank me later."

"I mean it Martin, I won't let you get away with this."

"But see, again, that's a lack of vision. Because I've *already* gotten away with it."

She stared Wat him for a long moment, her lips tight

before she shook her head and stormed from the room. The door slammed behind her. Wanda didn't see the big picture, not yet. But she would come around eventually.

In that big picture, her support, her anger—they didn't matter. What *was* important was Martin saw what was at stake and what needed to be done. And he knew without a doubt that his words to Wanda had been correct.

One day, she would thank him.

Chapter Sixty-Three

CHRIS STARED AT MAEVE. *Alvie's clones?* Chris was a pretty straightforward guy. Despite that, he'd been able to accept that they were not alone in the galaxy, especially after seeing Alvie for the first time. But clones? He wasn't really expected to buy that, was he?

Then the words she actually said hit him. "Wait, what do you mean they're clones *too*? Who else is a clone?"

Maeve winced. "Alvie. I forgot to mention that."

"Wait, you said he had one human parent and one alien. So how—"

"He does, technically. But he was cloned from an original subject who had an alien and human parent. He's the first successful clone ever created. My mom created him."

Chris knew his mouth was hanging open but he couldn't seem to get himself to close it. Alvie was a clone? Chris wasn't a science geek. He'd done well in school and college but most of the stuff Maeve did was way out of his league. But as he looked at the three little ones and Alvie, he simply couldn't wrap his head around the idea of them being clones. Clones were sci-fi extremism. *They weren't little baby aliens running around a secret base. Right?*

"Uh, so who was the original alien/subject/whatever he was cloned from?"

"No one is exactly sure. He was created from the DNA of a skull found down in Mexico. The skull was a thousand years old."

"Wait, so the original hybrid wasn't created in a lab."

"Well, at least not one of our labs."

Chris's jaw fell open. "Holy crap. Um, so someone found a skull and just took some DNA to create Alvie?"

"It was a little more complicated than that, but basically, yes."

Chris looked back at the three little aliens. One of them seemed a little smaller, its features finer. He squinted. It even had some very pale hair. "But isn't one of them a girl?"

Maeve stepped over to the glass, leaning in. Chris wouldn't have been surprised if she pressed her face up against it. "I think so. Even with clones it's possible to manipulate some aspects of the embryo. Or maybe the clone spontaneously became female."

"Spontaneously?"

"Every single human embryo has the potential to be either male or female. It's why men have nipples—just in case they end up being girls."

Surprise flashed through Chris. "Seriously? That's the reason?"

Maeve glanced up at him, and a brief smile crossed her face. "Learn something new every day, huh? Now, we need to get them out of there." She reached for the door.

Oh shit. Chris grabbed her arm as she reached for the control panel.

Maeve yanked it back. "What are you doing?"

"Okay, they're Alvie's clones. But we don't know what they're like. They weren't raised by you and your mom." He lowered his voice. "We don't know what's been done to them."

Maeve's mouth fell open but then she shook her head. "It doesn't matter. Whatever's happened to them, whatever some monster has done to them, we are not leaving them down here for the *other* monsters roaming these halls. They're coming with us."

A loud bang rang out from the hall, followed by a hissing sound, as if to emphasize her point.

Alvie stepped next to Maeve and took her hand. Maeve looked down at him, and Chris knew his argument had lost all effect. She looked back at Chris. "Whatever's happened to them, they are just like Alvie. He won't leave them here. And I won't leave him. Please step out of the way."

Chris stared at her, scrambling to come up with a way to convince her to come with him. He looked into the enclosure. The three creatures were huddled together, but one peeked its head out. Big eyes stared back at him. Chris could feel their fear.

"Damn it." He turned and keyed open the door. Chris started to step in, but Maeve touched his arm. "Let Alvie go first."

Chris backed up, and Alvie moved into the room. Chris stood in the doorway, leaving it open but blocking Maeve from entering. She peered around him, trying to get a better look.

Alvie moved forward cautiously. The creatures first reared back, letting out a small cry. Maeve put her hand to her mouth. "They're terrified."

Alvie stopped moving and just watched them. The one on the right looked at him before slowly standing and tottering over. Chris muttered a curse under his breath. There was a long burn mark that had healed over along the little guy's arm. Alvie reached out his hand, and the small one placed his in Alvie's. Then Alvie pulled him forward, wrapping his small arms around the smaller body.

Next to Chris, Maeve sighed.

Another series of loud noises came from the hallway.

"We need to get moving," Chris said quietly.

"I know, I know. Just give him a minute."

Chris glanced over his shoulder at the door. "Maeve ..."

"Alvie, we need to go," she called softly.

Alvie nodded but kept his gaze on the two little ones that still cowered in the corner. Then they moved forward cautiously. Chris noticed they each had some injuries, but the injuries looked older. They hadn't been caused recently, which meant the injuries weren't caused by the breakout. Someone, some human, had done that to them.

Something slammed into the lab door. Maeve whirled around, as did Chris. Chris knew he was running low on ammo. Whatever was outside the door, Chris really hoped it was alone.

"Maeve, get in the enclosure. I'll lock you guys in."

Maeve ran across the room for the closet in the back.

Chris growled. Was she ever going to actually do something he said? "Damn it. I said—"

She yanked open the closet door and pulled out a tranquilizer gun, expertly loading it and pocketing some extra rounds.

The door burst open and Chris whirled around.

Holy shit.

The thing looked like the Green Goblin from the Spider-Man comics Chris had read as a kid. It was six feet tall and green with pointy ears and muscular arms.

Chris pulled the trigger, but the thing moved so fast, all he hit was the doorway.

Shit.

Chris jumped out of the way as the thing lunged at him. He scrambled behind a lab table. The goblin leered at him from the other side.

"Chris, get down!" Maeve yelled. Chris dove for the ground as Maeve opened fire. The first shot hit the goblin in the chest. It yanked out the dart, but Maeve was still shooting. She strode forward, unloading dart after dart until the goblin crashed to the ground.

"Alvie, get them out of the enclosure. Chris drag that thing in there."

"Yes, ma'am," Chris said, then he grabbed the goblin by the arms.

Alvie ushered the other three out and Chris pulled the goblin inside. He slammed the door shut and looked at Maeve, who lowered her weapon, trying not to smile at the fact that she had just turned all GI Jane on him.

"So where did you learn to shoot?" he asked.

"John taught me. He thought if I was going to be on the base and working, I should at least have an idea what it was like to shoot."

"Remind me to send him a nice, long thank you letter when we get out of here."

"We are getting out of here, right?"

"Oh yeah."

Maeve met his gaze. "All of us?"

Chris looked at the four aliens and tried not to sigh.

I hope so.

Chapter Sixty-Four

MAEVE STRUGGLED to stay calm as Chris closed the cage on the goblin. That thing had been terrifying. She still couldn't believe she'd shot it that many times.

She felt eyes on her and turned to see the three little ones watching her from behind Alvie.

Oh no.

This was not exactly the first impression she was hoping for—her playing Xena, warrior princess.

Carefully and slowly, she laid the weapon on the table. She stepped away from it, keeping her hands in view and then knelt down. "It's okay. I won't hurt you."

The two boys ducked their heads, but the little girl stared at her.

Alvie placed his hand on the girl's cheek and she closed her eyes. When she opened them, she gave a little squeak and ran for Maeve, throwing herself into Maeve's arms. Maeve hugged her tight. "It's okay. You're all right. We won't let anyone hurt you."

The girl was incredibly light, but there was a strength in

her little arms. Maeve could feel her heart pounding away through her chest.

She's so scared.

Alvie placed his hand on the cheeks of each of the boys. Both looked at Alvie and then over at Maeve. Maeve held out one of her arms and the two ran to her as well. Maeve gave a small laugh, feeling tears in her eyes as she wrapped her arms around the three of them. And she felt an incredible sense of protectiveness.

I'll keep you safe. I promise.

Chris stood nearby. "Well, I guess they trust you."

One of the boys looked up at Chris and then ran to him, wrapping himself around Chris's leg. Chris gave a small cry and then looked at Maeve helplessly before awkwardly patting the little guy on the back. "You're okay. We've got you."

Maeve stood up, the two others in her arms. They were each only about two feet tall and she guessed they weighed no more than fifteen pounds each, if that.

"Do they have names?" Chris asked.

Alvie shook his head.

Chris pointed to each of them, ending with the guy attached to him. "How about Snap, Crackle, and Pop?"

Maeve looked at Alvie, who gave her a small smile. "Sounds good to us."

"Okay, little buddy." Chris reached down and patted the guy wrapped around his legs again before looking to Alvie for help. Alvie walked over and gently pried Pop from Chris's legs.

"Okay. No more side trips. We are heading out. Any objections?" Chris asked.

Maeve and Alvie shook their heads.

"Good. Everyone grab a baby alien and let's go." He

paused, shaking his head. "I cannot believe those words just came out of my mouth."

Maeve lowered herself down and Crackle hopped onto her back. Pop went with Chris and Snap, the girl, climbed onto Alvie's back.

Chris led them out of the lab. At the end of the hall, he put his hand to his lips as he waved them into an alcove. They stood waiting tensely as Chris took up position, the door to the stairwell in his sights. Maeve could hear some sort of movement on the other side of the door but she couldn't identify if it was human or otherwise. And apparently Chris didn't want to chance it either. They waited there for what felt like forever, but Maeve knew it was only a few minutes. Finally, Chris waved them to the stairwell and they headed up.

Chris had just stepped onto the landing outside the door to level ten when Alvie rushed up from behind him and shook his head, pulling Chris toward the door leading out of the stairwell. Maeve could feel Alvie's urgency, but it was different from when he wanted them to go to level eleven. Chris must have felt it as well. He looked down at him and nodded, opening the door. Maeve followed the two of them inside.

The door had barely closed when she heard the sound of something coming down the steps. Maeve stared down at Alvie. He was tense, his whole body rigid, but after two minutes he relaxed, looking up at Maeve with a smile.

I'll be damned. She tapped Chris on the shoulder. "I think we're all right."

"Why?" he asked, not taking his gaze from the door.

"Because Alvie says we are."

Chris gave her incredulous look. "What?"

259

Maeve leaned down so she was eye level with Alvie. "Can you tell when one of them is near?"

Alvie nodded.

"All of them?"

He nodded again.

"How?"

She felt a small pulse against her brain. Her eyes flew open. "You can do that with both humans and aliens?"

Alvie nodded.

"You guys want to let me in on whatever you're talking about?" Chris asked.

Maeve stared into Alvie's eyes. All these years and she had never known about this ability. Amazing. She ran a hand gently over his head before standing.

"Alvie can sense them."

"Sense them?"

"Telepathically. He'll know where they are before we do."

"Uh, okay." Chris looked between Maeve and Alvie. "Did you know he could do that?"

Maeve shook her head. "No."

Worry flashed across Chris's eyes and Maeve felt a prickle of concern take root in the back of her mind.

If you didn't know about this ability, what other abilities do you not know about? Maeve chased the thought away, but she couldn't quite remove the feeling of concern it left behind.

"I guess that's something in our favor." Chris took a step toward the stairwell. "So let's head back to—"

Alvie took Chris's arm and shook his head.

Chris's eyes locked on Maeve's.

"It's not safe," she said.

Chris's gaze flicked to Alvie before he gave an abrupt nod. "Okay, then let's try to find another stairwell." He started down the hall. Alvie moved ahead of him and Chris fell in step with Maeve. Pop, who rested on Chris's back, peeked at Maeve, who smiled in return.

Chris nodded toward Alvie ahead of them. "So you had no idea about this?"

"This exact ability, no. But Alvie's been having these bouts of depression. You saw him—he was sad, despondent. He'd have those horrible nightmares."

Chris nodded.

"Well, I think it wasn't him that was experiencing pain. I think Alvie was feeling what these guys were going through. He felt their pain, their sadness. I checked the dates— Alvie's last episode corresponds to an electric shock experiment on these guys. Alvie felt their pain and he couldn't do anything about it."

"But how did he know?"

Maeve shook her head. "That I don't know. But they're bonded in some way."

"And his ability to sense the other aliens, are you okay with that?"

"Honestly, it's unsettling. I didn't know he could do that. At the same time, all of these experiences, this environment, is new for him. Of course he's going to demonstrate abilities and behaviors I've never seen before. It would be strange if he didn't."

"Aren't you worried?"

Maeve opened her mouth to answer him and then shut it, thinking over his question. The fact was, in the last few hours, Alvie had seen *her* do things he'd never seen her do before—things that could easily trouble him.

"I guess not. I mean, Alvie saw me take down Henning, shoot aliens, run, fight—he's never seen me do anything like that before. He's never seen me violent."

"But that was to protect him, to protect us."

"Yeah, but are Alvie's abilities any different? Isn't he protecting us? And he doesn't seem overly worried that I'm going to turn my violence toward him, so I suppose I shouldn't be worried about him using his abilities on us."

"But he has. He got us to go to level eleven to get them."

"Yeah, but that was his way of talking. How else could he convey what he wanted? And if we hadn't, I think he would have made his way to the triplets on his own. He wouldn't have forced us." She paused. "But his abilities make you nervous, don't they?"

"It doesn't put me at ease." Chris walked forward quietly, not saying anything for a few feet. "But what about his ability to share his thoughts? These guys can't do that, right?"

"I don't think so. They're too young. They're babies, really. One day, they should develop the same abilities."

"I guess I'm glad Alvie's on our side," Chris grumbled.

Maeve watched him out of the corner of her eyes. "Are you really scared of him?"

"Alvie, no. But what if the triplets aren't as nice as he is? What if these other aliens have similar abilities?"

Maeve looked at Chris. He'd always been strong. She knew that in high school he'd been on the football team. He'd studied martial arts since he was a kid. He'd even gotten marksman trophies when he was younger, well before he joined the military.

"Well, welcome to the club."

Chris frowned. "What do you mean?"

"Men are always physically stronger than women. You are always more powerful. From childhood, women are encouraged to be nice and polite. Males are encouraged to fight and stand up for themselves. Woman are always at a physical disadvantage."

"It's not the same."

"Why not? Because Alvie might be more powerful than *you*? What about that weapon you're holding? Doesn't that even things up a bit? Aren't people beholden to the fact that those who are physically stronger or who have more powerful weapons are good people? Isn't that how life works, at its core?"

Chris shook his head. "No, it's not the same—"

"It *is* the same. And yes, it's an uncomfortable position to be in. And it's one you're not used to. But some of us are. And we simply need to figure out ways to defend ourselves as best we can. Or better yet, find a way to befriend those more powerful individuals so we don't have to defend ourselves."

Chris watched her for a moment. "But you don't think that, right? I mean, not about me."

Maeve smiled. "No. But I've had my Uncle John teaching me how to defend myself since I was a kid. And how to shoot. And how to stay safe. So no, generally I don't. But there have been moments."

"What kind of moments?"

"Guys who thought they were entitled to more than I thought they were entitled to."

Chris's jaw tightened.

"I was fine.

"So you're saying we have to rely on Alvie being nice, huh?"

Snap, who was perched on Alvie's back, let out a small cry. Alvie immediately pulled her around, cuddling her to his chest and humming softly.

Maeve smiled. "I think we're in good hands."

Chris smiled down at her. "I suppose we are."

A shrieking sound blasted down the hall, and all of them went still.

Shivers ran through Maeve, her eyes growing wide. She placed her hand on Crackle's back as he too shivered. "What the hell is that?"

Chris tensed, his weapon pulled into his shoulder. Pop lowered himself down on Chris's back, now peering over his shoulder.

Alvie turned and threw Snap at Maeve.

"Oh my god!" Maeve dove, landing on one knee, and she caught Snap in midair before she hit the ground. She pulled her into her chest as three beings slid out of the doorway ten feet from Alvie.

They were humanoid in appearance, seven feet tall, incredibly skinny, and a sickly pale white. They reminded Maeve of the Slenderman legends she'd heard of except that they had faces, although not human ones. When they blinked, their eyelids slid across their yellow eyes from the side.

"Back up, Maeve," Chris ordered.

Maeve clasped Snap to her chest, backing away from the nightmares as Crackle held onto her shoulders, his grip painful. Maeve's heart threatened to pound out of her chest as Alvie turned toward the creatures.

"Alvie, no! Run!"

And he did.

Right toward them.

Chapter Sixty-Five

MAEVE WATCHED in horror as Alvie ran toward the three creatures. The one nearest him opened its mouth, emitting a shriek and showing off three rows of razor-sharp teeth. It lunged forward, its teeth snapping at Alvie. Alvie stepped to the side, running along the wall and landing on the being's back.

Chris opened fire on one of the beings, but every place he hit turned insubstantial as his bullets passed right through.

"Its mouth, aim for its mouth!" Maeve yelled, swinging Snap around to her back next to Crackle and pulling up her own weapon.

Alvie clutched onto one of the thing's necks, looking like the world's smallest bronco rider. He placed his hands on either side of the being's head. Chris drew a bead on one of the things and pulled the trigger. Its head exploded in a mist of brain matter and blood. Maeve turned to the other one, but Chris beat her there, taking it out as well.

The third let out a shriek, which ended in a gurgle as it

slumped to the floor. Its eyes bulged before all the light in them disappeared.

Alvie hopped off the creature, moving slowly. He stood next to it, staring down, his shoulders dropping.

Maeve stood rooted in place. Alvie had just killed it—with his hands or his mind, she wasn't sure. She'd had no inkling that Alvie had that kind of destructive power.

Another ability I didn't know about.

Unease slid through her as she lowered her weapon. She could feel her arms beginning to shake.

Her gaze shifted from the monstrous vision on the floor to Alvie standing next to it, looking down. Sadness was written all over his slumped posture. She approached him slowly, reaching out tentatively for him.

"Alvie?"

He looked up at her, his eyes filled with tears and such pain that it broke her heart. Her emotions shifted from unease to empathy.

"Oh, Alvie." She dropped to her knees next to him, wrapping her arms around him as he shook.

Chris stepped in front of both of them, scanning the room. "Clear."

But Maeve kept her attention on Alvie. She touched his cheek, wiping away a tear. "I'm so sorry."

Alvie leaned his face into her hand. And then Snap crawled over Maeve's back and onto Alvie. Alvie pulled her tight into his chest as he took a stuttering breath, his eyes wet.

"What was that thing?" Chris asked.

Maeve still felt shaken by Alvie's actions and the attack. "I don't know."

"It was a Califax-AG3."

At the new voice, Maeve's head whipped to the side where a door was open, her gun back at her shoulder.

Next to her, Chris did the same. "Who's in there? Identify yourself."

The door opened and a man slumped into view. He sat along the floor, holding his stomach where blood had soaked through a bandage. "I'm Dr. Sheridan. And I could use a little help."

Chapter Sixty-Six

CHRIS HELPED LOWER the doctor to the ground of the lab as Maeve searched for a first aid kit. They'd closed the door to the hall after helping pull Dr. Sheridan out of the doorway. Chris recognized the name—Sheridan was the one in charge of setting up all the labs.

Alvie had ushered the three little ones over to the couch against the wall. Chris leaned down so only the doc could hear him. "Do you know what happened? How the security system broke down?"

Sheridan somehow managed to look down his nose at Chris from his position on the floor. "Of course I do. I'm the director of services."

"Right, well, Director of Services, what the hell happened?"

The man's face was ashen, his eyes glassy with pain. "It was not anyone in *my* area. My team did everything they were supposed to do. Even though we were rushed with everyone and everything arriving at the same time. I can't believe they expected us to—"

Chris struggled not to grab the guy by the lapels and demand answers. "Yeah, Doc, that's really awful. Now what happened? How did the system fail?"

Sheridan blinked at Chris's tone. "It was designed to fail."

"Designed to fail? What do you mean?" Maeve asked as she knelt next to him, placing her supplies on the ground next to Sheridan's chest.

Sheridan grimaced. "There was a back door in the security system. Someone accessed it and shut down the security in some of the containment units."

Chris sat back, stunned. "Someone *intentionally* let these things out?"

"Yes." Sheridan winced as Maeve peeled back his bandage.

"Sorry," she said quietly.

Chris watched Maeve inspect the man's injury without really taking it in.

Someone let these things out. Who the hell would be stupid enough to do that?

"That can't be right. It must have been a mistake. No one would—"

Sheridan shook his head and then blew out a breath between clenched teeth. "It wasn't a mistake. A code, a long code, was entered to let the creatures out. For some, the cages were opened. For others, weaknesses were introduced. I'm guessing to see if the creature could detect it."

"You think someone was testing them?" Maeve asked.

"Being where we are, that does not seem out of the question." The doc let out a shaky breath as Maeve finished cleaning the wound.

Chris wasn't a doctor, but he'd seen wounds before. He could tell this one had been caused by a single swipe across the doctor's abdomen, but now it almost seemed like the wound had somehow grown larger—as if the skin itself was being eaten away. He'd seen a case of flesh-eating bacteria once and that looked awfully similar to the doctor's wound.

While working on the wound, Maeve kept her face blank, but Chris saw the briefest of tremors in her hands. Maeve knew the doctor wasn't going to make it. But she quickly and carefully placed another bandage over the wound and then smiled at Sheridan.

"Now let me give you something for the pain," she said. She grabbed a syringe and, after releasing the air, inserted it into his arm. "This will only take a minute to take effect."

Sheridan smiled, letting his head fall back. "That already feels better. Thank you." He motioned for Chris to help him sit up. With a bit of work, they managed to get the doctor up, leaning him against the wall.

"Do you know how many species of these things there are?" Chris asked.

"Fifty-seven."

Chris felt his jaw drop. Next to him, Maeve turned a few shades paler. "Do you have files on them?"

Frowning, Sheridan nodded. "But you don't have clearance to see the other projects."

Chris snorted. "You do realize that point is completely irrelevant right now, right? We are going to run into every alien on our way out. So a little heads up as to how to survive that would be nice."

Sheridan shook his head and then tilted his head to the side, staring at Alvie and the triplets. "They're awfully cute," he said, his words a little slurred.

Frowning, Chris looked over at Maeve. *Morphine,* she mouthed back.

Chris touched Sheridan lightly on the shoulder. "Doc? You said you were going to show us those files?"

His head lolled back to Chris. "Oh, right." He frowned. "Where's my tablet?"

Chris looked around, spying the small computer a few feet away. He grabbed it and handed it to the doctor. "Here you go."

The doctor blinked a few times, squinting at the screen.

"It needs your password," Maeve prodded.

"Oh, right. What is my password?"

Chris struggled not to groan.

"Ah, yes—Dimaggio13. He was one of the greatest players that ever played the game, did you know that? Thirteen glorious seasons for the Yankees," Sheridan said to Maeve.

Maeve shook her head. "I didn't know that. Can you show us where the files are?"

"Files? Oh, right—all the creepy crawlies." Sheridan looked over at the triplets again. "Except for them. I always thought they were cute."

A noise from the hallway made Chris jump. "I got it." He strode for the door. Taking a breath, he glanced out but saw nothing except a ceiling tile now smashed on the ground. He stood silently listening but he heard nothing. Alvie stepped next to him.

"You sense anything?" Chris asked softly as he looked down at him.

Alvie shook his head. Chris watched outside for another minute, but he heard nothing except for Maeve and the doctor speaking quietly behind him. Alvie moved back to the triplets.

Chris wanted to head back to Maeve and hear what the doctor had to say, but he needed to stay by the door and hopefully he'd be able to keep them safe from anything that wandered down the hall.

Or scurried, or hopped, or teleported for all we damn well know.

Minutes passed, and then Maeve walked over to him.

"Did you get what we need?" Chris asked.

She nodded. "I guess so. But knowing what's out there doesn't exactly make me feel better. Some of these things—they have paralytics in their claws or they're huge. Those blue gorillas? Those were only babies."

"Well, Sheridan said only some of the containment units were opened. We won't have to face all of them."

"No," Sheridan said loudly. "You weren't listening. I said the *hacker* only opened some of the containment units."

"Right, so only some of the aliens are out," Chris said.

Sheridan shook his head. "The ones that got out, they freed the others. They're all out." Sheridan's voice shifted to sound like a wrestling announcer. "Every. Single. One." Then he giggled.

That is a man who cannot hold his morphine.

Chris turned his gaze back to Maeve. "Maeve, how many are there?"

Maeve looked up at him, her eyes huge. "Over two hundred."

Chapter Sixty-Seven

EDWARDS AIR FORCE BASE, CALIFORNIA

JOHN FORRESTER HAD LANDED at Edwards Air Force base ten minutes ago. He had grabbed a flight in an F15 and it had taken him no time to get here from Dayton. Now he was striding through headquarters at Edwards to the office Wanda had commandeered, clutching the folder that he hoped could make a difference.

He had been trying to reach Wanda ever since their phone call earlier and she hadn't gotten back to him. And John had used that time to reach out to everyone and anyone who might have some information about what was going on. And finally he learned one thing—some of the subjects at 51 had escaped.

He had finally reached her assistant, who told him Wanda could not discuss anything over the phone, but if he wanted to fly out to Edwards, she'd speak with him in person.

Wanda's aide saw him coming and quickly jumped up from his desk and opened the door. "She's expecting you."

He and Wanda had known each other since they had

worked together at the Pentagon. They mingled in the same circles. And now he was about to put that decades-old friendship to the test.

Wanda looked up from her desk as John walked in and he was taken aback by the bags under her eyes and the stress showing in her slumped posture. Wanda was always impeccably dressed. She usually looked like she'd just stepped out of a fashion shoot.

But not today. Today she looked like a woman with the weight of the world on her shoulders.

John shoved aside his concern for his old friend. Compared with his worries for Maeve, his concern for Wanda didn't even rank.

As soon as the aide closed the door behind him, John spoke. "Do you know what's happening in Nevada?"

Wanda nodded. "Yes."

"Did you order it?"

She shook her head. "No. Someone else is in charge out there."

"I don't understand. The base has never had a breach like this. What the hell happened?"

Wanda looked away. "I have a team looking into it."

A feeling of unease slid over John. "You know what happened. Why it happened. You—" He stopped short, horror overcoming him. "Someone did this, didn't they? Someone wanted to see the subjects in action, didn't they? It was Drummond, wasn't it?"

Wanda was always a good poker player, and her face showed no emotion. "Not to my knowledge. But how do you know Drummond?"

The old anger boiled up. "Let's just say I have a history with the man. You never should have approved him for the position."

"What kind of history?"

"The kind that tells me that if he is anywhere near these projects, it will not be good for anyone."

"Martin is, as you said, the head of the BOSAC, but I assure you he would never—"

John scoffed. "He would never endanger lives to fulfill his own agenda? Apparently you didn't do a deep enough background check on him. You should look into why he was banished to Thailand a decade ago."

"Thailand? What are you talking about?"

"I'm talking about things you should already know." He handed her the file. "You need to read this."

Wanda took the file. "What is it?"

"Everything you should have found out about Martin before you gave him control over people's lives." He paused, the thought that had been rolling around in the back of his mind haunting his every step. "Are they going to initiate the Manhattan Protocol?"

Surprise flashed across Wanda's face. "How do you know about that?"

"Wanda, I have been around this project from the start. I know all the security protocols."

"If the situation becomes untenable, then yes, the Manhattan Protocol will be initiated. But that will be hours and hours from now, if ever. Remember, that's a last resort."

John felt the breath leave his lungs. "And that will be Martin's call, right?"

Wanda nodded, tight-lipped.

"But you'll wait until the staff is out, right? You'll make sure everyone who works on the base is clear before you initiate the protocol."

"John, you know how these things work."

John did, but it still didn't lessen the blow. "There are good people on that base. They don't deserve this."

"Even if I wanted to, there's nothing I can do. My hands are tied."

And John realized then that whatever was happening was truly out of her control. "The President could."

And Wanda's facade of neutrality dropped as shock splashed across her face. "The President knows nothing of what happens at Area 51. It's need-to-know, and the President simply does not need to know."

John knew the arguments against allowing members of the executive or legislative branches into the know. As elected officials, their tenure with the government was up to the whims of the populace. In contrast, there were members of the government who had been with their agency for decades. The President or a senator might only hold office for four or six years, respectively. And no one wanted to take the chance of any of them using the information they learned from the A.L.I.V.E. projects or any of the other projects in a re-election bid.

But right now, things had gotten well out of hand if someone intentionally released the subjects. "There is precedent. Presidential intervention has happened. President Kennedy intervened. And it's needed right now."

Wanda shook her head. "I can't do that."

"But Maeve's there," he said quietly.

"I know."

John's head snapped up. "You know? You're risking her life and everyone on that base, and for what? Information? Information that could be gained another way? This is reckless. This is an abuse of power. And you're going along with it. You are better than this, Wanda. We are *all* better than this."

"John, if I could do something—"

"You *can*. You're just choosing not to, and you're signing the death warrant of dozens of Americans who placed their trust in us. Who dedicated their lives in service to this country, and now we're just offering them up as lambs to the slaughter."

"It's been done before."

"Yes, and history has judged them for it. This is our moment, Wanda. How do you want to be judged?"

Wanda sat in silence for a moment before standing, extending her hand. "Thank you for bringing this to my attention, John. I'll take it under advisement."

John ignored her outstretched hand. "Read the file, Wanda. And then tell me if that's the man you want making this decision. You know what the right thing is to do here. For God's sake, do it." He turned and stormed out the door, practically ripping the door of its hinges.

Wanda's aide jumped to his feet, but John ignored him as he stormed down the hall, struggling to come up with someone else to speak with. Someone who would have the power to intervene at Area 51. But the circle of those in the know was small, and the circle of those with the power to do anything was even smaller.

He pictured Maeve when he'd taught her how to ride a bike, and then he pictured Alice in her hospital bed as John held her hand, promising that he would look out for her daughter and for Alvie.

Oh god, Alice. I don't know what else to do.

Chapter Sixty-Eight

THERE WERE over two hundred aliens of various sizes and shapes roaming around the base. The only thing they had going for them was that the subjects had been split into two buildings, so only about a hundred were in this building. The bad news was they needed to get to the surface, and Chris was pretty sure most of the aliens would be heading there as well. Not to mention the elevators were out and that only left the stairwells, which the aliens also seemed to be using to make their way around the building.

"So, what's the plan?" Maeve asked.

Chris looked down into her hazel eyes and wished he had one. But right now 'plan' seemed too structured a word for what he thought they should do—try to get to the surface.

"We'll take the southwest stairwell. We haven't been in it yet." Chris paused. "But we'll have to leave it around level four. There's a security door we won't be able to get through."

"Why not?"

"We don't have clearance."

"Oh, you don't have to worry about that," Sheridan said.

"Why not?" Maeve asked.

Sheridan looked down at Alvie, who was staring intently at Sheridan's tablet. "He's so cute."

"Doc, why don't we have to worry about the security door on four?" Chris asked.

Sheridan patted Alvie on the head before swinging his head back toward Chris. "It's not there anymore."

"What do you mean?" Chris asked.

Sheridan shrugged. "One of them just ripped it out of the wall."

Chris stared at Sheridan. The security wall on the fourth floor was basically a vault door. It weighed tons.

Oh god.

Shoving his terror aside, he nodded. "Well, good to know." He nodded at Alvie. "What's he doing, by the way?"

"Memorizing every password in this place," Maeve said.

"He can do that?"

Maeve nodded. "Yup. And I made a copy of the alien files." She held up a USB. "I don't know if it will help, but I figured it couldn't hurt."

"Okay, good."

"What are we going to do with Sheridan?"

"You should take me with you," Sheridan said.

Maeve looked at Chris. They both knew he would not make it. And he would slow them down.

"We can't leave him to be found by them," Maeve said. And Chris had known she was going to say that. He also knew that the chances for them all getting to the surface were incredibly slim. Bringing the doc along would reduce those chances to practically non-existent.

"Hey, instead of going up, what if we went down?" Maeve asked. "You said they brought Alvie over in tunnels from one of the hangars."

Damn, I should have thought of that. "That's right. There's an entrance on—"

Sheridan shook his head. "That won't do you any good. All the tunnels will be sealed by now. It's the first act during an emergency protocol. And I oversaw the installation of all the seals myself. They're solid. That's not an option."

Chris closed his eyes. This just kept getting worse. He dropped his voice. "Maeve, I know taking him is the right thing to do, but I'm not sure he can walk. How are we going to get him out of here? I can't carry him and neither can you."

"There's an office chair," Sheridan offered. "It moves easily."

Maeve nodded. "Okay, I'll get it." She headed to the back of the room.

Chris watched her go, knowing bringing the injured scientist was the right thing to do. And also knowing it almost certainly confirmed that they were never going to get out alive.

Chapter Sixty-Nine

THE OFFICE CHAIR did slide easily. But even with it, it was slow going. And Chris knew the stairs would be impossible. But how the hell was he supposed to look Maeve in the face and tell her they needed to leave the man to die?

Alvie took point. Chris switched with Maeve so that he now pushed the chair. The doctor's head kept dropping, and blood soaked the bandage they had put on. But the doctor hadn't given a word of complaint. In fact, ever since Chris had taken over the chair, the doc had been quiet. Although every once in a while, he'd mutter something quietly to himself.

"There's something you should know about the tunnels," Sheridan said.

Chris groaned silently.

Great, now he's completely losing it.

"I know, they're all closed. We already talked about this, Doc."

Sheridan shook his head. "No, that's the thing. I've been thinking about that. I don't think they are."

"What do you mean?"

"I think the tunnels on the old base are probably still open."

"The old base? What's that?"

"This base has been around for decades. It's seen every generation of aeronautical innovation. But with each technological advance, older technology gets left behind. Some of the oldest hangars, they still have access to the tunnels. Of course, they'll only lead you off the base. And none of the newer tunnels link up to them."

"Where are these older tunnels?"

"The old hangars, the ones on the eastern side of the runways."

Chris pictured the base. Almost all of the buildings were on the western side of the runways. But Sheridan was right —there were some old hangars over there. But that wasn't going to help them get to the surface.

Besides they'd have to cross the huge expanse of open space that the runways were on. Doing that without getting any of them shot was probably going to be impossible. But maybe they wouldn't need to. If they got to the surface, maybe they could speak with some of the higher ups. Like Maeve said, they just needed time. Maybe they could even reach John back at Wright-Patt and have him intercede.

It wasn't a great plan. But at least it was something. He tucked away Sheridan's information just in case they needed a plan B.

They passed Alvie, who had stopped to re-adjust Pop on his back. Even though the triplets were small, Chris knew that for Alvie they must be pretty heavy. But he didn't complain. Come to think of it, Chris didn't think he'd known Alvie to complain about anything.

Sheridan was looking at him expectantly. Chris forced a

smile to his face as he focused back on the man. "Thanks, Doc."

"You're welcome," he said softly. Then his head tipped to the side and he stared, his chest unmoving.

"Doc?" Chris felt for a pulse at his neck. But there was nothing. *Damn it. Sorry, Doc*

Alvie let out a squeak. Chris looked up and had his weapon to his shoulder in an instant. At the end of the hall was a creature that looked like an octopus with six eyes and razor-sharp fins on each tentacle.

Oh shit.

Chapter Seventy

MAEVE HEARD Alvie cry out and her eyes grew wide at the thing undulating toward them. Chris unleashed a hail of bullets, but the octopus-like creature just slid out of the way.

She swung two of the triplets to her back, grabbing the back of Sheridan's chair. "I've got him," she said as Chris stepped from behind the doctor's chair.

"No. Leave him."

"We can't just—"

"He's gone, Maeve."

Maeve looked down at the doctor and saw he was slumped forward, not moving. She put a hand to his neck but couldn't find a pulse. She started to shake.

"Maeve, don't lose it on me now. We need to move."

Maeve looked up at Chris. He stared down at her, his eyes intense. "Run, Maeve, run."

Alvie grabbed her hand and pulled her down the hallway away from the thing rippling toward them at speeds that should have been impossible. Maeve pounded down the hall.

Alvie turned down a hallway, and Maeve saw an exit sign to the right. They had passed right by a stairwell. Alvie ducked into the stairwell as an explosion sounded down from the other hallway.

Maeve gasped and started to turn. But Chris pushed Maeve into a stairwell and slammed the door shut behind them. Debris battered the door as Chris held it shut.

"What was that?"

"Grenade," Chris said.

Maeve closed her eyes, picturing Sheridan's body. *Oh god.*

Chris took her arm. "We need to keep moving."

She looked up at him with tears in her eyes. "He died. They killed him."

"I know, and now we need to move so we're not next. Okay?"

She nodded, feeling numb as Chris gently took one of the aliens from her.

How did we end up here?

But she knew. Someone had let these things out. Someone had intentionally set up this little game pitting the humans against aliens. She hugged Snap to her chest, and Snap's little head rested on her shoulder. She was shaking. Her breaths came out in soft sighs. Someone had created these three and decided they didn't get a chance to live. Anger began to replace her sadness. If Maeve got out of this, she would make it her life's work to make sure whoever started all of this paid.

Dearly.

Chapter Seventy-One

GREG WALKED down the hall next to Leslie. He'd gotten rid of the fire extinguisher. He'd had to use it on another starfish-looking thing and emptied it. But he did currently have a machine gun of some type. He hadn't caught the name when Leslie had explained to him how to use it. And at least now he was confident he would not shoot off his own foot—although he couldn't guarantee anyone else's.

Now he and Leslie were on level nine, two levels lower than when they had first started their attempt to reach the surface. It was like some horrible video game—every time they went up a level or two something appeared to knock them back down.

The only good thing they had going for them was that the underground facility was a maze, which gave them lots of room to move around and hide. So far, they had found five stairwells. And by found he meant barged through an exit door in a blinding panic and sprinted either up or down one, depending on who was chasing them and from what direction.

But even in his panic, Greg had been mapping out the structure in his mind. The underground facility was at least twelve levels deep and shaped like a rectangle, though there were some offshoots unique to some of the levels. But the stairwells were all consistently located. Which meant there should be another one at the end of this hall.

All the stairwells ended at the first floor, where only two stairwells led to the ground level. They'd been forced out of the last stairwell by debris—someone, or more accurately something, had ripped part of the stairwell apart and flung it down a few flights. Greg wasn't sure if it was done intentionally to block them or by accident. He hoped it was the latter, because if the creatures were planning, well, that was just too terrifying to consider. He had enough real life nightmares to keep him company, no need to create some imaginary ones if he didn't need to.

"There." Leslie pointed down the hall where the exit sign was clearly marked with an arrow pointing around the corner.

Greg sighed with relief. *Yes*. "We haven't seen anyone, alien or otherwise, in a little while. Do you think everybody is out but us?"

Leslie shrugged. "Well, somebody has to be last."

Greg put his hand to his chest. "Personally, I think—" The sound of an explosion cut him off. The floor rattled and the walls shook. Greg put out a hand to the wall to keep his balance. "What the hell was that?"

Leslie glanced back down the hall in the direction the blast had come from. "Not sure, but I think it might be one floor below us."

"Well, that's good news, right? I mean, that means there are other people still fighting."

"You have a strange idea as to what constitutes good news."

"Well, not being the only ones in a building full of aliens, that kind of makes me feel better."

"Hate to burst your bubble, but it could have been an oxygen tank or hell, a Bunsen burner. This building is full of explosive chemicals. It could just be something knocked a tentacle into a table and blew himself up."

They had reached the door to the stairwell. Greg shook his head. "Nope, I'm going with optimism. Some human took out one of the bad guys. And I'm pretty sure we won't be seeing any more creepy crawlies."

He grabbed ahold of the stairwell door, yanked it open, and let out a scream.

Chapter Seventy-Two

MAEVE THREW up her hands as Greg screamed. "Greg, no!"

Greg stared at her, or more accurately, Snap, peeking over her shoulder. His weapon was pointed toward her and his hands were shaking so hard that Maeve tensed, waiting for him to accidentally jerk the trigger.

Chris grabbed the front of Greg's weapon and pushed it to the ground.

Leslie pulled Greg back, all the while keeping her weapon trained on the aliens. "Uh, Chris, you want to tell me what the hell's going on?"

"Well, we're taking three baby aliens for a walk along with the clone from which they were created. What are you up to?"

Leslie glared at him. "Not in the mood, Chris."

Maeve jumped in before Leslie could yell at Chris or just shoot him. "This is Alvie. And like Chris said, these are his kids—sort of. We're taking them to safety."

Leslie looked between the two of them. "Did you *miss* the termination order?"

"These guys aren't dangerous," Maeve said quickly. "I've known Alvie for practically my whole life."

Greg stepped forward, his gun still pointed at the ground as he inspected Snap sitting on Maeve's back. "He's a lot cuter than my guy."

"Your guy?" Chris asked.

"Yeah, think the alien from Predator, but slightly smaller and scarier."

Maeve winced. "Oh."

"So, Alvie, huh?" Greg stepped toward him.

"Back up right now, Greg." Leslie trained her weapon on Alvie.

"Whoa, whoa, whoa." Chris stepped in front of Alvie. Crackle hunched lower on his back. "Look, Les, I know what the order is. But this guy is not dangerous, and these little ones aren't either. And I'm not about to kill them just because. And I mean, look at these little ones, do you really want to hurt them?"

Crackle peeked out over Chris's shoulder and then ducked back down with a squeak. Alvie reached up and placed a hand on Pop's back.

"What the hell?" Leslie stumbled back. "What was that?"

Maeve winced. *Oh no, Alvie. Not helpful.* "Um, did you see something?"

Leslie nodded. "I saw a little girl playing with one of these small ones."

Maeve shook her head. "No, that was *me* playing with Alvie. He showed you a memory of us to demonstrate that we're not dangerous."

"How come I didn't get one?" Greg asked.

"I guess Alvie doesn't sense any threat from you," Maeve said.

Greg frowned. "Why does nobody seem to think I'm a badass? I *am* holding a weapon."

He started to lift it when Chris stepped forward, pushing the nuzzle back toward the ground again. "Yeah, okay, Rambo. No demonstration needed."

Maeve would have laughed, but her focus was on Leslie. Alvie's attempt to calm the situation only seemed to have frightened her more. "Leslie?"

Leslie flicked her gaze to Maeve.

Maeve put up her hands. "Leslie, it's okay, really. He won't hurt you. He can't speak, that's why he communicates that way. He's just trying to show you that he won't harm you."

"Yeah," Leslie drawled. "Not really feeling that."

"Oh, come on, Les. Look how cute they are." Greg stepped forward. "Who's the cutest little alien ever?"

"Greg, I swear to God, I will hog-tie you and carry you over my shoulder if you step near that thing again."

"Ha, like you'd really fulfill one of my fantasies." Greg slowly reached for Snap. "It's okay, boy. I won't hurt you."

"Girl," Maeve corrected.

"Right, girl," Greg said, his hand outstretched.

Snap cringed back, but then slowly leaned forward. She placed her cheek on Greg's hand and closed her eyes, giving off a little purr.

Greg smiled. "Aw."

Leslie watched the interaction, her whole body tense.

"Leslie, we have bigger issues than these guys. The *real* threats are out," Chris said.

Leslie nodded "I know. We already met a dozen or so."

"Did you take care of them?" Chris asked.

She shook her head. "Not all of them."

"Well, we need to get moving, because the ones we know about are not the type I want to run into. We're heading up or at least trying to."

"Yeah, we've been trying to do the same." Leslie paused. "You realize there's a chance these things have already overrun the security outside, right?"

Chris nodded. "Yeah. Backup plan is to get to the older tunnels, which are on the eastern side of the base. They should link up with Edwards."

Greg looked at them both, wide eyed. "The tunnels? They exist too?"

"What tunnels?" Maeve frowned.

Greg turned to her, his smile big. "Oh, you so need to read more on secret government projects. Back in the 1970s, the US got patents for these huge tunnel diggers. They could dig seven miles a day through rock, leaving the walls sheer. And allegedly they were used to create tunnels linking major US bases. The tunnels allow the government to hide projects they don't want people to know about and allow transport from one base to another. There's supposedly one under 51 that connects to Edwards Air Force Base and all the way out to Tulsa. In fact, 51 is supposed to be the hub. There's supposed to be something like twelve bases connected all through these underground tunnels. There's even supposed to be some sort of super train that links them all."

"If those did exist, wouldn't they be the first thing they close?" Leslie asked.

Chris nodded. "Yeah, but we ran into Dr. Sheridan. He said all the *newer* tunnel access points were closed. But on the old base, there are still some older access points that weren't updated. They can't be closed. And they're so old, he doubts anyone would even remember them."

Maeve paused. "But wouldn't they know there was another way out? I mean, the tunnels in general."

"They?" Greg asked.

"The military," Maeve clarified.

Chris gave her a grim nod. Maeve stared at him, the truth flooring her. "They're going to be coming through those same tunnels to clean out the base."

Leslie and Chris exchanged a glance.

"What?" Greg demanded.

Leslie spoke slowly. "If the tunnels exist, they will be blocking them off. And when they feel the threat of the aliens getting out is too great, they'll bomb the installation."

"But not with humans still inside, right?" Greg asked.

"They'll try to get everyone out. But once the threat is deemed too high, they will bomb the facility regardless of who's inside," Chris said.

Greg's mouth dropped open. "But they can't do that. We're American citizens. We—"

Leslie cut him off. "Signed away your rights. You're conducting research at a secret facility that no one knows about. We wouldn't be the first ones to have disappeared."

"So we can't get out?" Maeve asked.

"We can," Chris said. "If they take that step, it will be hours from now. We'll be fine."

The words sounded good, but as Maeve looked around the group she realized no one believed them.

Not even Chris.

Chapter Seventy-Three

GREG MOVED AS QUICKLY up the stairs as he could manage, but his legs were killing him. He must have walked for miles throughout this facility. Not including the sprints of terror and Stairmaster from hell that were all the other flights of stairs he'd been on.

I swear when this thing is over, I am going to start working out regularly.

Maeve was in front of him with Pop sitting on her shoulders. He rested his head on the top of her head, his four-fingered hands placed gently on the side of her head. Greg watched all the little guys in awe. They were amazing. Dexterity, intelligence, telepathy.

Why couldn't I have gotten one of these guys instead of Hank?

That thought led to a feeling of guilt. He had tried to kill Hank. And how had Hank escaped the container? Or had one of the other things broken in and let Hank out? And if so, was Hank still alive? And did someone break him out to help him or to eat him?

Ahead, Pop snuck a look at Greg. Greg smiled in response. And the corner of Pop's little mouth turned up.

Yeah, I definitely would have preferred one of these guys.

Leslie stepped next to Greg, keeping her voice low but keeping her gaze on the four aliens in front of her. "I don't get it. Hank was easily a nightmare come to life. And we haven't exactly run into any other aliens that I'd like to spend quality time with. You *know* how horrible these things can be. Why are you so sure these guys are harmless?"

Greg looked over at Leslie. "Because it's logical."

Leslie snorted, looking at him from the corner of her eye. "Okay, Spock, care to explain what you mean by that?"

Greg smiled and had to restrain himself from mentioning just how much more attractive the Star Trek reference made her. "Think about all the animal species on the planet. You have the horrific—sharks, cobras, alligators, jellyfish, even polar bears. Basically, humans just need to stay away from them. They are both terrifying and a danger to man."

Greg smiled as Pop snuck another look at him. "But then you have those that wouldn't even know how to hurt us: bunnies, chipmunks, butterflies, puppies. The alien world will be no less diverse. In fact, they'll be more diverse. If each alien species comes from a different planet, there's the potential that each planet has the same number of species as Earth. In fact, if they're nicer to their planet than we are, then they'll have even more species than we do. And on our planet, we have over 8.74 million species of animals. Plus, you figure they have to be as diverse as humans, of which there are seven billion. Yeah, some are real assholes. But there are others who aren't. It makes sense that the same would go for aliens."

When Greg stopped speaking, Leslie just stared at him. He began to feel self-conscious. "What?"

She shook her head before she smiled. "I keep forgetting with all your quirks, just how truly smart you are."

Greg stumbled a little. "Really? Cause that kind of sounds like a compliment."

"It is." Leslie stepped away from him, once again taking the back. Greg forced himself to not turn around and watch her. He'd play it cool, like the guys in movies who don't turn around when something explodes behind them.

He lasted ten seconds before he glanced back. Leslie smiled at him, and he smiled in return before facing forward again. *Wow.*

Chapter Seventy-Four

THE WALL of monitors in Martin's office was alive with scenes of destruction, mayhem, and death. His analysts were all busy making sure no one outside of 51 heard a word of what was happening inside 51. It hadn't been that difficult. They'd immediately shut down all cell phone and land lines. Internet connections had been dropped just as quickly.

Martin watched Area 51 security surround Buildings 34 and 39 as well as the hangars that the aliens had been brought in from. But it was a honeycomb of tunnels underneath the base. Aliens and humans had popped up from tunnels all over the base. Security was running thin trying to cover all of it. The camo guys had even been pulled in from their usual duty surrounding the base to help cover the interior.

On a screen second from the bottom, a camo dude stood at the corner of the dining hall, lining up his shot. He was so completely focused on the gray emerging across the street that he missed the other alien, a Croaxis-AG3, emerging from behind him. Martin tilted his head, watching the beast move. He'd wondered about its abilities. It looked kind of like a human-sized frog, except that it was purple in color. Its eyes were proportionally smaller than a frog's, and it walked on two legs. The Croaxis lumbered closer to the man and then opened its mouth. The camo guy turned, but the Croaxis quickly lowered its mouth, encircling the man's head. The man struggled for only a moment before the Croaxis yanked its mouth back. The body dropped to the ground, sans head.

Hm, cooperation? Or merely coincidental timing?

Martin referred back to his notes with a frown. There seemed to be quite a few instances where different alien species seemed to work together to defeat a human target. That in and of itself was worth the entire experiment. They'd had no inkling that the species could communicate. They assumed they came from different worlds. And maybe they did, but maybe their species had met before. Granted, they were clones, but still, there must be something there.

And what does that mean for us? Does that mean that every species that's visited this planet might one day return together? Was that what the Earth had in store for it? A joint invasion?

Martin frowned. That was not something he had considered before. And he was not happy to be considering it now. He pictured the Majestic 12.

Those fools. We're years behind it all because they failed to act.

In front of him, the screens shifted every minute, showing a different aspect of the base. They would continue to shift unless Martin tapped on the appropriate icon holding the feed in place. His eyes roamed over the pictures, pausing on a scene in the second row, three in. An alien with almost translucent skin slid from out of the air duct in Building 34.

Around the corner, a soldier walked carefully forward, his weapon at the ready. The alien walked, equally careful, from the other side. The soldier reached the corner first. The man started to raise his weapon, but then he dropped it, grabbing his head, his mouth open in a scream. The alien never touched him. Just watched him as he screamed and finally went still. Then the alien slid past him.

"Huh," Martin said, pulling up his files on the subjects. He flipped through until he reached Subject 47—Gliese-AG1, nicknamed Pasty. The subject had demonstrated an ability to transform its bones, making them flexible. But the telepathic abilities were not in the files.

Martin smiled. *See? Already learning new things*, he thought as he typed in the new information, noting the time and camera for further review later.

He shook his head. Wanda didn't see the big picture, but once he typed up his notes and presented them to her, all of them would see why he was right. This project had been going on for thirty years. And yet, within the last few hours they had learned more about these alien species than they had in decades of study. Great accomplishments required sacrifice. And this one was paying off extremely well.

Turning his attention back to the monitors, his gaze flicked from screen to screen. He'd focus on one monitor for a few minutes and make some notes before continuing on. In that time, he kept a running tally in the back of his mind on how many humans had been killed—forty-two so far. Granted, most were not soldiers, but the methods of death had been interesting nonetheless. A few research subjects had been killed as well but still, information was garnered. And information gathering was the goal of this particular game.

His attention was pulled to a monitor in the top right

corner. *Is that a group?* He sent the picture to the larger monitor on the wall to his right. Two men and two women were making their way up a stairwell. Martin tilted his head, squinting.

What is on their backs?

He sat upright in surprise—Subject 1 and his progeny. How on earth did they end up together? He punched in commands to bring the group into sharper relief.

Let's see who's with you.

His eyebrows rose when he saw Dr. Leander. *So you're still alive. How have you managed that?* Apparently the daughter was every bit as intelligent as her mother. He frowned at the other humans in the group. He recognized her guard, Garrigan, but the other two were unknown to him. The woman was obviously a soldier. And even though the man held a weapon, he obviously was not. Martin scanned the files, finally stopping at the files of Greg Schorn and his military guard, Leslie Cole.

"So what are you all doing with those subjects?" he murmured. The triplets had been kept on level eleven. There was no chance anyone associated with the other projects would have known of their existence. *So how did they find them?* He'd have to backtrack through the tapes to see when exactly they first linked up.

But first he zoomed in on Subject 1. He remembered the elation he'd felt at its birth. Because he'd known that was the beginning of truly understanding the alien threat. And then everything had come to a screeching halt.

But you're still around, aren't you?

Dr. Leander reached down and touched the subject's head, rubbing her hand over it, a gesture of comfort. When he'd heard that the former Dr. Leander had brought her child in to meet with Subject 1, he'd been only mildly surprised. She had taken to the subject like a mother to a child. But apparently that was a familial attachment the daughter also felt. In fact, as he watched, he couldn't help but notice the protective way even the triplets were being held, and he knew for a fact there was no history of interaction there to account for it.

Now that is interesting. He sat back, his hand on his chin. He had not considered the possibility of a team-up between aliens and humans—of actual affection and protectiveness between them. He'd seen the recordings of Subject 1—the being was fast, lithe, and had incredible balance. But what other tricks did he have up his sleeves?

He quickly ran a trace in the files of the path of Dr. Leander and Subject #1. He wanted to see exactly how they had drafted the rest of the members into their little group. He reviewed the tapes, backtracking Leander's progress, and he'd realized he'd been wrong. Subject 1 had been aggressive—to save his group. He'd taken out an alien threat with the aid of Garrigan.

He zoomed in on Subject 1 as he was astride the alien species known as a Califax. "Just full of surprises, aren't you?" he murmured. "But what happens when the threat is human? What will you do?"

He pursed his lips, scenarios running through his mind. Finally he smiled and pulled over his radio.

"Beta, this is Alpha."

"Beta here. Go ahead, Alpha."

"I have a group of four subjects and four friendlies who will be exiting Building…" He squinted, double-checking. "34 in about fifteen minutes from the southwest stairwell."

There was a pause at the other end. "Are the friendlies being chased?"

"Negative. They are travelling together. I'd like you to

set up a little reception for them when they finally reach the surface."

"Yes, sir. Are we protecting the friendlies?"

"Negative. The friendlies seemed to have switched sides. Consider all targets *priority* targets."

"Yes, sir."

Martin placed the radio back on the tabletop, wondering how the other aliens would react if the humans they were with were targeted by other humans. Would they go on the defensive? Would they kill one human to save another? Would they help *kill* the humans? And what exactly would that look like?

Martin pulled his gaze from the monitor and texted a note to his assistant to grab him some lunch quickly. It would take Leander's group some time to reach the top of the stairwell and then get outside. And his lunch should arrive just in time. He smiled.

Nothing better than a show with your meal.

Chapter Seventy-Five

SOMETHING HAD BEEN a few floors above them and heading down, so the group moved from the stairwell, back into the hallways on level four. None of them were interested in running into whoever or whatever it was.

Now they were headed for another stairwell, and Maeve prayed it was unoccupied and allowed them to just get to the damn surface. She felt like a rat, wandering through this tunnel and that hallway. She was sick of it on multiple levels.

Ahead, Maeve could hear voices. Greg, who'd been walking next to her, smiled and started forward, but Chris grabbed his arm, shaking his head. Quietly, they all moved into a small alcove. Maeve adjusted her grip on her weapon, her palms slick.

Leslie peered around the wall as the voices faded away. "Clear."

"I don't get it. Why didn't we catch up to them?" Greg asked.

Chris nodded to Alvie. "Most soldiers right now are

probably on a shoot-first-and-ask-questions-later frame of mind. So until we're sure, we need to keep these guys hidden."

Greg winced. "Oh, right. Sorry, guys."

"Let's go," Leslie said, stepping out of the alcove and turning at the end of the hall in the opposite direction the voices had disappeared.

Alvie let out a small cry when he followed. Maeve dropped to her knees in front of him immediately. "Alvie?"

But as she inspected him, she knew he wasn't hurt, at least not physically. Her heart pounded. The cry he'd made had been the same sound he'd made earlier when he was thinking of the triplets. If there was another one of him, how would they get to him? They couldn't possibly go back.

Alvie's eyes grew large, and he pulled himself from Maeve's grasp. She stumbled back, catching herself with her hands as Alvie started to run down the hall. "No, Alvie!" She scrambled to her feet as Chris leaned down, taking Snap from her. "Go get him."

Just then, voices came from behind them. "Move," Chris whispered urgently.

But Maeve was already sprinting toward Alvie, who had stopped in front of a door, his hand pressed against the glass plane that covered half the door.

Chris ran past him, two of the triplets in his arms. "Maeve, he needs to move."

Maeve nodded. "Go. We're right behind you."

She grabbed Alvie's shoulders as he stood transfixed, looking at the glass door.

"Alvie, come on, we need to—" Her words cut off and her mouth fell open as a being stepped in front of the window. Maeve stared, shock rooting her in place. The alien was tall, maybe six feet with a disproportionately large gray head, large eyes, and thin arms. A dark blue shirt and pants covered its body—a larger version of Alvie's outfit. In fact, the being himself looked like a larger version of Alvie.

A tear pooled down Alvie's cheek and he reached his hand up higher along the glass. The being reached its own four-fingered hand out, placing it on the opposite side of the glass from Alvie's.

Maeve watched in stunned silence. She sensed no threat from the being. It stared at Alvie with what felt like concern. Then it turned to Maeve. She felt the presence of something in her mind, like fingers rifling through her memories and an image of her standing in front of Alvie, defying Henning, took center stage.

The being nodded, its lips turning up ever so slightly.

The voices behind them grew louder. Maeve looked between the two aliens. *Damn it.* She griped the door handle and turned it, but it was locked.

Her gaze met the being's and she shook her head. "I can't." She looked down at Alvie. "Alvie, please, we have to go."

Alvie kept his gaze on the being before turning to Maeve and nodding. He took her hand and started to run down the hall. As they reached the end, Maeve couldn't help but look back. The being had moved to the edge of the door so he could watch them leave.

A lump formed in Maeve's throat. *I'm sorry,* she thought as she ran to catch up with the rest, and she wondered who exactly she was leaving behind.

Chapter Seventy-Six

THE TRIP to the stairwell from level four was happily uneventful. Now they'd made it another three flights without running into anyone, human or otherwise. Which was good because Maeve's mind was filled with thoughts of the large gray they had seen. Alvie was part alien and part human. Had the gray been the other part? Did they somehow recognize one another?

Maeve hadn't mentioned the gray to any of the others. She wasn't sure why. Probably because she felt guilty—she *had* left him behind. Would she have left a human behind? At the same time, she also couldn't shake the feeling that he'd understood. That he approved of her making Alvie and the triplets a priority.

With relief, she saw Chris wave them into the stairwell that would lead to the main foyer and safety. Maeve reached his side and he nodded inside.

"Watch out," Chris said softly.

Maeve's gaze dropped to the floor of the landing where Chris was carefully walking around a body. The poor man's mouth was open in a silent scream. Next to him was a woman in a lab coat, lying face down, deep gashes in her back staining her jacket.

Greg started to reach down. "Should we—"

Chris shook his head. "They're gone."

Greg snatched his hand back, wrapping his arms around Crackle. "Oh."

"Come on, we're almost there." Leslie gently pushed Greg forward.

He nodded, scooting around the two bodies. And Maeve noticed the tremor in his hands. *Poor Greg.* Her gaze strayed to each member of the group. *Poor all of us.*

And she hoped as she stepped onto the landing, that once they left the building, it would be smooth sailing. Because she really needed a break from all the excitement.

Chapter Seventy-Seven

MARTIN COULD NOT REMEMBER when a day at work had been so satisfying.

There was that time in the Congo when I had that overlord staked to the ground.

Martin mulled over the memory, the remembrance of the man's screams still making him smile. He shook his head. No. Even that paled in comparison to today.

On one of the screens in front of him, a soldier managed to set a large gray on fire. The man stood back, horrified, as the gray flailed and screamed.

Innovative. Martin made a note.

His phone rang and a quick glance told him it was Hamish. He ignored it.

A minute later a knock on the door caused him to scowl. "Go away."

"Sir, there's a problem."

Martin sighed. Why could no one just let him sit here and enjoy all his hard work? "Come in."

Hamish ducked into the doorway.

Martin glared at him. "This better be good."

"It's not. I mean, it's important, but it's not good news."

"Spit it out."

"Secretary Heig contacted the President about 51."

Martin narrowed his eyes. "She *what*?"

Hamish's words came out in a rush. "John Forrester met with her at Edwards. An hour later she contacted the President. He knows what's happening at 51."

Forrester.

Unbidden, he reached up and touched the scar at the end of his right eyebrow. Every time he looked in the mirror he remembered the bastard. He should have killed him years ago. He thought about it every once in a while. But he also knew that Forrester was undeniably prepared for that. And although he'd taken care of the Senator and his files, he was sure Forrester had developed one on him as well. And Martin had some secrets he needed to remain in the dark.

"Sir?" Hamish asked.

Martin waved him away. "Just go."

"Uh, yes, sir. Sorry."

So she actually did it. But what Martin had said was true. Even if the President decided to act, it would take hours. But that meant Martin needed to start wrapping things up. Martin looked up at the screens and scrolling images.

All that knowledge. But all good things must come to an end.

He picked up the phone.

"Delta Station," said a voice on the line.

"This is Director Drummond, ID Alpha Omega Two Three Tango Foxtrot."

"Identity confirmed, Director."

"Manhattan Protocol is a go."

"Yes, sir. Two hours until launch."

"Very good." Martin disconnected the call and set the countdown clock on one of the screens. He watched the screens for a few moments more, just enjoying the view. But he supposed it was time. They were getting closer to the surface, and they could not be allowed off the base—none of them.

He frowned, watching the few humans left in Buildings 34 and 39. Humans were crafty creatures, even the ones you did not expect to be. He frowned, pulling up one of the screens. Dr. Leander again. She had stopped with Subject 1 at a door. A tall gray appeared on the other side. Martin zoomed in.

You were supposed to be already off the base. And no one was supposed to catch a glimpse of you.

He frowned, not liking that Leander had seen the gray. In fact, the survivors left in the two buildings had seen much more than they ever should. And that just wasn't going to do.

He picked up his burner phone and dialed Henning. Henning picked up quickly. "Yes, sir."

"Our operation is coming to a close, and I need to make sure that everyone on the base does not get off."

"The aliens? Yes, sir, we'll—"

"No, not just the aliens. There should be no witnesses. Have your men run down any stragglers."

"Should we make it look like accidents? Because with autopsies—"

Martin watched the countdown clock—one hour, fifty-six minutes until the bomb was dropped. "Don't worry about that. Just make sure no one gets off the base alive."

"Yes, sir."

"And I have a special assignment for you."

"Yes, sir."

"Dr. Leander and her crew will be exiting Building 34 in a short while. I've arranged a welcoming party. But on the off chance they get by them, prepare a second reception."

There was an anticipation in Henning's voice. "It will be a pleasure."

Martin smiled. "I have no doubt."

Chapter Seventy-Eight

CHRIS STOPPED outside the door leading to the foyer, waiting for everyone to join him. It seemed surreal that they had finally made it. Part of him had thought they'd never escape the lower levels. But he knew it wasn't quite time to celebrate yet.

Leslie looked at Chris. "Okay, so we're here. Do we have a plan?"

Chris nodded to Alvie and the three little ones. "Well, these four are going to be the issue. We can't just wander out with them and expect everyone will be fine with it."

"They might think we're under their control," Greg muttered, and Maeve realized he was right.

"I'm not leaving them. They'll never survive on their own," Maeve said.

"No one's saying that," Chris said. "We just need to talk our way, or more accurately, their way to safety. And once we step outside, there will be humans as well as aliens we need to deal with."

"I'm not shooting any humans," Leslie said, her voice steely.

"No one's shooting any humans. But these guys aren't a threat. You see that, right?" Maeve asked, her eyes pleading.

Leslie glanced from each of the aliens to Maeve. "I don't think they should die. But the humans are my priority. I won't apologize for that."

"They're part human, too," Greg said softly.

Leslie opened her mouth and closed it. On the walk up, Greg had pestered Maeve for all the details on Alvie's capabilities and background. "I know that. I just—" She sighed. "I will try to get anyone we run into to listen, okay? That's the best I can offer right now."

Maeve opened her mouth to speak, but Chris clamped his hand on her arm and she closed it. Chris knew Leslie. Duty came first for her. But he also knew she would do the right thing when the situation presented itself.

"That's all we're asking," he said.

He turned to gaze at each of them. "Okay. Outside this door is a large foyer, then we need to go through the front doors and down the steps. We're in the center of the base, to the west of the runways and to the east of the dorms. I'm hoping help is waiting right there beyond the doors for us. If not, we need to head to the tunnels, and the closest entrance according to Sheridan's map is close to a mile away, underneath one of the hangars that was built into the side of the valley. That will be our destination. I'll take the lead, then Maeve, Greg, and Leslie will bring up the rear."

"Maybe one of us should go first. Maybe pave the way?" Greg suggested.

Chris met Leslie's gaze. "We're not leaving anyone in here."

"Maybe we could wait in the foyer," Leslie suggested.

"There's that big desk. We could hide behind it. Close enough to the front door to reach if we need to and far enough away from the stairwell that we'll have enough of a heads-up if anyone appears."

"I don't like splitting up," Chris said.

"Me either," Greg said.

"But it will be safer for these guys," Maeve looked at Chris. "You or Leslie should go talk to them. If they'll listen to anyone, it's you two. I'll stay with these four."

"I'll stay too," Greg said, and Maeve gave him a grateful smile.

Leslie nodded toward Chris. "You outrank me. You should go. I'll keep everyone safe until you give us the all clear."

Chris looked at each of them, hating the idea of walking out the door without them, but he also knew it was the right call.

"Okay. But I *will* be right back." He looked at Leslie. "And if you see any signs of a problem, you get them out of here, all right?"

"You got it," Leslie said. She turned to Greg and Maeve. "We're heading for the desk. You stay behind Chris. I'll bring up the rear. We say run, jump, duck—you don't question, you just do it."

Maeve and Greg nodded. And Chris watched Alvie do the same. "Greg, Maeve, and Alvie will take the triplets to leave me and Leslie free to maneuver. Okay? Everybody got it?"

Chris kept his tone brusque and all business, but he felt the weight of the responsibility on him. The responsibility for the lives of each person with him and four aliens. His gaze passed over each of the little ones. Someone had created half humans. He still couldn't wrap his mind around that. But he did know one thing: they deserved a shot at a life. They didn't deserve to be in the middle of all of this. He just wasn't sure he was going to be able to give it to them.

At the same time, he agreed with Leslie—he wasn't going to shoot his brothers and sisters in arms. They were following orders, and they didn't know Alvie. Chris would just have to convince them to spare these guys.

At the same time, if he failed, he knew he wouldn't be able to sit back and watch Alvie and the triplets be harmed.

No, not harmed, gunned down in cold blood.

He shuddered as an image of Alvie being shot floated through his mind. But what would he do? What *could* he do if it came to that? Would he be able to sit back and watch Alvie be harmed? Or Maeve? Because he was sure that no matter the cost to her, Maeve would protect Alvie with her very life.

And Chris knew he would do the same for her.

Chapter Seventy-Nine

MAEVE'S HEART was pounding through her chest as Chris pushed open the door leading into the foyer. Sunshine blazed through the glass windows, a startling contrast to the terror of what was happening underneath them. But across the floor she could see signs of that turmoil. Blood was smeared across the floor in a half dozen spots, one smudged trail leading to the front door. More blood was splashed in an arc across a few of the walls. Bullet holes also dotted the walls, and one of the floor-to-ceiling windows was smashed to pieces.

Maeve blinked hard at the light. Alvie turned his back to it as each of the triplets scrunched down low with a small cry.

"What's wrong with them?" Greg asked.

"Damn it, I forgot."

She reached into her pocket. "It's the light. Their eyes are really sensitive to it. Alvie's going to have trouble seeing." She pulled a pair of shaded goggles out. "I grabbed these in the lab with Sheridan."

"Hold on a sec." Taking the goggles, Chris knelt in front of Alvie, carefully adjusting them before gently placing them over Alvie's head and securing them. "That okay, buddy?"

Alvie nodded.

"You stay behind Maeve, okay?"

Alvie leaned forward, placing his forehead on Chris's. And Maeve wanted to cry. That was Alvie's version of a hug. Chris wrapped an arm around Alvie, his voice a little unsteady. "I know, buddy. We'll get them to safety."

He stood, and Maeve caught the flash of pain in his eyes before he covered it. "Okay. Time to go." Chris started for the door, looking out the window.

Leslie nodded at Maeve when Chris was about twenty feet away. "Okay. Get going."

They all trooped forward single file. Maeve hugged Pop to her, murmuring quietly. "It's going to be all right. Keep your eyes closed. You're going to be all right."

She kept murmuring reassurances as they crossed the tiled floor, their footsteps echoing loudly. She heard Greg doing the same behind her.

Ahead of her Chris stopped, putting up his hand. And then the windows shattered as bullets crashed through it.

Chapter Eighty

MAEVE DOVE for the floor as Chris's voice rang out. "Get down. Get down!" He yelled.

She crawled back behind the front desk, Snap curled in her arms. Alvie was already there, and Greg dove in to join them, followed by Chris and Leslie.

"What the hell?" Greg asked.

Chris looked at Leslie, shock splashed across his face. "That was aimed at me."

Leslie shook her head. "They must have seen the aliens. That's the only explanation."

"Then they have the worst shots out there," Chris growled as he held up his shirt sleeve, which had a bullet hole through it.

"There's got to be some kind of mistake. They wouldn't —" Leslie's voice cut off as the unmistakable sound of canisters hitting the ground reached them.

"Go!" Chris yelled. He grabbed Maeve's arm and Alvie's and pushed them toward the back of the foyer.

White smoke curled from three canisters in front of the desk.

Maeve slammed her mouth shut as Chris pushed her down a hallway. Greg and Leslie stumbled behind them. The hallway ended, and Chris kicked open the last door. Maeve stumbled in and barely got out of the way as Greg fell through the doorway. Leslie slammed the door shut as Chris yanked a drape off the window and shoved it in the bottom of the door.

"God damn it," Chris said.

"What's going on?" Greg asked, his eyes huge.

"Tear gas is not meant for aliens. They were trying to smoke *us* out," Leslie growled.

Maeve helped Greg to his feet. "What does that mean?"

"It means," Chris said, "that they're not just targeting these guys. We're free game now as well."

Chapter Eighty-One

MAEVE FELT the terror steal over her. She had thought they would at least have a chance to try and convince whoever was outside that Alvie and the triplets were peaceful. But apparently whoever was out there was not going to be interested in that. In fact, they seemed more concerned with wiping out everyone, alien or otherwise.

"But why?" Greg asked. "I mean, we're human, obviously."

"Something's changed. Maybe they think we're corrupted or infected or something," Leslie said.

Greg's words came out in a rush. "They have to have the building surrounded. How are we going to get out? I mean, I would just surround the building. They know all of us will break for the surface. We can't get out. We can't—"

Chris cut into Greg's panicked ramblings. "Okay. Enough. We didn't get through twelve floors of the world's most terrifying zoo to stop now. There's always a way. We just need to figure it out."

Maeve looked over the group. Chris and Leslie looked

pissed. Greg looked terrified, and she was pretty sure she looked the same. And Alvie—he just looked sad.

No. This was not how it was going to end. Maeve let her anger build up thinking about how much she and her mother had devoted to this program. Her whole life had been built around Alvie and there was no way in hell she was letting the government decide her life and Alvie's were now over. She'd given this government enough. She was not handing them her life. Not without a fight.

Now I just need to figure out how to get us through the armed barricade surrounding the building.

A thought crossed her mind and she went still. *No. I couldn't.* But the more she thought about it, the more she realized that as crazy and reckless as it was, right now, it was probably their only option. She looked around the group.

"Hey, guys? I think I've got an idea."

Chapter Eighty-Two

MAEVE CREPT QUIETLY DOWN the hall of the second sublevel. The gray tile on the walls and floor seemed so foreboding that Maeve shivered.

It's fine. This will work.

Alvie was just ahead of her. Chris walked next to her. "You don't have to do this," he said.

"It was my idea."

"Yeah, but Maeve—"

She shook her head. "No. This is the only way."

Greg, Leslie, and the triplets were upstairs, hunkered down in the front foyer once again behind the main desk. Leslie promised to protect them the best she could. But none of them had any illusions about their abilities to hold off against the base's security. It would be a bloodbath. Which brought them to their current situation. Alvie had indicated there was a large group of aliens located somewhere on this floor. And that's exactly where they were heading.

Ahead, Alvie stopped at the corner. He looked back at

Maeve and nodded. Beyond him, Maeve could hear pounding and screaming—and something that could only be described as a squelch. Heart hammering, she took a steeling breath and patted the handgun in the holster at her side she had taken from a downed security officer down the hall.

Chris grabbed her hand and gave it a squeeze. "Here we go."

As one, they all stepped around the corner, lining up across the opening of what had once been a cafeteria. Maeve's eyes widened. There were at least two dozen aliens in the large room beyond consisting of seven different species, each one slightly more horrifying than the next. A few human bodies lay crumpled on the ground. One hung from a light, another was sprawled over a counter. Maeve swallowed hard.

The three blue gorillas, each standing at least six feet tall in the back of the room, caught sight of them first and let out a yell. But that wasn't enough.

Maeve put her fingers in her mouth and let out an ear-piercing whistle.

"That's right, boys, here we are," Chris yelled.

Each alien went still for a moment and then turned toward them. Incisors, long tongues, sucker-type mouths all seemed to open and close in anticipation of their next meal or just their next kill.

And Maeve's heart pounded even harder.

"Well, I'd say that did it. Let's go." Chris grabbed her arm and pulled her back. Alvie backed up as well. And then they were full-out sprinting down the hall the way they had come.

Maeve focused on the entrance to the stairwell at the other end of the hall, three hundred feet away. Behind her, she could hear the alien horde following them. It wasn't just footfalls. There were yells and slurps, and even a scraping sound like nails over a chalkboard. She knew she should keep her focus ahead, but the sounds behind her were too unbelievable for her not to look.

And she wished she hadn't. The blue gorillas pounded down the hall, their large forearms punching into the ground with each stride. Behind them, every nightmarish vision she had ever had came to life, sliding, oozing, jumping, and running toward Maeve, Chris, and Alvie. Another alien raced along the hallway walls, it's long talons cutting into the walls. It looked like a crocodile except that it's arms and legs were longer, more humanoid in appearance.

But perhaps worst of all was the alien on the ceiling. It was a blob with no definitive shape as it hung upside down, matching the speed of the aliens on the ground below it.

"Oh god." Maeve legs trembled and she stumbled. But Chris grabbed her arm, keeping her on her feet. Alvie launched himself ahead into the stairwell. Maeve and Chris quickly followed him in while Maeve prayed no unfriendlies had made their way up the stairwell since they had been here.

Blessedly the stairwell appeared empty. Maeve hit the stairs and her thighs screamed in protest. She pushed past the ache, forcing herself not to slow down but to actually speed up. She'd reached the landing between floors when the first alien hit the doorway. The blue gorilla slammed into it, too large to fit through straight on. He was yanked from the opening and the alien from the ceiling oozed through.

Alvie was already at the first-floor landing. He yanked open the door and disappeared through. Maeve reached the door as the alien from the ceiling oozed up the side of the stairwell.

"Shit." Chris pushed Maeve through the doorway as the thing leapt for them. Alvie disappeared behind the front desk as Maeve and Chris burst into the foyer. Chris pulled Maeve away from the desk toward the other side of the room as the blob burst out behind them. He pulled his sidearm and started firing at the front window—one of the few that hadn't been broken in the original barrage. The thing oozed up the side of the wall and then the ceiling, racing toward them.

Ahead of them, the glass was a spider web of cracks but it held. There was no other exit.

"Chris?" Maeve yelled as she sprinted forward, not sure what the hell the plan was.

The hairs on the back of her neck stood up as the blob raced closer, almost on top of them. Chris grabbed Maeve, wrapped his arms around her, and dove through the window, turning so his back hit first. Maeve screamed as glass shattered around them, tucking her head into Chris's chest, crushing her eyes closed. They hit the ground and Chris rolled, keeping Maeve protected in his arms.

Maeve screamed as gunfire pierced the ground around them. Then the blob oozed from the window and the gunfire shifted toward it instead.

Chris pulled Maeve behind a parked car. "Are you all right?"

She nodded, trembling and trying to catch her breath. "What about—"

Alvie burst through the front door and Maeve's heart nearly stopped as gunfire hit the doorway behind him and the ground next to him. But Alvie moved as if he knew exactly where each shot was going to land.

And then all hell broke loose as the rest of the alien horde burst through the door behind him. Nightmare after nightmare poured through the door, emptying onto the grounds.

"Get under the car!" Chris yelled.

Maeve squirmed in next to him but kept her eyes on Alvie as he slid over the hood of another car and disappeared from view.

Run, Alvie, run.

Chapter Eighty-Three

THE GUNFIRE by the old headquarters sounded like a fourth of July celebration. If Mr. Smith was right, that would be Dr. Leander attempting to escape. He smiled, listening to the barrage of gunfire.

Don't think they'll be getting by that.

Henning ran along a sidewalk through the empty base. In his ten years working here, he'd never seen the place like this. He'd switched into camo gear. Now for anyone looking, he was one of the dozens of camo guys, who were yet another layer of protection for the base. The camo dudes had been hired years back to secure the hills surrounding the base. Technically they had no legal authority and were supposed to detain anyone they caught crossing into 51 territory, but Henning never let that stop him from giving any would-be trespassers a good scare.

But it was their job to make sure that nothing escaped or entered the base. Henning had actually been a member of the camo dudes until he'd been bumped up to inside security when the new projects had been brought in. And he realized that he was better suited to the perimeter of the base. Having to deal with the eggheads like that know-it-all Dr. Leander just pissed him off.

And he nearly let her ruin his career here. But with Mr. Smith backing him, he knew he'd get placed somewhere else where they'd appreciate all his hard work. In fact, most of the camo dudes had been pulling double duty while the base hired more security.

Henning ducked into the storage building at the end of the row and quickly ran up the metal stairs. He pushed through the door leading to the roof and made his way to the corner. He was down the block from the old headquarters, ground zero for the outbreak. Placing his rifle on the ledge, he knelt down, searching through the scope for his quarry.

Come on, where are you?

He was hoping Leander showed herself first. He'd be more than happy to take her down. A man crossed his scope and disappeared out of it. Chris. Henning had no issue with him and honestly he'd rather not shoot the man. But the rest of them? They were fair game.

He saw Leander's familiar dark hair and smiled. He adjusted his grip, but she was blocked by a truck. Damn it. He scanned, looking for a shot and finally found one—wide open.

Sorry about this, he thought right before he pulled the trigger.

Chapter Eighty-Four

GREG FELT like his heart was going to either pound out of his chest or bump up through his throat and out of his mouth. When the alien horde had torn out of the stairwell after Chris and Maeve, he'd known it was the end.

But as soon as the herd had started to slow and investigate the foyer, Alvie had leaped from his hiding spot and sprinted for the door, drawing them away.

Greg hugged the three triplets to him as the horde passed. And he tried not to vomit as he saw two climb along the ceiling. But none of them glanced toward the desk—they were all too focused on Alvie.

Alvie burst through the front door and gunfire rang out.

God damn it. Greg scrunched lower. His anger at the people outside grew, right along with his respect for Alvie. Alvie was leading them away so the rest of them had a chance to live. He was putting his life on the line with death facing him from both the front and the back.

And then all hell truly broke loose as the alien horde

burst through the front of the building. Gunfire, snarls, rips, screams—it seemed to go on forever. But then it quieted as the horde moved farther away into the base. Greg tried not to think about what that meant. Had they killed all the soldiers who'd been waiting outside the door? He knew he should feel bad about that but seeing as those same soldiers had tried to kill him not that long ago, he couldn't work up any sympathy.

"Leslie?" he whispered. She shook her head, listening. Greg could only hear sounds in the distance, but his mind still imagined the sound of the horde rushing past and he couldn't seem to stop shaking. And then to have their own people shooting at them—Greg didn't know what the hell to think about that except, *What the fuck?*

He glanced back at Leslie, who just gave him a confident nod in return. And her confidence took the edge off some of his own panic. Honestly, if she wasn't here, he was sure he would be in a puddle on the ground—a puddle of either his own pee or blood but a puddle nonetheless. But Leslie kept him going, kept him safe.

"Time to go," Leslie said.

Greg nodded, getting to his feet with some difficulty. "Okay, one of you scurry around to my back, okay?"

He was surprised when Crackle did exactly that. These guys were smart. He held Pop and Snap securely to his chest. "Can you manage all three?" Leslie asked.

"Yeah, and I prefer you to just worry about shooting somebody." He paused. "Um, have you changed your mind about that whole not shooting at humans thing?"

Leslie glared toward the front of the building. "Oh, yeah. Now come on. Stay low." She headed toward the same window that Chris and Maeve had burst through.

Greg tried to stay low, but with two aliens attached to his chest and another on his back, when he bent down he almost lost his balance. So he had to settle for hustling quickly across the floor with his shoulders hunched.

Leslie peered out the window. "Okay. We're good. Head for that truck over there and I'll cover you."

Greg peered out. "Um, you sure?"

"I won't let anything happen to you. Okay?"

Greg looked into her eyes and nodded. "Okay." He let out a breath as Leslie counted down. "3-2-1, go." Greg stepped over the windowsill, glass crunching under his feet. And then he was sprinting across the open space, waiting for the sound of a bullet to tear through the silence. But nothing happened. He reached the truck panting, and seconds later, Leslie was at his side.

"You guys good?" Chris called from the other side of the street.

"We're good," Leslie said.

"We're heading east," Chris yelled. "We'll cover you as you cross to us."

"Got it." Leslie grabbed Greg's arm. "Ready?"

He nodded, his mouth too dry to work up any words.

"Let's go." Leslie pulled him to his feet. They ran across the open space. Halfway across, Snap began to get agitated, gripping Greg's shirt. He patted her back. "Hey, hey, it's okay, little buddy. Calm down."

But Snap just grew even more agitated, struggling to get out of Greg's arms.

"Greg. Keep her quiet," Leslie hissed.

"I'm trying, but something's wrong."

Snap wrenched herself from Greg's arm, leaping onto his shoulder.

"Quit fooling around," Leslie ordered.

"I'm not." Greg tried to grab Snap but she leapt off his shoulder, slamming both her feet into Leslie's shoulders.

With a yell, Leslie crashed to the ground just as a gunshot rang out.

Chapter Eighty-Five

"GET DOWN!" Chris yelled as the shot rang out. More bullets chased Greg, who dove over a bench and then crawled underneath it. Pop and Crackle leapt from Greg and managed to reach Alvie and Maeve. Maeve grabbed them and scurried behind a truck.

Leslie crawled behind a planter, one hand to her chest and the other wrapped around Snap.

Chris scanned the buildings, looking for where the shots had come from. But they'd gone silent.

"Leslie?" Chris yelled.

"I'm good. We're good."

"Greg?"

He groaned. "Bruised but not shot."

"Maeve?"

"We're good," she called out, a tremor in her voice.

Chris was behind a building and none of the shots had been aimed at him, which meant he was most likely out of the sniper's range. He was pretty sure it had come from one of three buildings down the way.

"You guys sit tight. I'm going to find the sniper."

"We're splitting up?" Maeve asked.

"Just for now. You guys sit tight," Chris said, hoping he wasn't lying.

Chapter Eighty-Six

MAEVE WATCHED in fear as Chris disappeared from the side of the building. Alvie reached over and touched her cheek. She nodded at him. "He'll be back. He's going to find the shooter."

Alvie stared into her eyes and Maeve felt the fear he too had for Chris.

Maeve's head whipped to the side as Greg crawled in next to them.

"Jesus, Greg, give me a heart attack why don't you?"

Sweat lined Greg's brow. "Sorry, but my bench with the slats wasn't feeling too secure."

"Where's Snap?"

"With Leslie."

Greg peeked out and Maeve could see Leslie. She pointed to them and then behind them. Greg glanced over and saw a building fifty feet away. He looked back at Leslie and shook his head. She nodded, glaring at him.

He turned to Maeve. "Uh, I think Leslie wants us to head over there."

Maeve let out a breath, getting into a crouch, holding Crackle and Pop to her chest. She swallowed down her fear. "Okay. Alvie, we're heading there, okay?"

Alvie nodded.

"Get ready," Maeve said. Greg crouched low on his feet. Leslie counted down to three with her fingers and then leaned up with her weapon, aimed in the direction the shots had come. Maeve sprinted forward, Alvie at her side.

Behind her, Greg cursed as he stumbled, but he righted himself and reached the building just after them. No gunfire rang out.

"Alvie, take these guys," Maeve said, handing over Pop and Crackle. She would have preferred to hand them to Greg, but he was looking awfully pale. She pulled out her handgun, wishing it was a rifle. She was a lousy shot with a handgun, and besides, they didn't exactly have the distance. But it was the best cover she could offer Leslie and Snap.

She met Leslie's gaze and gave her a nod. Leslie burst from her cover, Snap tucked into her chest. She sprinted for them, and still no gunfire rang out.

As she reached their side, she flattened herself against the building. "You guys okay?"

"Yeah. You?" Maeve asked.

Leslie nodded toward Snap. "Thanks to her."

Maeve frowned. "What do you mean?"

"That first gunshot—it would have hit me. But this one, she knocked me down. I'm pretty sure she bruised my sternum but it's better than the alternative."

Maeve looked at Snap, whose little arms were wrapped around Leslie's neck, her eyes closed. "Is she okay?"

Leslie nodded, absentmindedly rubbing Snap's back. "Yeah. Just scared."

"I'll take her," Maeve said, reaching out. And she didn't

miss the look of thanks Leslie gave the little one. Apparently Snap had just won Leslie over to their side.

Greg ran his hand over Snap's back. "It's okay, little gal. No one's shooting us. So as of right this moment, there's not anything to be scared of," he said quietly.

"Oh I cannot believe you just jinxed us like that," Leslie groaned.

Greg gave her a small laugh. "You can't possibly think—"

A thump sounded behind them. And all of them turned to see an alien with the scales and mouth of a crocodile on top of an incredibly muscular body land on top of the truck seventy feet away.

Greg's mouth fell open with a groan. "Oh crap. It's Hank."

Chapter Eighty-Seven

GREG STARED at Hank in disbelief. How had he found them?

Leslie opened fire. Maeve was firing as well as she walked backward, Snap on her back. "Who the hell is Hank?"

"He's my project," Greg said as he backed up.

"You guys run!" Leslie yelled.

Maeve turned around, wrapping Snap in her arms, and sprinted. Greg ran next to her and Alvie somehow kept pace with them, Pop perched on his back and Crackle cuddled to his chest.

Man, that little guy's fast.

Behind them, an explosion sounded. Greg whirled around as Leslie stormed up to them. "Go, go, go!" she yelled.

Behind her he saw that the truck Hank had been on was now a ball of fire.

Leslie grabbed his arm, turning him around. "Move it, Greg!"

He nearly tripped over his feet as he turned because at the last second, he caught sight of a dark shadow bursting through the flames. "He's coming!"

Maeve, Alvie, and the triplets were just ahead of them. Maeve turned at the corner of the next building, ducking down an alley.

Greg started to follow.

"Look out!" Leslie crashed into him, rolling him away from the alley as a flaming piece of debris landed at the entrance, blocking the way.

She grabbed his arm and yanked him forward. Greg glanced back. "I—I think Hank threw that."

"Yeah, he's a real asshole," Leslie said, not breaking her stride. "Keep moving."

Greg ran but looked behind him, terrified Hank would follow Maeve and the triplets. But as Hank reached the entrance to the alley, he blew past it, keeping his gaze on Leslie and Greg. Greg felt a small relief that he hadn't gone after Maeve and company but complete terror that Hank seemed completely focused on them.

"Head for that hangar. I'll be right behind you," Leslie ordered as she took cover behind a dumpster and took aim at Hank.

Greg let out a yell, tripping and landing on his chest. Cursing his clumsiness, he scrambled to his feet and ran for the hangar door. He slammed into it with a groan, pushing on the door. It took him a second to realize it pulled open.

God damn it. He yanked it open and launched himself inside. There was a giant stealth bomber on the far side of the hangar and no movement. Crates two aisles deep lined the wall to the side of the bomber and Greg made a beeline for them.

He ducked behind the crates, sliding to the ground in

between the two rows. He struggled to hear any sound but he couldn't hear anything above the blood roaring in his ears.

He tried to calm his breathing enough so that he could at least hear what was going on around him. He thought he heard the creak of the door. He went still, straining to hear, but he couldn't make out any other noise. He waited, knowing Leslie would find him.

No sound came from the hangar, but he couldn't shake the feeling that he wasn't alone. He scurried to the back of the crate closest to the exit and glanced out and saw a Jeep ten feet away. Beyond it was the back door of the hangar.

Movement from the corner of his eye directed his attention up. His breaths came out in pants as his eyes lasered in on the movement. The alien moved along the rafters of the hangar, keeping in the shadows. He couldn't tell if it was Hank, but its large body was surprisingly agile. Then it swung down onto the wing of the stealth bomber, scanning the room. Its head swung back and forth, scanning the area.

Greg ducked his head back before Hank could catch sight of him, his mouth dry.

Now what do I do?

Chapter Eighty-Eight

CHRIS STAYED at the edge of the buildings, keeping low while scanning windows and rooftops for the shooter. The shooter had been quiet, which meant he'd probably moved to another position. Now Chris just had to figure out where that was.

A voice came from down the road. Chris ducked into a doorway. A few seconds later, two men in lab coats ran by.

"We should have saved him. We could have—"

"We didn't have a choice. Did you see that thing? We're lucky we got out."

"Stop right there," a third voice called out. Chris peeked out from his hiding spot and saw a man in fatigues stop the two men. He recognized him—Henning.

The two men stood with their hands up. The dark-haired one spoke quickly. "Thank God. There are—" Two gunshots cut off his words and both men slumped to the ground.

God damn it.

Chris tightened his fist. Why the hell had he shot the men? They were no threat. A chill ran through him.

They're cleaning up, taking out all witnesses.

He knew they'd thought that after the royal clusterfuck at the main headquarters, but Chris had hoped he was wrong. But Henning had no excuse for taking out the scientists. They were obviously no threat.

Henning moved slowly across the street and Chris leaned back, careful to stay hidden. He calmed his breathing, loosening his shoulders and getting ready to move.

In the glass of the car across from him he could see Henning's reflection. He looked up the street and then down before squatting down next to the men and rifling through their pockets.

Go. Chris burst from his spot.

But Henning heard his approach. He swung around, but Chris managed to kick the weapon from his hand before he could bring it around for a shot. It clattered down on the sidewalk, out of reach. Henning went to grab Chris around the waist and tackled him to the ground, but Chris slammed his knee into Henning's face. Then he shoved Henning's chin up and over his shoulders, slamming him onto his back. Chris went to kick him in the stomach but Henning twirled around, sweeping out Chris's leg.

Chris hit the ground and rolled, lessening the impact, and got to his feet. Henning had gotten to his feet as well, sliding a knife from the sheath on his waist.

"I spared you, you know," he said. "I had you in my sights and I let you go."

"Why are you going after us? Why did you kill those men?"

Henning shrugged. "I've been ordered to make a clean

sweep. We've all been ordered to—all non-security personnel are to be removed. It's nothing personal."

He lunged, swiping the knife toward Chris's chest. Chris leapt to the side, using his forearms to stop Henning's arm from swinging toward him. He grabbed Henning's wrist with one hand, holding the arm taut, and slammed his other forearm into Henning's elbow, breaking it.

Henning screamed, dropping the knife, but Chris had no pity for the man. He pulled his broken arm behind his back and forced him to his knees.

"It didn't have to be this way," Henning panted out. "You just picked the wrong company."

Chris shook his head. "What the hell's going on? I mean, I was getting people out of the building. I was doing my job."

Henning studied him for a moment. "Wrong place, wrong time, man. But I can get you out—you and that thing with you."

"Thing? You mean Alvie?"

"Yeah, they want him alive. He's your bargaining chip."

Chris felt cold. Why would they want Alvie? "Who wants him?"

"The powers that be. I don't have names. I just know they pull the strings."

"What about the rest of them?"

"The order is to kill on sight."

"Everybody?"

Henning nodded. "Yeah."

Chris pushed Henning's face into the pavement. "Why?"

"What does it matter? It's an order. Have you stopped taking those?" Henning laughed, his cheek scraping against the pavement. "It's that scientist, isn't it? She got to you.

What, you think you're going to be the hero? Get the girl? Save the day? You're not making it out of here alive unless you start following orders."

"Well, if I kill you that should improve our chances."

"Won't make a difference."

"Why not?"

"They've initiated the Manhattan Protocol."

Chris felt like all the air had been sucked from his lungs. The Manhattan Protocol, named after the Manhattan Project—the collaboration of top American scientists but also supported by Great Britain and Canada that had led to the creation of the first atomic bomb.

The Manhattan Protocol was using an atomic bomb to eliminate a contagion or threat. They were going to bomb the facility. They'd known it was going to happen, but Chris was hoping it would be hours from now.

"When?"

"An hour, and then this whole place will be toast." Chris slammed Henning's head into the concrete and knocked him out. Then he grabbed Henning's weapons and his radio. He scanned the area, but no one else was around. He started to jog back to where he'd left everybody else. Tension coiled around him. He needed to get all of them away from the base.

Waiting for reinforcements wasn't going to work, and talking their way out wasn't going to work. They were going to have to figure out another way off the base.

And as fast as possible.

Chapter Eighty-Nine

MAEVE CARRIED Snap and Pop while Crackle remained nestled on Alvie's back. They had run down the alley and sprinted down another one and now she didn't know where anybody else was. They seemed to be in some sort of loading area. There were crates piled around them. A metal Quonset hut stood to their right and another one to their left. Maeve didn't like their position. She felt too exposed.

Pop trembled in her arms. Maeve leaned her head down. "It's all right. It's going to be fine."

But her words were hollow. She needed to find the others. She had no idea how she was going to get any of them off the base on her own. Snap's head swiveled to the right and Maeve saw a door open.

Damn it.

"Alvie," she whispered.

But he was already moving to hide behind one of the crates. Maeve ducked in next to him, trying to calm the two trembling aliens in her arms. Alvie's head jolted up and he cocked his head to the side.

"Alvie, stay here," Maeve warned, hoping he wasn't about to bolt. Alvie's eyes pleaded with her. Maeve inched toward the edge of the crate and looked out.

Four soldiers were leading a tall gray alien from the hut. It was the same gray being that Alvie and Maeve had seen, or at least another one who looked exactly like him. He was being led to a truck, shackles around his ankles, a collar attached to a long pole around his neck.

Alvie let out a cry. Maeve placed a hand over his mouth, but the soldiers stopped.

"I got it," one of the soldiers said as he headed toward them.

Maeve's heart raced. They'd find them. Her mind scrambled, trying to figure out how she could get Alvie and the triplets to run while she created a distraction. She knew she wouldn't be able to outrun the soldier while carrying two of them.

She nudged Alvie and quickly crawled over to another set of crates. Alvie was right behind her, his small hand securely placed on Crackle's back. Maeve looked around, but there was nothing but fifty feet of open ground in front of her. Her heart raced because she knew they were going to get caught. At this point, there was no way to avoid it.

She placed Snap and Pop on the ground, and stared into Alvie's eyes. *Get them to safety.* His eyes grew slightly larger and he shook his head. She nodded and then inched her way to the edge of the crate, pulling her handgun from the holster, even though she knew she only had one round left. She peeked out. Two of the soldiers approached their former hiding place and Maeve swallowed. One and she might have had a chance, but two? She'd never be able to take down two.

They made their way around the sides. One counted

down from three with his fingers and as one they turned, they aimed their guns at the spot where Maeve and the aliens had been hiding.

One of the soldiers shook his head and looked over to where Maeve was hiding. She ducked back, her heart pounding. She looked over at Alvie, who had the triplets all curled around him.

I can't save them. The thought broke her heart.

Maeve felt eyes on her and glanced up, then gasped. The gray alien in chains had a perfect view of Maeve through the crates. She stared into his eyes.

Help us. Please.

Her head whipped back at the sound of a footfall only a few feet away. One of the soldiers was almost on them.

Then the gray started to screech, whipping back and forth. His arms raised, he yanked on his chains.

"God damn it. Leave it. Get over here and help with this guy," the soldier in charge barked.

The soldier near them hesitated for a moment, but then she heard his footsteps retreating. Maeve sucked in a breath, air rushing into her lungs. She peeked out and saw the two soldiers retreating. The large gray went quiet as the two soldiers approached.

"What the hell set it off?"

"Who the hell knows? Let's get him out of here."

They yanked the gray by the lead on his neck and he stumbled forward. Then the soldiers forced him up a ramp and into a truck. As the soldiers busied themselves strapping him into the truck bed, the alien's gaze once again strayed to where Maeve and Alvie were hiding. Maeve looked into the being's eyes again.

Thank you.

It nodded back at her. And then the back of the truck was closed, cutting him off from her view.

Maeve watched helplessly as the truck drove off. It had saved them. She had no doubt of that. Why? And where were those soldiers taking him?

A screech sounded somewhere not too far away, pulling Maeve back to their situation. Once they got out of here alive, she would find out where they were taking him. The screech sounded again, causing Alvie to tremble, his panic-stricken gaze latching onto Maeve's. And reality once again hit her.

If we get out of here alive.

Chapter Ninety

HANK HAD INFRARED VISION, and Greg knew he would see him standing there. But he hadn't charged.

Cold, cold. I need something cold to hide behind.

But it was a hangar in Nevada in July. There was nothing cold anywhere nearby.

Right, so I just make sure there's something between me and Hank at all times. He slid down so he was behind the crate. The Jeep was ten feet away and then it was only a five-foot run to the door, which was closed.

His shoulders dropped as the impossibility of the situation hit him. And then he pictured Leslie, her determination no matter what they faced. Where was she? She'd said she'd be right behind him. The idea of Leslie being hurt spurred him into a crouch.

I got this.

He peered over the crate and saw that Hank was gone from the wing. He frowned. *Where'd—*

Hank landed on the crate at the end of the row. Greg felt his eyes grow wide as Hank stared straight at him.

Oh god.

All thoughts of hiding disappeared as Greg scrambled to his feet and sprinted for the door. He heard Hank drop to the ground behind him. Greg had never run so fast in his life. He crashed into the door and tumbled out into the yard. He ran forward, praying, almost crying.

Don't let it end like this.

From around the corner of the Quonset hut behind the hangar, Leslie sprinted into view. "Hey, Hank, you bastard, over here," Leslie yelled before opening fire.

Greg tripped as he turned to see Leslie, standing out in the open. Hank switched direction with a roar as her bullets bounced off his skin.

"No!" Greg yelled.

He stumbled, catching himself with one hand as he started to fall and ran for Leslie. Hank sprinted along the ground, running parallel with him.

Leslie backed up, never letting up her assault. Hank roared and leapt, but so did Greg. He tackled Leslie just as Hank reached them, rolling them away and feeling one of Hank's talons rip through the skin on his thigh.

Greg screamed in agony. Leslie pulled her sidearm and emptied a single bullet into Hank's eye. Hank reared back.

Greg grabbed the grenade off Leslie's belt, pulling the pin. As Hank roared, Greg turned and aimed it at Hank's mouth. As soon as the grenade left Greg's hand Leslie grabbed him, rolling him down the embankment.

Pain crashed through Greg again and again as they rolled. Above them, an explosion sounded. Greg turned his head, crushing his eyes closed as organic material blew over the side of the embankment toward them along with a spray of blood.

Leslie rolled off him as the smoke cleared, glaring at him. "You idiot! What were you thinking?"

It took Greg a moment to find his voice. "Um, which part?"

Leslie pulled off her shirt, leaving her in a black tank top. "The part where you jumped in front of me."

He winced as she tore off a piece of her shirt and started to wrap it around his leg. "Um, I was thinking—" He stopped. "Actually, check that. I wasn't thinking. I saw Hank run for you, so I did too."

"You could have been killed."

"Yup," he said with a wince. "Not sure I won't still because that hurts like hell."

Leslie stared down at him, her voice softer. "You really are an idiot."

He nodded and closed his eyes, praying he didn't pass out from the pain. "No argument."

Chapter Ninety-One

A CHILL HAD CREPT under Chris's skin when Henning mentioned the Manhattan Protocol, and it refused to leave as Chris made his way back to the others. The base itself wasn't helping with the feeling. It was like an abandoned town. Cars and trucks were still parked along the roads, but there were no people. Just rows of empty buildings. It felt eerie.

Chris had left Henning unconscious in one of the buildings. He'd stripped him of all his weapons and communications, but he couldn't bring himself to kill him. Not in cold blood. Besides, if Henning was right and the Manhattan Protocol was initiated, his likelihood of surviving this was just as low as for the rest of them.

But Chris shoved thoughts of Henning's fate from his mind. He was much more concerned with the fate of a different group of people. Chris backtracked to where he'd left the rest of the group. He stopped at the building across from the old headquarters. A few carcasses of aliens were strewn across the ground. But so were the bodies of some humans.

Chris studied each body, but none were part of his group. He let out a sigh of relief, but it was tinged with worry and anger that American troops had been used so callously. But he didn't have time to focus on that. He strained but couldn't hear any movement near him. Where did they go?

A screech sounded from somewhere to his right. Chris paused, uncertain, then decided that right was as good a direction as any. He turned and slowly made his way down the street. An engine sounded from ahead and Chris ducked into a doorway, pushing himself against the wall and into the shadows. A military truck passed—a type he'd never seen before. The back looked like an armored truck.

It must be a containment unit.

He waited until it passed and then glanced out. No movement on the street. He closed his eyes and focused on Alvie, part of him not believing that he was actually about to try this.

Where are you, Alvie? I'm looking for you.

He waited for a moment, not sure what exactly he was waiting for. He opened his eyes and shook his head.

Well, that was stupid.

He was just glad no one had seen him do it.

He inched back to the edge of the building and looked out. He started to walk in the direction the truck had come from when he felt the slightest pulse in his mind, like a feather wiping across his brain.

Alvie?

A squeak sounded from down the road, and Chris picked up his pace. On the other side of the street, Alvie emerged, Crackle in his arms. And then Maeve stepped out with the other two in her arms.

Relief poured through Chris as he drank in the sight of her. Her eyes grew large at the sight of him, and then a smile spread across her face. Chris jogged across the street, still keeping an eye out for any movement. He stopped in front of her and looked down. "Hey."

"Hey."

He reached out his hand and cupped her face. "You okay?"

She nodded. "Yeah."

Chris looked behind her and frowned. "Where's Leslie and Greg?"

"We got split up. But I think Alvie might be able to find them."

Chris knelt down and looked into Alvie's eyes. "You okay, little buddy?"

Alvie leaned his forehead into Chris's with a sigh. Chris wrapped his arms around him. "It's good to see you too, buddy."

An explosion sounded from somewhere to their left.

Maeve put her hand on Chris's shoulder. "I think that's the direction Leslie and Greg went."

Chris nodded as he stood, helping Pop get situated on his back. "Well, then let's go find them."

Chapter Ninety-Two

GREG WINCED as Leslie tightened the bandage around his wound. "How's that?" she asked.

"Great," Greg said, feeling light-headed.

"We need to find everybody else. Can you walk on it?"

"Yeah. I'm all right."

Leslie helped him up, keeping an arm around his waist.

"It's okay, I got it," he said. He winced a little as his thigh throbbed but kept his balance, which he gave himself major points for. He glanced over to where parts of Hank lay and swallowed hard.

They started to walk, and Leslie nodded toward Hank's remains. "What you did—that was pretty incredible."

"I just kind of ran."

"Yeah, in a foot race with an alien who wanted you dead."

Greg stopped short and looked at Leslie.

"What?"

"You're right," he said slowly. "Hank wanted me dead."

"Yeah, they all want us dead. It's kind of their thing."

Greg shook his head. "No. Maeve ran off with Alvie and the triplets. They were the easier target—small, vulnerable. But he didn't go after them. He came after us."

"So?"

"So that shows thought. That shows a plan. He wasn't working by instinct." His gaze fell on Hank's arm, which lay on the top of a crate a few feet away. His mouth fell open.

"What?" Leslie asked.

Greg said nothing, just walked slowly toward the crate. He stopped next to it to inspect the arm. The familiar scales were there, the long talons. "There's only three," he whispered.

"Three? Three what?"

"Talons."

Leslie frowned. "One of them must have been blown off."

Greg shook his head, staring at the space on the hand where the fourth finger should have been. "No. Look—the wound has a clean cut, an *old* cut. It's already scarred over."

"That doesn't make any sense."

But Greg was afraid it made perfect sense. He looked around, his heart racing.

"What?" Leslie asked.

"This wasn't Hank. This was someone else."

"What? Who?"

Greg shrugged, the casual gesture completely undone by the tremors running through him. "I don't know. He must have been part of a different project."

"But it was going after you," Leslie said slowly. "Why would it do that?"

Greg stared at the remains. He remembered Hank faking his death. He could control his bodily functions to a level that most humans couldn't. But some could. Yogis were reportedly able to slow their heart rate to practically nothing. Tibetan monks were reportedly able to raise their body temperature to allow them to sit outside in freezing weather without experiencing frostbite. Hank seemed to have a similar ability to regulate some of his body's functions.

But that wasn't the event in his mind that he focused on. He remembered one time when he'd had an assistant, Randall. After only being there for a day, the assistant's behavior had shifted. He'd become angry at Greg. By the end of the week, he'd become so unhinged, he'd attacked Greg with a stool. Leslie had saved him, but Randall had been removed in restraints.

When Greg went to visit him in the mental hospital the next week, Randall was back to his normal self and beyond horrified at what he had done. He couldn't explain why he had reacted that way. He'd never been a violent person. If anything, he was the opposite. He'd just all of a sudden felt an overwhelming anger at Greg. The man had been baffled. Greg had been equally baffled and had written it off as some sort of psychotic break.

But what if it wasn't? What if the man had been influenced by Hank?

"Do you remember Randall?"

"Your assistant? The one who lost it?"

Greg nodded. "I've kept in touch with him. He's working at Los Alamos. He's had no other episodes and still can't understand what happened. He said he was overwhelmingly angry at me, but as soon as he left the building, it disappeared. But every time he entered the building, the anger grew again."

"Why are you bringing that up now?"

Greg swallowed, looking around, the hair raising on the

back of his neck. "I think Hank might have sent Randall after me. I don't think it was Randall's anger, I think it was Hank's."

Leslie looked at him for a long moment and then shook her head. "But I've been with you almost every day for the last two years. I've never become psychotically mad at you. Just normal mad at you."

Greg studied Leslie. She was strong, disciplined, and capable. Randall had been extremely smart but otherwise he'd been insecure and socially awkward.

"I think—" Greg hesitated. "I think it only works with certain personality types. You're too strong. Randall wasn't."

Leslie nudged her chin toward the remains. "Well, this guy wasn't exactly a shrinking violet."

"Maybe it's different interspecies versus intraspecies. All I know for sure is that this guy wasn't Hank. But I'm almost positive Hank put him up to this. Somehow he communicated his hate to him. He shared his emotions. Hank got this guy to come after me. Which also means—" Greg broke off, feeling a little light-headed and not from blood loss.

Leslie nodded, her face grim. "Which means Hank's still out there. And he's still looking for you."

Chapter Ninety-Three

GREG WALKED ALONG THE STREET, keeping close to the buildings. Leslie led the way, stopping every once in a while to listen. They were heading back to where they'd last seen Maeve and the gang. And hopefully they'd be able to track them from there.

Greg knew that he should be focused on his surroundings, because God knew what was out there. And it seemed they had both humans and aliens to worry about. But he couldn't get Hank out of his mind. That thing that had chased them hadn't been Hank. But he was the same species as Hank. Was it really possible for Hank to have conveyed his anger toward him?

He thought of Alvie and how he could sense the other aliens. That ability opened the door to a whole host of possibilities for alien abilities. And some form of group-think was not out of the realm of possibilities. In fact, ants essentially shared one brain, with the queen being the one in charge. Greg swallowed. What if Hank was the queen ant of his species?

Why couldn't I have gotten a nice worker ant instead?

Leslie went still, throwing out a hand to stop Greg.

He tensed, looking around. "What?"

She frowned. "I don't know. It's—" She paused and then smiled, shaking her head. "Damn it, Alvie."

Ahead, Chris peeked his head from around a Quonset hut at the end of the street. Greg smiled as Maeve and the aliens came into view behind him.

Thank God.

Leslie picked up the pace and they met up halfway. Chris grinned. "Knew you'd be fine."

Leslie grinned back at him, but Greg could see how worried she'd been. "Same here. And I'm glad to see our friends are still with us."

Greg walked over to Maeve and ran a hand over Pop. "They okay?"

"Yeah. How'd you guys get away from that thing?" Her gaze dropped to his leg. "What happened?"

"We had a close call with Hank's brother."

"Brother? That wasn't your subject?" Chris asked.

"No. But I think he probably was working on his brother's orders."

"How'd you get away?" Chris asked.

"Teamwork," Leslie said.

"A grenade," Greg said at the same time.

"Well, I'm glad you guys are all right. We need get out, and fast," Chris said.

"What happened?" Leslie asked.

"They've initiated the Manhattan Protocol," Chris said.

Leslie's mouth dropped open. "Oh no."

"Is that as bad as I think it is?" Greg asked.

Chris nodded. "They're going to nuke the place. We have less than an hour to get a safe distance from the base.

Any and everything within the base's boundary will be eliminated."

Maeve turned her stricken gaze to Alvie and triplets. "How are we going to get them out?"

"That's not the only problem. I saw men in uniform shooting unarmed civilians, not just aliens."

"Well, this just gets better and better," Leslie grumbled.

"We can use the tunnels. You said the old ones were still working," Greg said.

"Can you walk all right?" Maeve asked.

Greg felt his leg throb as if in response. "Walk, yes. Run? Not so much."

"Well then, let's get moving." Chris started down the nearest alley. In the distance, Greg could see a plane lying on a tarmac. It was maybe a quarter of a mile away. The tunnels were another half mile beyond that. So close and yet with everything they had been through, he knew it would be a miracle if they made it.

"But why would they create something like that?" Leslie asked.

"What?" Greg said.

"The tunnels," Leslie clarified.

"The Cold War," Chris said. "We wanted to make sure the Russians didn't know what we were doing, especially with our air force and weaponry. So a lot of the research was moved underground."

"And allegedly these things are huge. Eyewitnesses have said you can fit two 747s side by side in them," Greg said.

Leslie shook her head. "But that, I mean, there's no way—"

"The government would keep projects hidden from the public view?" Chris asked dryly. "Remind me again why we're hiding?

"They can't just create something like that," Leslie said.

Greg snorted. "With black budgets they can. I mean, honestly, how do you think we all get paid? It's not like there's some form being submitted to the Senate with 'Alien Maintenance and Replication' written on it.

"Okay, so if these tunnels do exist, how do we get to them?" Leslie asked.

"Sheridan's tablet could tell us," said Maeve.

"Yeah," Chris drawled, "but that's back on level ten. And I don't think I want to go grab it."

Alvie took Maeve's hand. She glanced down at him as a map of the complex popped into her mind with focus on a hangar.

She looked around at the humans. "I think Alvie knows where the entrance is. It's a hangar. Hangar 22 on the southwest side of the base."

"Um, Greg?" Chris asked, his gaze focused down the street.

"Yeah?"

"This alien of yours. Any chance he kind of looks like a human alligator?"

Greg frowned. "Yeah. How'd you—"

Chris nodded down the street. "Because I think he's right there."

Chapter Ninety-Four

EVERYBODY STARED down the street where a large alien, six feet tall with an alligator-like face and humanoid arms, studied them. Chris grabbed onto Greg's arm and started to back up slowly. "No sudden movements, anybody."

Maeve's voice shook as she spoke. "I thought you guys said you killed him."

"No, we killed his brother," Greg said.

"There's more than one?" Maeve asked.

"Yup. Hank has a very ugly twin brother," Greg muttered.

A screech erupted from Hank's mouth, sounding like a battle cry.

"Okay, everybody back up a little more quickly," Chris said.

They only made it another six feet when Hank leapt from his spot and raced toward them.

"Run!" Leslie yelled. They all turned, sprinting down the street. Maeve clutched Snap and Pop to her as she raced. Greg ran as best he could, his leg screaming in agony with each step. Chris wrapped an arm around his waist. "Grab onto me."

Greg threw his arm over Chris's shoulder and picked up the pace. The end of the street loomed ahead. And then there was the unmistakable sound of engines. Two pickup trucks swung into view at the end of the street. Men in camouflage leaned out each passenger window and opened fire.

Chapter Ninety-Five

MAEVE COULDN'T BELIEVE her eyes when the men in the pickups started to fire at them. Leslie shoved Maeve into a small alley. Alvie ducked in behind her and Chris, and Greg brought up the rear. Maeve sprinted along, Snap and Pop clinging to her. Her legs ached and she worried they were finally going to give out. But she pushed on, knowing stopping meant death.

Behind them, Hank let out a scream. At least, Maeve thought it was Hank. She didn't turn around to check. In response, the gunfire picked up. Maeve burst out of the end of the alley and across the street. Leslie grabbed her arm before she could duck into the alley directly across from them. She pulled Maeve to the left and down the alley that ran along the building there. Maeve ran on, glancing back every now and then to make sure her group was still together.

She burst out of the second alley. Leslie pointed at the Quonset hut ahead. "In there."

Maeve ran for the door and tugged it open before

spilling inside. She held the door open as everyone else spilled in behind her and then closed it quickly. Leslie was already at the window.

Chris helped lower Greg to the floor. "Anything?" he asked.

Leslie shook her head. "No. I think Hank is keeping the soldiers busy."

"Small blessings," Chris muttered, and then his eyes lit up. "Jackpot."

He crossed to a large cabinet on the other side of the room and slammed the end of his rifle into the lock. He pulled it open to reveal the interior, which was filled with weapons.

Leslie joined him, already reaching in. "Now we're talking." The two of them divvied up weapons for a minute, taking as many as they could reasonably carry.

Chris walked over to Maeve and handed her a machine gun and two magazines. "Okay?"

She took them with a nod. "Okay."

Chris turned to Leslie and Greg. "All right, now let's figure out how we're getting across the runway. Those soldiers will see us when we're out in the open."

"Could we get a car?" Leslie asked. "I mean, there are tons of them around."

Chris nodded. "I could probably hotwire something."

"We won't need to. There's a car lot next to the runway. All the keys are in a box by the entrance," Leslie said.

"Good. That's good. We'll head there." Chris looked down at Greg. "I'll help you over."

Greg shook his head. "No. I'm not going with you."

Chapter Ninety-Six

GREG SAT ON THE FLOOR, his leg throbbing, each person above him looking at him with their own variation of 'what the hell' on their face.

Maeve shook her head. "Of course you're coming with us. We're all getting off this stupid base."

Greg took a breath. He'd known ever since he realized the creature that had attacked them wasn't Hank what he'd have to do. And now that Hank was after them, that decision had become crystallized in his mind. "No, I'm not."

"What are you talking about?" Leslie asked.

"Look, I'm slowing you guys down. And I've got Hank on my tail. If I go with you, he'll be coming after you as well. If I stay, you guys have a chance to make it. If I go with you, none of us make it."

Maeve shook her head. "No, you can't do this. We'll figure out a way to—"

"Hank is tracking me. He's looking for me. He's not going to stop. There is no other way. Ask him." Greg nudged his chin toward Chris.

Chris narrowed his eyes. "Are you sure?"

"Yeah. Ask Leslie."

Leslie nodded. "I think Greg's right—Hank is tracking him."

Chris stared into Greg's eyes, and for a moment Greg had a small glimmer of hope. Then Chris nodded, his voice soft. "He's right."

Greg's stomach bottomed out at Chris's words. He'd hoped that maybe Captain America might have another trick up his sleeve. Swallowing down his fear, he nodded, letting out a breath. "Okay, it's settled, then. You guys go on and—"

"I'm staying too," Leslie said.

Greg stared at her. "What are you doing?"

"My job. Which is to protect you."

"Pretty sure the job description does not involve suicide. Besides, you're ruining my whole sacrificing-for-the-team thing."

Leslie rolled her eyes. "Yeah, well, you're my responsibility. I already let you get sliced. I should probably stay and make sure nothing else happens to you." Her tone was light, but Greg could read the seriousness in her eyes. She knew what she was saying. She knew the cost. Greg wanted to make a quip; after all, that was his go-to tactic. But he didn't have any. He nodded. "Okay."

Maeve turned to Chris. "We can't let them—"

Chris's voice was compassionate but firm. "There is no other way. Our chances are not high to begin with. But if Greg's got someone on his tail, those chances drop to almost nothing."

Maeve shook her head. "We can't let them. I'll stay, you guys—"

Greg took Maeve's hand. "And what about Alvie and

the triplets? Who will take care of them? Who will convince the military not to shoot them on sight? No, this is the only way. I know you want to save us all, but that's not in your power. So let me be the hero this time, okay?"

Tears sprang into Maeve's eyes, and Greg took a deep breath, trying to hold back his own emotions. How come in the movies they all looked so unemotional in these moments? He was barely keeping it together.

Maeve stepped forward. "No, no. We are not doing this. Yes, Hank's after us. Yes, humans are after us. But we are not giving up."

Greg shook his head. "Maeve, it's not safe—"

Maeve glared at him. "Safe? What the hell has been safe since we arrived on this goddamn base? We are not leaving you."

"How about a compromise?" Leslie asked.

Maeve narrowed her eyes. "Like what?"

"You six go ahead. We'll follow, but a few minutes behind. If Hank isn't following us, we'll head down the tunnels after you."

"But what about the soldiers?"

Leslie let out a breath. "Maybe we'll go through a different tunnel entrance. There's more than one, right?"

Maeve spoke quickly. "Yes. There are three on the other side of the base—Hangars 18, 22, and 26."

"Okay, then that's our plan. You guys go first. We'll follow you if it's safe," Leslie said.

"You will follow us, though, won't you?" Maeve asked.

"Absolutely," Leslie said.

Maeve knelt down next to Greg and hugged him. "Promise you'll follow after us. No more talk about sacrificing for the team."

"You got it," he said lightly, his throat feeling tight. "Okay, well, you guys get going. We've got this."

Chris looked at Leslie. She nodded back at him. "Like he said, we got this."

Chris took Maeve's arm. "Come on."

Alvie stepped back toward Greg. He leaned in, touching his forehead to Greg's. A vision of Leslie, terror on her face as he was hurt flashed through his mind. And in that moment he knew that whatever Leslie felt for him, it wasn't completely professional. That realization was followed by a rush of gratitude that left Greg almost dizzy.

But then another hangar appeared in his mind, Hangar 37, followed by the numbers 31827. It was a hangar Greg had never seen before.

Alvie leaned back and then followed Chris and Maeve down the hall. Greg sat back on his heels, watching them go.

What was that about?

He watched the door close quietly behind them and then turned to Leslie. "We're not going to be able to follow them, are we?"

Leslie shook her head. "No."

Chapter Ninety-Seven

MAEVE, Chris, Alvie, and the triplets had left the Quonset hut just a few minutes ago. But as Maeve walked, her steps grew increasingly heavy as she pictured Greg's face. Finally, she stopped. "We need to go back. Greg's not going to follow us. We need to bring him."

He and Leslie had agreed to follow behind them in ten minutes. But right now, ten minutes seemed like a lifetime, and Maeve was pretty sure Greg had only agreed to get her to leave.

Chris stopped, placing his hands on her arms. "Maeve, this isn't a game. This isn't a story where everyone is alive and well at the end. We have the United States military after us, and who knows what kind of aliens. And we are not guaranteed to get out. That's the reality. What Greg did, what Leslie did, was increase our odds. But it's not a slam dunk. Not by a long shot."

Chris knew they weren't going to follow. The realization floored her. "How has it come to this?

"I don't know, Maeve. But it has. Now come on. The lot is right up here."

Maeve spied the tall chain-link fence that surrounded one of the base's car lots. Inside the fence, Jeep Renegades and Cherokees and a few Hummers stood in silent formation.

Chris nodded to the edge of the building. "You guys stay here. I'll grab a car, and when I'm out of the lot you guys hightail it over, okay?"

Maeve nodded, amazed that she still had reserves of fear after everything they'd already experienced. "Be careful."

"I will. Alvie, anyone around?"

Alvie shook his head. And then Chris was gone, running across the space and slipping into the lot.

Maeve scanned the area, but trusted Alvie's senses more than her own. In the lot, she saw Chris pull keys from the metal box near the entrance. After looking at the label on the keys, he crouched low and made his way to one of the Renegades. Slipping into the driver's seat, he started the engine and pulled out of the spot.

"Alvie, let's go." She'd started forward when Alvie grabbed her hand. A picture of the pickups flashed through her mind. She whirled around as one of the pickups swung into view at the end of the road.

"Run!" she yelled, pushing Alvie forward. He sprinted toward the Jeep, Snap in his arms, and they were up and into it in a single leap. As Maeve reached the Jeep, Chris reached out for the twins. Maeve handed them over as she got in, taking them from Chris as soon as she had her balance. "Go, go go!"

Chris tore off down the street, and then he turned off

the paved surface, cutting across the ground surrounding the runway.

"We're heading there." Maeve pointed to the hangar in the middle of the five across the open space as Crackle and Pop crawled into the back.

Chris nodded but didn't say anything.

Maeve glanced behind her. Alvie was crouched low in the back, the triplets curled up with him. She wanted to say something comforting. But she had no words. She just reached down and squeezed his arm.

Behind them, the pickup followed their path, barreling across the runway. A second pickup appeared farther behind, and Maeve's pulse went up another notch. The gunman in the passenger seat leaned out and took aim. But he wasn't close enough for a shot, not yet.

Maeve looked ahead at where the hangar was that led to the old tunnel. And she remembered Chris's words—*we are not guaranteed to get out.*

And with two trucks giving chase, she knew that reaching the hangar was only the beginning of a whole new fight.

Chapter Ninety-Eight

GREG SAT ON THE FLOOR, watching the door where the rest of the group had disappeared. Leslie had been rifling around the hangar and had found a first aid kit. Greg swallowed a handful of aspirin and Leslie numbed his wound with some antiseptic. It didn't erase the pain but it definitely reduced it.

Carefully, Greg got to his feet. "Okay, boss, what's the plan?"

"Well, let's start toward the car lot. Who knows? Maybe we'll actually be able to follow them."

Greg joined Leslie by the door. She looked up at him. "Ready?"

Greg nodded. "Yup. Let's go."

Leslie opened the door slowly, scanning the area. Greg strained to hear anything, but it sounded quiet.

"Let's go," Leslie whispered. Greg followed behind her, his leg still aching. With a hurried limp, he followed Leslie into the shadows of the building across from them. It looked like a garage.

Greg started to go around the building when Leslie yanked him back. Greg's head whipped toward her and she mouthed one word—*Hank*.

Greg and Leslie turned away from the car lot and hurried down past two more Quonset huts. Greg hadn't said a word, not wanting to help Hank find them. So far, their change of direction seemed to have gone unnoticed.

But Greg was sure it was only a matter of time before Hank found them. And he couldn't help but wonder why. It had to be more than pure luck that Hank and his brother found them. They must be able to track them somehow. Greg thought about how Hank could tell when a camera was watching him. Could that be it? Could he somehow be focusing on Greg's electrical signal?

No, brain patterns.

Alvie could tell when an alien was nearby and whether they were good or bad. Hank must somehow be able to tap into the same information.

Leslie nodded toward a Jeep outside the hut and then gestured for him to wait. Greg nodded. Leslie carefully made her way over, glancing in the Jeep and flipping down the visor. Keys dropped onto the seat. Greg wasted no time hightailing it over to her and climbing into the passenger seat.

Gunfire sounded from over by the runway and Greg's pulse jumped. *Oh no.*

"Do you think they're shooting at our people?"

Leslie nodded. "Yeah."

Greg closed his eyes, wishing there was something to do to help them. But there was nothing. He was powerless.

"Any ideas about where we should go next? A backup plan?" Leslie asked.

"I was thinking maybe—"

A metal thud sounded right behind them. Greg turned his head, his eyes growing large as Hank grinned at them from a car twenty feet away.

Chapter Ninety-Nine

CHRIS SLAMMED the car to a stop only twenty feet from the entrance to the hangar. "Run!" he yelled.

But Maeve didn't need the encouragement. She sprinted toward the hangar door with Pop held to her chest as if it was the finish line in a race—the most important race of her life. But even as she pounded down the ground, she knew this was just one leg of the race. There were still miles and miles to go, both literally and figuratively.

Alvie ran next to her, Snap saddled on his back. Pop held on to Maeve's shirt, wrapping it around his small fists, his incredible balance keeping him in place. Chris brought up the rear with Crackle.

Maeve stepped under the overhang of the hangar entrance and automatically felt the temperature drop as the shade offered some relief from the blistering heat. Chris took up position in front of them, his eyes focused on the pickups as they kicked up dust racing toward them. "Someone get that door open!"

Maeve swung Pop around to her back, then held out her

arms, and Alvie leapt into them. She stepped up to the keyboard.

Alvie's fingers flew over the keypad, inputting the seven-digit code, and Maeve thanked God for Alvie's incredible memory. The door popped open. Maeve swung Alvie down behind her, stepping to the door's opening. "Got it."

Maeve nudged the door open, her weapon back in her hand as she scanned the room. There was no movement, no sign of life.

"Clear," she said, stepping in, holding the door open for Alvie and Chris. They hustled in and Chris stopped dead. "Holy crap."

Maeve gaped. "That's one way to put it."

While there was no sign of movement there *was* one thing in the hangar: a giant spaceship.

The black ship was shaped like a boomerang and each stretch of wing was easily one hundred feet long. Small windows lined the sides.

"You think that thing's operational?" Chris asked.

"You want to try and fly it?"

"Maybe some other time." He turned to Alvie. "Can you fly that?"

Alvie shook his head.

"Okay, enough with spaceships, let's find some technology we can count on, like an elevator leading down," Maeve said.

"Hold on," Chris said, cramming a pipe through the long handle of the door.

Maeve raised her eyebrows.

"What?" Chris asked.

"This is a multibillion-dollar facility, and you just locked a door with a twenty-dollar piece of tubing.

Chris grinned. "Sometimes the old ways are the best ways."

Outside came the unmistakable sound of one of the pickups coming to a screeching halt. Chris grabbed Maeve's arm. "Let's find the way down."

They sprinted across the large space. But even in that mad dash, she couldn't help but take in the spaceship and wonder which race of the aliens they had seen had created it. At the same time, most of the aliens seemed so primitive, little more than animals. Of course, they'd been locked up for their whole lives. Humans raised under such conditions wouldn't be able to drive a car or work a computer either.

But she forced her curiosity aside and focused on the more immediate issue. "There." She pointed to the undeniable outline of an elevator. The silence was loud until the door rattled behind them. And then gunshots sounded as whoever was out there tried to blast their way in.

Chris stabbed at the control panel, but nothing happened. "It must have been shut down."

The door bucked as someone kicked it with a curse. The door was not going to keep them out for long.

"Stairs?" Maeve asked, already moving toward the door to the left of the elevator.

"Yup," Chris said, running after her.

Maeve grabbed the door handle as Chris lined up next to the door. He nodded at Maeve and she yanked it open. Inside, it was extremely dark. Only the emergency lights running along the stairs provided any illumination, and that only extended about two feet up from the ground.

"Well, this sucks. All right, let's go into the creepy creepy stairwell toward the mythical tunnel that we hope still exists." Chris stepped into the dark.

Alvie followed him in, stopping first to pat Crackle's leg as he passed.

The door on the other side of the hangar rattled again, and then there was a loud explosion and the door blew off and into the hangar. Maeve quickly stepped into the stairwell, closing the door behind her and entombing them in the darkness.

Weapon at the ready, she let out a shaky breath and followed the rest of the group down the stairs, promising herself that if she survived this, she was never again going into any buildings that had more than one floor.

Chapter One Hundred

KEEPING his eyes focused on Hank on the car only twenty feet behind them, Greg yelled. "Go, go, go!"

Leslie quickly turned on the engine, peeling away from the curb. Behind them, Hank leapt from the car and raced along the ground toward them, moving incredibly fast. Greg had theorized that given open ground, Hank would have the speed of a cheetah. He'd never attempted to validate it because the idea of Hank being given space to run was too terrifying to contemplate. But as Hank raced after them, Greg could only conclude two things: one, he had been right about Hank's speed, and two, Hank running at full speed was indeed completely terrifying.

Hank leapt in the air and landed only ten feet behind them. Greg screamed and Leslie yanked the wheel to the side, swerving down an alley. Going too fast, Hank skidded right by the alley, and Greg sucked in a breath.

"I swear, if Hank or the bomb doesn't kill me, I'm going to die of a heart attack!" he screamed.

Leslie sped down the alley and bolted out the other side, just missing a military truck heading in the opposite direction.

"Shit!" Greg threw his arms over his face as Leslie missed the truck's bumper by inches.

The truck reversed and turned down the alley after them.

Greg groaned, knowing whoever was in the truck was not trying to help them. And behind them, he saw the ever-encroaching specter of Hank.

A shadow moved in his peripheral vision. He squinted at the roofline of the building next to him trying to make out what it was racing along its rooftop. Leslie blasted through the intersection, turning the wheel sharply, and Greg slammed into the side of the car, losing sight of the creature. But then it leapt off the building and his heart all but stopped.

"Leslie?"

"What?" she yelled, her voice tense.

"There's another one."

"Another what?"

Greg couldn't believe what he was about to say. "Hank. There's another Hank."

Leslie's head whipped toward him, her eyes huge before she turned back to the road, gripping the steering wheel even tighter. "God damn it, how many of those things did they make?"

"I'm hoping only three."

The truck behind them picked up speed, and gunfire slammed into the back of the Jeep. Greg yelled and ducked as Leslie swerved down another alley.

"Oh shit."

Greg looked up, and his eyes grew wide. There was a

giant dumpster halfway down the alley. They'd never be able to drive around it. Leslie slammed on the brakes, the front bumper just touching the dumpster.

"Get out!" she barked at him.

Greg fumbled for the door and all but fell out of the car. Leslie was already climbing over the hood of the car. Greg stepped on the bumper, the pain in his thigh making him suck in a breath. Leslie landed on the ground and pulled him along the hood. "I've got you."

Behind them, the truck turned into the alley and then slammed on its brakes. Leslie grabbed Greg's arm and pulled him away.

Greg sprinted next to Leslie, ignoring the pain throbbing through his leg. Doors slammed behind him as the soldiers began to give chase.

Oh, come on.

A screech sounded and then a man screamed, followed by gunfire. Greg glanced back, nearly tripping over his own feet. Hank had one of the soldiers impaled on his hand and was using him as a shield as he battled the other soldier. Hank reached out with his other hand and swiped his talons across the soldier's midsection and then his neck. The soldier impaled on his arm, who by some miracle was still alive, grabbed the grenade off his belt and pulled the pin.

The explosion shook the alley, causing windows to shatter.

"Only one left," Leslie said.

Greg nodded, not having any breath to speak.

A shadow crossed over them and jumped down from a landing on yet another dumpster. Leslie pushed Greg behind her and opened fire. But the bullets did no damage to Hank.

And then she pulled the trigger and nothing happened.

"I'm out," she said quietly.

Greg stared at Hank, who watched them, tilting his head.

"We're dead."

Chapter One Hundred One

THE STAIRWELL WAS BLACK, with only the dim emergency lights piercing the darkness. Maeve couldn't stop shaking. Being on the run from humans and aliens in broad daylight was terrifying. She didn't even have a word for what it was while in a pitch-black stairwell.

Maeve made her way down the stairs as quickly as she could. Alvie was quiet next to her, which gave her some sense of comfort. And she wasn't seeing any signs that the aliens had made it to this side of the base. So they just needed to avoid the humans at the top of the staircase.

"You okay?" Chris asked as they hurried down the stairs.

"Um, no?" she said.

"Well, only twenty more flights or so to go."

"Oh, good. We're practically there."

"That's the spirit."

Maeve smiled in spite of her terror. Thank God Chris was with her. She knew he took his job seriously but he had such an easygoing nature and confidence that it made even terrifying situations like this one a little easier to bear.

"You okay, little buddy?" Chris asked of Alvie, who was in between them.

Alvie nodded.

She still couldn't believe all Alvie had been through. He had spent his entire life in a lab, and now he'd been forced out into the world in the worst way possible. And yet, he seemed to be coping. He had more reserves in him than she realized, and she was so grateful for that.

Alvie stopped, and Maeve bumped into him. She grabbed his shoulder to keep the both of them from pitching forward. "What's wrong?"

An image of the door leading to the stairwell popped into her mind a split second before Alvie grabbed her hand, hurrying forward.

"We need to go faster," Maeve said, hurrying along with Alvie.

Chris picked up the pace. "Why?"

Maeve didn't answer because she didn't need to. The door opening at the top of the stairwell spoke for her.

"Oh Dr. Leaaanderrr," a voice sang above them.

"Who the hell is that?" Maeve asked in a whisper.

"Henning," Chris growled. "We need to go faster." Now they were all but sprinting down the stairs.

But even with the blood pounding in her ears, Maeve heard something hit the stairs a flight below them and start to roll down the steps.

"Look out!" Chris yelled seconds before the grenade exploded.

Chapter One Hundred Two

HANK DROPPED OFF THE DUMPSTER, disappearing from view. But neither Leslie nor Greg gave any thought to trying to sprint forward. Hank was still there, and Greg got the distinct impression he was enjoying the anticipation.

Greg backed up, Leslie doing the same next to him. "Uh, Leslie, you've got a plan, right?"

"Well, I'm out of ammo. Our escape route is cut off, and I'm pretty sure any hand-to-hand combat will result in both of us getting sliced to death. So no, Greg, nothing's really coming to mind."

Greg laughed nervously. "So we're relying on divine intervention?"

"Yup. So start praying."

Greg stared at Leslie and then down the long alley. He heard Hank's nails on the concrete before he saw him. Too soon, he stood walking slowly down the alley, saliva dripping from his mouth. Hank was in no rush. He looked like he was actually savoring the moment.

Leslie reached over and squeezed Greg's hand. "You're a good man, Greg. And I have been lucky to know you."

"Right back at you—except for the man part. You're a good woman. A great woman, an amazing—"

"Shut up, Greg."

"Good idea."

But Greg wanted to look Leslie in the eyes and tell her how truly amazing he thought she was. How grateful he was to know her. But at the precise moment, Hank charged, and Greg could do nothing but scramble back, praying for a miracle.

Chapter One Hundred Three

THE FORCE of the blast blew Maeve off her feet. Her head smacked into the wall. She thought she might have blacked out for a minute, although the complete darkness of the stairwell made it hard to be sure.

She opened her eyes to see Crackle on her chest, his hand on Maeve's face. Alvie knelt down next to her.

"I'm okay," she said as she started to sit up. Her head swam. Both her neck and the back of her head ached. "Chris?"

"Here," he groaned. "God, that sucked." The sound of footsteps pounding down the stairs echoed through the space.

Maeve scrambled to her feet and cautiously made her way toward him. He reached out for her hand. "Let's go."

"Alvie," she called, but he was already moving ahead of them.

"Where did the grenade—" But her words died away as the next landing came into view. Or more accurately, where

389

the next landing should have been. A gaping hole stretched across it now.

"Ah, shit," Chris said. Alvie moved forward and with a quick run, leapt across the chasm.

Maeve shook her head. "I don't think I can do that."

"We'll climb the rubble. You see that ledge? We'll use that."

Maeve nodded. "Okay. Let's—" Gunfire crashed into the landing next to her.

"Get behind me!" Chris yelled as he opened fire. "Go across Maeve. Now!"

Swinging Crackle around to her back, Maeve ran to the wreckage. She lowered Crackle to the ground. "Go to Alvie." Crackle scampered across quickly. Maeve placed a foot on the bar and it shook. "Oh, come on," she groaned.

She stepped on it and it held. Heart in her throat, she inched along the beam, trying to lean against the wall for extra support, her arms out. Behind her, Chris kept up a barrage of gunfire, keeping Henning and whoever he had brought with him away.

"I'm over," Maeve yelled as soon as she touched down on the other side. "Alvie, take Pop and Crackle and go."

He stared at her, shaking his head.

"Go, Alvie. Get them out of here." With one last look, he turned and fled down the stairwell.

Maeve pulled her weapon into her shoulder. "Come on, Chris." She opened fire.

Chris wasted no time. He sprinted for the beam and gingerly made his way across the top.

"Keep shooting!" he yelled as he landed on the other side, Snap wrapped around his neck. He knelt down. Snap jumped off and ran for Maeve, hiding behind her legs.

Chris shoved at the beam, moving it inches. Slowly it headed for the hole and then dropped.

"Let's go." Chris grabbed Maeve's hand with one hand and scooped Snap up with the other. In darkness, they fled down into the stairwell after Alvie.

Chapter One Hundred Four

LESLIE AND GREG sprinted down the alley. The sound of Hank grew closer and closer behind them, but Greg didn't turn to look—his imagination was terrifying him enough, no need to have that image confirmed. Ahead was the Jeep blocking the way. And the dumpster.

"God damn it." Leslie jerked to a stop in front of the dumpster and whirled around. Greg came to a stop next to her.

From the corner of his eye he saw a shadow swooping down.

Oh god, there's another one.

He pushed Leslie down, throwing himself on top of her as Hank lunged. Talons ripped Greg's shirt and he tensed, waiting for the pain. But then Hank was gone, shredding Greg's shirt as he flew into the air.

Greg looked up in astonishment as Hank scrambled, arms and legs moving as he was carried off. Greg stared at the being holding him, terror running through him even as he acknowledged that the being had saved their lives. Large wings as black as night extended from its body. It held Hank in his arms securely as Hank struggled. At first Greg couldn't see his face, but then it turned and Greg caught a glimpse of a dark humanoid face with red eyes. And then before Leslie or Greg could say anything, it ripped Hank in two, dropping him to the ground before flying off.

Leslie sat up slowly, her mouth hanging open. "What the hell was that?"

Greg didn't look at her, his attention still focused on the creature, which was now no more than a dark blur in the sky. "I think it's Mothman."

"What are you talking about? I swear to god, Greg, if that's a reference to another one of your video game characters, I will—"

"No, Mothman. He was a giant creature with wings that supposedly terrified residents of West Virginia for a few decades. Humanoid in appearance except for its giant wings. There were even isolated cases of it being seen at NASA's Johnson Space Center."

"You're kidding me."

Greg gave a nervous laugh. "Well, while normally that would be possible, the fact that we just saw a six-foot-tall bat-man fly off with Hank would suggest I'm not."

"So what the hell is it?"

"I'm going to go with alien, based purely on every other thing we've seen."

Leslie glared at him.

"Okay, I'm guessing he's some sort of hybridization gone wrong or gone right, depending on what the end goal was."

"But it looked part human. I mean, its face—it looked *really* human."

Greg pictured the being that had saved their lives. It was

humanoid in appearance but those wings... Greg was horrified.

They merged alien and human DNA.

"So did it save us on purpose? Or was it just after Hank?"

Greg looked over at Leslie and brought himself back to the conversation. "I don't know."

"What the hell is wrong with these people?" Leslie said through gritted teeth. "They combined human DNA with some bat thing? Who the hell does that? Why the hell would they do that?"

"Well, the military has a long history of looking for every possible threat and then running off and creating it."

"What are you talking about?"

Greg waved his hand toward the southwest and the Nevada testing site. "The United States has tested over a thousand bombs to prepare should any other country set off a bomb. I mean, they seemed to bomb things just cause they could. They set off one bomb in the atmosphere not far from Hawaii just to see what the signs would be if the Russians did the same thing. There was even a plan to bomb the dark side of the moon."

"What? Why?"

"To demonstrate our military might. Basically, in our past, the military acts like a bunch of Neanderthals running around with big clubs, bashing everything in sight."

"But the human toll—"

"Not a factor. We tend to play with technology long before we fully understand it and more importantly, before we understand the harm it can cause."

"So you think these creatures are the military waving a big stick?"

"I think these creatures are evidence that the military is terrified of something."

Chapter One Hundred Five

EVEN AS THEY raced down the stairs, Chris took a little solace in the grenade toss. Henning had miscalculated throwing it. It would slow him and his men down as well as they tried to get across the destroyed stairs.

Above them, Chris could hear footsteps pounding down the steps after them. Chris picked up his pace but Alvie bounded ahead of him anyway. Chris had worried the little guy wouldn't have been able to keep up with his smaller legs. But Alvie didn't bother using every step. He went down two or three steps at a time.

Maeve was behind him and Chris stopped. "Give me Pop."

"But—"

"No time. Hand him over."

Maeve did, and Chris quickly pulled him into his chest; Crackle was still perched on his back. Maeve had taken Pop from Alvie as soon as they caught up with him. The extra thirty pounds made little difference to him, but he was sure Maeve was reaching her physical breaking point.

"Move, Maeve. Move."

Maeve scampered down the stairs ahead of him. They were at least ten flights down. Chris knew they had to reach the tunnels soon.

If they actually exist.

But he didn't entertain that thought for long. Because if this stairwell simply led to a basement or boiler room, they were dead. Ahead, Alvie led out a small cry.

"He's at the bottom," Maeve whispered.

A few seconds later, they reached the landing next to Alvie. Maeve quickly grabbed the twins from Chris as he reached for the door. The footsteps on the stairs continued toward them.

Chris reached for the handle and tugged but it wouldn't budge.

"Is it locked?" Maeve asked.

"I don't think so. I think it's stuck," Chris said as he pulled on the door. "You guys get back."

"We're coming, Chris," Henning sang down the stairwell. "You should have killed me when you had the chance."

"Don't worry. I can take care of that now," Chris yelled.

Henning laughed. "It's too late now, because you see, I brought some friends." And the rapidly approaching footprints accentuated his words.

Chris knew they were only a few flights away. He pulled out his shotgun and aimed to the left of the handle and pulled the trigger.

The handle and part of the frame disappeared. Chris reached into the hole, grabbing onto the jagged wood, still warm from the shot, and yanked. The door flew open.

"Go!" Chris yelled.

Maeve ran through the opening with the triplets and

Alvie. Chris yanked a grenade off his waist, waiting at the doorway for Henning and his friends. When they were a flight away, he ripped out the pin. "I brought some friends too," Chris yelled, tossing the grenade up the stairs.

Chapter One Hundred Six

MARTIN GRITTED his teeth as he watched the Jeep speed across the tarmac. They were actually escaping. His men trailed behind the Jeep, but Martin's anger only grew hotter at the sight of them.

They're letting them get away. Idiots.

He stared at the screen as Dr. Leander vaulted from the car for the hangar and then watched in disbelief as she propped Subject #1 up so he could input the code. All that wasted potential. Cooperation between humans and an alien species.

But then he paused, tilting his head to the side as Dr. Leander and company disappeared into the hangar. Perhaps it wasn't entirely wasted. Subject #1 did show aggression, at least in defense of himself and his human friends.

Maybe I've been looking at this wrong. Maybe we need some who will fight with us, not just for us.

Here he'd been trying to build an alien race, when the first successful cloning subject could hold the answer. He just needed to convince the race that the human race needed saving and that they needed to do it.

Martin gave a small laugh. *Maybe that's the direction we should be heading.* His gaze strayed to where a Blue Boy had grabbed a man in camouflage and slammed him headfirst into the pavement.

Of course, they all show a little promise, don't they?

Martin sat back, content. This experiment had provided him with more than he'd ever believed possible. But even he could see it was time to end it. Leander and company escaping through the old tunnels indicated a flaw in the base's security system. And as much as Martin was enjoying watching what these subjects could do, he would not risk releasing them on the general population. It was time to wrap things up.

Leander and company heading into the tunnels meant he'd have them all within his control within an hour at most. All the other aliens he needed had already been evacuated. And the rest, well, he still had the recipe for them if, after reviewing the recordings, he deemed them necessary.

Looks like my job here is almost done.

Martin picked up his phone, dialing quickly.

"Delta Station."

"This is Director Drummond, ID Alpha Omega Two Three Tango Foxtrot."

"Identity confirmed, Director."

"The bomb is a go. The bomb is a go. I repeat, the bomb is a go."

"Sir, we have thirty-two more minutes before detonation."

Martin watched his security force enter the old hangar. "Negative, Command. The situation has changed. The bombing will commence immediately."

"Yes, sir."

Martin disconnected the call, already dismissing everything that had happened in the last twenty-four hours and all the lives that were about to be lost. Instead, he focused on the future and where the A.L.I.V.E. Project would next head. He began to hum as he wrote up his ideas.

Chapter One Hundred Seven

LESLIE AND GREG made their way to the pickup that had chased them. Greg carefully avoided looking at the remains of either of the men. Of course, for one of them, that was a little more difficult as his remains were spread all over the place.

Greg got into the passenger seat and tried not to grimace as Leslie put on the windshield wipers to remove some of the blood and tissue.

"Okay," Greg said, feeling like he'd aged a hundred years. His mind could barely take in everything that had happened. "What now?"

"Well, let's see if we can follow Chris and Maeve. If not, let's find a closer tunnel entrance."

"Okay. Sounds good," Greg said although at this point he would agree to anything that Leslie said. His mind was slowly turning to mush.

"Turn on the radio," Leslie said, nodding to the radio between the seats as she reversed out of the alley. "Let's see what's going on."

Greg grabbed the radio, fumbling with the knobs for a minute before he figured out how to turn it on.

"—repeat. Evacuate the base immediately or find deep shelter. The bombing will commence in five minutes."

Leslie slammed on the brakes and stared at Greg.

"But—but Chris said they weren't going to bomb it for another forty minutes."

"Something happened. Something changed. Where's the next closest entrance to the tunnels?"

He scrambled to remember what Maeve said while picturing a map of the base. "Other side of the base. We can't make it in time, can we?"

"Not if we run into any interference. So we just need to find a place to lay low until—"

"Leslie, when this hits, it will be the force of, well, you know, a bomb. Even if we somehow survive that, the whole place will be radioactive. Granted, within an hour, the air should be clear, but that's still an hour of not breathing in the air. Pretty sure I can't hold my breath for that long."

Leslie slumped down in her seat. "So this is it?"

Greg glanced over at her. "I think it might be."

Behind her, he could see the old runway, the place where the U-2 spy plane had first launched. Where the stealth bomber had launched. To the southwest, they tested atomic bombs. At least he was going in the middle of a place with an incredible history.

All the aliens he had seen in the last twenty-four hours flew threw his mind, ending with an image of Alvie. He pictured Alvie leaning into him when they left.

Hangar 37. Greg jolted.

"Greg?" Leslie asked.

Greg put up a hand, straining to remember. Hangar 37 and something else. What was it? 31827?

"I think we need to go to Hangar 37."

"37? Why?"

"Do you know where it is?"

"Yeah, the southern part of the base, it's not that far from here." Leslie hit the gas, looking at Greg from the corner of her eye. "Why are we going there?"

"Because I think Alvie may have told me a way to save us."

Chapter One Hundred Eight

MAEVE SPRINTED FROM THE STAIRWELL. There was a set of propane tanks next to the entrance along with a handful of crates. But Maeve didn't even think of stopping. They needed to put as much distance between themselves and their pursuers.

Ahead of her was a giant cavern carved out of the rock. The walls were sheared smooth, and there was a train track running through the side of the cavern. Maeve stared at it in shock even as she sprinted forward.

I guess the rumors about the supersonic train are true. I can't believe it's real—just like every other thing I've seen today, she thought.

Unfortunately, there didn't seem to be any train service today. But she did spy a utility truck over by the side of the tracks.

"Alvie, the truck!" she yelled.

Maeve sprinted for the yellow pickup with blue stripes and lights along the roof. She skidded to a stop at the driver's side door and nearly cried with joy when it opened easily. And hanging from the ignition were the keys.

Oh, thank you, Jesus.

Maeve climbed into the driver's seat and turned it on as Alvie scrambled in next to her. Snap, Crackle, and Pop leapt into the truck as well. All four of them huddled together on the floor of the passenger side.

An explosion at the stairwell caused her heart to leap. *Chris.* Her head whipped back toward the stairwell. He was sprinting towards them.

"Come on, Chris!" Maeve yelled, putting the truck in gear.

Gunfire rang out from the destroyed stairwell. Apparently someone had survived.

Maeve stomped on the gas pedal and the truck roared to life. She pulled it to a stop and Chris ran around the back. Chris let off a burst of gunfire, aiming for the propane tanks. They exploded, and Chris dove into the passenger seat. "Go, go, go!"

Maeve needed no encouragement. She slammed down on the accelerator. The back of the truck fishtailed as she peeled out.

In the rearview mirror, she saw Henning crawl from behind the wreckage of the stairwell, his radio to his mouth. "Chris!"

He glanced behind them.

"Is he doing what I think he's doing?"

Chris nodded. "He's signaling someone ahead of us. We're not out yet."

Chapter One Hundred Nine

MAEVE KNEW UNDENIABLY that there was an armed force waiting for them ahead. But she also knew that behind Henning and his men was an atomic explosion. So she kept her foot on the gas.

"Damn it." From the passenger seat, Chris tossed the radio that had been on the passenger seat in the back. "Dead."

Up ahead, she could see the tunnel split into two.

"What's the closest base?"

"Nellis Air Force Range borders the base."

"I don't think I want to be that close."

"There's Creech, but I think we should head to Edwards. I know some people stationed there."

"How far away is that?"

"About two hundred seventy miles."

Maeve glanced at the gas tank—it was close to full. "Okay." They rode in tense silence. Alvie crawled down to the floor of the truck and pulled the triplets into his lap.

"That's got to be weird," Chris said quietly.

"What?"

"Hugging cloned versions of yourself. I mean, that's weird, right?"

"It's weird. But … I don't know. I mean, clones are basically identical twins. In this case, for Alvie, there's just a bit of an age difference."

"They are cute."

"Yeah. Alvie looked almost identical to them when he was little."

Chris frowned. "I still don't get that. He's a clone. Shouldn't they *be* identical to him?"

Maeve shook her head. "They have the same genetic makeup, but the environment can still play a role. These three could have been impregnated in one host or three. Either way, it wasn't the same host that Alvie had, which means there will be some differences. And they haven't been raised like Alvie. His first year he had my mom and Greta. I don't think these guys had that kindness."

"How do you think it will affect them?"

Maeve sighed. "I don't know. But maybe Alvie will be able to soothe whatever harm this last year has done to them."

And I really hope he has the chance to do that.

"You think we're going to make it?" Chris asked.

And Maeve knew he wasn't looking for reassurance. He knew what lay ahead of them—it was not going to be any easier than what was behind them. He was asking to see whether or not she really understood that after everything they had been through, that Alvie may never have the chance to make up for whatever horrors were inflicted on the triplets.

So Maeve didn't answer because she didn't want to. Because right now she had to hope. Hope that all they had gone through to survive hadn't been for naught. Hope that as they raced down these tunnels created decades ago by members of the government who wanted to keep certain aspects of America's research private, that they were racing toward safety.

And not racing toward their deaths.

Chapter One Hundred Ten

"DO YOU SEE IT?" Leslie yelled to be heard over the wind.

"Uh ... " Greg scanned the road ahead, looking for any sign of the hangar.

"There!" He pointed to a new hangar, the number 37 clearly visible above the doors. Greg frowned. Why would Alvie send them to a new hangar? All the new hangars were cut off from the tunnels.

Leslie stomped on the gas, speeding down the last few feet before slamming on the brakes. "Time."

Greg fumbled for the door handle. "About five minutes."

"Then move it." She vaulted from the car.

Greg hobbled after her, ignoring the ache in his leg. Leslie tried the door, but it was locked. She reared back and kicked it open. Greg followed her inside and nearly collided with her. She had stopped short just inside the doorway.

"Leslie? What's wrong?"

"Do you know what that is?"

Greg looked at the plane that took up most of the

hangar, his hope fading away. "A plane? Like dozens of other planes on this base?"

Leslie shook her head, a smile spreading across her face. "There is no other plane on this base like *that* one. Oh, Alvie, I love you."

Greg stared at the plane. It was a large jet that look no different than a million other planes he'd seen at airports. "Les?"

"It's a smaller prototype of the doomsday plane. Now go get the door open. I'm going to open up the elevator."

"What's a—" But Leslie was already running across the hangar and ducking under the wing of the plane.

For the first time, Greg noticed the large elevator doors on the opposite wall. He hobbled over to what looked like a door in the silver metal. There was a keypad next to it.

"Um, open the door. How do I open the door?" He started punching numbers into the keypad, but the light glowed red at him.

"Oh, come on," he groaned. 31827 flashed through his mind and he quickly punched it in. The light glowed green and the door cracked open and then began to lower to the ground. "Yes!"

Leslie ran back toward him, the elevator doors opening behind her. "Get in."

Greg scrambled up the ramp. Leslie followed behind him and hit some button at the top of the ramp before disappearing into the cockpit. Greg followed her, grimacing as he whacked his leg into a counter as he stepped into the fuselage. A counter ran along the right side of the plane and was loaded with electronic equipment. He could spy what looked like a kitchen toward the back and what he thought was maybe a bedroom. In front of him were a dozen large leather chairs. He frowned. What the hell kind of plane was this?

He leaned against the doorway of the cockpit. "Um, any particular reason you're so excited about this plane?"

Leslie was already sitting in the pilot's chair, flipping switches. "You mean there's something I know that you don't?"

Greg felt red seep into his cheeks. "So it appears."

"It's a doomsday plane—to be used by the President and members of congress in the event of a nuclear attack."

"A nuclear attack?"

Leslie nodded. "It's got an electromagnetic pulse shield as well as thermo-radiation shields. It's basically a flying bomb shelter."

"So you know how to fly this thing?"

"Fly? No. But I'm pretty sure I can figure out how to drive it. Take a seat."

Greg slumped into the co-pilot's seat as the bird came to life. It jolted, and Greg's panicked eyes turned to Leslie.

"It's okay. I just released the brakes."

"Oh," Greg said as he felt the plane begin to move. "Is it going to fit in that elevator?"

Leslie nodded, not sparing him a look. "Yeah. It was made for large-sized aircraft. I'm guessing they tested them underground or maybe even moved them from base to base. I'm going to send us as far down as we can go to escape the bomb's impact. What's our time?"

"Uh," Greg looked at his watch. "A minute." He cringed as one of the wings scraped the side of the elevator. But a few seconds later they were safely within.

Leslie bolted from her seat. "Get into the fuselage and close the cockpit door behind you."

"Why—"

But Leslie was already gone. He heard the outer door open. Seconds later, the elevator doors closed and they began to descend. Greg hobbled into the fuselage, closing the cockpit door. As he did, he realized that Leslie had lowered coverings over the windows along the fuselage.

That's why she wanted us in here.

He strapped himself into one of the big leather seats, realizing this was the first time he'd ever been in a first-class chair.

Better late than never, I guess.

Leslie ran back up the ramp and closed it. She strapped herself in next to him. "Time?"

He glanced at his watch. "Thirty seconds."

Leslie took his hand. "It's been a pleasure serving with you."

Greg squeezed her hand back. "Thank you for everything. For protecting me."

She gave a small laugh. "Given our current predicament, I'm not sure I deserve thanks."

"Well, I'm pretty sure I would have been dead a long time ago if you hadn't come back for me." He paused. "Why *did* you come back for me?"

She looked away. "I just needed to know you were safe."

"See? Who else would have come back for little old me?"

"I'm guessing quite a few people, if you let them get to know you."

"Maybe." He glanced at his watch. "Ten seconds."

Leslie grabbed the collar of his shirt and pulled him into her, her mouth on his. Greg's heart raced, and he wrapped his hand around the back of her head. She broke away first, leaning her forehead against his.

"Just in case this is the end," she whispered.

"Well, that's a pretty good way to go." He glanced at his watch. 3-2-1. He wrapped his arms around Leslie as the deadline passed. And then the ground shook, like an earthquake. Everything unsecured in the plane crashed to the ground, and the ground itself undulated like a wave.

Greg held Leslie tighter.

Good-bye.

Chapter One Hundred Eleven

A RUMBLE SOUNDED from behind them and then grew. Maeve swerved and then quickly regained control. "What the—" But the sentiment died in her throat. The bomb. They had set off the bomb early.

Her chest ached, picturing Greg and Leslie. Tears sprang to her eyes and she gripped the steering wheel.

"God damn it!"

Chris slapped the dashboard with his palm. "Fuck!"

Alvie hugged the triplets as they let out a wail.

No one said anything else. What was there to say? The United States Government had just killed dozens of their employees to cover up a secret they'd been hiding for decades.

Chris reached over and took Maeve's hand, squeezing it. She clasped it tightly, needing to know that someone else felt the injustice and the grief of the moment. They drove like that for another twenty minutes, no one saying a word. The emotions in the cab of the truck spoke for them—fear, exhaustion, anxiety, worry, and grief.

A light blinked up ahead in the distance. Maeve pulled her hand from Chris's and put it back on the steering wheel. She squinted. "What is—"

Gunfire raked the front of the truck. Yanking the wheel to the side with a yell, she felt the truck drop as one of the front tires, or maybe both, were punctured.

Chris reached down and grabbed all the little ones as Maeve hit the railway tracks. The truck went airborne and then with an ear-shattering crash, slammed onto its side.

Chapter One Hundred Twelve

CHRIS GROANED as the seat belt cut into his ribs, but at least it kept him from dropping onto Maeve, who lay still in the driver's seat, her head against the window. Alvie was next to Maeve, his hand on her face, squeaking anxiously.

Slowly, Chris released the triplets, who were squirming in his arms. He punched the seat belt. "Alvie, get them out of here. I'll get Maeve."

With one last look at Maeve, Alvie clambered up the dashboard, each of the triplets following in his wake through the passenger door window.

With shaking hands, Chris undid Maeve's seat belt. She let out a groan, and Chris felt relief pour through him. "That's a good girl. Time to wake up, Sleeping Beauty."

Maeve's eyelids flickered open. It took her a moment to focus on him. "Chris?"

"Hey there. Time to go." Gently, he pulled her up. There was a gash on the side of her head. Gunfire raked the underside of the truck.

Shit. Chris pushed Maeve against the back of the seat so

she was leaning against it. Then he turned and kicked out the windshield.

He looked into Maeve's eyes. "I need you to move quickly. Can you do that?"

Her eyes cleared. "Alvie. The triplets."

"They're out," he said, hoping that they hadn't been caught in the gunfire. "Now it's our turn."

With a grimace, she nodded. "Let's go."

Chris crouched at the edge of the dashboard, his weapon ready. He and Maeve ducked out of the windshield frame. The hood of the truck blocked the movement from the shooters, who were still aiming at the underside of the truck.

They ducked around the back of the truck. Alvie and the triplets looked up at them with big eyes. Maeve dropped to their side, frantically running a hand over each of them. "Are you all right?"

Alvie stared into her eyes, and Maeve nodded back. "Good." She turned to Chris. "Plan?"

And once again, she impressed the hell out of him. She'd been through more combat than most soldiers saw in a lifetime and here she was, still focused.

The gunfire on the truck quieted. "Whoever is ahead of us is undeniably going to make their way toward us. Let's make for that wall there." He nodded toward a cement wall about twenty feet away.

Maeve shook her head. "No chance."

"Maeve, there's no other—"

"Chris, that's where they store the fuel—gas and propane. Didn't you see those stations as we drove by? We'd be sitting next to a bomb."

"Oh. Right. Well, let's not do that, then." He looked around.

Alvie pointed to a spot farther down the track, away from where they needed to go. It was a series of crates.

"Works for me," Chris said. He popped his head out and gunfire forced him back. "Small problem."

"What?"

"They're already here."

Chapter One Hundred Thirteen

MAEVE LOOKED at the four aliens in her charge in desperation. This couldn't be it. They couldn't die here so close to freedom, not after everything. She glanced around wildly.

There has to be something.

Her eyes lit on the fuel depot. She whirled back to Chris. "You have any grenades left?"

"One. Why?"

She nudged her chin in the direction of the gunmen. "How far away are they?"

"Maybe fifty feet?"

"How long until they're in range of the fuel depot?"

Chris grinned, pulling the last grenade from his belt. "Any second. Get ready."

Maeve turned to Alvie. "Give us Pop and Crackle. We need to run."

Pop leapt into her arms as Crackle climbed onto Chris's back. She hugged Pop quickly, running a hand over Crackle's back. "Hold on tight, guys. You ready, Alvie?"

Alvie nodded, Snap in his arms.

Chris ducked his head out and yanked it back in. "Here we go." He nodded at Maeve, then pulled the pin. She crouched, ready to go. Chris stood up and flung the grenade for all he was worth. And his aim proved true.

The blast shook the tunnel. Maeve sprinted for the crates, Alvie next to her and Chris right behind. Gunfire erupted when they were only ten feet away from the crates, but the gunmen were too far back to reach them. Maeve ducked around the crates, sliding to the ground.

Alvie rolled in next to her and Chris, the least elegant, crashed to the ground, careful to keep from crushing Crackle. He looked up at her with a grin. "Well, so far so good."

Maeve laughed despite the fear racing through her. "Only you would think that. Okay, what's next?"

Chris peeked out and pulled back in. "Most of their guys are down, but there are three still standing holding their position."

Maeve glanced back the way they came. "Do we go back?"

Chris squinted. "I don't— Oh shit."

Maeve looked back down the tunnel. Two lights were growing brighter with each passing breath. And the two lights could only be one thing—a car.

She looked at Chris. He stared into her eyes and slowly shook his head. And she heard the words as if he had said them out loud.

We're trapped.

Chapter One Hundred Fourteen

CHRIS TRIED NOT to let Maeve see how the sight of those headlights terrified him. But that terror wasn't for him—it was for Maeve, Alvie, the triplets. None of them deserved this. Chris had signed up to be a soldier. He had signed up for the risks. Maeve had only been trying to give Alvie the best life possible. And the triplets and Alvie hadn't had any choice at all: the government had brought them into existence. And now they were planning on snuffing them out without anyone being the wiser.

A steely calm settled over Chris. He turned to Maeve. "How much ammunition do you have left?"

She released the magazine and then slammed it back in. "I've got one magazine left and ten in this clip."

He nodded. "Okay. I have about the same. So make sure every shot counts. Every shot should be a kill shot."

Maeve grabbed his arm. "Chris?"

"*Every* shot, Maeve. They don't get to take us or them without one hell of a fight, got it?"

She nodded, determination replacing the fear in her eyes. "Got it."

"I'll take the incoming truck; you keep our other new friends busy."

She nodded, taking position on the other side of the crate. She took a deep breath. And Chris wanted nothing more than to tell her it would be okay. To tell her that she was brave and incredible and that she was the most amazing woman he had ever met. But this wasn't a romance novel. This was real life. And if they had any chance of making it, he needed them both to keep their head in the game.

Chris looked down at Alvie. "I'm glad I got to know you, Alvie. You deserved better than this."

Alvie reached up and touched Chris's cheek. A feeling of love wafted over Chris, making him gasp. Gently, he removed Alvie's hand. "Thank you."

Then he turned, more resolved than ever to give each of them a shot at making it out alive.

Chapter One Hundred Fifteen

MAEVE WAITED, alternating between complete terror and overwhelming anger that this was happening. She heard the squeal of brakes down the tunnel and tensed.

She glanced at Chris and he nodded at her with a smile. "You've got this."

She stared into his eyes, knowing it was probably going to be the last time she ever did so, and forced herself to turn away, bracing the gun with one arm as she aimed down the tunnel.

Behind her, Chris pulled the trigger. And it was like everything slowed down and sped up at the same time. Bullet after bullet slammed into the crates covering them, a few chewed up the ground near Maeve, forcing her back. But she kept shooting. She hit one man in the chest and forced another to take cover. The third man ran for their truck and Maeve got him in the thigh before shooting him in the chest.

And she felt no guilt.

Then six more men appeared from the tunnel behind them.

No, Maeve moaned inwardly even while she ejected her empty magazine and popped in a fresh one.

Chris let out a yell. Maeve whirled around and saw the blood pooling at Chris's side. She scrambled over to him, pulling him back behind the crate. She stepped over him and aimed for the gunman closest. She caught him in the shoulder.

But there were five more men behind him.

And seven on the other side.

The impossibility of their situation threatened to choke her, but she shoved it aside. She heard gunfire behind her, but she could only focus on one side at a time. She just aimed for man after man until her weapon was empty.

Then she ducked back behind the crate. "I'm out."

Chris grabbed her hand. "You did great."

Tears sprang to her eyes. "You too."

The gunfire continued to blast beyond them, but Maeve ignored it. She just stared into Chris's eyes and waited for the bullet that had her name on it.

And then everything went quiet, and Maeve realized that of all the bullets that had been spent in the last few seconds, none had hit their crate.

Crazy, irrational hope bloomed in her chest.

A voice boomed down the tunnel. "Dr. Leander? Captain Garrigan? I'm Agent Bileris with the Secret Service. It's all right now. President O'Donnell sent me on behalf of Commander John Forrester."

Maeve's gaze flew to Chris, whose shocked look mirrored her own. And then she smiled and so did Chris. Alvie leapt into her arms and Snap, Crackle, and Pop crawled all over them. Maeve began to laugh until tears ran down her cheeks and she sobbed.

Chapter One Hundred Sixteen

MAEVE SAT with Snap and Pop in her lap in the office of a hangar on Edwards Air Force Base. Alvie sat next to her with Crackle. Chris had been whisked off to the hospital ward. A group of men in black fatigues who had identified themselves as US Secret Service had escorted them from the tunnels to the hangar. Maeve, Alvie, and the triplets had been placed in the office. A medical doctor had come in to see if they needed any help, the woman's eyes growing large at the sight of the aliens. But she'd kept her cool and just asked after injuries.

Maeve had asked for some food and blankets. The doctor had left, promising she'd have them delivered. Fifteen minutes later, they had arrived, delivered by the Secret Service. And now they'd been sitting here for almost two hours. No one had come to speak with them. Maeve thought she should probably get up and demand some answers. But she honestly wasn't sure if she wanted them.

Alvie leaned his head on Maeve's shoulder. Maeve leaned her head on top of his. She could feel his exhaustion.

The triplets were already asleep, their soft breathing the only noise in the room. "Go ahead and sleep. It's okay."

She wasn't sure if it was, but Alvie closed his eyes, leaving Maeve awake to worry about what happened next. A kill order had been put out on Alvie and the triplets, and now they were being held by the government. That could not possibly end well.

She knew she should stay vigilant, but everything that had happened in the last twenty-four hours was catching up with her, and quickly. Before she knew it, her eyelids were closing. She blinked them open a few times, trying to stay awake. But then she gave up the fight. Whatever was going to happen, would happen. Better if she was a little more rested to face it. So she let herself drift off to sleep.

"Um, Dr. Leander?"

The voice cut through Maeve's sleep and she jolted up, disturbing everyone in the process, though Snap and Pop just readjusted in her lap and fell back asleep. Crackle did the same on Alvie's chest, although Alvie stayed awake, carefully watching the agent who'd woken them.

Agent Bileris from the tunnels looked at her from across the room. He was about Maeve's age, with brown hair and blue eyes. He would have been handsome if he smiled. But Maeve had yet to see that expression on the serious agent's face.

"Sorry to disturb you, ma'am, but there's someone who wants to speak with you."

Maeve looked around the room, wondering why he was even asking. "Uh, okay, I guess show them in."

Agent Bileris shook his head. "I'm afraid for security reasons, I can't do that. I'll need to bring you, and only you, to him."

Maeve shook her head. "Absolutely not. I am not leaving them."

Bileris gave her a small smile. "I was told you would say that."

"And who told you that?"

"Captain Garrigan."

Maeve's chest tightened. She hadn't received any word on him since he'd been taken away in the ambulance. "Is he all right?"

"A few stitches, some rest, and he'll be fine. He suggested there may be two people who you would find acceptable to watch them." Bileris reached back and opened the door.

And Greg and Leslie stepped into view.

Maeve gasped, getting to her feet and practically running across the room. "You're alive." Holding the two sleeping aliens with one arm, she wrapped the other around Greg.

Greg hugged her back, careful not to disturb Snap and Pop. "Of course I am. I had the badassiest soldier in the entire military protecting me."

Maeve looked over at Leslie, who smiled down at Snap and Pop. "How are they? How are you?"

"We're okay, I think. You heard about Chris?"

"Yeah, we saw him before we came here. He's fit to be tied. He keeps trying to sneak out of his hospital room and get back here."

Maeve laughed, relief flowing through her. "How did you guys survive? Did you get off the base before the bomb?"

Greg shook his head. "Oh, no. We were there for that."

"Alvie saved us." Leslie looked down at Alvie with an

expression Maeve hadn't seen on her face before—pride. "He sent us to a plane that could withstand the radiation."

"There is such a thing?" Maeve asked.

"So it seems." Greg reached out his hand to Pop. "Hey, this guy's awake. Hey, little man."

Pop looked up at him and touched his cheek. Greg went still then smiled. "Nice job, buddy. That's your first thought transfer."

"What did he show you?"

"All of us," Greg said as Pop climbed out of Maeve's arm and into Greg's.

Bileris cleared his throat, watching them and trying really hard not to look shocked. "Dr. Leander? We need to go."

"Uh, right. Can you two watch these guys? I'm needed to meet with some unknown person," Maeve said.

Leslie nodded. "We've got them."

Maeve looked into her eyes. "No one takes them anywhere without me."

"Maeve, I promise, I won't let anyone take them." Maeve watched her for a moment and then nodded, handing her Snap. And for the first time, she saw the tough soldier soften as she cuddled Snap to her chest. "Hey there, little one," Leslie murmured.

Maeve hid her smile as she turned to Alvie, kneeling down so she could look into his eyes. "I have to go speak with someone. I'll be right back." She hugged him and felt his concern.

But she didn't say anything to ease his concern because it would be a wasted effort. And she had the distinct impression denying the agent's request was not an option. So she kissed Alvie on the forehead and then turned, catching Bileris's amazed expression as he watched the two of them.

But he quickly snapped his focus back to the mission, opening the door for her. "After you."

Taking a deep breath, Maeve stepped out into the large hangar on Edwards Air Force Base. When Bileris and his team had caught up with them in the tunnels, he explained that John had contacted the Secretary of the Air Force, who in turn had contacted the President. The President had then sent Bileris's team down to extract Maeve and any other Area 51 employees. They were too late to stop the bombing, but they had seen Maeve escape through the tunnels and had hurried to help.

From that point on, everything was a bit of a blur. They'd been hustled into a truck, then an elevator, another truck, and then they'd been driven into this hangar and hidden away in the office. Now, Maeve realized there were a dozen armed guards in the hangar, and her trepidation increased. She stopped walking.

"Why are these guards here?"

"To keep you and your friends safe."

"And when you drive me out of here, they're not going to go in and grab Alvie or the triplets?"

"No, ma'am. You have my word."

Maeve crossed her arms over her chest. "Yeah, see, you work for the government, and that same government just tried to kill all of us."

"That was *not* the government I work for. The government I work for protects its people."

"And if that other government shows up here?"

Bileris smiled. "Then *my* government will make them regret it."

Maeve stared into the man's face and then nodded. "Okay."

Agent Bileris led her to a Jeep. Maeve hopped in the passenger seat as Bileris climbed into the driver's seat.

"Can you give me a hint as to who I'm meeting?"

"I'm afraid not. And all contents of this meeting are top secret. No one can know you spoke with him."

Maeve felt her jaw drop open. *It can't be.* Bileris drove them to the other side of the base, pulling in front of a terminal. She glanced out at the runway and saw a large 737 waiting on the runway, the United States seal emblazoned across it.

She began to feel light-headed as Bileris led her inside. It was the waiting area for both pilots and passengers. Rows of chairs, a few TV screens, and two counters were spread across the room. But besides those pieces, the room was empty save for two men in suits standing on either side of a door across from them.

Bileris headed toward the men. They nodded at him and opened the door.

"Good luck, Dr. Leander," Bileris said before gesturing for her to enter. Maeve stepped inside, and the two men in suits inspected her. But Maeve ignored them, her focus entirely on the dark-skinned man who turned away from the window with a smile. He walked over to her, extending his hand. "Dr. Leander. It's a pleasure to meet you."

"You too, Mr. President."

Chapter One Hundred Seventeen

PRESIDENT GRAHAM WILSON gestured to a table and chairs a few feet away. "Why don't we sit?"

"Uh, sure." Maeve took a seat. There was a tray of food and some water bottles on the table over by the window.

"Would you like anything?" he asked.

"I wouldn't say no to a cup of coffee."

He smiled, the wrinkles around his eyes deepening. "Me either." He nodded to one of the agents, who poured two cups and brought them over, along with the pot, sugar, and milk. He placed the tray in front of them and went back to his post.

Maeve focused on pouring in some milk and sugar while trying to calm her mind. President Graham Wilson was sitting across from her. He'd sent the Secret Service agents. He'd saved them. But what did he want with Alvie?

"I hear you've been involved with the A.L.I.V.E. Project for most of your life. That's a rather unorthodox upbringing."

"Perhaps. But I wouldn't trade it for anything."

The President eyed her over his coffee mug. "No, I don't suppose you would. I know you've been through a lot today, so I won't bother forcing you through a round of small talk. Let me tell you where we stand—I've been read into the A.L.I.V.E. Project. I was not aware of the project until it was brought to my attention six hours ago. I do not agree with the termination order, and to be honest, I'm not sure how I feel about the program."

Maeve took a long drink of the coffee, needing the caffeine. "How did you learn of it?"

"Apparently Commander John Forrester has some very powerful friends."

Maeve smiled inwardly. *Thank you, Uncle John.*

"Were all the species destroyed with the bomb?"

The President poured himself another cup of coffee, holding the pot up, silently asking Maeve if she wanted more. She nodded, extending her mug. And Maeve couldn't help but think this was completely surreal—she'd been running for her life from the US Government and aliens created by that government and now the President of the United States was pouring her coffee.

After filling her cup, the president placed the pot back on the table. "They're still going through the site. It will take weeks, if not longer, to climb through every possible corner and make sure the site is clean."

"Have they found any … " Maeve swallowed. "Bodies?"

"Over two dozen humans and another seventeen non-humans, although both those numbers are expected to go up—on both sides."

Maeve thought of all the dead she had seen. Those numbers eclipsed the President's numbers by a wide margin. "Did any escape?"

The President eyed her and then looked away. "We have

people looking into that. At this point, we do not believe that is the case."

But you can't really know that for sure, can you?

And when dealing with an alien population, who knew what their survival mechanisms would allow them to do? It could allow them to hibernate for years before making their presence known. Or they could head straight for a population. Or take up residence in the desert surrounding the base. The nightmare someone had unleashed on the world was almost unimaginable.

"Who put out the termination order?"

The President frowned. "I don't know for sure, but my suspicions say it is the head of BOSAC, Martin Drummond. I have my people trying to uncover evidence that links him to the situation, but they've warned me they may never be able to do so."

"How's that possible?"

"Whoever initiated the order is well plugged in behind the scenes, and from what I am told, Martin is someone who excels at operating in the shadows. I'm the President, yes, but I'm not omnipotent. And this incident has greatly outlined the limits of both my power and my knowledge."

The words hung in the air between them. He was right. There was a whole other government at work, using taxpayer money that the elected officials had no knowledge of. And that secret government was still at work.

"What about the people in the tunnels? The ones who were shooting at us?"

"They've received medical treatment and are being questioned. So far they all seem to be following the same script—they were simply following orders. Although I'm told one of them, Andy Henning, had a burner cell phone

435

that someone was using to contact him during all of this. My people will track the caller down."

I don't think so. Whoever had been behind this had covered himself or herself well. And like the President said, he or she was extremely well wired in behind the scenes. Maeve wrapped her arms around herself, suddenly feeling cold. "What will happen to Alvie? To the triplets?"

The President leaned back. "Well, that is a dilemma, isn't it? We can't exactly let them go. Their very existence would cause quite a bit of chaos. And after all, they were created by the United States Government."

Maeve crossed her arms across her chest. "I thought the United States had abolished slavery."

The President smiled, tipping his chin to acknowledge the point. "We did, but that only applies to humans. There is no mention of aliens in the Constitution. They are not subject to the same rights."

"Alvie and the triplets are part human."

He raised an eyebrow. "So I've heard. But that also makes them a unique case."

"So they're what, property? They don't deserve to be locked away. They haven't done anything wrong."

The President smiled. "Well, it just so happens I agree with you. And I assume you wish to continue with them."

Maeve nodded.

"I'd like to meet them one day, once my agents have determined that they are safe, of course."

"They're safe," Maeve said quickly.

"I believe you. And Alvie seems to have some impressive abilities."

Maeve went still. "What do you mean?"

"I've seen some of the feeds from 51. I saw him take

down that one alien with his hands. Do you know what that was?"

Maeve swallowed. With everything that had happened, she had forgotten about that. She shook her head. "No. I don't."

"But if anyone could find out, it would be you. He also seems to be able to communicate with some of the other ones. Is that true?"

"I'm not sure if it's communication or more that he can sense them, their moods."

The president sat back, nodding his head, his hand on his chin, his gaze on Maeve. After a few seconds, Maeve began to feel uncomfortable.

Finally, the President spoke. "I think the A.L.I.V.E. Project could be beneficial for this country. I think Alvie and his—" The President eyed Maeve. "Clones?"

She nodded. "Yes."

"Huh. Well, I think they could all be very helpful."

"Helpful with what?"

"Well, Maeve, you've seen quite a bit in just the last few hours. But believe it or not, this is only the tip of the iceberg. And I think you and the clones may be just the thing we need to delve deeper into that iceberg. What do you say?"

Maeve looked into the President's eyes and knew that although he had phrased his request as a question, it wasn't —not really. Either she agreed or she would never see Alvie and the triplets again.

So she nodded her head, while promising she would do everything in her power to keep Alvie and the triplets safe.

"Yes."

Chapter One Hundred Eighteen

DENVER, COLORADO

One Month Later

MAEVE STEPPED outside the ranch house and looked at the mountains in the distance. The President had agreed to allow them to live on the ranch. There was a fifteen-mile perimeter around the land, armed with electronic surveillance and human surveillance, and there was a flyby at least a few times a day.

There were some concerns about satellite access, and if that ever became a problem, Alvie and the triplets would need to be moved to an underground location. But Maeve didn't think that would be an issue. She'd given them a makeover. Gone were the blue scrubs. Instead they wore kids clothes. And whenever they were outside, they wore baseball caps and sunglasses. From a satellite feed, they'd look like normal kids.

The world at large, however, remained blissfully unaware of them.

They were only about an hour from Denver's airport,

and Maeve had a feeling that was the main reason they were here. She had heard rumors on and off about what was happening underneath Denver's largest airport. Greg had filled her in one day when he and Leslie stopped by to visit. She shook her head. No need to borrow trouble. Besides, she'd accepted the deal knowing that one day, someone would come asking for a favor. And she, along with Alvie and his family, would have to pay up.

Chris stood up from the rocking chair. "Morning."

Maeve handed him a cup of coffee as he kissed her gently on the lips. "Morning. Where's our little family?"

Chris nodded toward the brook. "Their favorite place."

The willow tree with the tire swing stood at the edge of the brook, and Maeve glanced over as the sun began to set. She noticed Snap sitting on the swing, Crackle and Pop playing by the water's edge, with Alvie sitting against the tree, a look of contentment on his face. Their puppy, a black and white retriever mix named Hope, trailed after them, her tail wagging. Hope had been a gift from Uncle John. That visit had brought the four aliens a great deal of joy.

For Maeve, it had been less enjoyable. John had explained about his and her mother's history with Martin Drummond. The man had been around since the beginning of the A.L.I.V.E. Project, and Maeve had a feeling she had not seen the last of him, even though no one seemed to have seen him in weeks.

And even though the last few weeks had been peaceful, Maeve knew it couldn't last. The government was still playing catch-up with the A.L.I.V.E. Project and the destruction out at 51. But soon they'd come here and want something from all of them. Maeve just hoped they didn't ask for more than they could give.

At the brook's bank, Snap tried to get out of the tire

swing, but her foot got caught and she stumbled to the ground. Alvie was at her side in a second. He wiped the dirt off her, leaning his head into hers. Maeve smiled at the sweetness of the scene. Alvie had proven himself an incredibly attentive big brother. Soon, Snap was scampering over to her brothers.

Chris put his arm around her shoulders. "Ah, they grow up so fast."

She laughed. "Actually, these guys don't."

He raised an eyebrow. "Must you be so literal?"

She leaned up on her toes and kissed him. "Yes."

Chris held her close. "Well, I guess I can put up with it. But only for the next two decades or so. Then we may have to renegotiate."

"Deal." She wrapped her arms around him, her gaze straying back to the triplets.

They're safe, she thought. But the darker, more realistic part of her mind didn't agree.

It whispered to her from the dark recesses of her mind.

For now.

Chapter One Hundred Nineteen

DULCE, NEW MEXICO

IT HAD BEEN AN INTERESTING MONTH. Martin had lost his position at BOSAC. But he didn't really mind that. He considered himself to be retired from that line of work and now on to his second career. The President had agents breathing down his neck trying to find him, but it didn't matter. Martin had prepared for this day. If he was being honest, he'd longed for it. He'd had enough with government oversight and had squirreled away enough money to finance his work for decades.

He glanced to the glass wall that took up the back of his office. From his seat at the desk, all he could see were the rock walls of the cavern and the lights rimming it. He stood up and walked over to it, looking down. His lab came into view.

It had been built in the heart of the mountain, hollowed out decades ago thanks to the United States Government and then forgotten about. Vats with organic material were strewn along the back. Containment units were built into the back walls on the far side.

But one inmate was sitting quietly at a lab table, his shock collar on as the scientists studied him. The large gray looked up to Martin's window. And even though the glass was shaded to prevent anyone in the lab from seeing in, Martin had the distinct impression that the gray could see him. For a moment he felt the presence of something in his mind.

He hit the button on his belt and the presence disappeared at the same time the gray screamed. Other screams rang out from the containment units. Martin smiled. All the collars were linked. When one misbehaved, all were punished.

His intercom buzzed and with a sigh, he walked to the desk to answer it. "Yes?"

"Sir, your daughter called. She wanted to know if you were going to be able to make it this weekend."

Martin frowned. He'd promised to visit her for dinner. He glanced at his monitor. There were still some video feeds he wanted to review. "Tell her I can't make it. The usual response—work, sorry, you know the drill."

"Yes sir. Flowers?"

"Yes." He paused. "What about her doctor's appointment? That was today."

"She re-scheduled for tomorrow."

He frowned. "Send Louis in to make sure she makes the appointment, *however* he needs to get her there."

"Yes sir."

Martin disconnected the call his daughter already slipping from his thoughts. He walked over to the corkboard—his collection of photos and reports from 51. And right in the center was a still photo of Dr. Leander with Garrigan and the four aliens. They had all disappeared. The Secret Service had swooped in and taken them away. Martin had been searching for them, but so far had had no luck. But he knew it was only a matter of time.

The President had gotten to them, but he was a novice at the game of intrigue. Martin was a master. He'd have the aliens in his custody soon enough. Until then, he had plenty to keep him busy.

His phone beeped and he picked it up. Hamish's panicked voice came through. "Sir, there's been a problem. Someone hacked into the central computer."

Martin sprang to his feet. "You assured me that could never happen."

"I assured you it couldn't happen from an external source. This source was internal."

Martin seethed. One of his own. "Who?"

"Hatcher. He was stopped on his way out of the facility. Security has him at the south entrance. They want to know what they should do."

"Hold him. I'm coming to them." Martin strode out of his office and down the long hallway. He paused at the end of the hall. One door was to his right and a hallway extended to his left. He pictured what was behind the door. His greatest creations.

But he bypassed it and made his way down the hall. After a series of hallways, he reached the end of the building. He stepped out into the cavern and nodded to one of his security team, who quickly opened the door to the waiting SUV. Martin climbed in as the man hustled around to the driver's side. It took them five minutes to wind through the cavern toward the exit.

Ahead, a large fence fifty feet tall blocked the exit, barbed wire running through it. A guard post stood on either side of the fence. And right now a small group composed of two security guards and one man on his knees stood on this side of the fence.

Martin stepped out of the SUV as soon as it stopped. "Stay here," he ordered his driver, slamming the door.

He stalked over to the group. "Report."

"Sir, the subject had a USB on him when he tried to leave. We detained him and called your office immediately."

Martin stared at the man on the ground. Kevin Hatcher —one of his programmers. Kevin's glasses were gone, his lip was busted, and his right eye had begun to swell. Apparently his security had left a few details out of their report.

Martin crossed his arms over his chest. "So, Kevin, what exactly were you thinking?"

Kevin looked up, his chin wobbling, tears in his eyes. "I couldn't do it anymore. I couldn't turn a blind eye. It's wrong."

Martin nodded, his voice soft as he pulled his Beretta from its holster. "I understand. Not everyone has the stomach for this kind of work." He shot once. Kevin's eyes sprang open, his mouth forming an 'O' as he fell to the ground.

Martin looked at the two men. "The USB?"

One of the security guards handed it over. "Here you go, sir."

Martin pocketed it. "And did you two look at the files on the drive?"

The men nodded. "Yes, sir. We wanted to be sure it was worth calling to your attention."

"Very good. And what files are on here?"

The men exchanged a look. Martin knew his mild tone had put them at ease. One, the beefier of the two, even smiled. "It's mainly pictures. Stuff in vats, and I'm not sure what the other ones were."

"No files?"

The beefy one spoke quickly. "There was one. But it didn't make any sense. It was called Ariana." He paused. "Isn't that your daughter's name?"

Martin smiled slightly. "So it is." He pulled the trigger two more times before the men could even breathe. Both collapsed to the ground, the same look of surprise on their faces as on Kevin's.

Martin walked back to the car, seething.

Idiots, all three. He opened the door and his driver looked over. "Anything I can do, sir?"

"Send a disposal unit." He paused. "And don't look at things you shouldn't."

"Yes, sir."

The driver turned the car around, and Martin had already forgotten the men lying at the tunnel entrance. He had too many other things to focus on. He pictured his daughter. No one was allowed to find out about her. Not until he had everything else lined up. *And then*, he smiled. *And then it would be a very good day indeed.*

www.vinci-books.com/dead

After an explosion at Area 51, reports of strange new creatures emerge...

After escaping Area 51, Dr Maeve Leander is on the run. But with the Department of Extraterrestrial and Alien Defense (D.E.A.D.) hot on her heels, the odds of survival are shrinking. There is only one thing Maeve is certain of: she will do whatever it takes to keep her children out of D.E.A.D.'s reach.

Turn the page for a free preview...

D.E.A.D.: Chapter One

UNDISCLOSED LOCATION

Three Months Ago

The room had no windows, just dark-tiled walls. The only light came from the monitors and the backlit keyboard. And there were no other humans. This was Guardian's domain.

Guardian's eyes scanned the three rows of four monitors on the wall. Focus shifting from box to box, Guardian took all of it in. These screens were meant for only Guardian and the computers that provided answers to any question Guardian might imagine.

Right now, all of them were filled with images of violence.

A Kecksburg-AG2 ran down a man in a white coat, digging his talons into the man's back. A Kingman-AG1 turned a corner and the soldiers standing there grabbed their heads collapsing to the ground. For hours, Guardian watched the violence play across the screens. Area 51, reputed to be one of the safest military bases in the United States, was being torn apart.

On the monitors, the images flashed, continually changing, yet Guardian missed nothing. The scene in one box drew Guardian's focus more than any other. Subject One, who'd found his clones and been helped by a group of humans, stopped at a door, staring up at Orion1. The two placed their hands against the glass. Guardian frowned. *What is that about?*

Soon the woman with Subject One rushed him along, although she turned to look back at Orion1. Was that guilt on her face? Compassion? Guardian wasn't sure. Emotions were not Guardian's strong suit.

An hour later, Orion1 saved the same subject and his clones by distracting a group of guards. *He's important to him.* Guardian did not know why, just that it was true.

An ache started behind Guardian's eyes. It happened sometimes when too much time was spent in the box. But Guardian couldn't leave, not yet. Things were moving fast and Guardian couldn't yet see what was coming. But things were beginning to happen, to change. It was only a matter of time now.

But I need to know everything so I can prepare. Guardian's hands flew over the screen. *I need to see.*

D.E.A.D.: Chapter Two

TRIBUNE, KANSAS

Today

The dishes were still in the sink from breakfast. It was the first sight that greeted Sandra Gillibrand as she walked into the kitchen after being at work for twelve hours. She'd just completed a double shift at the diner. She was glad for the work because they needed the money, but her feet were killing her, her back was aching, and she wanted nothing more than to crawl into her bed and just declare that today was officially over.

"Mom?"

Sandra took a breath and turned around, her smile in place. "Hey, honey, did you get everything out of the car?"

Her son Luke nodded, his big brown eyes staring out at her from under a mop of light brown hair. "Can I go see if Sammy is here?"

Sandra hoped the disappointment wasn't on her face at the mention of Luke's imaginary friend. At age ten, he was too old for them. But Luke had hit all his milestones at later dates than most kids, so being that friends were one area where Luke really struggled, she supposed she should be happy that he was at least role-playing how to be a friend. And she hoped that maybe, just maybe, it would help with making real friends.

Luke had been diagnosed with Asperger's Syndrome two years ago. While having the diagnosis at least helped Sandra to have a better idea of what to expect, it hadn't made Luke's life any easier. The kids at school still gave him a hard time. He just couldn't read people. He assumed everyone was a friend. As a little boy, his open embrace of the world had made her heart sing. As he'd gotten older, it terrified her.

Now he stood looking at her expectantly, framed in the doorway of the old kitchen. The notches from his growth chart were lined up next to him. When had he gotten so big?

"Please, Mom."

She stood, indecisive. She didn't like him going out to the old barn. Their house sat next to the O'Hare Farm, a giant, sprawling, two-hundred-acre working farm. Corn was their major crop. Sandra and Luke's house had been on the farm that O'Hare had bought the land from decades ago. Now all that was left of that past was the barn and the house.

Out the window, the shadows were already beginning to form. While she did not like him being out there, he'd had a rough day. Some kids had teased him at lunch and the teacher had called Sandra at work to let her know. She assured Sandra that Luke was fine and the kids were punished. But the idea of her son being the target of bullies just broke her heart. She'd felt helpless all day, with an ache in her chest.

But Luke had looked no worse for wear when she'd picked him up at school. He'd sat in a booth at the diner and done his homework and then worked on his computer, coding something or other until the end of Sandra's shift.

While she felt like she'd been run over a few times his eyes were bright at the thought of 'playing' with Sammy. She sighed. *Maybe I need an imaginary friend.* "Sure, honey, go ahead. Just come in when it's dark, okay?"

He gave her a quick smile and then turned for the back door. But then he ran back to her, giving her a hug. Tears sprang to her eyes and she rested her head on his for a moment.

"Thanks, Mom." Luke sprinted back for the door.

The hugs were new, too. He'd overheard her talking to a friend late one night about how she would give anything for him to hug her more. And he'd taken it on as his mission to make sure he did. And today, those hugs helped push away the anxiety that always seemed to be gnawing at her.

Sandra watched until he disappeared into the barn. Then she went and got changed into sweats, pulling her pink terry-cloth robe on over them before heading back to the kitchen. She stared at the pile of dishes again and just could not bring herself to clean them. Not today. She reached for the cabinet above the refrigerator and pulled down the bottle of Merlot she'd stashed there. She had one glass a week, her small little concession to relaxation.

She poured herself a generous amount in a plastic cup with a dancing elephant on the front. Yup, I'm a class act. She tilted her cup toward the refrigerator, where the last picture taken of her and her husband, Noah, was prominently displayed. They'd both been deployed on the same day, her to Afghanistan, him to Iraq. He'd been killed a month later in an ambush. And then she'd learned she was pregnant.

I miss you, Noah. She took a sip and sighed, closing her eyes and letting the warmth flow through her.

"Mom!" Luke's terrified scream ripped through the house. Sandra's eyes jolted open and she lunged from the chair, spilling her wine across the table. Heart pounding, she sprinted across the kitchen and ripped open the back door as Luke screamed again.

Her eyes went wide and her heart pounded as she saw the large shapes lumbering after Luke, chasing him into the fields. "Luke!"

One of the shapes turned toward Sandra at her yell. Sandra's breath hitched and her eyes went wide. The shadows made it difficult to see clearly, but it was big, muscular, blue, and most definitely not human. The creature let out a cry and ran toward her, its arms pounding the ground like an ape.

Stumbling back into the house, Sandra slammed the door shut and locked it. She ran for the pantry, grabbing a stool on the way. Standing on it, she reached along the top shelf until she felt the barrel of the shotgun. She scrounged around for the box of shells and pulled it down. The shells spilled across the floor.

The back door thumped and Sandra's head whipped up. Shaking, she grabbed a handful of cartridges and shoved them into the pocket of her robe as she stepped out of the pantry. The door thumped again. She swiped the phone off the counter and dialed 911, putting it on speaker as she kept her eyes trained on the back door.

"This is Greeley County Dispatch. What is your—"

"Something's trying to break into my house!"

"Ma'am, did you say something is trying to—"

The rest of the words were drowned out as the back door splintered. Sandra screamed as a creature stepped in with a roar. Its body was shaped like a gorilla. But it was blue. And its face, good God, what was wrong with its face?

The creature turned to Sandra and roared again. The hair along her arms and neck went ramrod straight. Sandra pulled the trigger, catching it at the waist. It grunted as it lurched to the side. She pulled the trigger again and caught it dead center. Its knees sagged as it fell to the floor but was still alive.

"Ma'am? Ma'am?" the dispatcher called out.

Her hands shaking so hard she wasn't sure how she managed it, she dispensed the two shells and then reloaded. She didn't wait for the thing to stand fully upright—she unloaded on it again and again.

It dropped to the ground, fully splayed, half its head gone. Sandra's heart threatened to pound out of her chest.

"Ma'am, deputies are on the way," the dispatcher called out. "Are you all right?"

But Sandra didn't respond. She ran into the pantry, grabbed two more handfuls of shells, and shoved them in her robe pocket. Making a wide circle around the thing, she ran out the back door, more terrified than she'd ever been in her entire life.

"Luke!"

Grab your copy...
www.vinci-books.com/dead

D.E.A.D.: Chapter Three

Luke ducked into the cornfields, running as fast as he could manage. Behind him, he could hear the creature crashing through the stalks of corn. He'd gone to the barn to find Sammy, but he hadn't been there. He'd looked up in the rafters and then on top of the roof, but there'd been no sign of him.

When he'd come out, the two creatures were standing in the drive, staring at him. He'd smiled at first, thinking maybe they were friends of Sammy's. But something about them scared him, scared him more than anything in his life. He'd backed up and they ran for him. He screamed for his mom but they blocked the way to the house, so he'd run for the farm.

He could hear their heavy breathing even above the sound of their fists pounding into the ground. They ran like apes, but they weren't apes. They were blue, hairless, and their faces were no animal he'd ever seen.

He glanced over his shoulder. One was right behind

him. It reached out a giant paw. With a scream, Luke dove to the side, rolling along the ground. It lunged after him. He tried to get up, but his knee hurt too much.

The thing stopped, tilting its head at him. Luke scrambled back and screamed.

D.E.A.D.: Chapter Four

Blood pounded in Sandra's ears as she barreled down the drive. She paused for only a few seconds at the large path that had been carved into the cornfield. Then Luke screamed.

"Luke! I'm coming, Luke!" Her hands slick with sweat, Sandra tore through the field, barely feeling the rough ground cutting up her bare feet. All she could picture was that thing going after her son.

Screams, different from Luke's, sounded from ahead, sending chills through her. It sounded like something was being torn apart. Not Luke. Please don't be Luke.

Something came flying at her and Sandra dove for the ground with a roll. Heart pounding, she looked back at what had nearly hit her as she got to her feet.

It was an arm—a hairless blue arm. Ahead, an object lay across the path carved in the field. She backed up, her eyes wide. It was one of the things, or at least part of it. One leg, some of its waist. She'd seen the aftereffects of IEDs in Afghanistan, but this was something different. She stepped over the parts and spied the other half of the body twenty feet away.

She moved forward, the shotgun securely in her arms, terror stealing over her. What could rip that thing apart?

"Luke?" she whispered. But there was no response. She followed the string of broken stalks, searching the area until the trail ended. She looked around but couldn't see him anywhere. She searched for another twenty minutes, pushing through the towering corn, her panic growing. She knew she needed to get help but she couldn't bring herself to leave.

Finally, though she forced herself to backtrack out of the field. She wasn't going to be able to search the field herself. She jogged back toward the drive, hoping the deputies had arrived.

Luke, where are you? She tried to keep her mind from going to a dark place, but it was so hard. Luke was a sweet soul. He didn't understand danger the way other people did. He didn't know how to fight. To be honest, the fact that he'd even run away from those things had shocked the hell out of her.

He's okay. He has to be. As she stepped out of the corn-field, a bright flashlight shone in her eyes. She put a hand up to block the glare.

"Sandra?" The flashlight lowered and Deputy Dave Carson stepped forward.

"Dave, thank God." Dave had been friends with both her and Noah in high school.

"Jesus, Sandra, what the hell's going on? I saw that thing in your kitchen." He glanced down. "Your feet are bleeding."

Now that she was talking out loud, the reality of what had chased Luke hit her full force. She started to shake so hard, she thought she might split apart. "Luke. One of those things went after him. It chased him into the cornfields. I can't find him."

Grab your copy...
www.vinci-books.com/dead

Fact Or Fiction?

At the end of my books, I like to do a section where I discuss what in the novel is fact and what is fiction. For *A.L.I.V.E.*, this section proves to be particularly difficult. There is rumor, there is belief, and there are two sides to each 'fact.' Unfortunately, due to the amount of research, I can't include every fact here. I'll try to hit the bigger facts. And I'll let you know what I played around with and what I left alone. And as always these are in no particular order.

But first let me say that once you start looking into the idea of the reality of aliens and UFOs, the amount of information you find is overwhelming. Both sides of the coin are equally adamant about their position. Having said that, let's see what I found!

Wright Patterson Air Force Base and UFOs. Wright Patterson Air Force Base is an actual air base just outside Dayton Ohio. It has been the center of UFO rumors since Roswell. The Foreign Technology Division is an actual division that was homed at Wright-Patt and later renamed NASIC. As explained in *A.L.I.V.E.* it's job is to analyze any and all foreign air technology, usually from foreign countries. However, there are rumors that after Roswell, the alien ship either in its entirety or parts was taken to Wright-Patt for inspection. And there have even been reports by individuals who worked at Wright-Patt, such as June Crain, who testified, usually at the end of their lives that they saw UFO wreckage and in a few cases, alien bodies at Wright Patt.

Roswell. I don't speak about Roswell except in passing in this novel. Everyone knows the story- a UFO allegedly crashed in Roswell New Mexico. The rancher came out and found an unusual material that seemed unlike any other material. It would not break and even if bent went back to its original shape. And the military put out a press release shortly thereafter claiming they had in fact collected a downed UFO. Then the military changed their mind and said it was a weather balloon. We all know that story. But what I found particularly interesting was how many times the military put out an explanation for the alleged Roswell crash. The last one was in 1995 and said that the Roswell crash was the result of a balloon cluster that was being tested over New Mexico. That's almost fifty years later. Why on earth are they still writing about it? And why would someone mistake balloon material for a metal?

Phobos 2. Phobos is the name of the moonlet surrounding Mars. In 1988, two Russian probes were sent to investigate the moon. Phobos 1 proceeded without any problems. But Phobos 2 failed as soon as it came in line with the moon. But not before it relayed a picture of something between Phobos and the moon-a narrow cylindrical object. One of the Russian scientists even went as far as to claim that Phobos 2 had been destroyed by the object.

Alien Implants. The idea that humans are abducted and implanted with a small metal object is not my creation. There is actually a doctor named Dr. Roger Leir who in his free time, removes small pieces of metal left in alien abductees.

Exoplanets and the Goldilocks Zone. Exoplanets are planets outside our solar system. As mentioned in *A.L.I.V.E.*, there are over three thousand exoplanets that have been discovered and that number is growing daily. The Goldilocks Zone is also an actual term. It refers to a planet whose location from the sun allows it to be not too hot and not too cold to promote life.

Alvie. Alvie is a fictitious character. He is however based on a skull found in Mexico in the 1920s. The star child skull is a unique structure that does not match human dimensions or characteristics. DNA test allegedly showed that it had a human mother and non-human father. For those interested in reading more on the star child skull you can Google the term.

Maeve's Dreams. Obviously, Maeve's dreams are fictitious. They were however inspired by how the star child skull was found. In the 1920's a fifteen year old girl was visiting relatives in Mexico when she discovered two skeletons in a cave in Copper Canyon. One skeleton, the star child skeleton, was buried underneath the human skeleton. But the human skeleton's arms were reaching down into the ground, holding onto the star child skeleton. The teenage girl removed both skeletons from the ground and left them in the cave to retrieve them later. That night, a flood washed away most of the skeletons except the skulls of each. The human skull was lost decades ago but the star child skull has remained in private hands since then and now resides in the United States.

Janet Flights. There are unmarked flights that leave McCarran airport in Las Vegas and have been reported to be seen landing at Area 51 in Nevada. The planes are white with a long red stripe down the side. These flights are called Janet flights and some have traced them to the United States government.

Majestic 12. Rumors of the Majestic 12 have been on the fringes of UFO lore for decades. Allegedly, the Majestic 12 had been created by executive order by President Harry S. Truman after the Roswell crash and a rash of UFO sightings. The committee was composed of scientists, military and intelligence agents whose sole focus was preparing the United States to defend against the alien threat. Some argue it was disbanded a few short years later. Others say it shifted into the shadows. And some say it never existed at all.

Mothman. I don't know if Mothman is real. He's a bit of an urban legend. A tall humanoid creature with large wings like a bat was reported to be seen in West Virginia back in the 1960s. But that was not his only sighting. There were also rumors and eye-witness reports of a similar creature who was inhabiting on Johnson Space center in the 1980s.

US Atomic Bomb Testing. The information on the US atomic bomb testing is true. I was personally shocked to learn how many bombs we had set off just to see what the effect would be.

Project A119 was real as well—there was a plan to bomb the far side of the moon back in the late 1960s. Luckily, it was never enacted.

Phoenix Lights. The Phoenix Lights are a real event that occurred in 1997. And to be honest, this is one of the most compelling UFO sightings I read about. A huge, slow moving triangular shaped craft was seen above Phoenix and was witnessed by hundreds of individuals as it covered three hundred miles in about an hour. The craft was the size of at least two football fields, according to eye-witness reports. The government said that it was not a UFO but the people on the ground beg to differ. If you're interested in reading more about the sighting, simply Google Phoenix Lights.

Foo Fighters. During World War II, pilots repeatedly reported aircraft of incredible speeds watching them during aerial battles or simple flights. In fact, both allied and axis troops reported the sightings.

Aurora Crash. The crash of a UFO as reported in *A.L.I.V.E.* is accurate to the best of my abilities. There were newspaper reports back in 1897 that spoke about UFOs being seen over Aurora Texas on and off for a year before the final crash. And as mentioned, the citizens of Aurora recovered a body from the crash. They gave the pilot a burial, complete with a tombstone. Later, the tombstone however was removed due to too much interest in the site.

Kecksburg Crash. There was also a highly public crash in the woods of Kecksburg Pennsylvania back in 1965. Some say the project that crashed was a UFO. Others suggest it was a meteor and still others argue it was a Nazi time travelling bell. Seeing the crash, many citizens went to investigate but reported being turned away by the US military. And more importantly, they reported that the military then took something from the site under tarps.

Doomsday Plane. There *is* a doomsday plane. As mentioned in *A.L.I.V.E.*, the doomsday plane was developed to hold members of the government and military in the event of a catastrophe. It is said to be able to withstand a nuclear blast. It can fly for days without needing refueling. The prototype in *A.L.I.V.E.* is a figment of my imagination but is based on the idea that the real doomsday plane may have been created at Area 51 and therefore, there might be another in mothballs still hanging around the base.

Tunnels under US Military Bases. The US did in fact get patents in the 1970s for tunnel diggers as described in *A.L.I.V.E.*.

Area 51. Area 51 is of course a real base. It was denied by the United States for the majority of its existence. And it was the overabundance of evidence of that existence, including Russian satellite photos of the base, that finally led the United States government to admit that it does indeed exist. The history of Area 51 however is still much debated. There is little doubt that cutting edge aeronautical vehicles were tested and perhaps developed there. But as for aliens, that is all rumor. For an interesting history of *Area 51: An Uncensored History of America's Top Secret Military Base* by Annie Jacobsen.

So now I suppose a reasonable question is: what do I believe? Well, I do not believe we are alone in the universe. That seems mathematically impossible with the size of the universe. And I have to admit, some of the eye-witness testimony from pilots or government workers and just normal people with nothing to gain and lots to lose, can be very compelling. But I suppose we'll all have to wait for definitive proof to determine who's right.

But I also wonder, whether or not we'd be allowed to see that definitive proof. Most think tanks that have researched how they believe society would react to the news of intelligent alien life seem to have reached the same conclusion: we as a society will lose it once we learn of their existence. I'm not entirely sure they're wrong. After all, we've all seen the footage of people on Black Friday losing it when they learn of the existence of a low price on a flat screen TV. I'm afraid those types of reactions may have doomed us from ever having a clear picture of what exactly is going on above our heads.

Even so, it is fascinating to read the accounts from astronauts, members of the military, and just ordinary folk that come across something they cannot explain. This series will pull from those accounts and ask - what would we do if we ever came across an alien species?

Thanks for reading. I hope to see you next time!
RD

About the Author

Author, Criminologist, Terrorism Expert, Jeet Kune Do Black Sash, Runner, Dog Lover.

Amazon best-selling author R.D. Brady writes supernatural and science fiction thrillers. Her thrillers include ancient mysteries, unusual facts, non-stop action, and fierce women with heart.

Prior to beginning her writing career, R.D. Brady was a criminologist who specialized in life-course criminology and international terrorism. She's lectured and written numerous academic articles on the genetic influence on criminal behavior, factors that influence terrorist ideology, and delinquent behavior formation.

After visiting counter-terrorism units in Israel, R.D. returned home with a sabbatical in front of her and decided to write that book she'd been thinking about. Four years later she left academia with the publication of her first book, *The Belial Stone*, and hasn't looked back.